Our Bloodline

BY

KC KEAN

Our Bloodline
Featherstone Academy Series #3
Copyright © 2020 KC Kean

This book is licensed for your personal enjoyment only. This book may not be re-sold or given away to other people. If you would like to share this book with another person, please purchase an additional copy for each recipient. If you're reading this book and did not purchase it, or it wasn't purchased for your use only, then please return to your favourite book retailer and purchase your own copy. Thank you for respecting the hard work of this author.

All rights reserved.

This is a work of fiction. Names, characters, places, brands, media, and incidents are either the product of the authors imagination or are used fictitiously. The author acknowledges the trademark status and trademark owners of various products referred to in this work of fiction, which have been used without permission. The publication/use of these trademarks is not authorised, associated with, or sponsored by the trademark owners.

Our Bloodline/KC Kean – 2nd ed.
ISBN-13 - 979-8-697755-52-5

To my Dream Machine,

The coolest kid on the block, who has lived this life more than once.

You are the best brother, son, grandchild, cousin, nephew, friend, and all round human being.

I'm sorry COVID's had you staying home with me for a while, and now you have even more of my traits. As if you weren't outspoken enough as it was LOL.

You have better one liners than me, and your wit already drives me crazy!

You make me proud every day!

I love you my handsome boy,

Always & Forever

ALERT

So, just to be on the safe side, if my dad, or my nan happened to recommend my book to you, and you've made it this far, I bow down to thee. But PLEASE they are not allowed to read this book or know ANYTHING that goes on LOL so act casual in future conversations.

They have been the craziest supporters, but they'd recommend it to anyone that'll listen LOL

KC KEAN

"This is my family, here in this room. Nobody else. This is my safe place and wherever we are I'm home."
- Parker Steele, Featherstone Academy

PROLOGUE
Totem

They used to underestimate me, but now they fear my very existence.

What I have now is not enough, it will *never* be enough.

I want it all; I'm done living in the shadows. Soon, Featherstone will be mine.

I feed off power, and I'll do whatever it takes to have more, to be more than my bloodline ordains.

To do this, I need a following, an heir to walk beside me. Believing in my vision and the carnage we can cause.

I've destroyed everyone that has tried to stand in my way, biding my time, and all I need now is her.

My Little Moon.

OUR BLOODLINE

ONE

Luna

NINE DAYS BEFORE THE GAMES

My heart pounds in my chest as my palms sweat in anticipation of the conversation that's coming.

Climbing into the Rolls Royce with Parker close behind, I get as comfortable as possible in the leather seat. Nervously rubbing my hands down my black skirt while staring out of the window, not actually taking any of the scenery in.

We're heading back to Ace block with the thumb drive we received from West, which has all the documents and files he gathered on The Games. Yet, my mind is solely focused on what I'm about to ask Parker.

"Hey, angel. Are you okay? You seem a little distant," Parker says quietly from beside me, pulling my attention away from the Academy grounds.

Turning slowly to face him, my eyes trail over his tattooed fingers, lingering on the skull and anchor ink, before running up his perfectly buttoned shirt, to his lush plump lips. His curly brown hair has my fingers itching to play, but it's his hazel eyes that hold me captive.

The more I look at him, the louder my heartbeat thumps in my ears. Wetting my lips, I pause, searching for the right words.

"I… I have something I want to talk to you about, alone. I just don't know how to say it," I murmur, undoing my blazer buttons and loosening my collar. This is causing me too much anxiety, my whole body feeling as though it could burst into flames at any moment.

Worry crinkles the corners of Parker's eyes as he frantically searches mine.

"Angel, you know you can talk to me about anything, right?" He reaches his hand across the armrest between us, lacing our fingers together. The gentle squeeze of encouragement he offers helps settle my nerves a little.

"I need you to hear me out before you say no, okay?" I don't want him to shut me down without listening to everything I have to say. This is a big deal, I know that, which is why I'm scared of his rejection, even under the circumstances.

Covering up his anxiety, he tries to muster a smile, but my emotions are affecting him. I want to run my thumb between his eyes and take away the worry lines that mark his skin.

"Luna, just talk to me. I don't know if you've noticed, but I struggle to say no to you because I want to make you happy."

Blowing out a breath, I push my insecurities to the side and focus. "While I was in New York, I had time to talk with Rafe and Juliana. We talked about a lot of topics, and even though I didn't want to talk about you guys, they continued to push the subject until I did."

Offering him a weak smile, I can see by his face that my words are adding to his confusion. I try to squeeze his hand, just as he did mine, offering reassurance while my brain continues to try and formulate the right words. My apparent fear of rejection taking over. He doesn't say a word, giving me the time I need to go at my own pace.

"One of the topics we talked about… was you." He nods gently, maintaining eye contact with me, and I can feel my chest begin to flush pink as my breathing becomes heavier. "I have some information and a really big question to ask you. I know I pushed you all away when I came back, but I want you to know, I would have always told you everything."

My emotions are starting to show, my mask of indifference slipping as my lips quiver and I'm unable to contain the shake in my hands. Parker must feel it too because he leans in close, somehow looking deeper into my eyes.

"Breathe, angel," he whispers, and I feel the air that passes his lips caress my face. It somehow helps ground me enough to calm the frantic beating in my chest.

"Parker, I know your bloodline," I breathe out, and his whole body stiffens. "But I don't want you to take it." Pausing, I take a deep breath to center myself again. "I want you to share mine."

Silence surrounds us as he slowly slouches back into his seat, sinking into the leather as he processes my words. I know I'm throwing a deep conversation at him here, and

I want to give him my full support, but he may need some time to wrap his head around all of this. He needs to chat with the others, I just don't want him to push me away.

"What do you mean by 'you want to share yours'?" he quietly questions, squeezing my hand tightly, leaving me confused.

"I, err, do you not want to discuss the first part of what I said?" I stutter, surprised by his calmness, even though he still hasn't moved.

"No, not really. I'm more interested in the part where you said 'I want you to share mine' and what that means."

Locked in his gaze, we can't seem to pull away from the emotions pulsing between us. He waits patiently for me to answer, treating me delicately like he always does.

"I want you to marry me and share my bloodline."

The words leave my mouth in a whisper. I know he heard me, so there's no taking it back now. He stares at me for what feels like hours, maybe even days, and I slowly start to backtrack.

"I know you don't love me, Parker. That's not what I'm saying here. I want you out of your father's web—"

My words are cut off by Parker's lips on mine. His lips are usually soft and gentle, so it takes me by surprise when he crushes his mouth to mine. Parker releases my hand, dropping it into my lap so he can cup my face. Slowly catching up, my palms find his chest as I respond to the demand of his lips, allowing him access to take me entirely. My brain can't process the dominant touch from Parker, but my body melts against him, offering him complete control.

A throat clears, forcing us to separate our lips. We take a moment to catch our breath as he rests his forehead against mine. The emotion that plays in his eyes mirrors my own, as I fumble to gain control of myself.

"Yes." As simple as that. He is willing to put all his trust in me without question or concern.

"Parker, I really need you to think about this, and chat with the guys, okay? There's more at stake here than just getting married. We're a team no matter what, and we need to be open with everyone."

Before he can respond, Oscar's calling us from outside. "Will you two get your horny asses out here? Or at least make room so I can join you."

Parker sighs, but smiles at my exaggerated eye roll. Ian offers a simple nod as he holds the door open, giving us space to step out.

"Are you okay?" Oscar asks, suddenly in my face. His messy blonde hair moving with the breeze as he strokes his thumb gently over my cheek. The emotion I feel when I look at him too, completely overwhelms me.

"I'm fine," I say with a gentle smile, reining myself in. Happy with what he sees on my face, he plants a gentle kiss to my lips and steps back.

"Jess isn't feeling too great, so I'm going to drop her off, and meet you up there." I search for Red to check on her myself.

She's standing by the automatic doors, looking nervously around. Slipping past Parker and Oscar, I make sure she's okay.

Smiling, she shakes her head at me. "I'm alright, just tired, that's all." She doesn't seem physically exhausted, but maybe she just needs a mental break.

"Are you sure? We can have girl time if you'd like?" I offer, resting my hand on her shoulder.

"Nope, I'm going to make a hot chocolate and curl up on the sofa with a book, a sexy reverse harem one." I raise an eyebrow at her but nod in understanding. She clearly needs some alone time to relax.

"Make sure you eat, Red. Otherwise, I'll be forced to

put you under full Oscar surveillance," I say with a wink, and she gives me a copy of my own eye roll as Oscar leads her to the elevator. Sassy bitch. She makes me chuckle.

"That sounds like a good idea. I can monitor your food intake, bathroom breaks and definitely make sure there are no boys," Oscar adds, and she growls at him as the elevator doors shut.

I feel Parker step up behind me. His hands find my hips as his lips brush against my neck. Tilting my head backward, I feel him smile against my skin.

"You save me time and time again, angel. I'll discuss it with the guys because like you said, this decision affects all of us, but I'm yours. I want to be Parker Steele."

Parker

My heart hasn't calmed its rapid beating in my chest since those words passed her lips.

I want you to marry me and share my bloodline.

It has repeated over and over in mind while we're supposed to be sorting through all this information for The

Games. My gaze keeps straying back to her, but I can't help it. She's already the center of my everything. I've known it since she willingly tattooed the feather on my arm, I just didn't truly understand this feeling yet. Since our conversation in the Rolls, I see her in a different light. Truly my angel.

I'm obsessed with the way her emerald green eyes sparkle when she laughs with us, and when her mouth scrunches up and her nose wrinkles when she reads something she doesn't like about The Games.

My heart kicks into overdrive at the thought of what she's offering me. A family, a level of security I've never truly had.

"From the unauthorized files, I was also able to compile a list of recommended weapons. We should be able to get them from the vaults," Kai says, pulling me back to the present.

Luna hums in response. "I don't know about you guys, but I can get us plenty of access to weapons from the Gibbs vault. If you print the list out, I could go down on Saturday to see what could be useful. From what their experiences said, they weren't given time to go to the vaults, only being able to take weapons they had in their room."

"I'll go with you, princess. We can go before or after we meet the agent, whatever you want to do," Roman offers, and she smiles lightly as she closes her eyes.

"Great, on Sunday I'm meeting my grandmother. It's about time. I haven't spoken to her since Washington, and she might be able to add anything we've missed," she says, not opening her eyes and her voice getting softer.

Nobody responds as we all sit and stare at her, she looks so peaceful my heart could burst. Oscar strokes his hand through the waves of her brown hair as we all watch her drift off.

"She's working herself too hard," Kai whispers, not wanting to disturb her.

"You're right. Between classes, the additional training and the life-changing revelations coming out of nowhere, she hasn't really had time to rest," Roman adds, staring down at her now sleeping form.

Taking this as my opportunity to finally say the words out loud and discuss it with my brothers, I clear my throat as quietly as possible. "While she's sleeping, now might be the time to tell you about what she asked me on the car ride over."

Three heads whip around to look in my direction,

confusion in each of their eyes.

"What are you talking about?" Roman questions, but I shake my head.

"We need to move this conversation into the kitchen if we don't want to wake her." I nod my head in that direction, and they quietly maneuver out from underneath her, while making sure not to disturb her peaceful sleep. Oscar runs into her bedroom, reappearing moments later with her pillow and the blanket from the bottom of her bed.

I stand and watch him delicately cover her up, as do the others, before heading into the kitchen.

It's instinctive to walk into the kitchen and turn the coffee machine on for her. Shaking my head, I step back to the fridge, which is closer to the door, and grab a bottle of water, handing some out to the others as well.

"What the fuck's going on, Parker? I was comfortable with her lying against me," Oscar whines, but he must see the seriousness on my face because he immediately stops talking.

Propped up against the fridge, I watch as the others get comfortable waiting for my response. Kai takes a seat at the kitchen table, while Roman leans against the wall, and Oscar sits on the countertop.

Damn. What am I supposed to say? If this is how I feel now, what must Luna have felt like in the car? Rubbing my hand rhythmically over the feather tattoo on my arm, I try to pull strength from it, to find the best way to repeat her words.

"While Luna was in New York, she found out my surname, what bloodline I stand for." I pause, still not looking up from my feet, as everyone remains silent around me. "She doesn't want me under Rico's control. Luna wants me to take her bloodline… by marriage."

Releasing a deep breath, I feel a little better now I've finally spoken the words out loud. No one has said anything, and as much as I don't want to look at their reactions, I have to. This is life-changing, and Luna makes me stronger, so discussing it with these guys is nothing in the grand scheme of things.

I look to Roman first, my other source of strength, and the way his eyes tighten I can see his brain working overtime to understand what I just said. Glancing to Kai, he's as frozen in place as Roman, openly gaping at me. Bringing my eyes to Oscar, I'm surprised to see him frowning, hurt in his eyes, and his usual mischief nowhere to be seen.

"So, she asked you to marry her?" Oscar mumbles, lost in his own mind as he tastes the words against his lips. Finally lifting his gaze to mine, his frown deepens. "What does that mean for me? This is supposed to be about all of us, but it can't be if she marries you." There's no venom toward me in his voice, but I can tell he's upset.

"It doesn't have to make anything different, Oscar," Luna says, gaining all of our attention. She leans against the doorframe with her gaze fixed solely on Oscar, her tired eyes tracking his every movement. Attempting to smooth out her ruffled hair, it's clearly too much effort, so she wraps her arms around herself.

"What does it mean then?" Roman asks, his knuckles white as he grips the countertop as though his life depends on it.

"Can we sit back in the lounge? I really am tired, but I want to have this conversation." She offers a soft smile, and it eases some of the tension in the room. Kai is the first to move and plants a kiss on her head.

"Let me grab you a coffee, Sakura. I'll catch up with you guys in a minute," he mutters, before busying himself around the kitchen. There's a tightness in his shoulders, more so than usual. He's trying to act fine, and give Luna what she needs, but the internal turmoil seeps through him. Tapping his fingers obsessively beside the coffee machine is only one of the noticeable signs.

Patting Roman on the shoulder, I lead the way into the lounge with him right behind me. I can hear Luna murmuring to Oscar, but I don't catch what she's actually saying. They soon follow us into the lounge though, taking a seat on the other sofa. When Kai steps in with Luna's coffee, he sits with Roman and me.

Taking a deep breath, Luna wastes no time getting straight into the conversation. A completely different person to the one sitting in the car earlier. I don't think the guys would believe me if I described the emotions she showed, or how her fear took over earlier.

"While I was in New York, as I mentioned to Parker earlier, Rafe and Juliana wouldn't let up about having a conversation about you guys. A lot of which was focused on Parker and his bloodline." She places her hand on Oscar's knee in reassurance, stopping the slight bounce in his leg, as she looks to the rest of us. Each of us sitting tensely, side by side, as she explains. "After The Pyramid, I vowed that I would tear them all down, and I meant it." Her eyes search mine, but she won't see me arguing with her, we're all in agreement there.

Roman shuffles beside me, leaning forward with his arms propped up on his thighs as he focuses on her words. Looking past him to Kai, I'm surprised to see him as relaxed as me. Clearly, we know Luna would only ever put us all first.

"It took a lot of discussions before Rafe finally told me Parker's bloodline. Yet when he said it, it didn't make me feel any better for him. It actually made me sick in the pit of my stomach, knowing that one significant word would strengthen Rico's hold over Parker." Hands clenched tightly in her lap, Luna's eyes flash with anger as she looks directly at me. "I refuse to let that fucker control and destroy you, Parker. Because he will." I can't help it as my body ignites with goosebumps knowing how much she really does care for me.

Besides Roman, this is the first time someone is willing to put me first. To give herself so selflessly, simply to allow me to be myself, it completely floors me. My heart drums in my ears as I truly feel accepted.

"This is my family, here in this room. Nobody else. This is my safe place, and whenever we are together, I'm home." The words flow freely from my mouth, without thought, which only seems to make them more powerful. Bracing my elbows on my knees, my hands clasped together, I stare straight into Luna's eyes.

I feel Roman's hand squeeze my thigh in support, and when I meet his gaze, the contentment I see is surely a reflection of my own. A sniffling sound makes me frown. Glancing over to Luna, I'm shocked to see her face buried in Oscar's chest, shoulders shaking. He's gently stroking his fingers through her hair, as she clings to him with her arms wrapped around his neck.

Is she crying? Did I break her?

I look to Roman and Kai for guidance, but they're both staring in shock too.

"It's okay, baby girl. I understand now," Oscar says in her ear, loud enough for all of us to hear. His eyes finally meet mine over the top of her head. "You want to protect Parker and offer him a real family in the process. With you, with *us*. A family that's without expectation or hatred." His words hit me square in the chest, making me feel lighter than I ever have before. I watch as he brings his fingers beneath her chin, tipping her face back to capture her eyes. "Luna, tell me how we do that together, and I'm all in."

She stares into his eyes for the longest moment, her

tears stop, and a smile takes over her face. Lifting up off his chest, she looks around at us all with her puffy eyes.

The crazy joker, O'Shay.

The quiet, observant, Fuse.

The hot-headed, alpha Rivera.

And me, the obedient bastard. Soon to be Parker Steele.

KC KEAN

TWO

Parker

SIX DAYS BEFORE THE GAMES

Checking myself out in the mirror one last time, I can't stop the slight tremble that runs through my fingers as I straighten my silver feather cufflinks. My tattoo tingles on my arm at the memory, as my heart soars, knowing I have more happy memories to come. I'm not nervous, excitement courses through my body as if it knows what today means for me. Today is another stepping stone toward being who I'm supposed to be.

Tucking my white shirt into my navy pants, I run my

fingers through my curly brown hair one last time before I head into the lounge. The guys are all sitting patiently on the sofas, with some football game on the television, but the second they hear the bedroom door creak, they each cast their gaze in my direction.

The sound of heeled footsteps catches all of our attention, as Luna waltzes into Roman's apartment as casual as ever. She is the most beautiful woman I have ever laid eyes on, and today she'll be officially *ours*. Her heels instantly take me back to the night of the Fall Ball, when I willingly handed over, not only my virginity but my soul. Look how far we've all come since then.

"Holy fuck, baby girl. You look divine," Oscar says, as he stands to approach her. Luna rolls her eyes at him as he grabs her hand and twirls her around.

Luna's off-white dress sits just above her knees, the lace paneling teasing me with her stunning body that lies beneath. Her golden skin pops with the angelic color, somewhat symbolic for my angel.

"You look beautiful, Sakura," Kai murmurs, wrapping his arms around her from behind, even though Oscar refuses to let go.

Her eyes stray to Roman, who slowly stalks her way,

an instant reminder of the power and control he has. I can see from the sparkle in her eyes, she loves offering that submissive side of herself to him.

I don't know exactly what happened at the vaults yesterday, but they came back different. Not completely whole, but a lot less broken. There is a new softness between them, another layer of comfort that they take from each other. After that, everything went to hell. Luna was finally able to sit down with the agent, and nothing went her way, *our* way. We're a team, a family, so if anything affects our girl, it affects us too.

"Princess, you are stunning as always." He steps in beside her and brings his lips down on hers. The gentleness surprises me, as he delicately cups her face, consuming her.

I stand exactly where I am, watching them all with her, letting them have this moment because I'm sure as hell going to be getting mine soon enough. Luna must feel my eyes on her, as she pulls back from Roman, with Oscar and Kai still caging her in, and stares at me with her eyebrow raised. With that one look, she's taunting me, sending a nonverbal challenge, daring me to stay on the sidelines.

Not today, not ever again, I think, as I smile at her taunt.

Joining the group, I stand to her side and place a gentle kiss on her cheek. The four of us wrap our arms around each other, cocooning her in the middle. Surrounded by my family, with my angel between us, I've never felt this content. My best friends relax as we all bask in this moment together. This is us.

Looking at Luna, it blows my mind how she instinctively touches us all. Her back leaning against Kai, her head on Oscar's shoulder while her hands reach out touching both Roman and I.

"I can't fucking breathe, you Aceholes," she groans, making us finally give her some room. "Are you ready?" She turns to face me, straightening my collar, waiting for me to answer her question.

"You know it, angel," I answer, looking around at the others.

Since our talk, everyone has been one hundred percent on board. Rafe and Luna's grandmother, Maria, have offered a lot of help and guidance in what is expected in a traditional Featherstone marriage.

"How are your tattoos?" I ask, and the guys all look at me with wide smiles and pride in their eyes. They're topless already, in only their sweatpants. Stepping back, they all drop their waistband a little, showing off their hips where the brand new ink marks their skin.

The Diana, Goddess of the Hunt symbol, sits perfectly in black strokes. Three arrows pointing upwards, with a crescent moon wrapping around them. I haven't gotten mine yet, the tradition states that the party who marries into the specific bloodline by law has to be marked by a specific bloodline within Featherstone. The tradition for multiple parties in a Featherstone marriage is that one is legally married, while the others bear the bloodline symbol. It didn't state anything about who had to tattoo the others, so Luna did it herself. Which I think only strengthened the emotional bond between them, making it even more personal. By the end of today, we will all wear the tattoo of the Steele bloodline.

My angel agreed to leave no one out, making us all one family. I will become Parker Steele, while the others will have a double surname, with Steele at the front. It fits perfectly for each of them as if it was always meant to happen.

Roman Steele-Rivera.

Oscar Steele-O'Shay.

Kai Steele-Fuse.

"You better get someone to FaceTime us, understood? I hate that we can't go. I know we have to keep it under wraps, so this is my compromise. I want to watch, okay?" Roman says, looking between Luna and me.

"I promise, baby," Luna whispers, rising up on her tiptoes to plant a kiss on his lips.

Oscar moves in, tapping her on the shoulder expectantly. He doesn't say a word, just closes his eyes and puckers his lips for her. When she releases Roman and catches sight of him, her eyes soften instead of the eye roll I was expecting.

Lifting her hands to his jaw, she strokes his cheek as she presses her lips to his. Glancing at Kai and Roman, they're just as surprised as I am at the delicateness Oscar shows in return. Usually, when Luna and Oscar are together they bite and nip at each other, always wanting to leave a mark. Right now in front of us, they're taking their time, and they've never looked hotter together.

Kai seems to have had enough and steps up behind her, kissing down her neck and making her moan into Oscar's mouth. Turning between them, she crushes her mouth to Kai's, whose grip on her hips has his knuckles turning white. Huh, apparently Kai can get a little feisty.

"Hurry home," Kai murmurs, placing a kiss on her

head and maneuvering her to stand in front of me. The shy smile on her face gets my heart racing, and I reach my hand out intertwining our fingers.

"Let's go and forge our own path, angel."

Kai

Roman holds his door open for me as I silently enter, his grey wooden floors, white walls, and black gloss furniture coming into view. Parker and my Sakura should be calling any minute now for us to watch the ceremony. I'm trying to exude a calm demeanor even though I'm nervous inside.

The three of us decided to go to the gym to work out while we waited, instead of sitting around in foul moods. We sparred until our bodies ached, pushing through the lingering aggression we had. It helped a little, but I'll feel better when my Sakura is home. I hate that we couldn't be there with them.

After our chat the other day, it was without question that we all agreed this is the right decision. Making sure Parker is the legal partner while we all wear the mark of her bloodline and incorporate her surname with ours. The contentedness that has settled over my soul is indescribable. Luna continued to say that it's all about Parker's safety, but we all know it's more than that. If it weren't, none of us would be doing this, including her.

Taking a seat on Roman's sofa, I place my phone on the table, ready for it to ring. I've already set up the Bluetooth connections between my phone and Roman's television, so when they do call we can watch the ceremony on the big screen.

Oscar is already here, sitting on the other sofa, but we're all too on edge again to talk. The anxiety in the room is palpable. No one is happy that we are so far away, but we can have a do-over. We can go all out when it's safer and really show our girl she is the only one for us.

Roman takes the seat beside me, his leg bouncing in anticipation as he finally breaks the silence.

"I can't believe this is happening," he mutters, rubbing a hand through his damp brown hair. "She is so willing to put others first, taking care of us without question. She doesn't even realize the impact she has on us. What do I offer her in return? Nothing, I just keep the past a fucking secret and—"

"Shut your mouth, Rome. You can't stay in the past, man. She's moved on from all of that, and you need to as well. We all need each other, but Luna is our glue. Don't project your own insecurities onto her," Oscar says in exasperation, frowning at Roman. I can't deny that I'm slightly impressed with him talking sense and standing his ground.

Before Roman can respond, my simple ringtone fills the room and I rush to answer it. Within a few seconds, the screen comes to life.

"Is this thing even on?" Luna murmurs, with the phone in her hand, the camera directed at her chest.

"Of course it's on, angel. Honestly, how are you so good at tech but a simple video call throws you off?" Parker chuckles in the background.

"Fucking Acehole." I love it when she mumbles that at us, most of the time I don't think she realizes she's saying it out loud.

"Hey, baby girl. As much as I love looking at your tits, I love looking at your beautiful face even more," Oscar calls out, and their faces instantly appear on the screen.

Parker's chin is resting on Sakura's shoulder as he stands behind her and holds the phone up, while she crosses her arms and glares. Everyone chuckles except Luna, but her face softens at the sound of our laughter.

I can't see very much around them, with the direction they're holding the phone, but I can see they're at the courthouse. Pale blue walls and a few orange cushion chairs are all there is to the room.

I know Rafe and Juliana should be there somewhere, as the two witnesses needed, but I can't see them yet.

"Are you all set?" I ask, and they nod in response.

"Yes, this very nice man who works here is going to hold the phone," she says, glancing to her left and a sigh can be heard in the distance.

"Who the fuck just sighed at my princess? Get him on the screen! I swear to god I'll come down there and—"

"Baby, chill the fuck out," Luna snaps, stopping Roman's rant from escalating any further.

"Relax, Roman. I know everyone's emotions are high right now, but she doesn't need us adding to that pressure," I whisper. He takes a deep breath, looking at the ceiling to calm himself down, clenching his hands on his knees as he focuses.

Oscar jumps on the sofa with us, getting in the frame so Luna can see him too.

"Miss Steele, are you ready to begin?" a man asks quietly. Luna nods, blowing a kiss toward the phone, before handing it off to someone.

They stand together in front of an older man in a suit, in the small room. Nothing at all like our Luna deserves, but she looks beautiful all the same. Not a single ounce of worry or tension appears on her face as she smiles brightly at Parker.

The way this guy is holding the camera, I can finally see Rafe and Juliana standing beside them. I notice Rafe is beginning to get emotional like he doesn't know what to do with himself.

I feel a hand squeeze my shoulder, but I don't see who it belongs to because I can't pull my eyes away from the couple on the screen. Parker and Luna stand with their hands joined between them as the officiant goes through the motions.

"Do you, Parker Manetti, promise to love and cherish this woman, in sickness and in health, for richer for poorer, for better for worse, until death do you part?"

I see his mouth move as he says 'I do' but my brain is frozen on his name. It completely slipped my mind that Luna found out his surname in the midst of the whole marriage talk. Glancing to my left, the other two also look in a state of shock.

"Do you, Luna Steele, promise to love and cherish this man, in sickness and in health, for richer for poorer, for better for worse, until death do you part?"

"I do," she responds confidently. She looks brighter, her body completely relaxed.

"I now pronounce you, husband and wife. You may now kiss the bride." The officiant steps back as Parker pulls Luna toward him, his fingers tight around her waist. Luna's hands rise to his neck. The smile they share hits me straight in the heart as they lean in to kiss each other. The respect and appreciation they feel for one another blows me away.

Whoever is holding the phone has clearly had enough and interrupts their perfect moment.

"Here, I'm done. Take your damn phone," he grunts, handing the phone over, which is aimed at the floor as one of them grabs it off him. It must be Luna because Parker's voice booms through the speakers.

"Watch yourself, that's my wife you're talking to."

"Holy shit," Roman mutters in awe.

A quick apology comes from the guy as we hear Rafe

grumble in the distance, and Luna's face fills the screen.

"Hey," she murmurs, and I wish I was there with them. Holding her, and basking in the happiness of their moment, *our* moment.

"Hey, princess," Roman says, admiration written all over his face. "Are you both okay?"

"Yeah," she whispers, her eyes looking away from the phone a moment. "I wish the three of you were here with us. Especially now, since Parker thinks it's his job to growl at everyone who looks at me or speaks to me the wrong way. Rafe isn't helping the matter either." She rolls her eyes as she focuses back on us and it makes me chuckle. Parker's face appears beside her again, but he's still squinting his eyes and frowning at someone in the distance.

"That was beautiful, baby girl, but I need you here with me now, so I know this is real," Oscar whispers. Looking past Roman, the strain all over Oscar's face catches me off-guard. His eyes are tight, and he's biting at his lip. He looks as though he's been on an emotional rollercoaster.

"I just need to get my tattoo, and we have to have lunch with Maria, and we'll be straight back," Parker says softly, clearly hearing the strain in his voice. Concern fills Luna's eyes as she nods in agreement.

"See you soon, Aceholes," she murmurs with a wink, trying to lighten the mood before the screen goes black.

We sit in silence for a moment, digesting everything we just saw. Luna is ours, now and forever. This is next-level crazy, but this whole world is. We're protecting our brother and committing ourselves, and our souls, to the girl of our dreams all at once. Our foundation is built, and we have plenty of time to find ourselves and each other in this world.

"Manetti," Roman grunts, lost in his own mind. "Fucking Manetti. All that worry and stress, and it didn't even fit him anyway." He sighs, scrubbing a hand down his face. "I need to keep busy until they get back." He jumps to his feet and starts pacing the floor.

None of us ever truly knew what his surname was, but now it doesn't even matter. I understand what he means though, the distress it has caused Parker, all for a simple seven-letter word.

Looking at Oscar, he's lost in his own head. I can tell by the gloss to his eyes as he stares out of the window. As much as I'm always battling my internal demons, this brings me a sense of fulfillment I never thought I'd have. I have to push down my own emotions right now, these guys need me. Luna needs them at their best when she gets back, ready to fight and survive.

With The Games upon us, and the constant shit thrown our way, there is a lot to do.

Parker was right, this is our family, and Luna is our home. I'll do whatever it takes to be what they need.

KC KEAN

THREE

Luna

SIX DAYS BEFORE THE GAMES

Finally, back from lunch with Maria, and my brain is reeling. The Games are being moved forward, and apparently, Rico is banging Barbette Dietrichson. Someone in Featherstone Academy clearly wants me dead. Veronica wants me to join a new movement, which I think relates back to Totem somehow, based on what Rafe said.

All I want to do is spend time with my best friend, Red, and my Aceholes and draw my art on people's skin. Instead, I'm dealing with Veronica breaking into my room, and Rico trying to claim me. I can't stop the shudder that runs down my spine at the thought.

Pulling myself into the present, I look around my guys. Parker and I are still in our dressy outfits, while Kai, Oscar, and Roman are rocking their grey sweatpants like it's their mandatory uniform. At least they're wearing different colored t-shirts so they're not completely matching. Although, the thought of them all color-coordinated makes me grin.

"Now, I hope Agent Dominic Bridge keeps his word because when we survive The Games, it'll literally give me a day, two at most to track him down. If not, then Featherstone will take great pleasure in killing me for that instead." I frown at this shit.

Oscar surprises me with a kiss to my cheek, "I'm pleased with your confidence, baby girl. We're going to tear these bastards down," he growls in my ear.

He hasn't stopped twirling the ring on my finger since we got back. It's my grandmother's wedding ring, and I almost cried at the emotion and memories it holds. A magical, vintage art deco inspired French platinum ring, with a petalled setting for the beautifully cut diamond. The slim tapered shoulders only enhance the gem, while also giving it an elegant finish.

Jewelry has never been my thing, at all, but this ring represents more than just the legality, there are a lot of emotions tied to it as well. Which I'll make time to process eventually. My eyes flicker to Parker's hand, where my grandfather's ring sits. A classic platinum court wedding ring, which looks like it was always meant to be placed on his tattooed ring finger.

When we were FaceTiming the ceremony earlier, there was an ache in Oscar's eyes I hadn't seen before. I was a little relieved when we had to cut our lunch with my grandmother short. I don't like the reason why though. I'd rather The Games weren't moved to November, but my Oscar, my big mouth, needs me.

Relaxing further into Oscar's lap, I keep my hand in Parker's which rests on Roman's thigh, and my gaze on Kai sitting on the coffee table. Leaning my head on Oscar's shoulder, he wraps his arm around me, refusing to drop my hands as he continues to roll the ring between his fingers. A part of me wants to be irritated with the action, but I can see the comfort it brings him.

The silence that surrounds us as we enjoy each other's company is bliss, as the sun sets through the floor-length windows.

"Let's forget all the shit for now, baby girl," Oscar murmurs, loud enough for everyone to hear. "We're all safe in here, so why don't we focus on what actually matters today? Not what they're distracting us with?"

Goosebumps flair up my neck where his breath skates across my skin, and it continues to blow my mind how the smallest of caresses from one of them has my body reacting so much.

"And what is that?" I ask, knowing the answer, but wanting to hear them say it.

"Guys, I think our Sakura needs a reminder," Kai says, surprising me. Leaning toward me, from his spot on the coffee table, he strokes his finger over the lace midsection of my dress. Sending a shiver down my spine as he winks at me.

"A reminder? Of what?" I'm confused. Glancing around them all, there's a wicked gleam in their eyes, and I'm definitely slow at catching up.

"I agree, Kai," Roman adds, his grip on mine and Parker's hands in his lap tightening. "Our girl needs an official claiming after today."

Oscar's mouth finds my neck, his lips tipping up

against my skin in agreement with Roman's words.

"What do you say, baby girl? Today hasn't really happened unless we consummate it." I roll my eyes at his thought process, but I can't stop the slightest moan from passing my lips as he continues to trail kisses all over my neck.

"I can't deal with Oscar being right so much at the minute," Roman groans, moving his hand to squeeze my thigh. My eyes shut on their own accord as my head tilts further back.

"Let's take care of our, Mrs. Steele," Parker adds, and I'm fucking lost to them.

Without warning, Oscar's hands drop to my waist, lifting me off his lap slightly to turn and face him. My thighs come down on either side of his, with Roman to my left. Oscar's blue eyes hold me captive as his fingers dig into my hips, holding me in place.

I don't know who leans into who first, but our lips meet in the middle as we slowly burn each other's touch to memory. My fingers rake through his sexy blonde hair, gripping hold as I take more and more from him. I feel his hard cock beneath me, and there's no holding myself back as I grind against him.

Moans fill my ears, but I can't tell you who they belong to. A hand strokes down my back, and I know it's not Oscar's because he still has one holding my hip and the other cupping my chin.

"So beautiful, princess," Roman murmurs beside me.

Pulling back a little from Oscar, my thumb strokes over his swollen lips as my eyes take a moment to focus. Finally, able to see through the sexual fog, I turn my gaze to the left, and my breath catches in my throat at the pure need on Roman's face. His hooded eyes rake over me as his chest rises in rapid succession.

His lips crash to mine, taking everything from me just as I did from Oscar. Someone unzips my off-white dress, baring my skin to the cool air. The delicate stroke down my spine tells me it's Kai undressing me, making me need Parker too. I need all of my Aceholes touching me right now.

"Parker," I breathe out against Roman's lips, but he must already know because light kisses trace over my right arm.

Holy Fuck. Having them all touch me at once is like fireworks, and I never want it to end.

"Somebody sort the mattresses out. My baby girl needs

spreading out," Oscar grunts, pressing his cock against my core, grinding me against him harder.

The kisses down my arm and the caresses on my back stop as I hear Kai and Parker rush to pull my mattress out and bring Roman's over. I really just need to buy a giant bed.

Roman pulls his mouth from mine as he stands from the sofa. Coming up behind me, in between Oscar's legs, he slowly pulls the straps of my dress down my arms. Revealing my bare pierced nipples to Oscar, whose grin widens with pleasure.

"Rome, look at these jeweled babies," Oscar whispers, as his thumb teases against my pebbled peaks. Without wasting another moment, his lips close around my nipple to his left, his tongue swirling, forcing a groan from my lips.

Roman leaves my dress to fall at my waist as his hand trails over my ribs to cup my left breast, rubbing my nipple between his thumb and forefinger. My back arches with the pleasure that rolls through my body, and Roman doesn't miss an opportunity to bite down on my shoulder.

"Fuck," I moan, as Oscar chooses that moment to sink his teeth into my breast. I hiss as the bite takes over my senses, the lick of pain running straight to my core.

A thump draws my attention to the right, seeing Kai and Parker arrange both of the mattresses for us. They catch me staring, and what a sight I must be with Oscar and Roman devouring me. The want on their faces, darkening their eyes, only makes me want more.

"Bring her over," Parker calls out, as I watch him slowly start to undo the buttons on his white shirt.

Roman's mouth leaves my skin as he looks in Parker's direction. Oscar does the same, releasing my nipple with a pop, as we all stare at Parker shedding his clothes.

What a fucking sight.

My eyes instantly fall to his new tattoo as I take him in. My bloodline tattoo, still red and sore but so bold, and the meaning behind them all getting it heightens my lust.

Forcing Roman back so I can stand, Oscar's grip loosens and my dress pools at my feet. I feel all of their eyes rake over me, as I slowly make my way to Parker, without a stitch of clothing on.

"Baby girl, do you ever wear a bra and panties?"

"Why would I add another layer between my body and yours?" I throw back with a grin as I sink to my knees in front of Parker. As he takes out his cufflinks and drops his shirt to the floor, I make myself useful and unfasten the button on his pants.

"What the fuck?" I moan, as my eyes take in his cock in my face, no boxer briefs blocking my view as I slowly unzip his pants, teasing him like he's teased me in this shirt all day.

"Like you said, angel. One less thing in the way." He grins down at me, until I slowly drag my tongue up his hard length, making him throw his head back in pleasure. A curse leaves his lips in the midst of a moan, as I wrap my mouth around him.

Wanting to give him more, I pull his pants down to his feet and slowly drag my nails up his thighs, taking him deeper into my mouth. Hollowing out my cheeks, I suck on him like a lollipop, and the grunts that tumble from his lips only makes me do it more.

Suddenly lifted in the air with an arm around my waist, Roman growls in my ear. "Princess, you're going to have him coming too quickly, and we don't want that yet, do we?" I can feel his bare chest against my back, as his other hand strokes circles around my belly button.

My feet still aren't touching the floor as I realize they're all undressed. How did I miss that? Clearly, I was too busy enjoying Parker's dick in my mouth, and now I have four wanting my attention. I wet my lips as I try to decide where to start.

"Kai, come taste our wife," Roman says, maintaining his hold on me as his other hand trails down to slide through my folds. Holy shit, that feels so good. "Fuck, Kai, you better make it quick, she's dripping."

Not needing to be told twice, Kai is instantly on his knees in front of me. His arms go under my thighs, resting them on his shoulders as his tongue caresses my entrance. Mixed with the press of Roman's cock in my back, I'm flying.

I can't help the moans that pass my lips as he sucks my clit into his mouth, his teeth grazing across the sensitive nub. My eyes can barely stay open, but I spot Oscar and Parker as they step up on each side of Kai and simultaneously bite down on my nipples, tugging my piercings, making my cries louder.

My head falls back on Roman's chest as their onslaught on my body increases. The licks and nips on my nipples and against my clit sending me higher and higher. As Kai's tongue circles my clit, he slowly thrusts two fingers into my core, and I know I'm not going to last much longer.

"You're so close, princess, I can feel it. Your muscles are tightening, and your pulse is thumping. Open your eyes and watch them make you cum," Roman murmurs in my ear, as his grip on my waist tightens.

I'm lost to the bite in my skin from his grip and the press of his cock against me. Mixed with the tugging on my piercings shooting heat straight to my center, it only adds to Kai's unrelenting touch at my core. Grinding my hips against his face as he rubs against my g-spot, my fingers wrap in his dark hair, pulling him closer as I explode against him.

None of them stop until they're sure I've ridden out every last drop of my orgasm, leaving me spent and weak in Roman's arms. My forehead is sticky with sweat as Oscar swipes the loose tendrils of hair out of my face.

"Sit her on my dick, Rome. I need to feel her," Oscar says with a grin as he sits on the mattresses. Without question, Roman places me exactly as he wants, my knees coming to rest on either side of Oscar as he pulls my core straight onto his thick length.

"Fuck," I moan at the sensitivity, but he gives me a moment to adjust. Roman comes to stand at my side with his cock pointing in my direction. Opening wide, I take him deep into my mouth as my hands rest on Oscar's shoulders for leverage, lifting myself up, then sinking back down on his cock, and his eyes roll back in ecstasy.

Humming around Roman's cock, I look up to see the fire in his hooded gaze as he rests his hand on the back of my head. Hands cup my breasts from behind, as kisses are trailed down my spine. Catching a glimpse of dark ruffled hair, I know it's Kai.

Oscar takes over my movements, his fingers marking the flesh at my hips as he lifts me up and down on his cock. While Roman thrusts into my mouth and Kai cradles me from behind, his dick nestled between my ass cheeks as his hands touch me everywhere.

Parker, where's Parker?

"Holy shit," Roman mutters, releasing his cock from my mouth and turning my head around.

Holy shit is right, when I see Parker slightly crouched at my other side with the tip of his cock in Oscar's mouth. I can see Oscar's brain working overtime as he considers the weight on his tongue. Kneeling up a little more, I bring my tongue to lick where his lips touch Parker. They both moan in sync and Oscar's grip on my hips tightens as he thrusts up into me.

Leaning closer to Oscar's ear, as Kai continues to twist my nipples between his fingers, I whisper, "Do you want to taste my Parker Parker?" I ask, and he groans in response. It turns me on watching him experiment, losing his larger than life persona to let someone else take the lead.

Deciding these are my guys, and this is my show, I take control. Placing a kiss to his damp neck, I lift off him completely. He takes the hint and kneels in front of Parker, who stands just off the mattress back at his full height. Turning to my right a little, I know I'll have the perfect view from here.

"Rome, fuck me, baby," I murmur. "Kai, get your cock in my mouth like this."

No one argues as Oscar tests how much of Parker's length he can take, and it's hot as fuck. Roman surprises me, peppering kisses over my shoulder blade as he lines himself up at my entrance, from behind. I expect him to go slow, so I'm taken back by the power behind his thrust. Kai cuts off my moan with his cock filling my mouth.

Watching beads of sweat form on Parker's head as he watches Oscar, is so raw I'm mesmerized. Oscar cups his balls with one hand, clearly picking up on what Parker enjoys. Running my hands around to the globes of Kai's ass, I thrust him deeper, matching the brutal pace Roman has set.

This is all too much for my senses, I can't get enough of the ecstasy in front of me as Roman and Kai fill me, bringing me close to the edge all over again.

"Fuck, Oscar," Parker grunts, gripping his blonde hair. Which only encourages Oscar to take him deeper, bringing his other hand to stroke over Parker's ass. "Fuck. Fuck. I'm gonna cum, Oscar, let go."

I watch through watery eyes as Kai continues to dominate my mouth. Oscar grips the back of Parker's thighs and swallows him down, making him thrust into Oscar's mouth with jerky movements as he cums down his throat. I love how his knuckles are white from the tight grip on Oscar's hair.

It sets me on fire watching him orgasm at the hands of my Oscar. As I watch him go all alpha, taking what he wants, with Oscar encouraging him over the edge. Rome continues to stroke his cock against the walls of my core. The sound of skin on skin with the groans filling the room plays the perfect soundtrack as I find my climax, screaming around Kai's length.

"Fuck. That's it, princess, squeeze my cock," Roman

moans, as he continues his brutal pace.

Kai pulls my head back, forcing me to meet his gaze. His jaw is slack as he takes me in, meeting the back of my throat with every thrust. I can see his control slip as his legs tremble. I drag my teeth against the bottom of his cock, and he growls above me, grunting as he cums. He looks deep into my eyes the whole time, letting me see the man behind the mask.

Slipping from my lips, he glances at Roman. "Come inside her, Roman. Let her know how you feel," Kai groans, surprising everyone with his dominant side.

It's so hot that he can control us all, forcing us to chase our release. Roman pulls my body back against his as he sits on the mattress. I try to take a moment to figure out my bearings, but it's not needed. His hands scorch into my hips, his cock still inside me as he grinds me against him.

"Show me how you reverse cowgirl, princess," he murmurs, sending a tingle up my spine.

I love hearing Roman tell me what he wants, giving me a glimpse of my Acehole. The one who lets me see the fire in his eyes, instead of the stone-cold exterior everyone else gets.

Doing exactly as he says, I grind myself against him

again and again. Loving the feel of his grip getting tighter on my waist. Kai steps into my line of sight, crouching before me.

"Cum for him one more time, Sakura." He presses the pad of his thumb to my clit, as his breath fans against my face.

Panting, I trail my fingers over his lips as I burn with pleasure all over again. Roman moves a hand to my hair, wrapping it around his wrist as he pulls.

That's all I needed to find my ecstasy again. The vice-like grip my pussy has on Roman sends him over the edge with me, riding wave after wave together.

Looking past Kai, I see Parker slowly sinking to his knees in front of Oscar, who stands wide-eyed, staring down at him. Not wasting a moment, Parker sucks him down, straight to the base, and Oscar has to lean his hands against his shoulders to remain on his feet.

Roman's forehead rests against my back as we try and catch our breath. Fuck, if this doesn't bond us, I don't know what will.

Kai takes me from Roman's lap, placing me gently on the mattress, and with a wink, Roman stands and approaches Parker and Oscar. I don't know what he's saying, but he leans in and whispers in Oscar's ear. Whatever it is, it only adds fuel to the fire as Oscar thrusts into Parker's mouth, matching his momentum.

All the pent up sexual tension around us encourages Oscar over the cliff, and we watch him climax.

Oh. My. God.

Flopping down, flat on my back, I sink into the mattress. I don't move a muscle as I bask in the sex cloud I've found myself on. Closing my eyes, as I try to cool my body temperature down, I could fall asleep. I can hear the guys murmuring around me, but I'm too out of it to pay attention. I feel someone run their fingers through my hair before I'm lifted into their arms. I don't open my eyes as I rest my head on their shoulder, letting whoever it is carry me wherever they want. Although, I'd be lying if I didn't know the woodsy scent beneath me was Oscar.

The light scent of my coconut bubble bath milk fills the air, forcing my eyes open. I'm surprised as I'm gently placed into a fully drawn bath. Oscar smiles, placing a kiss to my head as I groan at how good the water soothes my aching body. He climbs in behind me and pulls me against his chest.

We don't speak as we relax together, but I feel his

breath against my ear as he goes back to twirling my ring on my finger. The sound of the others walking around in the lounge and kitchen, the only noise. Stroking my hand down his thigh, I can't believe how good this feels. Lying with Oscar in our post-sex haze, feeling the water lap against my chest. His hand cups my cheek and tilts my head back a little to look up at him. Frown lines mark his forehead, with his jaw set tight, but the softness in his eyes tells me he's okay.

"I love you, Luna."

My breath catches, my heart beating rapidly in my chest. Turning around to face him fully, his hand remains on my cheek, as I look into his wild blue eyes. A rare moment where he's letting me see his soul, my hands lift to his chest, feeling his heart beat just as fast as mine.

Frantically searching his face, the pureness of his words settle over me. Releasing a deep breath, I smile softly at him, and as foreign as the words feel on my lips, my heart takes over and speaks the truth.

"I love you too, Oscar."

OUR BLOODLINE

FOUR
Parker

THE NIGHT OF THE GAMES

I can't breathe. I can't fucking breathe. This motherfucker has his arm locked around my neck, as I watch Luna fight with Veronica over the gun in the back of the moving SUV. The gun is between them as Veronica tries to overpower my angel.

He has my left arm hooked up near my head, which only makes trying to fight him off harder. He growls in my ear as I try to force my way out of his hold, but it's no use. I'm struggling to fight back and my airflow is dropping. I can feel myself getting lightheaded as little black dots fill my vision.

Luna throws her head forward, smashing her skull into Veronica's face, and I hear Veronica's scream fill the SUV. I see Luna wince in pain, and I hate seeing her like this, but I hate it even more that I'm useless to her when she needs me most.

I grunt as I try to push my legs off the floor, trying to get more leverage, so I can try and land a hit with my free arm. Glancing at Luna, I barely see when she swings her arm around, the barrel of my gun connecting with the side of Veronica's head. She falls dramatically into the seat behind her, but Luna doesn't waste a second. She turns, aiming the gun in my direction, without even a breath of hesitation she pulls the trigger and the hold around my neck instantly falls.

Leaning forward, I dip my head between my knees. Gasping for breath as the fog in my mind slowly begins to clear. Without warning, the SUV screeches to a stop. I try to brace myself against something, but my body doesn't react quickly enough, and my head bounces off the seating opposite me. I stumble backward, my vision still blurry as I try to gain my balance, but I don't know if it's from the impact.

Luna!

Moving my head around slowly, I search out my angel. I falter when I see her.

My heart pounds in my chest, the ringing in my ears is thunderous. The window behind her has shattered, covering my angel in tiny shards of glass. It takes a moment for her green eyes to open, fluttering as she tries to process what just happened. As I start to crouch down, I notice the gun at my feet. Luna must have dropped it when her head smashed the window.

Looking back up, I try to find who stopped the SUV. Time stills as the driver pulls a gun from the cup holder beside him, aiming it straight at Luna's shocked face. My body feels weightless as it moves on its own accord.

"Luna!" I scream, but I don't hear the word.

I feel like a useless bystander, watching as my life slips between my fingers in slow motion, seeing the shock and fear flicker across her face as she sits frozen in place. Everything we have lived through and survived so far, for it all to end here in the back of some SUV is not acceptable. Our scars run deep as we continue to pick ourselves up and march on. This is not how it ends, how *we* end. My heart pleads for my body to kick into motion, to do something, anything, to protect my angel.

My finger slips through the trigger guard as I lift it off the ground. Dropping to my knees, I finally feel my training instincts takeover. My eyes focus solely on this motherfucker, pointing a gun at my wife. *My wife*, my angel, my Luna. I haven't even been able to express my heart to her yet.

In a smooth, practiced skill, he clicks the safety off, keeping the gun aimed at Luna. My hand raises instinctively, fingers wrapping around the grip as I level the gun in front of me. Without a second thought, I fire.

It feels as though time is not on my side, the bullet traveling slowly through the air. The bang from the gun finally registers in my ears as the bullet blasts through his skull. A large splatter of blood coats the interior of the SUV, myself, and Luna included, making me see nothing but red. As his now lifeless body falls forward, hanging over the back on the seat.

My eyes frantically search over him, making sure he really is dead and no longer a threat to my angel. Slowly, I click the overhead light on and reach impulsively for Luna. Her hands lift to my chest. The delicate touch of her fingertips against my skin makes me sigh in relief. A quiet sob leaves her mouth as she inches closer.

"I'm okay, angel," I manage to force out, and her mouth finds mine. The touch of her lips calms my racing heart and frayed nerves. I feel the blood of death between our lips, and rest my forehead to hers instead. Running my fingers through her hair, pulling out the small pieces of glass, I try to distract myself for a moment. Making sure there aren't any deep cuts, I lean back and cup her face.

"I'm sorry I got blood on you when I shot him," I murmur, looking deep into her emerald eyes and she smiles up at me.

As I look at her, she reminds me of Diana, the triple goddess, just like our bloodline's symbol. The research I found on the tattooed symbol runs through my mind. Diana Triformis: Diana, Luna, and Hecate were all one. Diana as a huntress, Diana as the moon, and Diana of the Underworld. Just like my beautiful fallen angel before me, a goddess, a warrior, a queen.

Leaning back, she takes in the scene around us, and my eyes follow her gaze. Veronica is still knocked out, but an almost muted shouting catches our attention. Luna leans over her mother to pick up the phone wedged between the seats. I grab her arm, worry taking over as she presses the speakerphone button.

A guy starts yelling on the other end, about some shit her egg donor apparently promised. There isn't a chance in hell he's getting his hands on my angel. I'll fucking kill him with my bare hands before he even gets that close. He'll be another reason for me to have blood on my hands, and I won't regret it.

The line cuts off after his idol threat, and there was no denial when Luna called him Totem. As if we need to be dealing with the man that wreaked havoc on Featherstone years ago, on top of everything else.

I watch as Luna looks for something on the floor of the SUV, pulling her phone out, rushing to answer the call. It must be Maverick if she's asking about Jess, and the way her shoulders relax after a moment's pause, I know she's okay. Looking in my direction as if to make sure I'm still here, I wrap my hands around her waist and pull her into me as I sit down on the seat behind us.

I need to touch her, make sure she's real. I'm too busy running my hands over her stomach to process what they're saying on the phone. My head rests on her shoulder blade as I breathe her in. I hear her call a quick goodbye on the phone, but she whips round to face me.

"Parker, I know where we need to go," she says frantically, and I nod subconsciously in agreement.

"Let's move their bodies to the back and then we can leave, angel. Do you think they have something in here we can tie Veronica up with? As much as I'd rather toss them out, I think we need to show up with a statement," I say, begrudgingly lifting her off my lap.

Stepping out of the SUV, the road is dark around us. We move the dead bodies to the back, piling them up to one side as we tie Veronica up on the other. Handcuffing her to the 'oh shit bar' above her head, we bind her legs together and put duct tape over her mouth.

Luna climbs in beside me as I take the driver's seat, I can't help but appreciate the strength and determination she has. Her eyes are blazing again, ready to take on the world.

"Let's go get our family, angel," I say with the same confidence that's in her eyes.

I'm ready to show Featherstone exactly where I belong.

Arriving at Beechwood Hall, which Luna had added to her

mobile navigation app, I'm surprised by the actual size of it. I assumed it would be big, but this place is crazy. Surrounded by farming crops for miles before you even get here, with wrought iron gates guarding the entryway inside.

With Veronica awake in the backseat trying to scream against the tape for our attention, I can't help but chuckle at the way Luna just turns the volume up on the radio. Devil by Barren Gates fills the space around us, all too fitting right now.

After a brief stop at the security checkpoint, we're soon driving down another long road before the Manor house actually comes into view.

My breath picks up again as my defense mechanism kicks in. It hadn't truly slowed after shooting the driver, but I know he deserved it. If I hadn't, he'd have taken my angel away from me, and nobody gets to do that. Ever. My blood starts to boil again as the memory floats in my mind. Gripping the steering wheel, I try to focus. I can feel the anticipation of seeing my father, but I refuse to let it consume me this time.

I don't think either of us really focus on our surroundings, both wanting to find the others so we can take this all on together, as a team.

Coming to a stop in front of the massive building, I pay little attention to the outside as Luna's eyes run over the whole exterior.

"Are you ready, angel?" I ask, running my thumb over her knuckles, needing to feel her any way I can.

"As I'll ever be," she says with a soft smile. My heart screams at me as my pulse throbs in my neck and my palms sweat. After what we just went through, I don't want to step in there having not said it. I need her to know what she means to me.

"Don't you dare, Parker. You can tell me on the other side of this, and I can say it too. The chance of death will not be the reason, do you understand?" Her breathing is erratic as she searches my eyes, refusing to say the words under these circumstances.

I nod in understanding and offer the next best thing. Pointing my finger to my eye, to my heart, and to my angel.

Her eyes well with emotion and her hands shake as she repeats the action to me.

I feel like my heart has stopped, I could die a happy man right now for my girl. My throat is clogged with unspoken emotion as I try to process this overwhelming sense of belonging and peace.

"Fuck you, Parker Parker, for making me feel," she whispers, pressing her lips to mine.

Pulling apart, we both step out of the SUV, and I drag Veronica out of the back. Funny how she doesn't look at all put together as she usually does. Her ragged hair is a mess as I drag her barefoot beside me. This vile bitch has done more than enough to our girl, and I refuse to let her do anymore, especially since she is connected to my father, and apparently, Totem.

I have no mercy as I make quick work of uncuffing her and retightening them behind her back. Tearing the bindings on her legs, I leave the duct tape in place, not wanting to hear a word from her mouth.

The long entrance is silent, all the noise coming from the room straight ahead. I can hear Roman, Oscar, and Kai all shouting, clearly wanting answers on our whereabouts.

Trying to cover the ground between us and them as quickly as possible, I drag a stumbling Veronica along with me by the handcuffs as Luna jogs beside me. The sound of her boots hitting the ground fills the space around us. In true Luna fashion, she throws open the arched wooden double doors, letting them bounce off the walls on either side of us.

The instant relief I feel at the sight of my brothers is indescribable, and it's reflected back in their eyes too. Veronica whimpers beside me, but I tighten my grip on the handcuffs and ignore her protests.

"Princess, why are you covered in blood? Parker?" Roman murmurs, rage filling his eyes as he grinds his jaw in anger.

"What the fuck is going on?" Rico snarls, and I instinctively recoil at the sound of his voice. It feels as though my heart may truly shatter against my chest this time.

Luna pulls me forward with her as I drag Veronica along with me. She trips over her own feet so I let her fall to the floor in front of us, looking pathetic. It seems we already have everyone's attention.

The Ring sits before us at a table elevated on a small platform. Maria's hands are planted on the table, anger rolling off her in waves as she sneers at my father. The tension that fills the room could be cut with a knife, and the fear emanating from the crowds sitting around the tables is embarrassingly noticeable.

We continue to stand on the red carpet walkway as

other guests and students sit at tables on the other side of the red rope dividing us. Luna stands taller and takes another step toward the front with her hand firmly in mine, and her voice fills the room.

"Please, Rico. Do tell me where you thought we would be?" she asks. "It wouldn't happen to be knocked out cold in the back of an SUV with Veronica, would it? On our merry way to see Totem?"

Rafe bursts forward from the crowd to the left where Rico is sitting, ready to snap his neck. "I'm going to kill you," he growls. It actually warms my heart at the loyalty and devotion he always shows my angel, his daughter.

"It's okay, Dad. We're here now," Luna says softly, trying to calm him. Wanting to show this room that she can handle herself, and the vipers set on tearing us down. "Still no response, Rico? I'm disappointed. I'm waiting for you to ask how we still made it here, and Barb, where's she? I'm sure she would love to know too."

This fucking girl has ovaries of steel. Bigger balls than anyone I have *ever* met.

Everyone subtly looks around for Barbette Dietrichson in the crowd as I squeeze Luna's hand in support. Focusing my gaze back on my father, Luna pushes on when she doesn't get a response.

"Okay, well, you'll be glad to know the SUV is parked outside in one piece. Unfortunately, the other passengers are dead."

Rico's snarl turns into a grin as he stares down at Veronica at our feet.

"Not everyone, little girl," he grinds out, which is all the encouragement Luna needs. I can feel it in my bones. I knew she would need to do this. Lay this bitch to rest so she's no longer lingering behind every dark corner.

She calls out to Veronica, who whips her head around in fear, frantically trying to move away from Luna. This is Veronica at her lowest, her appearance is all she seemed to care for, and sitting before us is a broken shell of a woman who knows where this is heading.

Without a wasted moment, Luna raises the gun and pulls the trigger, hitting straight between this bitch's eyes. Everyone watches as Veronica's limp body drops to the floor, blood spraying the ground around her. The few people sitting closest to us jump back, trying to avoid the splatter.

I hear commotion continue around the room, but my mind is focused on the weight that was just lifted off

Luna's shoulders. I can't help but wish for the same. To no longer have my father darken my path.

"Parker, come here, son. Standing beside her does not help you earn your bloodline from me," Rico grunts, and I can feel Luna glare at him. She's made sure to keep me away from him, so this is new to her, but not to us. She'll finally see how he tries to control me.

I glance back over my shoulder, my eyes instantly connecting with Roman, who gives the smallest of nods.

"I'm good where I am. Thank you, Rico," I finally say, finding strength in my family who surround me.

I see the evil glint in his eyes. I've seen it before, he'll try and make me pay for this show of disobedience. This man is nothing like I once feared, I have the courage and the strength to push back at him. I'll forever wonder how I share blood with him, especially when we look nothing alike and share no traits. A replica of my mother through and through.

"If you continue to stand there with her, you lose any right to my bloodline, and I don't need to remind you what happens in Featherstone to people who lose their bloodline," he threatens, and I grin, feeling his noose around my neck loosen.

I smile down at Luna, who squeezes my hand before releasing it to stand in front of me.

"I don't need your bloodline to survive, Rico," I say with absolute clarity.

"Have it your way, you just signed your death wish," Rico throws back with a laugh, an actual laugh at the threat of my life. What a fucking dick.

"Nah, I don't think he did," Luna says with a smile of her own. I step in behind her, gently moving her hair over her shoulder as I unfasten the clasp of her necklace and place it in her hand. "You see, he doesn't need to be a Manetti," she continues, looking at me to continue.

The ring from her necklace falls into her hand as I take in the room again, excitement filling my bones, because I'm finally able to say it to everyone. Dipping down the waistline of my jeans a little near my left hip, I show off my Steele bloodline tattoo. Luna slips the ring onto her delicate finger showing it off with pride to the room, along with a little sass.

My heart pounds in my chest, but not from fear of his presence like it usually would. I can't pinpoint my exact emotion, but I know I'm fucking positive. My angel beside me, and my brothers behind me, offering their support, I know I've got this. Excitement bubbles up as I stare Rico down.

"Hi, my name is Parker Steele and this is my wife, Luna."

OUR BLOODLINE

FIVE

Luna

The room erupts in chaos at Parker's words. Gasps bounce off the walls around us as the crowd watches this all unfold. The look in Rico's eyes is exactly what I was hoping for. Hatred burns in them as he stares me down. This motherfucker didn't even see it coming. His face continues to turn red with anger as his fists slam into the table in front of him. The tumbler of alcohol in front of him falls to the ground, smashing on impact.

I already know there are no more bullets in this gun. I checked on the way over here, and I knew I only had one remaining to put between Veronica's eyes.

Looking down at her as blood pools around her lifeless body, I feel like I could almost float away without the weight of her dark cloud hanging over me.

My gaze whips back up to Rico at the sound of his chair crashing to the floor as he steps down from the platform, ready to charge at us. Bring it on, motherfucker, let me wrap my fucking hands around your throat, watch you take your last breath.

Parker steps in front of me on instinct, as I feel the rest of my Aceholes circle around me, ready to protect me from whatever Rico plans to do. Oscar stands to my left, with Roman to my right and Kai behind me. Not wanting to be a damsel in distress, I try to get through the smallest gap between Oscar and Parker, but Oscar's arm flies out at the last moment, stopping my movement.

"Baby girl, I need you to stay where you are," he says loudly, over the chatter that's increasing as worry ripples through the crowd.

"Oscar, I—"

The crunch of knuckles smashing into someone's face pauses my argument. Standing on my tiptoes with my hand gripping Parker's shoulder for balance, I'm surprised to find it's Rafe laying hit upon hit on Rico. Catching a glimpse of Rafe's side profile, my heart stops at the rage I see in his near-black eyes.

Rafe hits Rico so hard he falls to the floor. With one of his giant hands wrapped around Rico's neck, the other hits him square in the face, forcing more blood to pour from his nose.

Before it can go any further, security guards dressed in black with the red Featherstone Academy logo on their hoodies pull Rico out of Rafe's grip.

Fuckers, I was enjoying that.

They try to restrain them both, but I refuse to let them get a hold of my Dad.

"Let me get to him," I snap, as I try to get past Roman's side, but he stands firmer than Oscar. "Please, I need to stop them from taking him anywhere!" I yell in frustration, making Roman frown down at me, struggling with making the right choice.

The decision is taken out of everyone's hands as glass shatters.

"That's enough!" someone shouts, their voice booming around the room, forcing everyone into silence. It's my grandmother, who is now standing on the podium along with the other members of The Ring. Juliana Gibbs, Betty

Morgan, Reggie Rivera, Travis Fuse, Patrick O'Shay, and John Dietrichson. The only one with a snarl on their face is Dietrichson, which isn't a surprise at all.

"Somebody clean that shit up off the floor," she says, flicking her wrist in annoyance at Veronica. "I couldn't stand the woman alive, never mind dead and staining the carpet," Maria adds, glaring around the room.

I have to cup my hand over my mouth to stop the chuckle bursting out. As if on cue, more security guards step into the room from behind us, making quick work of picking Veronica up in a less than caring manner.

I watch as they carry her from the room. Her eyelids are open, revealing her soulless eyes, which are no different from when she was alive. The tape around her mouth only adds to her pathetic state as blood drips from her skull, leaving a trail behind them.

"Now, if you've quite finished, my granddaughter has been through quite an ordeal at the hands of another member of The Ring. You can bet your ass we will be investigating this further." She clenches her hands at her sides, the only hint of the real rage she's trying to control. "Rafe, please escort Luna and the guys to their room."

The look she gives the security guards holding Rafe's

hands behind his back, is enough to burn holes right in between their eyes, leaving no room to question her wrath if they don't listen.

They reluctantly release him, and Rafe heads straight for us, trying to search my face for clues on how I really feel, without trying to draw too much attention to our emotions.

Parker's hand rests on the small of my back, moving us toward the door we stormed in through.

"Wait a goddamn minute," John Dietrichson growls. "She only needs escorting by her apparent husband, the other's will fucking stay here."

Why do these fucktards always have to underestimate me? Us?

As if in sync, we all stop and turn back in their direction, my Aceholes coming to stand beside me. Parker and Oscar to my left and Roman joins Kai to my right. All at once, raising their t-shirts, and revealing their Steele bloodline tattoos with pride.

I can't keep the smug ass grin off my face as I note the surprise in Dietrichson's eyes. Glancing around the room, I notice others in the crowd staring in shock.

Turning, we leave the room together as one. Leaving

death and destruction in our path.

Silently following behind Rafe, he takes us through the entire grounds, leading us to a separate two-story building. Pristine gardens and spotlessly clean paths are all I can see between the two buildings. I'm sure we'll get our fill of the areas for The Games soon enough, but curiosity has me wanting to catch a glimpse now.

Rafe holds the door open for us as we step inside. The feel in here is completely different, surprisingly calm compared to the main building. Warm neutral tones coat the walls, with thick hand woven rugs scattered all over the floor.

A large stairway sits in the middle with corridors leading off in all directions underneath, but Rafe takes us up the stairs. A large golden chandelier hangs from the ceiling as he heads to the left.

"Are we fucking there yet?" Oscar mutters, making me grin.

Fuck. A lot has happened tonight, none of which we planned for, and the sound of his whining helps settle my overthinking brain.

"Stop whining, O'Shay," Rafe grunts, continuing down the long corridor.

"Actually, I think you'll find it's Steele-O'Shay," Oscar huffs in response, as I feel his fingers lace through mine. Looking up at him suddenly beside me, he winks. "Fine, I guess I'll just hold my baby girl's hand to get me through it," he murmurs, bringing my hand to his lips.

Rolling my eyes at him, I notice the silence still from the other guys. Before I can glance around to check everything is okay, Rafe is stopping in front of a door at the very end of the hall.

Standing beside him, I see him enter a code into a pin pad before placing his thumb against a scanner. What the fuck? Is that on all the doors? Looking across to the opposite door, I notice the same setup there.

The sound of the security locks clicking open draws my attention back around as Oscar pulls me through the open door.

Walking straight into the lounge, there is an oversized, grey, double corner sofa in the center of the room. I want to sink into the giant cushions, but I don't want to ruin it in my current bloody state.

Taking in the rest of the room, the walls are a dusty

pink, with all the furnishings made from solid oak. A huge television hangs on the wall, lined up perfectly with the sofa, and grey curtains frame the windows.

"Obviously this is the lounge, the bedroom is through the door straight ahead, with an en-suite attached. The kitchen is to the right, while the main bathroom is through the other door," Rafe points out, as his hands swing around the room offering direction.

"Thank you," I mutter, and he finally turns to stare into my eyes. Stepping into my personal space, his hands come to rest on my shoulders.

"Darling, I don't know what you've been through tonight. I know you need time to process everything and take care of yourself. So, I'll give you tonight, but tomorrow I need someone to give me all the details because someone has to pay for this." He tries to remain calm, but he's unable to keep the growl from his voice. Grinding his jaw, he trembles with rage.

"Veronica paid for it, Dad, don't worry."

"No, Luna, someone has to pay at my hand. Seeing my daughter step into the room, covered in blood, after those fuckers drugged and tried to take you, nearly destroyed me."

His hands wrap around me as he holds me tight. My arms instinctively squeeze him back as I relax into his hold, feeling more of my anxiety slipping away. I feel him brush a quick kiss to the crown of my head as he steps back.

"This is one of the Steele rooms, Maria had it set up for you. I'll be in the room across the hall, okay? All of your fingerprints have been registered to access the room, and the pin pad code has been set up as your wedding date, so don't pass that information on."

With a nod, he stalks out of the room.

The door barely clicks shut behind him, when Kai is in front of me, hands cupping my face as he searches my eyes.

"Hey, Sakura," he whispers, the pad of his thumb caressing my cheek. I start to feel the events of tonight take their toll on my body, my eyes closing with the emotion that builds inside of me.

"Hey, handsome," I barely offer in response, my body swaying into his, wanting to feel him close to me.

"Holy shit! Grandma Steele outdid herself!" Oscar calls from behind me. Forcing my eyes open, I see him at the doorway to the bedroom. The grin on his face forces a smile of my own. "Guys, we're not gonna need to mess around with mattresses tonight," he says before stepping further into the room.

Resting my head against Kai's chest for a moment, I take a deep breath, soaking in his musky scent as I try to find my center. Before I can force myself to stand unaided again, Kai moves swiftly, wrapping an arm under my legs as he lifts me against his chest.

I continue to soak in his presence as I let him carry me toward the bedroom, where Parker and Roman have already followed after Oscar.

Casting my gaze around the room, I see what Oscar means. The biggest bed I've ever laid eyes on fills the space, easily able to fit the five of us, plus more if desired. Mustard and navy bedding covers the sheets, clearly tailormade to fit the frame, while plain grey walls frame the room. Little furnishings decorate the room in hints of mustard and navy too, making the space cozy and fresh.

I hear the shower turn on in the en-suite before Oscar steps back into the room with us.

"Good, right?" he asks with a waggle of his eyebrows, and light chuckles fill the room. I can feel him relax, knowing he lightened the atmosphere a little. The softness in his eyes as he looks at me touches my soul. "The shower is about as big as this bed. I thought you and Parker might want to wash away the grime of tonight together?"

I nod in response, making him smile as he bounces on the bed.

I catch Roman picking up a card from the dresser in the far end of the room, reading over whatever it says.

A smile ghosts over his lips as he looks over to us. "Maria also filled the room with fresh clothes for us." Turning the card around to us, he shakes his head. "The note says, I hope your men are big enough to fit in these clothes, otherwise, send them back. The men, not the clothes."

I smile along with my guys as Oscar laughs out loud, clapping his hands like a seal in delight.

"Let's get you cleaned up, angel," Parker says, coming to stand in front of Kai, who slowly lowers me to my feet.

Placing my hand in Parker's, I let him lead the way. I don't close the door all the way, opting to leave it open slightly, before I peel out of my sticky outfit. Only then do I realize my Aceholes are still dressed as cowboys. Parker lost his hat back at the party, but I watch as he steps out of his chaps and cowboy boots.

Kicking my combat boots off, I drag my black leggings down my legs, wishing for a pair of scissors to just cut them off, it'd be easier. Pulling my black sports bra over my head, the fresh air against my bare skin sends a shiver down my spine.

Parker grabs my hand, hauling me into the shower behind him. It really is huge in here. Four showerheads hang from the ceiling, while jets shoot water from the walls too. We can definitely conserve water and shower together in the future.

Letting the water hit my skin, I will it to wash everything away. I feel Parker step up behind me as he undoes the hair tie still barely intact. My hair falls around my shoulders as he maneuvers me under the spray better, my eyes shutting as I relax into the heat.

I feel him step away, but he's back within moments, and I feel a soapy cloth run along my bloodstained skin. The smell of vanilla fills the air around me as my sweet Parker Parker washes my body and cleanses my soul.

I can't bring myself to move, but I manage to open my eyes, trusting him enough to let him see me vulnerable. Tilting my head back, his fingers run through my hair as he begins to wash the blood out. I tense as he lifts his hands to my head. After being knocked out in the gazebo, head butting Veronica, and smashing it against the window of the SUV, I'm nervous it'll be sensitive. He's so gentle though, his fingers running through my hair as he slowly lathers shampoo into my scalp over and over again, making sure to get rid of every speck of dried blood.

I know he's done when his fingers gently wrap around my neck, stroking a comforting trail from my ear to my chin. I look down to see the cloth at our feet.

I swiftly pick it up, along with the body wash beside it. Lifting it to Parker's skin, I return the favor, and I watch his eyes close instinctively just like mine did.

Working meticulously to ensure not a single drop of grime and blood remains, I rub the cloth over his skin There is nothing sexual in our movements, but the moment is just as intimate. My fingers linger over his feather tattoo, and his new ink on his hip, loving the connection I feel. I notice the raw red marks around his neck, gently making sure I don't add to his pain from where he was strangled.

Happy with my work, I lean up on my tiptoes and place a soft kiss to the corner of his mouth.

"Thank you, Parker. If you hadn't shot that guy, I wouldn't be standing here right now," I whisper, watching as his eyes flicker open.

"You are my life, Luna. I'll do whatever it takes to keep you." The determination in his eyes leaves no room for question. His hands coming to rest on my hips, as the need to touch each other takes over. "Let's get you dry, angel. Before the guys give up on waiting patiently," he says with a gentle smile, and I nod.

I need my Aceholes right now. I need to feel that sense of family and belonging they offer me without question.

OUR BLOODLINE

SIX

Roman

Slowly blinking my eyes open, I stall at my surroundings, before it dawns on me that we're in the Steele suite at Beechwood Hall. Luna faces me, her breath rhythmically blowing against my chest as she sleeps soundly. The sunlight trying to sneak in through the curtains tells me it's at least morning.

Parker is curled up behind her, the true meaning of a big spoon and little spoon, holding her protectively. I can't imagine how they must feel, but a new level of tenderness falls between them. The way they swung open the doors into the conference room yesterday, covered in blood, with

Veronica a ragged mess, I knew we were lucky to see them alive.

After they came out of the shower last night, Oscar, Kai, and I had agreed not to badger them with questions. Instead, we'd let Luna and Parker sleep off the events from yesterday, and discuss everything as a whole group today, Rafe included. I didn't want them to have to relive it over and over again. As much as I hated not being fully in the know, I know it was the right thing to do.

Attempting to stretch out, I feel the weight of an arm slung over my waist, and a leg hitched over my thigh. Glancing past Parker, I see Kai laying flat on his back with his arm thrown over his face.

Fucking, Oscar. Who knew this little shit was so damn cuddly?

Trying not to wake him as I slip out of the covers, I push his leg off mine and place his arm on Luna's waist. Crawling to stand at the bottom of the bed, I stretch my arms above my head as I take them all in.

I had no idea this is what our family would look like: my brothers and my princess. Luna was destined to be mine from day one, an agreement between the bloodlines or not, she's mine. She is *ours,* and that doesn't bother me in the slightest.

I always knew I would be expected to share her with West, but when she brought up the subject of marrying Parker legally, I couldn't have been happier. Her love and protection of him, matching my own, only made me want her more. I'm just happy she's alive and a part of my life.

Heading for the bathroom, I quietly shut the door behind me and turn the shower on. A bed for all of us is perfection but laying with those fuckers is like sleeping in an oven.

Letting the rainfall shower wash over me, I try to calm my need to slit everyone's throat who've brought destruction to me and mine. My chest burns with anger, as my pulse throbs for all the wrong reasons. Their time will come, I just need to make sure I don't let my hotheaded tendencies take over.

After using the vanilla body wash I smelled all night on Luna, I shut off the water, wrapping a fluffy grey towel around my waist, and step back into the bedroom. Last night, after Maria's note about clothes, I searched through the dressers finding clothes in a variety of sizes. It'll do until our duffel bags are brought up with our own items of clothing inside. Throwing on a pair of tight black boxer briefs, I rub the towel through my hair and head for the kitchen.

My princess is going to need her coffee this morning, and I'm going to be all sweet and shit, and have it ready for her.

The kitchen is massive, all high-end steel appliances with pure white walls, and charcoal grey cabinets and backsplash. The dining table is big enough to seat twelve, and there are six stools at the island in the center of the room.

Fiddling with the fancy as hell coffee machine, I figure out how to turn it on before I pull ingredients out of the fully stocked fridge to make bacon and eggs for everyone.

Grabbing the pans from the bottom cupboard, I'm all set when I notice a multi-functional system on the wall. Clicking through the touchscreen pad, I see you can link your phone up through Bluetooth to control the lights and other electronics throughout the suite, or play music.

Opting to click through a few radio stations, avoiding all the pop and country songs, Body On My by Pitbull and Loud Luxury comes through the speakers. Music isn't really my thing, but sometimes a song just has the right vibe, and my body starts to move.

Lost in my little bubble as I sing along to myself, I fry up the bacon and make enough eggs for everyone, absorbed in what I'm doing. So, when the song ends, and clapping starts behind me, I jump out of my skin.

Whirling around, spatula in hand as my weapon, I frown at Luna and the guys all standing at the door with smiles on their faces.

"Don't fucking do that," I grunt, taking a deep breath, trying to calm my beating heart.

The fact that my princess is standing in just a long t-shirt that falls to her knees, does nothing to relax the beating in my chest.

"Please, continue, Rome. The way your ass was shaking was really working for you," Oscar says with a chuckle and an exaggerated wink. I glare at him in response.

"No fucking bacon for you now, asshole," I say, pointing the spatula in his direction, before turning back to the stove. My cheeks heat slightly at their attention, but I refuse to be embarrassed.

A hand slides up my spine coming to rest on my shoulder, as lips gently kiss my back. I know the feel of my princess' lips, and my eyes shut instinctively as her touch sends electricity coursing through my veins.

"Hey, baby," she murmurs against my skin, and the emotion that washes over me, grounding me, leaves me speechless. "Ignore him, you looked sexy as hell." Her lips lift against my skin.

Turning the heat down on the stove, I drop the spatula and turn to wrap my girl in my arms. I feel her lips against my chest as I pull her in close, soaking in her presence for a moment.

"Take a seat, princess. The coffee is done, I'll bring you a mug over." Kissing her gently on the head, I walk my girl over to the breakfast bar. I feel her eyes track me as I rush back to make the drink as promised, and it gives me goosebumps. I love feeling Luna's attention on me.

Kai and Oscar take a seat with Luna, while Parker takes over cooking the food. Placing the mug down in front of her, she catches my hand before I can step away.

"Everything okay?" she asks, and I nod.

"Everything's fine, I just want to take care of you. Even if that means making you a cup of coffee, because you're too independent to let me do anything else," I add with a smile, as she gives me her classic eye roll in response. The perfect reminder that my girl is here, but there is still a lot to talk about.

"I'll have a coffee too, Rome!" Oscar calls out as I turn back around, but I shake my head.

"You know where the machine is."

"No fair. Luna got one," he whines, and Parker chuckles beside me.

"That's because she has a golden heart, and a magic pussy," Parker chimes in, and I can't help joining in with the laughter.

"Hell yeah I do," Luna laughs along, and I know what Parker meant now, back at Ace when he said this is our family. Our sense of home. I just need to make sure I belong here. Pushing my self-doubt to the back of my mind, I help Parker plate everyone's food and take a seat at the breakfast bar with the others.

We all dig in, having not eaten since mid-afternoon yesterday. A dark cloud begins to form over us all in anticipation of the conversation we all know we need to have.

"Would you like me to call Rafe, Sakura? So, we only need to have this conversation once?" Kai asks, staring at Luna with gentle eyes.

"That would probably be best. I'm going to take another shower and get ready while you do."

Rising to her feet, she walks around the island placing kisses on each of our cheeks before heading out of the room, all of our gazes following after her.

"How bad is it, Parker?" Kai murmurs, and we all look to Parker expectantly.

"It's not great," he sighs, swiping a hand down his face.

My blood is already simmering with anger. God, help those motherfuckers.

Luna

Slipping into a pair of black skinny jeans and a burnt-orange turtleneck, I frown at myself in the mirror. This is one of the very few outfits Maria has arranged that isn't a damn dress. I don't know what she thinks we're doing here, but I need breathable clothing if I'm gonna kick ass.

Although she did think of everything, right down to phone chargers and toiletries, so I can't complain too much. The guys all got dressed while I was in the shower, scrubbing away the memories of the blood coating my skin.

I hear the main door knock, but I know this is going to get heavy, and I have a call to make first. Quickly tapping the screen on my phone, the ringing tone fills the room.

"Luna? Luna, I swear to god, this better be you calling! I have been going out of my damn mind over here!" Red shouts through my cell, and my anxiety relaxes a little.

"Hey, Jess. You okay?"

"You only call me that when things are serious. What's going on, Luna?" she quizzes me instantly, knowing me inside and out, even when she isn't standing in front of me.

"It's a little hectic, but we're okay." I try to be honest with her, but I don't need her worrying. "How are things at Maverick's? All good?" I ask, trying to change the subject.

I hear her shuffle on the other end of the line, and a door clicking shut behind her.

"It's fine, everything's fine. Don't worry about me, just stay safe, okay?"

A bang sounds from her end and I hear her shush someone. At least she's bossing someone there just like she does with me.

"Alright. One other thing before I go, I need you to stay away from Trudy. She was somehow involved with them drugging us and taking us."

"What?" she whispers, devastation etched into her voice. I know the feeling, I thought we could trust her, but shame on me.

"Yeah, something Veronica said, you know, before I killed her."

Silence consumes me as I wait for her to respond. I don't regret it, but in a short period of time, I've killed two people, with good reason. I just don't want her to think I'm becoming a monster.

"Thank god." She sighs. "That bitch had it coming, and when I see Trudy, I'm going to give her a piece…"

"Keep away from her, remember? Let her sweat it out. I'll deal with her eventually," I mumble, absently running my hands over the comforter at the bottom of the bed.

Shouts from the lounge catch my attention, and I frown in confusion.

"Red, I'm gonna have to go. I'll check in as often as I can, okay?"

"Yeah, of course. Love ya, captain. Make smart choices!" she shouts, and it melts my heart.

"I love you too, sassy pants. Behave."

Ending the call, I drop my phone to the mattress as I rush for the door, wanting to know what all the noise is about.

Swinging the door open, I'm surprised to see most of The Ring in here, all of which stop their shouting to glance in my direction.

Great, this talk just got a whole lot bigger.

SEVEN

Oscar

A knock sounds from the door and Kai stands to answer it. It'll be Rafe. Finally. I'm ready to know what happened last night to Luna and Parker before we all arrived at Beechwood Hall.

I messaged my sister last night, but she hasn't responded, making me a little worried. We text all the time, but I wanted her to know where I am. Niamh is fifteen and lives back in Ireland with my mother. Lucky for them, I've never been able to leave the States, having to stay with my father. It's all worth it though if it keeps her out of harm's way. As much as I despise my father, I was surprised my mother saw the damage he was causing too. When I pushed for her to take Niamh and go back to her homeland, she actually fucking listened.

A bang draws my attention to the entryway, where Kai is gaping at all of the people stepping into the room. Rafe, Juliana, and Maria, we kind of expected, but I watch as Reggie Rivera, Travis Fuse, and dear old dad, Patrick O'Shay, follow them into our room too.

What the fuck?

Without a moment's pause or an explanation for why they are here, all hell breaks loose.

"What the fuck is going on, Oscar?" my father growls as he storms in my direction. Rafe instantly lifts a hand to Patrick's chest, stopping his movement. My eyes are solely focused on my dad's angry face, but I can hear Kai's father shouting too.

Another boom sounds around the room, bringing everyone to a halt. Glancing around, I see my Luna in the doorway leading to the bedroom with a surprised look on her face. Me and you both, baby girl. The glare on her face could cut ice as she stares everyone down.

"Does someone want to tell me what the fuck is going on?" she demands, and I feel my cock stiffen in my pants.

Damn, I love it when she's feisty.

"Really? You think you have the right to ask *me* what's going on?" My father looks her up and down, disgust clear on his face. "You've got some explaining to do if you think you're going to be connected to my family, to my son!" my father shouts, and my blood instantly boils.

"Shut the fuck up, Patrick. That's my wife, and you'll do well to remember that. Disrespect her again, and we will take great pleasure in putting you six feet under. You hear me?" I growl, feeling my pulse quicken and my face heat with anger.

Nobody, and I mean nobody, insults Luna like that. He needs to learn that now before I show him where my loyalty truly lies.

My father fumes before me, his body stiff as he clenches his jaw, fire burning in his eyes, but I hold my ground. I want him to see how serious I am. I don't look at the others, yet I can feel the tension rise as my brothers stand by my words. I hear Roman growl beside me, and a glimpse of a tattooed hand rests on my shoulder in support.

"Patrick, right?" Luna says, stepping further into the room. Her confidence vibrates from her with each step she takes, as she keeps her facial expression neutral. Everyone else is still frozen in place. My father barely offers a nod in response before she continues, "If you ever step into my bloodline's territory again making demands, I'll shoot first and ask questions later. Do I make myself clear?"

He scoffs at her in response, and Rafe instantly wraps his fingers around Patrick's throat. Good. Let him see the army she has. Those who are willing to protect her no matter what. He shoves against Rafe's chest, but he doesn't budge, reminding Patrick O'Shay who has the upper hand.

"Let's take a seat at the table, shall we?" Maria Steele asks, heading for the kitchen without a backward glance, and everyone starts to follow.

I don't move until Luna nears, holding my hand out to lace my fingers through hers. Placing her hand in mine, she squeezes my shoulder with the other. I was all set to offer her comfort, yet here she is, returning the favor to me instantly.

Looking to the kitchen, I see the guys have all waited in the lounge for us. Parker steps toward me, concern in his eyes.

"We've got your back, Oscar. Okay?" he offers, squeezing his hand around the back of my neck, and damn does it relieve more of the tension building inside of me.

"The same goes for you too, Kai," Roman adds, getting a nod in response.

He won't have any issues, Roman was always meant to marry Luna. My father can fuck right off. I'm a fully grown adult married to someone I love. It's as simple as that.

Leading us into the kitchen, everyone has taken a seat at the table already. Maria and Rafe hold up the two ends of the table, while Juliana, Reggie, Travis, and Patrick all sit in a line. Leaving this side of the table free for us to join them. Luna sits in the middle, with Kai and Roman to her left, and Parker and I, to her right.

"So, what can we do for you?" Luna asks, always willing to charge head-on into anything. Her fingers stay threaded through mine in her lap, while Parker rests his palm on my knee. They're both grounding me as I continue to calm the storm brewing inside.

My father goes to respond, but Travis Fuse cuts him off.

"I'd like you to explain to me why you are married to my son, along with three other men, and the first I hear of it is in a crowded room? With your bloodline inked on his skin?" Cool, calm, and collected. I wonder where Kai gets it from?

Luna leans forward, dropping my hand to her lap as she braces her arms on the table, staring deep into his eyes. Silence engulfs us as everyone waits to see what she says.

"Travis, can I be honest with you?" she finally asks, not waiting long enough for him to respond. "I don't really care to explain myself to a man who chooses to cause his son so much pain, then shows up here acting like he gives a shit. Unless you're here to contribute to the current situation, I highly recommend you shut the fuck up."

He flinches slightly at her words but doesn't back down. Luna taps the table with her finger as the room grows more uncomfortable, and she doesn't stop.

"Does anyone have any serious questions?" she asks, looking to everyone at the table, and I love that Rafe is struggling to hide his grin at her sassy attitude. She has us all by the balls, and we love it.

Travis frowns as my father finally finds his tongue.

"I don't think you have too much room to talk about family since we all watched you shoot your own mother square between the eyes last night," he snaps. I'm close to killing him right now, for insinuating Luna has no understanding of family.

"That woman merely provided working ovaries. Don't pretend to think you understand any of this," Luna sneers back, pointing her finger at him, but he just shakes his head.

"Yes, Patrick. You'll do well to not speak shit about things you know nothing about," Maria interjects, likely trying to move the conversation along to keep Rafe calm.

"My son does not know commitment, sugar, and he doesn't have time for this shit when The Games are here," he spits, glaring from Luna to me. "Get your shit, we're leaving. Your mother and sister are waiting back in the room."

My hand instinctively pounds into the table in front of me as I start to panic. "What the fuck do you mean? Where is Niamh?" Parker's hand grips my leg tighter, forcing me through the fog of rage taking over my mind.

His Cheshire cat grin tells me he knows he has my attention, that I'll do just about anything to protect my sister.

"She's here, of course. Didn't want to miss one of her big brothers finally making it through The Games now, did she?"

This is why she hasn't been answering my phone calls or texts. She knew I would be upset that they are here.

She's returning to the life I tried to protect her from, the one where he's forcing us to participate in his Featherstone authorized clinical trials.

Taking a deep breath, I try to control my anger. "For the second time tonight, *Dad*, Luna is my wife, and this is my family." Gesturing to the guys beside me. "We will be entering The Games together so I'm staying here, but I want to see Niamh." Parker's hand squeezes my thigh harder, almost to the point of pain, except I'm too on edge. My heart is racing, and I can feel my hands shaking as I hide them under the table.

His mouth opens as he goes to argue, but Reggie Rivera speaks up. "Patrick, shut your fucking mouth before you make this any worse. Our bloodlines are connected now whether we like it or not." He pauses, turning to Luna with a soft smile. "No offense against you, Luna. I'm ecstatic you are now officially a part of our family. It's these dickheads who need to catch up." He wags his finger at my father and Travis, before turning back to them. "We need to stand together if we want any chance of coming up against Totem, and this new fucking movement."

Nobody says a word as they digest what Reggie said. My father swipes a hand down his face in frustration but doesn't argue. His age showing through the strain on his face. His blonde hair thinning on top, and his skin much paler than usual.

"This damn movement," Travis mutters. "I've been slowly watching numbers add to the group, all while Totem manages to stay in hiding."

"He's gone global," Maria huffs. "The rumors are spreading that he's gotten himself an army of followers believing in his shit. Totem's coming for Featherstone, it was inevitable. We must keep on our guard because somehow he always manages to be one step ahead."

"But ultimately, what does this new movement want?" Luna asks, glancing around the table. Her expression is neutral, but I know she's as surprised as me that they're openly discussing this in front of us.

"They want to run Featherstone, overrule The Ring, and lead us down an even darker path," Juliana answers, her icy cool demeanor unwavering. No one talks after that, each of us trying to imagine what that would look like.

"Luna, why don't you and Parker explain what happened yesterday? Catch us all up," Juliana eventually continues, scanning the group.

"How do we know one of them isn't involved with

Totem?" Roman questions, glaring at Patrick and Travis sitting on the other side of the table.

"Well, if they are, they'll know what went down anyways," Rafe growls, joining Roman in his stare down, and Luna shakes her head, exasperated.

"To make a long story short, when we got to the tent we were ambushed and assaulted. Both Parker and I were hit in the back of the head, which knocked us out. We woke up in the SUV, and I could hear Veronica mentioning that someone intentionally gave Parker and me a sedative to keep us unconscious for the ride, but obviously it didn't work." She sits back in her chair, glancing at Parker before continuing. "Veronica was explaining to Totem that she was on her way with us. When she realized Parker and I were awake, she attacked me."

"Fucking bitch," Juliana interrupts, but nobody complains, only nodding in agreement with her statement.

"We fought until I managed to head butt her, and shot the guy strangling Parker." Luna's voice breaks at the end ever so slightly, and it hurts my heart, hearing the pain flutter in her throat.

"Take your time, baby girl," I whisper, stroking her shoulder and kissing her temple in comfort as if no one else is here. She smiles softly at me before straightening her back and continuing.

"The driver slammed on the brakes, and I didn't have enough time to hold on to anything so my head smashed against the window. By the time I was able to focus, the driver had a gun pointed at my head. I truly thought I was going to die in that moment." She pauses, pain etched all over her face as she loses the ability to mask her emotions. Clenching her fists, she blinks rapidly. "Until Parker pulled the trigger, saving my life."

Wow. They literally saved each other from death. My brain can't function, knowing things could have ended much worse.

"I'll fucking kill everyone behind this that is currently still breathing," Rafe fires, throwing his chair back as he stands.

"In time, Rafe. Now, sit down," Maria says sharply.

"I'm done with waiting around, Maria. This new movement keeps fucking trying to kidnap my family. I refuse to just let it all pan out. This is my limit." His knuckles are white as he clenches his fists at his side, his chest rapidly rising with each breath he takes.

Luna stands from her seat, rounding the table and

wrapping her arms around his neck tight. He instantly pulls her toward his chest, clearly needing to feel her to calm down. I can hear her whisper in his ear, but I can't tell what they're saying. They eventually separate and retake their seats, Rafe slamming his chair back to its feet.

Clearing his throat, Travis looks to Luna. "How do you know they were taking you to Totem?" The way he clenches his hands in front of him is the only real tell that he seems nervous. Luna stares him down for a moment, likely deciding how much to tell him.

She relents with a sigh. "Because I spoke to him."

You could hear a pin drop, it's that silent.

"What do you mean you spoke to him?" Rafe asks, his calm persona gone again.

"As I mentioned, Veronica had been on the phone, she must have dropped it to come at me. After Parker and I killed the men and tied up Veronica, I found the phone, and he was still there." She pauses, taking a moment to look around everyone, but it must be obvious that we all want to know what was said.

"Princess, I'm gonna need you to tell me what was said in that conversation," Roman says, trying to remain calm, but a slight pink flush is creeping up his neck. He can't deal with all of this being out of his control. I see him, with his alpha tendencies, but he takes the weight of the world on his shoulders for us. Always has, it just got a whole lot heavier being at Featherstone and with Luna too.

Looking into his eyes, she nods in agreement. Luna must be able to see his struggle too, and reaches her hand out to hold his, knowing he'll need the support when she finishes her story. I can feel it in the pit of my stomach, whatever she's going to say will change everything.

"He said, 'I love a little challenge, but you're starting to annoy me. Your mother promised you to me when you were a baby. Now I've waited patiently, and your time is up. Do as I say, or it'll only get worse'. When I said it would be a hard no from me, he ended the call with 'just remember, I'm coming for you'."

Fuck. If we were unsure if Totem was involved to begin with, there's no question now. Why does everyone want to take my baby girl from me? My hand instinctively searches for hers, lacing our fingers together.

It takes me by surprise when my father talks again "No one else falls at the hands of that man, we're all in agreement there." Who the fuck is this guy? He must see the question in my eyes and shakes his head at me. "Oscar,

I only ever want what is best for you. I lost your brothers to The Games because of Totem, I refuse to lose anyone else. Everything I have done and continue to do, has always been to protect you," he exclaims, but I just scoff.

"Yeah. Forcing different drugs into my system is so protective, Dad. Thanks."

"What?" Luna shouts from beside me, frantically searching between us.

"Oscar, those drugs were to try and make you unaffected by the weapons and gasses being made. I was trying to find a defense mechanism for you." He throws his arms out wide in desperation, but it means nothing.

My heart pounds, ready to explode in my chest. I can't talk about this again, the memories of being strapped to the medical bed with constant wires linked up to my body never brings me comfort. IV drips, heart monitors, medical patches, and the constant feeling of blood being drawn from my body, overwhelms my senses.

Closing my eyes, I try to shut them all out, but it's no fucking use. Anger rises from the pit of my stomach, my mind lost to the prick of my skin, and the beeping of the machines. The feeling of being unable to breathe as different gasses were released into his science chamber, rendering me unconscious, feels all too real.

My fist slams down on the table, the sound of something shattering as it falls is the only sound I hear, but I'm too far gone to give a shit.

"Fuck you!" I grind out, looking my father dead in the eye.

I need to get the hell out of here. It's all a mind fuck with my father, and the longer I stay around him, the worse it will get. It's always been a proximity thing with him, the further away I am from my father, the better I feel.

Kicking the chair behind me out of the way, I head for the door. Feeling someone's hand wrap around my arm has me reaching my breaking point. Not looking to see who it is, I rip my arm from their hold, charging out of the room.

I need to be alone. I can't control my rage when I'm like this. Stepping into the bedroom, I slam the door shut behind me. Trying to take deep breaths does nothing to calm the shake in my body.

Raking my fingers through my hair, I pull at the ends, willing to do anything to ease this fucking tension and sadness that's taken root within me. Fuck him and fuck this shit. I step into the en-suite still needing more distance between us.

Bracing my hands on the vanity, I try to catch my breath, but my eyes catch my reflection in the mirror. My blonde hair is stuck out in every direction, my heated face is red from the anger I'm consumed with. My eyes are frantic, unable to focus fully on myself. I look like a wild beast and feel like a caged animal.

My fist reels back on its own accord, smashing into the mirror before me. Pain shoots up my hand and into my arm as the punch lands perfectly on my reflection. It calms the adrenaline coursing through my veins, but not enough to stop the frantic beating of my heart. My vision is coated in red as blood carelessly drips from the top of my cut hand, small glass shards sticking in my knuckles.

"GET. OUT!" Luna screams, venom in her voice, but I can't bring myself to see what's going on.

"Please, son," I can hear my father plead, but I could care less.

"Oscar," I hear Parker murmur from the door, but my eyes are locked on the damage I've done to my hand.

"Roman, get him out of here before I kill him with my bare hands." The calmness to her voice only makes her words more deadly. "Dad, I need you all to go to. Oscar needs us right now."

"Of course, darling. Orientation starts this afternoon at three p.m. I'll get here fifteen minutes before, okay? I love you," I hear him say, as I hang my head and rest my hands on the top of the sink, watching the blood slowly go down the drain. Silence temporarily embraces me as the door shuts behind them.

"Osc..." Parker starts again, but Kai barges in, interrupting him.

"Shit, Oscar. What did you do?" He tries to step into the en-suite, but I shake my head at him over my shoulder. Roman barges past Kai, his eyes scanning the scene before him.

"I need some space right now, Roman." I feel heat trailing up my neck as I try to breathe through the pounding in my chest.

"Oscar?" Luna murmurs, her voice almost lulling me down from the fight or flight state I find myself in. I can't bring myself to look at her, dropping my gaze back to the vanity as I prop myself up against it, no longer caring about my bleeding hand. "Oscar, let me help you."

"Let *us* help you, Oscar," Parker adds, stepping up beside me.

This time when I feel a hand on my arm, I don't feel

the instant burn to pull away. Squeezing my eyes tightly shut, I can't hold my vulnerability in any longer.

"We've got you, Oscar," Kai murmurs, coming to stand at my other side, and little by little, I feel my family piecing me back together. Finally finding the strength to look Luna in the eye, it blows me away when I only see the same love and care in her eyes, even when I'm in this unstable state-of-mind.

Roman wastes no time turning the faucet on, my hand numb as he cleans the cuts. I register the sting, but I don't wince with the pain. I'm at a loss for words as Luna wraps her hands around my waist from behind, resting her head against my back, comforting me in ways I haven't experienced before. I never want to hurt her, or any of them.

"You'd never hurt me, Oscar. Never."

I frown down at her hands, as though I'd be able to read them like her face. How the hell did she read my mind?

"This dumbass doesn't realize he's talking out loud," Roman says with a grin, and on instinct, I give him the finger, with my non-injured hand. Dick.

The soft sound of Parker chuckling fills my ears, making me feel a little more present.

"Tell me something real, Oscar," Luna murmurs against my back, and it warms my tainted soul.

Thinking for a moment, the words come naturally, "You make me laugh louder, and smile brighter. That is why I love you."

Her hold on me gets tighter, and I begin to feel lighter at the truth in those words.

Surrounded by my brothers, with the feel of my Luna against me, helps lower the fire burning through my veins. Always willing to care and protect each other. This is what family is, blood is just blood, thick and sticky. Whereas these people standing here with me, at one of my lowest moments, offer me much more than anyone else ever has.

EIGHT
Luna

A knock sounds from the main door, and I'm already sick of it. We haven't even been here twenty-four hours yet, and every time someone knocks on that door, nothing good comes from it.

This morning it was the majority of The Ring in our room, and glancing at the clock, I know it's Rafe because it's time for orientation. I'd much rather stay here, in our little cocoon snuggled up with my Aceholes.

From what it sounds like, orientation is just a formality and nothing will be going down tonight, so there is no need to change in preparation.

After this morning, Oscar seems much more like my big mouth, his smile is back on his face, and the cheeky glint in his eyes is back in force. When he finally came back to us, we decided to make use of the entertainment system in the lounge. Kai wrapped Oscar's hand, and luckily, the cuts on his knuckles aren't too bad.

Watching Oscar break down, showing his vulnerability, floored me, and the guys too. I hate feeling helpless, and the only time I do is when one of my men gets lost in their mind. Luckily, Parker seemed to know what to do. Choosing some superhero movie, one of Oscar's favorites, we all relaxed into the giant sofa with all of the blankets, doing nothing except simply being together.

I sit in the corner with my feet up on Roman's lap and Oscar's head in mine. I run my fingers through his blonde hair in hopes to give him comfort. Oscar's legs are tangled with Kai's, who is lying in the opposite direction, laptop in hand, silently working away as always, and Parker is leaning against Roman on the other end of the couch.

It was just what we needed. Oscar needed a relaxed atmosphere to bring himself back into the present, and it was necessary for the rest of us too after recapping yesterday's events.

I killed my mother. I repeat the words over in my head, trying to feel anything, but yet again, I say those words with no remorse. I feel like Arya Stark ticking off every motherfucker that has crossed me.

Patrick O'Shay has joined Rico and Dietrichson, high up that list right now after what he did to Oscar. By a mere fraction, my heart won out over my brain earlier, either care for my husband or seek revenge for him. If he hadn't been so unresponsive, I'd have gone right for his father's throat, but Oscar needed more from me at that moment.

Parker is at the end of the sofa, closest to the door, so he stands to open it while the rest of us untangle ourselves.

I wanted to scream at Kai's father earlier, demand for him to tell me where his sister is, but I know that's not going to be how this works. Shaking my head, I stop my mind from wandering off again. I need to focus on one thing at a time, but there is just so much shit going on right now.

Closing his laptop, Kai places it on the coffee table, stretching his arms above his head. His loose white top lifts slightly, giving me a peek of his abdomen, and I can't help but lick my lips instinctively.

"Kai, put it away, man. You're making our girl horny,

and we have serious business to attend to," Oscar says, grinning up at me. I glare down at him and look back to Kai, who has lifted the hem of his t-shirt over his head, giving me a full view of his abs.

"Holy shit, yes please," I blurt out, making Roman chuckle beside me as Parker opens the door. "Screw you, Aceholes." I push Oscar's head from my lap so I can stand.

Rafe steps into the room offering a soft smile, calming me. I never realized how much his smile affects me, making me feel safe. He steps further into the room, looking past me to Oscar.

"Are we all good now, Mr. Steele-O'Shay?" Rafe asks with a wink at him, and Oscar bounces up off the sofa.

"Hell yeah I am, old man," he says with a cheeky grin, but drops his usual façade as he rounds the sofa to stand in front of Rafe. "Thanks for asking. And I know I haven't really said anything to you yet, but thank you for letting us marry your daughter." In a flash, they're fist-bumping and slapping each other on the back.

What the fuck?

"Give me a sec, guys, I need to piss before we go down," Oscar calls over his shoulder, before disappearing into the bedroom.

I raise my eyebrow at Rafe, but he seems just as surprised as I do. Looking to Roman, he shakes his head slightly. Since when did Oscar sound so sincere to anyone but me? My heart flutters in my chest.

"I can't decide if the real Oscar is better or scarier than the joker he usually is," he murmurs, looking at the door Oscar just went through, and I giggle.

"Does it matter? He's still our Oscar," I say, and everyone smiles.

Kai steps by me, placing a kiss on my temple as he passes.

"You ready? By the time we're done with this, Ian should have brought everyone's belongings up," Rafe says, making me pause.

"Ian, as in, Ian the driver?" I ask, and he nods in confirmation.

Roman steps up beside me, wrapping an arm around my shoulder.

"Yeah, Ian the driver. He actually brought Oscar and me here without any bodyguards, and we actually weren't drugged or knocked out. He was a godsend, princess, well done for making good allies."

Wow. Who knew on my first official day of classes

at Featherstone, I would ask a driver his name, and he would show such loyalty? I wonder if he'll let me take him everywhere with me, once I survive The Games of course.

We take the same path back to the main building of Beechwood Hall, the sky bright with the sun out, not a cloud in the sky, but the chill in the air makes me shudder. Wandering aimlessly on autopilot, we step into the exact same room that I shot Veronica. Not that you'd know, they clearly have an excellent clean-up crew. Not a single blood drop can be seen on the cream carpets.

The layout of the room is completely different today. There aren't any large tables set up, instead, the space is empty except for the long oak table that seats The Ring members. The anxiety seems to kick up a notch at our arrival, the chatter that filled the room dims to a mere murmur, and I smile wide at everyone around the room.

They're all sitting there already, Rico and Dietrichson to the right, with Travis and Patrick separating them from Juliana, Maria, Reggie, and Betty Morgan. Juliana offers a soft smile, which looks out of place when she's in her 'ice queen' mode. She sits rigid, her face completely blank, devoid of any emotion. With her pure white fitted power suit on, she looks as though her gaze alone could slice you in half.

Looking further down the line, my fists clench at my sides as my eyes fall on Rico and Dickhead Dietrichson. They're already glaring in our direction, but I make sure to keep my face neutral. I don't want these wankers thinking they impact me. Watching Rico clench his hands on the table, I can tell he's itching to pay us back. Dietrichson's top lip rises with a sneer, showing his veneers. Fuck them.

Standing on either side of the doors we've just walked through, are other students from Featherstone. I spot Wren, with Becky and Brett, but I don't recognize anyone else from classes. It blows my mind that they are here by choice. I'm slowly learning it's irrelevant how I feel, these Featherstone students know what they've signed up for.

The family members stand on the opposite side of the room, all with pleased smiles on their faces. Not an ounce of fear or worry for their child's safety.

All the students are dressed casually, like us, while their parents think this is a business dinner with men wearing three-piece suits and some women wearing cocktail dresses. What the fuck is that about?

Rafe squeezes my shoulder as he goes to stand with the other parents, looking completely out of place in his denim jeans and henley t-shirt, as the doors shut behind us. Standing in the center of the room, Maria nods for us to join the other students, and we slowly make our way over.

A middle-aged man steps to the center of the room, smiling as he looks us all over.

"Fantastic, we're all here! Let's get to it, shall we?" he says, clapping his hands in front of himself in excitement. "Good afternoon, for those of you who don't know me, my name is Harris Franks, and I teach Laundering, Fraud and Gambling at Featherstone Academy. I can see a few of my students here."

This is the guy who teaches Red's L.F.G. course? He looks like a fucking sleazeball, with his slicked-back hair, pointed shiny shoes, and a wandering eye, inappropriately checking all the students out. He clearly loves himself too, his speech screams Barbette Dietrichson. I see her across the room, smiling proudly at him. I roll my eyes at her usual shit, ready to get on with it. I feel one of my Aceholes stroke a finger down my back, and it relaxes the tension in my body, making me almost shudder at the contact.

"So, this is your Orientation, which is simply an

introduction and run through of what is to be expected." He points his arm toward the far wall to our left where there is a map of Beechwood and all of its grounds. "The Games will officially start tomorrow. You will have three games to complete in total, which will take place on Monday, Wednesday, and Friday… if you survive that long." He chuckles, and I want to punch him in the face. He's so fucking cliche, attempting to play the typical villain.

Roman wraps his fingers around my clenched hand, forcing me to unclench it so he can intertwine our fingers. I look up to him, and he offers a comforting smile while stroking his thumb over my knuckles. I think he's trying to calm me down. I'm obviously not covering my annoyance as well as I thought.

"You won't find out what The Game for the day will be until that morning. Tuesday and Thursday are your well-deserved relaxation days. We've decided this year to hold a gala dinner on Friday for all those participants that complete all the challenges. Okay?" he asks, leering at us all. He's overplaying his role here, like the creepy hand guy from Scary Movie Two. "Perfect, so without further ado, let's do a roll call. When I call your groups, along with your bloodline and skillset for Featherstone, you will simply step forward."

He claps his hands again, and rushes to grab a tablet from a chair propped up against the right side of the wall. Nobody speaks a word as we all wait for him to proceed.

"Okay, group one is Wren Dietrichson, Ace, skillset for Business and Embezzlement. Rebecca Brown, Diamond, skillset for Infiltration, and Brett Rhodes, Diamond, skillset for Drug Trafficking."

Wren steps forward with a conniving grin on her face like she's fucking amazing. I hope I get the chance to ruin that fucking face. Barbette smiles brightly at her daughter, and they make me sick. Becky steps forward, and I watch as Harris Franks runs his eyes over her body from head to toe. A part of me wants to feel sorry for her but she's too much of a bitch for me to truly care. Brett stands there like he fucking runs the world, someone needs to remind him and Becky that they're Diamond. I really need to stop rolling my eyes.

"Group two is Neil Portman and Eliza Walker, Jokers, who both produce narcotics for their skillset."

A scrawny blonde girl steps forward, with a guy just as small, barely touching five feet, two inches with shoulder-length brown hair. They're holding hands and smiling wide.

"We have a lone runner, Conor Starker, Club, whose skillset is torture." Harris shudders as he speaks the words, and the guy steps forward. He must be over six feet tall, with tattoos on his shaved head and a scar running down his cheek.

I mean, even I would be nervous of running into him in a dark alley.

"Group three is Taylor Doherty, Heart, and Zoe Borg, Spade, who both have skillsets in Espionage and Extortion. Along with Freddie Richards, Spade, who is training in all things trafficking."

"Finally, we have group four, the Steeles." Fuck that sounds good. I hear one of my guys hum in agreement beside me and it makes me smile. Harris flicks through the documents on his tablet before continuing. "Sorry, there are a few of you, right?" he says, looking at me with a wink. Roman growls, draining a little color from Harris' face.

"Get on with it, cunt face," Oscar grunts, and he instantly looks away.

"Yes, sorry. So, we have Kai Steele-Fuse, Ace, trained in Business and Technology. Oscar Steele-O'Shay, Ace, who specializes in Science and Combat. Roman Steele-Rivera, Ace, Skilled Assassin." He gulps, glancing quickly in his direction, before continuing. "That leaves Luna Steele, Ace, our resident thief, infiltrator and weapons expert, and Parker Steele, Ace, with his own chosen skill sets, Tech and weaponry construction."

I fucking love that he actually says 'chosen', letting everyone know Parker is paving his own way. No Rico Manetti needed.

We all step forward as one, and the sound of a palm slapping on wood draws my attention to where The Ring are sitting. Rico's eyes are blazing with fury as he stares us down. Motherfucker wants my Parker Parker. Over. My. Dead. Body.

I hold his gaze and grin, unable to stop myself from adding fuel to the fire.

"That's all of the participants for this year's Games. Good luck. We'll be back here tomorrow at eight a.m.," Harris says, but I don't shift my gaze.

I feel Roman lean in close, his breath blowing against my ear. "Don't worry, princess. We'll kill him. Whatever it takes." He kisses my cheek and I nod.

We'll make him suffer for everything he has done,

payback's gonna be a bitch.

NINE

Roman

My heart is thundering in my chest, but I wear my indifferent mask. I need to show a strong front so the others don't panic and see my strain too.

It's seven fifty on Monday morning, and we're making the slow walk back over to the main hall to find out what the first game will be. I can feel a dark cloud building over our heads, only getting stronger and darker with each step we take.

On instinct, the four of us guys walk perfectly to protect our girl. Not that she needs it, but it appeases us at least. Oscar takes the front, leading the way, with Kai and Parker on either side of Luna, while I take up the back. I frown at the sky, the sunny fall day completely luring us into a trap, hinting that today could be a good day.

We're all in black from head to toe, wearing matching black pants, t-shirt, combat boots, with leather jackets hiding our guns by covering our shoulder holsters. We don't know what to expect, so we all brought a gun and a knife. Just another casual Monday in the fucked-up world of Featherstone.

Oscar stops just outside of the doors leading into the building, and turns around opening his arms, waiting expectantly for Luna. She doesn't waste a moment before stepping into his embrace, and I can feel their love for one another from here.

Yesterday, when Oscar showed such vulnerability, I was in shock. I've never seen him like that, but he didn't shy away or hide from us in the end. He let us take care of him, mainly Luna, who we all turn to when we feel lost. Somehow, she's able to pick us back up again.

Parker and Kai join in the hug, wrapping their arms around our girl, and I refuse to let my worries stop me from joining the moment. My arms stretch wide, not actually touching Luna, but I rest my head against hers. Breathing her in, I let her vanilla scent consume me.

We've all trained for this, even Luna. She may not have realized it at the time, but as hopeful as Rafe was about her not having to attend Featherstone, he still made sure she was prepared.

"I still think we should have had #TeamAceholes printed on our t-shirts," Oscar grumbles, making Luna giggle, and it relaxes the atmosphere. As annoying as this asshole can be, he's always able to break the tension. Not that I'm going to tell him I appreciate it, because I'll never hear the end of it.

"We are not wearing matching slogan t-shirts, Oscar," I respond, making him groan.

"But think of the Christmas cards we could do? Thanksgiving would be so awesome if we—" I slap this douche around the head, effectively shutting him up. "Ow, Rome. If Luna suggested it you would've worn them," he whines, rubbing the back of his head.

"Damn right I would, but she isn't a fucking pussy like you. So I have nothing to worry about," I say confidently, until I hear Luna chuckle, but it sounds way more wicked than usual. Stepping around Kai, she strokes her hand down my back.

"I'm going to remember that, baby. I just might surprise you," she purrs, before heading in through the door, giving me no option but to follow her inside, with a semi in my pants. A simple touch from my princess, mixed with her voice, and I'm having to count backwards, the concentration distracting my thoughts. I do not want to walk in there with my cock noticeable through these damn pants.

Parker pats me on the shoulder as he passes, clearly aware of the effect she has on me. Kai and Oscar follow behind, and I adjust myself discreetly as I step inside.

Walking down the hallway, it's almost eerily quiet, and as we turn into the main room I'm surprised to see everyone else is already there waiting. The tense atmosphere swallowing us up.

I cast a glance to my father, who offers a reassuring smile from the large table that sits The Ring. It doesn't do anything to help the situation, but I appreciate the sentiment. The deep wrinkles around his eyes show his strain and worry, and I'm glad my mother isn't here. When this is all over, I'm taking Luna to meet her again.

A smaller hand grips my shoulder, and I already know it isn't Luna because she's in front of me. My skin crawls, knowing the only other person here with the balls to touch me. Glancing down, I'm not wrong.

"Get your fucking hand off me, Wren," I grunt, shrugging her off. This girl is just never going to learn. I shouldn't be surprised that she wants to cause a scene. She's been too quiet since we've been here, but she doesn't know we have the footage of her setting up security cameras in Luna's room. It definitely doesn't help that the last time I saw her, I was trying to convince her to come with Oscar and me for some alone time so that we could interrogate her.

"Roman, baby, don't be like that. We were having so much fun at the party on Saturday night, weren't we?" She tries to be seductive, but her voice just grates on me.

"No, no, we weren't, Wren. Now, fuck off."

This conversation now has everyone's attention in the room. I look to Luna, and she's sneering at this bitch hanging off my arm. Fuck. Her protectiveness is doing nothing to help the situation I've got going on in my pants. My heart swells knowing she has claimed me as one of her Aceholes.

Wren glares up at me, a sinister glint flickering in her eyes, and I already know she thinks she's going to ruin me with whatever comes out of her mouth next.

"Does your little whore of a wife know you were trying to fuck me at the party? Hmm?" She walks her fingers up my chest, and before I can grab her wrists, Luna does it for me.

Hanging off my arm, Luna keeps her grip on Wren's wrist as she looks up at me.

"Hey, baby."

"Hey, princess." I can't help but grin at the calm approach she's portraying because her eyes give away the fire building inside.

"Is this bitch talking about Saturday night, when I had to practically force you to be in her presence? The same Saturday night where you were luring her into the gazebo ready for me to fuck up her face?" She smiles sweetly up at me before turning her gaze to Wren. "That Saturday night?"

Wren stares with her mouth open as Luna's words slowly sink in. She tries to pull her arm out of Luna's grip, but she doesn't relent. Instead, she drops her arm from me and steps right up into Wren's face.

"I swear to god, I'm coming for you, Wren Dietrichson, and you won't even see it coming. Now get your hands off my husband." She pushes Wren back, releasing her wrist as she does, but the blackness that takes over Wren's eyes tells me she's not done.

Lifting her arm, she goes to slap Luna across the cheek. Luna doesn't waste a moment, stopping the hand coming toward her face, while simultaneously forming a fist with her right hand. The crack that vibrates off the walls when Luna punches her straight in the face gives me too much pleasure, and I can't help but smirk. Which is nothing compared to the slow clap that Oscar starts, making Parker laugh behind his hand as he tries to keep a straight face.

Wren wails on the floor, clutching her nose to try and stop the blood from going everywhere. Real tears prick her eyes as Barbette scurries over.

"What the fuck have you done? I'll have your head for this!" she yells, as the room breaks into chaos.

I pull Luna away from them, spinning her behind me, where I know the guys will be.

"Quiet!" Somebody shouts, and the room comes to a stop. Looking to see who spoke, I'm surprised to see Juliana Gibbs glaring daggers at Barbette as she braces herself on the table with clenched hands. "When you're quite fucking done, Barbette, we'll continue. Like mother, like daughter is all I can say... touching people without their explicit permission." Standing to her full height, she straightens her blazer. "Now, sit the fuck down."

Following her own words, Juliana takes a seat, watching as the Dietrichsons begrudgingly do as they're told. Barbette's death glare burns holes into Juliana, while Wren cups her nose. I can't say she didn't ask for it.

Looking behind me, I see Luna standing in the middle of the other guys. Parker behind her, and Oscar and Kai to each side while she tries to fake glare at me.

"You didn't have to move me away," she mumbles, and it only makes me smile more. Leaning in to whisper in her ear, I grip her waist.

"Princess, don't play me. I can see the sparkle in your eyes. You're wondering when I'll be able to manhandle you like that in private." I bite down on her earlobe. "Soon, princess. Real soon." I growl, feeling her shudder against me.

Standing back, I turn to face The Ring as everyone else is, only to see Maria Steele looking at me with a raised eyebrow. This woman has me made, but I can see the humor in her eyes, so I flash her a wink as Harris Franks comes to stand in the center of the room. I can't handle the sight of him, he thinks he's slick in his pinstripe pants and gelled back hair, but he looks creepy as shit.

"Good morning, students. Let's not waste any time and get straight to it, yes?" He rubs his hands together in front of him as he looks at us all. "Perfect, this morning we will be doing The Tunnel over in Zone A. You'll get all the information upon arrival. If you'd like to follow me, we'll be making our way over there in your groups."

He raises his arm to the open door before leading the way. Everyone starts to filter out behind him while we keep to the back. Wrapping my fingers around Luna's, I expected a little more information before we left, but true to Featherstone standards, they keep all the details under lock and key.

Luna must be able to sense something, as her other hand comes up to squeeze my shoulder.

"Baby, we've got this. We just need to stay focused, okay?"

I nod my head in agreement, unwilling to meet her eyes when I feel like this. I don't want her to see weakness in my eyes, at the fear of something happening to one, if not, all of us.

Bringing her hand to my lips, I brush a kiss against her

knuckles. Pulling strength from her as I force confidence and positivity into each step I take.

Whatever they try to throw at us, I have to concentrate on our skill and ability to overcome this. We won't be broken by Featherstone and the minions it creates.

Bring it on.

OUR BLOODLINE

TEN
Oscar

The anticipation in the back of the SUV is almost suffocating. The Tunnel, that's all he said. I'm sure we'd have more to discuss if we knew what it actually meant. I'm trying to remember if we came across that specific game when we were digging through all the files from West, but my mind doesn't want to work.

Pulling my gaze from the trees lining the road outside of the SUV, I glance to Luna who is sitting across from me in between Kai and Roman. She's slightly leaning into Roman, clearly picking up on the dark vibes I'm also getting from him. Although, being close to Luna has relaxed his tense shoulders and the tightness around his eyes.

Kai twiddles his thumbs, obviously itching to have his laptop in hand so he can research more into this damn thing, instead of us going in blind.

"I really don't remember reading about The Tunnel, does anyone else?" Parker asks, breaking the silence, but we all shake our head.

"No. It's fucking typical that the first game is something we don't have more information on," Luna murmurs, speaking the truth we're all thinking.

A huge white building comes into view, and I instinctively point it out, getting everyone's attention. It looks like a super modern two-story business building. All white exterior walls with floor-length windows to the ground floor, but nothing above.

"Any guesses where the dark shit happens?" Kai grumbles, and I hum in agreement. Top floor with no natural light to filter in. Perfect.

As the SUV comes to a stop, I don't wait around for someone to open the door. Stepping out, I hold my hand out for Luna, who rolls her eyes at my chivalry but takes it all the same. As she stands beside me, I wrap my arm around her shoulders and place a kiss to her head. I just need a moment to soak in her calming energy before we walk into the building.

Before we joined Featherstone Academy, none of us were worried about coming here and taking part in The Games. But that was before we had something to live for, *someone* to live for. Now, everything is different, and I think that's what has been playing on Roman's mind too.

A hand squeezes my shoulder, and I glance to see who is offering me support. Parker comes to stand on the other side of Luna, as Roman comes to stand in front of me. Instinctively, we all nudge in a little, creating a private circle and blocking ourselves off from the rest of the world.

Luna's hand comes to rest on my back, and I close my eyes for a moment. No matter what, I feel like things will change when we step in there, and I just want to feel the normalcy of this moment. Letting them see the real me, the one behind the mask. I want the concern in my eyes, and the inability to lighten the mood right now, to show what I am incapable of saying.

"I feel like we need a pep talk, and to slap each other's asses like it's a football game or something," Luna jokes, and I can't help but smile as I peer down at her. She's already staring in my direction, and offers me a wink when I meet her gaze.

How does she always know what we want and need? Knowing I couldn't lighten the mood like I usually would, she took that weight off my shoulders. Using her positivity, I smirk as I lean down and turn quickly. Before she even knows what's happening, I have her over my shoulder in a fireman's lift. Raising my hand, I spank her ass good, making her squeal.

"Alright boys, who else wants a turn?" I say with a grin, and as cheesy as they may think I am, they all slap Luna's ass.

"You fucking, Aceholes. Stop it. Put me down!" I can't tell whether she means it or not, but she's chuckling along. Bringing her down, so her legs wrap around my waist, she brings her arms around my neck and leans her forehead to mine.

"Oscar Steele-O'Shay, you're making a scene," she mutters, but I just shrug.

"Baby girl, let 'em watch."

She hugs me tight, before patting my shoulder to put her down. I comply begrudgingly, but I know we need to walk in there strong, and me carrying her in will only make her appear weak. Luna is the motherfucking strongest one here.

Stepping up to Kai, she reaches for his hand and begins walking to the entryway. I watch as her ponytail swishes back and forth for a moment, while Roman and Parker follow beside them. As if sensing I'm not there, she glances over her shoulder, and the sparkle in her eyes encourages me to join them.

Finding my game face, I'm ready to take on whatever they try to throw at us. No one is hurting my family. No one.

"Each of you will pull a card. You will either be a traveler or an interceptor, quite literally," Harris Franks says, gesturing to the large display on the wall.

There is so much information scattered across it, I don't know where to look first. Glancing to my left, I see Kai's observant eyes, and Roman's calculating mind digesting the pictures and notices as quickly as possible.

"The Tunnel is simply that. A tunnel for which a traveler is to go from one end to the other while surviving what lays in wait." He lifts his arm, indicating behind us.

What looks like an ordinary wall, is actually the divider between us and The Tunnel, apparently.

"If you happen to pull an interceptor card, you'll be an obstacle in there." Glancing around us all, his smile only widens. "Now, I know some of you are here in groups, but this is a solo game. Which means you will enter alone, but you won't be put against a member of your own group if you choose opposite cards. Understood?" he asks, but he still hasn't really explained what it is we're actually doing.

"What do we even have to do in there?" Wren whines, and as much as I just had the same thought, her voice still fucking grinds on me. Even more so now she sounds nasally from Luna's punch. I'd rather not know the answer if it means I don't have to listen to her.

Harris rolls his eyes as he sighs, clearly not giving a shit that it's Barbette's daughter who is asking a question. "Travelers will enter from the left, and have to make it out of the door straight ahead, which will bring them out to the right."

He points specifically at the sides of the space he's talking about. It's not that long, maybe fifty yards or so, but knowing Featherstone, a lot can happen in that space.

"If you choose the interceptor card, you'll be escorted

around to the other side where there are doors. It's your job, if you choose, to stop the travelers by any means necessary."

"That's barbaric," Luna whispers beside me, and Parker squeezes her shoulder. She's not wrong, but the only way out of here is literally the light at the end of the tunnel. So fucking cliché.

"Let's get a fucking move on," Rico grunts, gaining everyone's attention. All the members of the Ring are sitting on high-back black velvet chairs like they're royalty, while family members are seated at the entry into The Tunnel on shitty plastic blue chairs.

"Okay, there are fourteen cards placed face down on the table here. If you would all like to come and choose one, we can proceed with The Games," he says, clearing his throat.

Everyone tentatively steps forward, the choice playing a role in our fate. My fingers brush against the closest one, the guys doing the same, while Luna leans across the table, grabbing one from further back.

Holding our cards close to our chest, every single one of us steps away from the table, peering down like it'll stay a secret forever.

Traveler.

Great. Looking to the others, we stand in a makeshift circle again. Wanting to just share with each other first, before the rest of the room. Without any prompt, we all turn our cards around, reading each others instantly.

Luna and Kai both have interceptor cards, while Roman and Parker have matching traveler cards to mine. My heart begins to thumb heavier in my chest, as the situation starts to set in. Blowing out a breath, I muster whatever smile I can, and they all do the same. At least I'm not the only one nervous, I just don't know which role is worse.

"Okay, if we could have travelers to my far left please, and interceptors to my right, we can begin."

Grabbing Luna's chin, I crush my lips to hers, only for a moment, but enough to feel her. Bringing my lips to her ear, I whisper, "I love you, baby girl."

Turning, I walk away without a backward glance. I showed her my vulnerability and my emotion, now it's showtime. In a room filled mostly with sadistic idiots, I let my rage at the world brush the surface, shutting down everything else.

Roman and Parker come to stand beside me, and I watch as they lock their emotions down too. Focusing solely on doing whatever it takes to come out the other side alive.

"Perfect. If the interceptors would like to follow Barbette, she will lead you around to the other side. Please remember interceptors, you don't technically have to fight, but it's dark in there, and there will be trained Featherstone men joining you. So, you could get a little caught up either way," Harris speaks, and I watch as Rafe nods at Luna as he stands with the other family members.

It almost feels too tame, but I'm not in there yet, and it's also round one. I'm sure if we make it to round three, it'll be much more cut-throat from the start. Although, I have a feeling in the pit of my stomach telling me that we're not all going to make it out of these Games.

I watch as Luna leaves with Kai, and the other interceptors leave, including Brett, Becky, Taylor, Conor, and Eliza. That leaves Wren, Freddie, Zoe, and Neil along with us three as the runners.

"He's still not giving us enough information, Rome," I murmur to him, and he nods in agreement.

"We just focus, and slay whoever we need to. When we get in there though, you call out for Luna and Kai. I wouldn't put it past these fuckers to go against their word and have us kill each other off," he mutters, and he's fucking right.

Looking past him to Parker, I'm surprised by the sheer look of determination on his face, his jaw tight as thunder flashes in his eyes.

"Okay, so the members of The Ring will be able to see what happens inside from the monitor above the exit door. You may watch it too, if you make it out of course." Tapping his fingers on the tablet in his hands, he continues to drone on. "Did any of you bring weapons?" he asks, looking over to us.

I don't move a muscle, and neither does anyone else as we continue to stare him down.

"I sure hope you did, because we won't be providing you with any," he says with a smirk, and I just want to beat the shit out of him for enjoying all of this.

I have a blade and a handgun. Although the handgun is going to be useless if it's dark in there, I'll keep my blade ready. I can feel it's weight against my side in the holster under my leather jacket. I can picture the leather-wrapped handle and it's razor-sharp tip. My fingers are itching to grab it now, ready for a fight.

"You will run in the order we call your name, no

questions or amendments." Harris smiles as Rico claps his hands, excitement playing in his eyes. I'd love nothing more than to use my blade to slit his throat. "Freddie Richards, you're up first."

He nervously steps forward, no weapon currently in hand, as someone prepares to open the door for him. With bated breath, I watch the door shut behind him, the space around us now eerily quiet. To say The Tunnel is mere steps in front of us, we can't hear anything. So, either nothing is happening, or the space is soundproof.

Glancing across at The Ring, I look at my father, whose eyes are fixated on the screen at the exit. I see his head flinch a little at whatever is happening, but that's my answer. For Freddie, The Games have already started, and until we can see the screen or them come out of the other door, we will stand here unaware of what lurks inside.

After what feels like an eternity, the door at the opposite end of The Tunnel bursts open, and Freddie falls out, dropping to the floor. There is blood in his hair and dirt on his arms. His eyes frantically look in our direction, fear etched in every molecule of his being before he passes out.

Screams fill the room at the state of his condition, but I know not to pay them any attention. Instead, I keep my eyes trained on The Ring, just as I know Parker and Roman are doing, making sure we show no reaction or care to what is going on around us.

"Oh my god. I can't go in there. You can't make me!" Wren cries out. "You may as well kill me now!" She screams, which only makes Rico chuckle.

"That can be arranged, sweet cheeks," he purrs, and that instantly shuts everyone up, although the death glare old man Dietrichson sends him shows the tension between them.

"Let's continue," Harris interrupts, and that's what happens. One by one, we're called out.

Neil Portman, from Joker, enters next and eventually makes it out of the other side, with a similar reaction to Freddie. His unconscious form is carried away.

Parker is called next. He glances at Roman and me before entering The Tunnel. His eyes are devoid of any emotion, as my palms begin to sweat. It's fucking hard locking your emotions up when you can't control what happens in there.

It feels twice as long as the others before he steps out of the other doors, but when I glance at my watch, he wasn't even in there for ten minutes. I release the breath I didn't realize I'd been holding, scanning him from head to toe. Blood and dirt cover most of his body, including his face. Darkness seeps into his eyes, but he remains on his feet.

He shakes the ends of his leather jacket while mouthing 'off', and I nod in acknowledgment. His eyes burn into ours as he mouths his next words, 'call out.'

Holy fuck. Luna and Kai were in there when Parker went through. Roman was right, some slick motherfucker's trying to break the rules, and it won't take many guesses to figure out who.

A chair is brought out for Parker to sit on, which he plants right in front of the monitor. He hasn't looked over at The Ring once, not even subconsciously to check his father's reaction and I've never been prouder of his new-found strength.

"Zoe Borg, you're up next," Harris calls, and she slowly makes her way over. Looking up to the ceiling, she takes a breath before stepping inside.

I'm not even sure if a minute has passed before Parker's eyes instantly fall to us, and he shakes his head. A siren sounds and medics step inside The Tunnel from Parker's end. Moments later, Zoe's lifeless form is being carried out, droplets of blood trailing their path.

Holy fuck. That makes this situation a little more real. Catching Parker's gaze again he mouths, 'Brett' and I can't say I'm surprised. He'd make a perfect understudy for Rico. Sick bastard. He couldn't just go in there and survive like everyone else.

"Right then, Oscar Steele-O'Shay, you're up."

OUR BLOODLINE

ELEVEN
Oscar

Shrugging my leather jacket off, like Parker advised, I drop it to the floor beside me, leaving my black t-shirt underneath. There's no use handing it to Roman when he's going to have to do the same. I can't help but glance back one last time at him, before nodding at the guy to open the door.

I'm surprised to see a dimly lit space, with another door leading into The Tunnel. Stepping into the tiny space, there isn't even any room to stretch out my arms. The door behind me is slammed shut, and I guess that's my cue to get on with it.

Pulling my blade from my holster, I open the door in front of me. Darkness overwhelms my senses as I look around the area. My eyes try to adjust to the blackness but with the light flickering above my head, my sight isn't adjusting.

Moving into the long room, I shut the door behind me. My heart pounds in my chest, ready for a surprise attack. Gripping my blade tighter, I release a breath and relax my tense shoulders.

"Luna," I call out, and the words barely leave my lips, before I hear her voice. She sounds distant, but she's definitely to my left. Maybe closer to the exit.

"I'm here, Oscar. Kai too. Just focus straight ahead, we won't be near you, but there are a lot of guys in here who—"

"Shut her the fuck up, before I gut her myself," some guy growls to my right. I can hear their footsteps approaching. My heart rate spikes. This motherfucker just threatened my wife.

Trying to keep my emotions at bay, I catch movement from the direction the voice spoke heading toward me. I don't know if these people have weapons or not, but I refuse to leave them alone when they endanger my family.

Cracking my neck, I feel him near. He's close enough to attack but trying to creep up on me. Letting the fireball of anger overcome me, I spin my body to the right, grabbing his shoulder with my left hand, I lift my blade and stab him straight in the neck. Instantly, I feel the blood trickle over my hand.

I wish it were lighter in here so I could see the fear in his eyes as the pain and reality wash over his features. His hand pats my arm frantically, trying to grab onto something, but moving now will do him no good anyway.

"You'll do well to remember who you're fucking threatening. You'll forever wish you'd stayed in the corner and left my wife alone," I spit out, as he drops to his knees. "It won't matter now. Not where you're going," I growl, listening to him gurgle on his own blood. "Can you die quietly somewhere else? You're getting on my fucking nerves."

Twisting the blade, I pull it out of his neck, letting his body fall to the floor in a heap. I feel his blood swipe across my skin, flickering up from removing the blade, but there's no use wiping it when there is more to come.

"Which motherfucker is next?" I grunt, moving forward.

I feel my boots squish on the ground beneath me. Mud, this is why everyone has come out covered in dirt. Parker had it up his jacket sleeve and down the side of his pants. Who pushed him to the ground? Someone is going to pay for that.

I can't stop my eyes from frantically searching around me, but I'm never going to adjust to the darkness if I keep it up. Focusing straight ahead, I start to see the space come into view more. The floor is uneven for as far as I can tell, with what looks like large rocks placed around the room too. Trying to see if there is anything else I can pinpoint, my eyes start to take in the outline of men standing around, ready to attack.

My brain tries to calculate how many people are actually in this room, but I'm cut short as someone charges at me. Pity they can't run quietly, because they give themselves away. Swinging my arm upwards, my elbow connects with their face, throwing them backwards.

"Just keep walking, Oscar," I hear Luna say, and I'm not sure if she actually did, or if it's my imagination using her voice as an encouragement to carry on.

Continuing to put one foot in front of another, I feel someone step up behind me. Before they get a chance to touch me, I drop to a crouched position and swing my blade up and over my head. I feel as the tip of the blade punctures skin, keeping the pressure going, and sinking the steel all the way to the hilt.

The attacker groans as I stand and turn, all while holding the blade in place. Punching out, they connect with my cheek. My head snaps to the side with the impact as they hit again, meeting my stomach this time.

Fuck.

Shaking my head, I focus. Pulling my blade from their body, I swipe my left fist out, hearing the crunch of my knuckles against their face. My knuckles are still sensitive from yesterday, but I still crush their nose in the process. Not wanting to waste any more time here, I thrust my blade forward again, stabbing them in the abdomen. Pulling my six-inch blade out, I do it again and again. Feeling them lose the strength to fight back, I pull my blade out for the final time and push him to the floor.

Bracing my hands on my knees, I try to catch my breath. Sweat trickles down my back, and my t-shirt sticks to me with a mixture of blood, sweat, and filth. Pushing my hair from my face, I stand to my full height, feeling the sticky substance of blood coating me everywhere.

The longer I'm in here, the more my eyes adjust, but now I'm a little disorientated, and I don't know which fucking direction I should be going in.

"Oscar? Oscar, are you okay?" Luna shouts, trying to remain calm, but I can hear the panic in her voice.

"I'm just fine, baby girl, don't you worry," I call out, keeping all emotion from my words. I'd rather give her nothing, than too much. I'm sure Kai has his hands full keeping her at bay enough as it is. If it was up to her, she'd be over here slaying them all with me, one by one.

Her voice came from my left though, and I know she was near the exit when I stepped in, so that's the way I head. Trying to keep my pace up, the door is in sight, the handle inches from my fingertips. When something is smashed against my shoulder, knocking me to the ground, making me drop my blade.

Holy shit. Pain ricochets through my body as my shoulder throbs with the impact.

"It's about time someone taught you a lesson, O'Shay," I hear from above me, and I instantly know it's Brett. He should have kept his damn mouth shut. I've wanted an excuse to fuck him up since his drunken sneers and groping of Luna.

He lifts what looks like a bat over his head, ready to drop it on me again, but he'll not get the upper hand twice. Placing my feet on the ground, I throw my injured shoulder into him, the momentum knocking him on his ass. I grapple to get the bat out of his hands, bringing it down between us to add pressure to his chest.

He laughs maniacally as he releases the bat to claw at my face, like a bitch. His fingers prod at my eyes, trying to blind me, and I push the bat from between us to fight him off. Dropping a hand from my face, he punches me in the stomach before I can hit him. His hips push up, and he quickly has the tables turned. Leaning over me, his hands wrap around my neck, choking me.

Blinking through the pressure, I force myself to remain calm. Panicking isn't going to save me here. I feel the mud seeping into my clothes, as he pushes me further into the ground with his weight on top of me. I can hear Luna, but she sounds even further away than before.

Closing my eyes, I remember all the times I would practice scenarios like this in the gym at high school with guys. Only this time, I remember what else I have in my holster. Moving as slowly as I can so I don't draw attention to the movement, I try and grab my other weapon. His fingers are digging into my neck, biting the skin, as my vision becomes blotchy, the darkness seeping in.

I fiddle with the gun wedged between my body and my arm, feeling my fingers wrap around the handle fills my body with relief. I click the safety off, and if he hears it he doesn't falter, only continuing to add pressure to my airways.

My head is fogging as I fight to breathe. I'm not dying at the hands of fucking Brett Rhodes, not a chance in hell. I'm going to make him suffer. Aiming the barrel of the gun, I pull the trigger. The scream that fills the room is like music to my ears.

His hold on me instantly falls away as he rolls to the side. Gulping in as much oxygen as I can, I rise to my knees, my head swaying close to the ground as I push through the burn of breathing.

"Oscar! Oscar!" Luna's cries fill my ears, forcing me to stand, anything to show her I'm okay.

"Luna, I only like it when you cry out like that when we're fucking, okay?" I say, my voice croaky, trying to relax the moment. I don't need her to worry, and I need to teach this motherfucker at my feet a lesson.

"Screw you, Oscar. I heard the gunshot and I… and

I…"

"I know, baby girl. I know," I murmur back, feeling her emotions in every breath.

I hear Kai murmuring to her too, so I focus my attention on this little prick. I really wish he could see the devil in my grin right now, because I'm going to take a lot of pleasure from this.

"How's your little dick doing, Brett? Hmm? Did it turn you on when the bullet just blew it to pieces?" I have never loved shooting anything as much as I enjoyed making him lose his dick.

He cries out, rolling in pain, but I'm far from fucking done. Lifting my foot up, I bring it back down hard on his ankle, putting all my weight behind it. The sound of his bones breaking only offers me encouragement as he wails in pain.

Crouching down beside him, I whisper in his ear. "How does it feel to be helpless? Maybe I should do to you, what you longed for Tyler to do to Luna. What do you say to that?" I growl, fury filling my body again as I remember his words. "Maybe I should put a bullet through your skull, lay you on your front and fuck you like you tried to do to my wife?" My words only add fuel to the fire, wanting to give him a taste of his own medicine, and if that means dropping to his level for a moment, then I will.

"Please, please…"

"That's it, Brett, beg me. Beg me to save you," I spit out, as I force his head to turn so he's looking in my direction. He doesn't stop me, his hands are too occupied holding his junk together. "Unfortunately for you, I can be a little sadistic from time to time, when people cause my wife pain. So, I'm going to make you wish I'd killed you today, but instead, you're going to enjoy your life without your little manhood in your pants. Living in constant fear that I'm going to hunt you down and finish the job."

Standing tall, I wrap my hand around his crushed ankle, making him scream louder as I drag him along behind me to the exit door.

"I love you, baby girl."

"I love you too."

Stepping through the door, I find myself instantly face to face with Parker. His eyes are filled with rage as he tries to search every part of me at once. Looking past me to Brett at my feet, he pulls the gun from his holster. Aiming down at Brett he doesn't waste a second before pulling the trigger, shooting him straight between the eyes.

Dropping the leg in my hands, I look at him with a raised eyebrow.

"Nobody touches what's mine," he says, turning to sit back in his chair as someone comes to pick Brett's body up.

Screams and shouts fill the room, but I refuse to pay them any attention. If they want to approach us, then they best be prepared for us to aim them down too.

"You sappy fuck," I chuckle, and he shakes his head at me as we get comfortable.

Glancing to the other end of the room, I spot Roman instantly, his eyes widening at the state of me. God, I must look bad. Looking down at myself, I've got blood and dirt wrapped around every part of my clothing and exposed skin. My fingers trace my cheeks, feeling it all on my face too. My abdomen is killing me, but I won't let any of these fuckers see.

It's all totally worth it to be standing here.

KC KEAN

TWELVE

Luna

"I love you, baby girl."

"I love you too," I respond automatically, but how the fuck is he strolling out of here so casually? The pounding of my heart is still ringing in my ears, and my breath is still coming in short bursts as I try to calm down from what we just saw.

We've been in here so long our eyes are much more adjusted than the travelers. I thought I might cry when I watched Parker complete The Tunnel, but watching Brett wrap his hands around Oscar's throat plays on repeat in my mind.

Leaning my head back on the wall behind me, Kai finally moves back a little, reminding me why I'm mad at him. I shove at his chest, and he doesn't move.

"When we get out of here, we're seriously going to talk. I can't even deal with you right now. He was in danger, and you didn't let me help." I'm keeping my voice low, but he sure knows how fucking mad I am.

Of course, when we first realized they weren't going to pull us out when the guys did the challenge, I promised to stay to the side. But I didn't agree to stand by and watch them get hurt, that wasn't the fucking deal.

"Sakura, I'd rather you be mad at me than have you both in danger. You heard the guy when we came in here. We could only attack, no helping." His lips brush against my ear, intoxicating my senses, but I'm still furious. "I'm not staying trapped in here, being outnumbered in the dark. Besides, Oscar knew what he was doing. We've practiced scenarios like that a lot."

Is he serious? They've practiced strangling each other? And I thought my training was intense. The knowledge helps relax me a little, but I'm still on edge, and I will be until Roman has made it through too.

As if reading my mind, the door to our right opens

again, slamming shut behind the next person. It's either Roman or Wren, that's all who is left.

"Luna?" Roman's deep voice rumbles through the room, and my heart pounds in my chest again.

"I'm here, Rome," I respond, as Kai leans back from me slightly.

"I find it rather insulting that not one of you called out my name, you know," Kai chides, and I can't help but chuckle. He's clearly listening to Oscar whine too much, and now he's picking it up.

"Shut up, Kai. How's our girl doing? Is she mad at you yet?"

"Like you wouldn't believe," Kai says back, placing a kiss to my forehead.

"Princess, you need to relax. Kai, I need you to keep her busy until you hear the door slam on the other side, I can feel her pulse from here."

Before I process what he just said, Kai's mouth comes down on mine. Lost to the feel of his lips, my hands clench the opening of his leather jacket, bringing him closer to me. His fingers trail around my neck, cupping the back of my head as he lets me explore his mouth. While his other hand grips my hip.

A grunt sounds out around the room, reminding me why we're in here, and exactly why Kai is trying to keep me occupied.

What a load of fucking Aceholes.

My grip on his jacket instantly turns into trying to shove him away, my palms flat against his chest. He holds me in place tighter, moving his lips to my neck. My head falls back as my body encourages the distraction, wanting all the attention he has to offer.

Changing tactics, I bring my lips to his, intensifying the moment. I relax into him, and when he least expects it, I bite down hard on his bottom lip.

The moan that pours from him gives me goosebumps as heat tingles at the surface of my skin. I taste blood on my tongue with the force of the bite, yet he's kissing me harder, wanting more.

Holy fuck.

His fingers are holding my hip in place so tight, I know I'll have fingertip bruises there later.

"All good, princess," I hear Roman shout before the door slams shut behind him.

Kai doesn't release me like I expect him to. Instead, he deepens our kiss. Taking more from me and leaving me vulnerable. Pulling his lips away, he leans his forehead against mine. Before I can yell at him, his finger is against my lips stopping my words.

"Sakura," he whispers huskily. "Before you go crazy on me. Please remember that we will always do what we have to do to protect you. As much as you can handle yourself, the fear in us is real and unavoidable. Luna, you are our wife, and that means everything to me."

The truth and emotion in his words almost has me to my knees. I don't know how to process the rawness he lets me see. Behind this quiet and observant man is a soul so passionate, he leaves me needing more.

Out of nowhere, it dawns on me, and I feel a fool for never seeing it earlier. I may not like the way he feels the need to protect me, but I think he'll go above and beyond to do so because of his sister. Leaning back I try to see into his eyes, but the darkness that surrounds us makes it difficult. I have to respect the pain he must feel, and the fear he must have of losing me. As much as I fear for my Aceholes, his anxiety must be ten-fold.

In the distance, I hear the door open again for the final time, but I'm too focused on my handsome in front of me. Raising my hands to cup his face, I tilt my head back and kiss him on the forehead for a change. Trying to portray my feelings the same way I'm recognizing he does.

"Watch out," someone suddenly yells, and Kai quickly turns to protect me. I can just about make out Wren casually walking along the path with no one attacking her, like this is just one big set up for her to breeze through.

A movement directly to my right catches my attention, I'm not quick enough to respond. The glint of a blade enters my vision, as I feel the sting against my cheek.

What the fuck?

Not willing to waste any time contemplating what is going on, I pull my own blade from my holster. Pushing Kai forward, I swing my right arm to the side, throwing whoever this fucker is into the wall. The right answer is to always strike first, ask questions later, and that's no different right now.

I stab my knife straight into their gut, forcing all my strength into the handle of my blade. My hand aching against the cross-guard in protest. The scream that rings in my ears is definitely female, and if it isn't Wren, it could only be one girl.

Becky.

Stupid fucking bitch.

Pulling the blade from her stomach, I repeat the action, feeling as the blade penetrates her skin.

"I saved your life once, I won't make that same mistake again," I grind out. I can't make out her eyes, but I pull the blade out of her body and wipe it on my pants.

Kai's arm comes protectively around my body, holding me against his chest as he tries to process what just happened.

My heart is pounding, and my breathing is heavy as I watch her fall to the floor, sobbing in pain.

"Sakura, you're bleeding," he says, his hand clamping tight on my shoulder as his finger trails through the cut on my face.

I'm too in shock to register the pain and suddenly taken by surprise when the overhead lights turn on. Blinking at the intrusion, it takes me a moment to adjust to the light. Looking at my feet, I see the fear in Becky's eyes as she hangs on to her life by a thread.

Before I can finish the job, Kai is spinning me around to look me over. His eyes fall quickly to my cheek, and he frantically starts looking for something to stop the bleeding. As he goes to take his leather jacket off, a black bundle of material is thrust between us.

To our right stands Conor, shirtless, with concern on his face.

"I'm sorry, I saw her move, and I tried to warn you, but my shout didn't give you enough time to prepare," he murmurs quietly, his voice gravelly.

Kai stares him down for a moment, before taking the top from his hands, bringing it to my face and applying pressure.

"It's not your fault, but thank you," I mutter, not really sure what else to say.

"No worries, I'm here if you need me. Trudy said you'd make her pay for her mistakes, no matter the threat she was under. Even still, she begged for me to help you guys with whatever you need. So, here I am."

He's walking for the exit before I can even catch up with what he said.

"Come, Sakura. We need to get this looked at," Kai mutters, keeping the cloth to my face as he guides me by my arm to the door. It is instantly thrown open, and I can see a thunderous Roman from here.

He blocks Conor's path, staring him down for a moment until he finally lifts his hand. Without question, Conor takes it, something passing between them before he lets him by.

"Just fucking pick her up, Kai," I hear Oscar groan, getting frustrated with the time it's taking to be reunited. The smile that graces my lips surprises me. I barely did anything in there, yet I feel utterly exhausted. Clearly worrying about the safety of my Aceholes, while also having someone slice your face can be tiring.

Kai lifts my hand to the top of my face, encouraging me to keep the pressure going as he scoops me up in his arms. It's no use arguing, and I feel myself wanting to let him take care of me after my revelation earlier.

Glancing to the door again, Oscar and Parker are standing side by side as Roman steps up beside us. His hair is a mess, and there is blood caked on his hands and cheek, but he looks nothing like Parker or Oscar. Both of which are covered in it, Oscar more so, after tumbling on the floor with Brett.

Shit.

We did it. The relief that washes over me has me leaning into Kai's hold.

The Steele's – One, Featherstone – Nil.

THIRTEEN

Kai

Someone hurt her. Becky hurt my Sakura, and I wasn't fucking quick enough to defend her. I sit and watch as Parker cleans the rest of the blood from her face, another scar to add to the list since she's been at Featherstone. The cut doesn't need stitches, but the doctor Rafe sent up to our room had to medically glue her skin shut.

I can't stop my knee from bouncing. Even as Oscar glances my way from his seat beside me on the large sofa, he can see my growing agitation. As soon as we stepped out of there, we barely stuck around to hear what's scheduled next, and I'm supposed to be the observant one.

All the screaming and shouting about Parker killing Brett, and Becky bleeding out in The Tunnel, as we left Zone A, was irrelevant since we needed to get Luna out of there. I just hope we didn't miss anything vital, but knowing Featherstone, whatever they tell us today, might not be relevant tomorrow.

I don't know what I expected from the first stage of The Games, but it almost felt anticlimactic until they went back on their word. Dietrichson and Rico definitely had a hand in forcing Luna and me to stay in there as Roman, Oscar, and Parker went through, which only fuels my anger.

Then, to hear Oscar struggle with Brett's hands around his throat, I was almost a goner. I know how hard it was for Luna to not rush to him. I felt it too, but while she was showering this morning, we'd promised each other that we would protect her at all costs even if it means sacrificing ourselves in the process.

"Do you know how fucking satisfying it was to shoot Brett in the dick? Man, I can't tell you," Oscar says, shaping his hands as though they were a gun, replaying the moment for us.

"In the dick?" Luna repeats, trying to process his words as Parker grabs another cleaning swab.

"Yeah, baby girl. I was going to let him live a long and sexless life until Parker got all trigger happy wanting to protect my honor, oh and yours too, Luna." The waggle of his eyebrows and the smile on his face makes Parker groan in response, but he doesn't correct him.

As Parker finishes off cleaning Luna's face, Roman flicks the television on, kicking back on the sofa. It's late afternoon, but it feels like midnight already. Tomorrow is downtime for us to do as we please, which means we'll likely spend the whole time relaxing here in private. Everyone else has showered and changed into comfortable clothing. Luna looks just as beautiful as ever in a pale pink tank top and grey loose shorts.

"Is it wrong that I'm turned on because you did that for me?" Luna questions, almost to herself. Her eyes are heating with desire in front of us.

A car blares on the screen, grabbing my attention, but it's all just a bit too much. Watching what happened in The Tunnel has me at a loss compared to usual, not having the same level of control I'm used to. I'm usually able to predict situations and their potential outcomes, but today, I had no idea what was planned.

I need to figure out how to push through the haze in

my mind. I can't fight free of it. My mind keeps repeating the vision of Becky attacking Luna over and over again, making myself feel even more helpless. The memory of Brett strangling Oscar definitely doesn't help either.

I need to calm the erratic beating of my heart and the pounding in my head. I've let my Sakura and my brothers down. I can't forgive myself, nevermind expecting her to forgive me. Sitting in here with all this noise around me definitely isn't helping.

Not wanting to draw any attention to my current mood, I quietly stand from the sofa. I head straight for the bedroom, not glancing back to see if anyone notices. Clicking the door shut behind me, my head falls back to rest against it with a thud, leaving the light off since the glow from the afternoon sun fills the room.

I stupidly stepped away to check behind me when that guy called out and focused on the wrong threat. If I'd have looked to my left, this wouldn't have happened. What ifs eat me alive, just as they did the day my sister was taken. I usually have full control of my fears and anxiety, but it's all too fresh. The fear of losing Luna now consumes me as I internally rip myself to shreds for letting her get hurt.

I need a shower. I let the others clean off when we first

walked in, now I need to wash the grime away, hoping it will improve my mood. It surprises me as I step into the en-suite that a brand-new mirror has been fitted so quickly after Oscar shattered the last one.

Not wanting to look at my reflection right now, I turn the shower on, letting it heat up as I take off my clothes. Stepping under the water, I let it rain down on me as I take a deep breath and relax my body a little, but I'm not finding the mental calmness I was hoping for.

Continuing to stand motionless under the spray, I let my failure wash over me as I scramble to find my usual logic. Pushing through, I consider the same question I always ask myself when I feel like this, 'Is there anything I can do about this situation right now?' As always, the answer is no, but asking myself and being able to answer, helps alleviate some of the pressure building in my chest.

I make quick work of washing the blood and dirt from my body and step out of the shower.

I step back into the bedroom with a towel wrapped around my waist. Only to find Luna sitting at the bottom of the giant bed, patiently waiting for me.

"I'm mad at you," she states, her emerald green eyes never wavering from mine as she twiddles her fingers in her lap. She sits ramrod straight, with a frown on her face, but the gentleness in her eyes softens the blow. Even mad at me, my Sakura is still the most beautiful being in the whole world.

"I'm sorry, Sakura. I should have never let her get so close to you, I…"

"Wait, what?" She stops my apology with a deeper frown, her nose wrinkling in confusion. Before I can respond, she's processing what I said. Shaking her head and waving her hand at me, she continues, "That's not what I'm mad about, Kai."

"Well, I am. How can you trust me to keep you safe when shit like that happens? When it could have been avoided?" I argue, my fists clenched tight at my side.

Slowly standing, she looks me over from head to toe. "Kai, I'm mad because you wouldn't let me help the others. They just told me about the pact you made this morning, and I get it, I think. But I'm still fucking mad at how helpless it made me feel." She swings her arms out to the side, glancing down at her feet for a moment, before meeting my gaze again. "We need open communication between all of us. It's not me against all of you, we're a team, and you guys don't get to make decisions or pacts like that behind my back. Especially not now that we're married. I lectured those Aceholes out there, and now it's your turn."

The hurt is evident in her eyes, and I'm left speechless. I'm royally fucking up today. I don't move a muscle. I want to make it better like I usually can, but right now, I don't know how.

Sighing, she claps her hands in front of her, eyes closed for the briefest of moments. "Now I have that off my chest." Exhaling again, she places her hands on her hips and stares me down. "Tell me what's going on with you."

Her stance screams, 'don't fuck with me'. The smallest part of my brain, that is functioning, recognizes the opportunity to show her I can communicate just like she asked me to.

Clearing my throat, I rub a hand on the back of my head, trying to ease the tension rising in me.

"I'm not dealing too well with what happened back there," I murmur, struggling to find the right words to describe what I mean. "She cut your face because I stepped in the wrong direction. How can I expect you to trust me when I screwed up like that? As your husband, it's my job to protect you." I can barely meet her eyes.

"What are you talking about, Kai? I trust you." I feel her eyes burning holes in my skull, trying to understand.

Shaking my head, I sigh. She can't actually mean it, has she looked at the damage Becky did? Will it heal? Yes, but it wouldn't even be there if it wasn't for me.

"Get out of your head, Kai," she demands, the determination in her words only fueling my own.

"It's not that simple, Luna. I can't lose someone else so important to me. I can't," I grind out, frustrated that she doesn't get it. Clasping my hands together at the back of my neck, I try to take deep breaths.

"I hate it when you call me that," she murmurs, standing chest to chest with me. "I. Trust. You. With. My. Life. Kai. What more do I need to say?"

"Saying it and feeling it are completely different things, Sakura. I need to get out of here because this isn't relieving any of the tension growing inside of me." I try to move around her, but she grabs my arm.

"You don't get to storm out of here, Kai. Tell me how I can help." Her eyes plead with mine.

"There is no helping. I need to feel control and right now, I don't," I respond, fighting myself more than I'm fighting her. I've never had anyone try to console me when

I feel like this, but it's almost like she's pushing too hard, taking more of my control away, and she doesn't even realize it.

"Well, what would you usually do when you feel like this?" Her grip on my arm tightens, making sure she has my attention.

The stress in her face holds me captive, frown lines mark her soft skin as she tries to understand. Her need to help compels me to respond.

"I either fight or fuck until I feel better." Her eyes light up with both options, but I'm shaking my head before she can speak. "I will not fight you, Sakura. Ever."

Her pouty lips at the disappointment has my cock twitching, her hand relaxing on my arm.

"As sad as that makes me, I can definitely get down with option number two, handsome," she says with a grin, but I don't smile back. Looking to the ceiling, I try to put this the lightest way possible.

"When I'm like this, sex is different. I need full control," I murmur, my heart beating faster with the thought of her laying bare before me, watching her trust me like she says she does. It feels like forever before she answers, her voice quieter than I expect.

"And what would that entail exactly?"

My eyes shoot to hers, surprised by her response.

"No, Sakura, that's not…"

"I asked what that would entail?" She is more determined this time. Searching her pretty green eyes, I only see the truth.

"Restraining you," I whisper, and she shivers. My cock tents under my towel, as I watch goosebumps appear up her arms. The picture in my mind of her tied up and at my mercy completely distracts me from the self-loathing I'm feeling.

"And if I trust you like that, give you the control that you need, would that make a difference?" Before I respond, she cuts me off, "Don't give me any of that shit about 'that not being what you're saying.' Just give me a straight yes or no answer," her words are rushed, her chest heaving slightly.

"Yes."

The pause that follows my answer has my palms sweating until she mutters the sweetest words.

"Show me."

Luna

My heart feels as though it's about to break through my chest. It's beating so hard, but I want this. I want to help him gain the control he needs, and I trust him enough to show me how it can feel.

Once upon a time, I believed I would never trust anyone to see me in such a vulnerable position. Yet, my Aceholes always find a way to give me more than I ever thought I would want. Now he has me curious, but I'm nervous as hell.

I can see the appreciation in the slight sparkle that is back in his dark eyes as he looks me up and down. It turns me on to see him happy to stand there, visualizing what it would look like.

"Are you sure?" he asks, finally bringing his eyes back to mine. Filled with heat, but still wanting to make sure I'm okay.

I nod slowly in agreement, shaking my hands out to try and lose the nerves building up inside of me.

"I need words, Sakura."

My hands instantly land on his damp chest, as my eyes watch a droplet of water trail down his neck. Gaining my attention, he tilts my face up to his with the gentle press of his finger beneath my chin. His eyes swing back and forth between my own, making sure I'm not doing this just for him, but I'm really not.

"Yes," I murmur, finally finding my tongue.

"I could start fires with what I feel for you," he murmurs, looking deep into my soul, leaving me breathless. Lost in him, in *us*, I let my emotions rise to the surface. Goosebumps cover my body, my mouth dry, with the words slipping from my tongue without pause.

"I love you, Kai." His eyes widen as his heart pounds against my hand, and I continue, "I love who you are, what you stand for, and how you always take care of those close to you. I want to give myself to you, just like you've already given yourself to me."

My heart is in my throat as I watch every aspect of his reaction. His pupils explode, as he blinks repeatedly, and the feel of his other hand grips tightly on to my waist.

"I love you too, Sakura, with all that I am," he mutters before his lips meet mine. We'll never know who moved first, only that the electricity that flowed between us was more charged than ever.

Feeling his fingers move to the back of my head,

holding me in place, I relax my body. I want to show him that he can take control without resistance from me, we both need it now.

My hands slowly rise to his neck, feeling his pulse throb beneath my fingertips as his tongue dances against mine. His hand on my waist hauls me in closer to his body, standing us chest to chest. As close as we are, I need him closer.

Clearly needing the same, he leans back just enough to lift my tank top over my head. Bringing my breasts back to his chest as his lips come back to mine. The moan that passes my lips is raw with need. His hands slip into my shorts, pushing them over my hips and letting them fall to the ground.

As I lower my hand to open the towel, he wraps his hands around both of mine at his neck, stopping my movement. Slowing his assault on my lips, I peel my eyes open, meeting his gaze instantly.

Kai holds my stare a moment longer, just to be sure before he steps back from me.

"Into the en-suite, Sakura. Hands on the vanity." It takes a moment for me to process his words, while he looks at me expectantly. Releasing a shaky breath, I do as he says. I feel as though he knows he needs to ease me into this, just like I would expect him to.

Stepping up to the vanity, I place my hands against the cool surface, my eyes finding my reflection in the mirror. The thin gauze strips protecting the cut to my right cheek barely hold my attention, as I see the flush slowly rising up my body.

I watch as Kai steps into the room naked, with his length on full display. Glancing over my shoulder at him, he shakes his head with a tut.

"Eyes forward, Sakura," he says, voice firm and laced with desire. I follow his instruction as I see the tie he places on the vanity beside my hand.

My pulse kicks into overdrive, knowing what it is though, arousal playing at the edges of my nerves. Kai's hands find my hips, pulling me backward toward him, stretching my body out, as my legs instantly separate.

"Further," he murmurs, and like a puppet on a string, I do as he says.

His hand ghosts over my ass cheeks, tingles lighting up my skin at the contact. Moaning at the touch, it catches me completely off guard when his hand comes down on my ass with surprising force.

Fuck.

Before I can glare at him through the mirror, his hand is stroking the now heated skin, soothing the pain. My mouth falls open, shock and desire fighting in my mind. Without pause, he repeats the motion on the other side, a groan finally passing my lips.

"You like that, Sakura," he states, not lifting his eyes from his marks, smiling at his handy work. "How wet would you be if I traced your pussy right now?" Tilting my hips up, I encourage his question, knowing the answer already. "Answer me," he demands, and I can't help but comply.

"Drenched," I barely say, before his palms come down on my body again. Harder, the sting ricocheting through my body, my clit thrumming with need. Looking at his reflection in the mirror, desire floods my body. Sweat glistens on his chest, as it rises slowly with his heavy breathing, offering me a glimpse of his raw side instead of his usually controlled demeanor.

"Please, Kai," I moan out, my hands clenching on the vanity. At my words, his hand slowly trails down my thigh, and when he begins to stroke back up, his fingertips ghost over my core.

"Fuck, Sakura," he murmurs to himself, his eyes watching as he slowly slips two fingers inside of me. Pleasure ripples through me at his touch, and I push back into him, needing more. But just as quickly as his fingers enter me, he pulls away.

Releasing an agitated sigh, I glare at him through the glass, but I can already see the change in him. A slight glimmer in his eyes, and the strong set to his shoulders, tells me his control is slowly coming back.

Panting, I watch his cock in the mirror glistening with pre-cum, making me wet my lips instinctively. The blue tie now dangling from his hands pulls my attention away, my heart beating rapidly in my chest.

"If you need me to stop, just say so, okay?"

Holding his gaze through the glass, I nod in agreement, seeing the fire in his eyes increase.

"Words, Sakura."

"Yes," I murmur instantly, but he shakes his head.

"Say, yes, I understand."

Releasing a sigh, I look over my shoulder at him, "Yes, I understand."

With a smile of appreciation, he steps away for a moment, coming back with a thick, fluffy grey towel, placing it beside the sink on the vanity. I don't need instruction, I know he wants me to shift to stand in front of it. Resuming the same stance, of my legs shoulder-width apart, I do as he wants.

"Lay your face on the towel, Sakura, and place your hands at the bottom of your back."

He isn't forcing me to do it, he's wanting me to make the decision myself. My heart swells, I'm giving him exactly what he needs, control. Kai still manages to gain that power while giving me the freedom to choose this.

As I slowly go to lay my face on the towel, Kai shuts the door to the en-suite. I pause in place, my eyebrow raised in question, as I continue to get comfortable. Lifting my hands to the bottom of my back, he must understand that I want an explanation from the look in my eyes.

"Your screams in here are mine, no one else's," he murmurs, the heat in his words zapping my core. Leaning forward, with my face in the fluffy towel, my ass in the air, with my legs spread and my hands behind my back, I feel vulnerable. The sexual tension outweighs my nerves.

I want this. No, I need this.

Laying the tie gently over my arms, he does nothing more with it, letting me feel the weight of the soft silk on my wrists. My eyes close as I relax into my surroundings, enjoying the feel of his presence behind me, my desire evident as I feel it on my thighs.

I'm suddenly lost to the pleasure as he sinks his cock all the way home. The little foreplay from earlier, mixed with how wet I already am, gives him the perfect friction inside of me. His cock drags against my walls until I feel his hips rest against my ass.

He doesn't move for a moment, giving me a second to adjust, my pussy squeezing him as I try to catch my breath.

"Fuckkk," he breathes out, his cock twitching as his hand strokes up my spine. The rare cuss from his mouth only adds to my pleasure.

Slowly he pulls all the way out, leaving me empty, until he thrusts straight back in harder, faster.

"Holy shit," I groan, my right hand slipping from my back.

Without missing a beat, he grabs the end of the tie, wrapping it around my right wrist and pulling it so my hand is on my back again. His next stroke inside of me intensifies with the feel of the restraint. I moan uncontrollably, as he holds my wrist in place and continues to slam into me. I can feel my face flush with the sensations, my nerve endings desperate to reach my climax.

I feel the silk of the tie wrap around my left arm, tightening to hold my hands together. My body can't catch up with the caress against my skin, as he doesn't slow his cock from pounding into me. I struggle to keep my balance, and in an instant, the room is spinning on its own accord.

I'm suddenly turned around, the tie releasing easily, letting my arms fall to my side before Kai lifts me. My legs instinctively wrap around his waist as he brings his lips to mine. Making the most of the opportunity, I run my fingers through his dark hair, holding him close to me.

The press of cool wood at my back catches me by surprise. Pushed up against the door, I watch as he pulls my hands from his hair, making quick work of wrapping my wrists with the tie again. Tighter this time, before securing it over the hook at the top of the door.

Pulling my arms down a little, I feel the restraint, but I know I could lift my arms up enough to unhook them if I wished. Before I can catch my breath, Kai thrusts into my pussy, mixed with the stretch in my arms, I moan long and loud. My legs squeeze him tighter as his mouth finds my nipple, biting and tugging on my piercing.

"Fuck, Kai. Fuck," I chant, lost to the ecstasy dancing

along my skin.

My gaze falls on the mirror, allowing me the view of Kai's muscles coiling with tension as he fucks me into the door. His hands squeeze my thighs as he holds me in place, taking everything from me, while I freely let him.

As if lighting a stick of dynamite, I feel the ripple of my orgasm start in my toes, swirling against every inch of my body, before I finally explode against him. I scream as wave after wave of my orgasm hits me. I've never climaxed without stimulating my clit before, and it feels as though it lasts forever.

Looking deep into Kai's eyes, I force myself to let him see how I feel. This is everything. The grin on his face is pure Kai, my handsome. Just when I think I've finally ridden out my orgasm, his fingers dig into my thighs, and his cock slams into me erratically, bringing me to the edge all over again.

Watching as his jaw drops open, Kai's eyes roll to the back of his head as he fills me with his cum. The pulsing of his cock inside me sets my orgasm off again, my wrists pulling at the restraints as my body spasms with ecstasy again.

My heart pounds in my ears, as I slowly catch my

breath, my head hitting the door with a thud. That was intense as hell, and I fucking loved it. Kai's head rests against my chest, our sweat mixing between us. When he finally lifts his gaze to mine, there is a new level of softness in his eyes.

"You trust me, Sakura," he murmurs, tasting the truth on his tongue.

"I told you I did," I whisper, my throat raw from my screams.

He nods in response, before quickly releasing the tie from my arms. My hands fall to his shoulders as I refuse to look away. The loving smile he offers me melts my heart. A glimpse into the soul of this man.

Without moving his eyes from mine, he walks us to the bathtub, turning the faucet on. Just as he sets me down, a bang comes from the door.

"Hey, you made her scream, dickhead. Let me in so I can shower with her," Oscar shouts from the other side, and we both roll our eyes.

"You mean fuck her in the shower," Kai calls back, his eyes on my lips.

"Well duh, what else was I supposed to mean?" Oscar grumbles, and I chuckle.

I fucking love my Aceholes.

OUR BLOODLINE

FOURTEEN

Luna

My eyes are still barely open, but my hand knows how to lift the mug to my mouth, gifting me with the strong taste of coffee. A chuckle from beside me at the table interrupts my moment, and I pop an eye open to glare at Parker.

"What? You are all cute with your bedhead and the inability to open your eyes," he says, trying to defend himself, but it's the look in his eyes that softens my glare. His eyes always say so much, and the love emitting from them right now makes me pause.

After telling Kai I loved him yesterday, being the first

one to say it, doesn't seem so scary anymore. The beating of my heart always increases just from thinking about it. Parker and I have our special hand gestures right now, and it warms my heart just as much.

Pointing to my eye, my chest, and then right at him, his smile widens as his face glows with happiness. He's quick to repeat the movement and place a kiss to my forehead.

"Now let me drink my fucking coffee in peace," I mutter, only making him laugh louder. I don't know whose idea it was to get up before nine a.m. when today is our relaxation day before the second lot of games tomorrow.

Kai and Roman went to the on-site gym, while Oscar went to see his sister, leaving Parker and me to wake up. My body aches in all the right places today after Kai wrecked me yesterday. It still blows my mind how I trusted someone enough to restrain me. I never believed I would experience anything like that. Kai, always the observant warrior, knew exactly just how far he could push me.

Closing my eyes, I drink the rest of my coffee, feeling Parker's gaze on me the whole time. I can't help but peek at him from the corner of my eye, sitting beside me shirtless with only a pair of grey jersey shorts on. His curly hair is still damp from the shower, making me itch to run my fingers through it. If I wasn't so tired I would lick his feather tattoo right now. Every time I look at the ink, it makes my heart leap in my chest.

"Remind me why we are awake again?" I ask, giving him my attempt at puppy dog eyes, and he shakes his head at me.

"Oscar wanted to go see his sister then spend the day together, and because you're all lovey-dovey, you smiled sweetly and said yes." He takes a sip of his own coffee, amusement in his eyes as he continues to stare at me.

I flip him off with a roll of my eyes.

"Angel, why don't you get in the bath and relax? That way you won't get your face wet," he offers, indicating the fresh bandaging on my face.

"It's not as bad as you're all making it out to be," I grumble, but the thought of climbing into the bathtub sounds good.

"If you say so, angel. Now, the bathtub should be ready, since I turned the water on when I got out of the shower." I stare at him for a moment in surprise.

"Why didn't you lead with that?" I ask, rising to my feet, and remembering my manners. "Thank you," I whisper, leaning over to kiss his lips.

"You're welcome." He pats my ass and winks at me. "Now, let me finish my fucking coffee in peace." He smirks, throwing my own words back at me.

Heading straight for the bathroom, I turn off the faucets, the water and bubbles at the perfect height, as the smell of lavender fills the room. Taking off one of the guy's long tops, I throw my hair up into a messy bun on the top of my head and step in, the heat instantly beginning to soothe my body. Lying back, careful not to make the water splash on to my face, I let my mind drift.

There is so much going on at the minute it's hard to know what to focus on. Of course, The Games are the priority since we're here right now, but I have so many unanswered questions. It might be a good idea to speak with Rafe today too. I can't stop thinking about the fact that Dominic knew about my 'Meu Tesouro' embroidered bag.

A light tap sounds from the door before Parker sneaks his head in.

"Sorry, angel. Jess is on the phone, and apparently, you are only alive if she actually speaks to you," he says with a raised eyebrow, and I smile.

"It's fine."

He places his phone on the side of the tub, hitting the speakerphone button so Red's voice fills the room.

"Luna?"

"Hey, Red," I respond, as I sit up, the water still hitting my shoulders.

Parker doesn't hang around for girl talk, blowing me a kiss from the door before shutting it behind him.

"Luna, Parker said you were cut on your cheek. Are you okay?" Her voice is higher pitched than usual, filled with worry.

"I'm fine, it didn't even need stitches. Becky's aim could have used some work," I answer casually, trying to calm her.

"Becky? Becky did it? I hope you buried her," she growls through the phone, and it makes me smile.

"The last time I saw her, she was bleeding out on the floor. I didn't look back to check if she was still breathing or not," I answer honestly.

"Why do you always attract the crazy bitches, captain?"

Chuckling at her words, I shake my head. "Same way I attracted you apparently."

"Not funny. Now, tell me everything."

I hear her moving around on the other end of the phone,

the sound of banging in the distance.

"There isn't much else to say, except Brett is dead. Otherwise, it was the usual fucked up Featherstone event," I respond casually, before she squeaks down the phone.

"Brett's dead? How?"

"Oscar and Parker." I sigh, ready to talk about anything other than what happened yesterday. "Is everything okay there, Red? I hate leaving you," I say, trying to change the subject.

She doesn't answer for a moment, making me worry, but she eventually sighs. "It's fine. I'm just at Maverick's, he's now decided I can't go to classes unless someone he trusts can watch over me. Aid and Wes- uhhh, and, uh, when, uh, he tries to make me do more Combat training, I want to throttle him."

"Do you need me to talk to—"

"Nope. No, don't talk to him. I'm fine, it's all handled, no stress," she interrupts, sounding flustered. Clearly, she doesn't want to rock the boat, and I won't get involved if she doesn't want me to. I just want her to be safe while I'm not there, and I'm glad he's taking it seriously.

"Okay. Oh, actually I have a huge favor to ask. I think I want to go through the bag the agent mentioned. Do you think you could get it to Ian, the driver at Ace block, and have him bring it up here?" I don't know what it is, but I feel like I have the strength to do it now, and I don't want to lose my courage.

"No, of course, I'll have Ai-err…" clearing her throat, she tries again. "I'll get that sorted now, and send you a text as soon as he's on his way. Okay?"

"Thank you. You know you can talk to me about anything, right, Jess? I'm always here. I'm sorry I forced you to stay with a tutor. I just need you safe, and he's one of the few I trust," I murmur, hating that I'm making things difficult for her.

"Is that Luna?" I hear someone ask in the background, and I frown in confusion.

"Is West there?"

"Uhh, yeah. He's friends with Maverick, and he wants to speak to you," she answers, and I can tell she's already handing the phone over, her voice getting quieter toward the end.

"Luna?" West calls out down the phone, and the concern in his voice makes me smile. I may not remember a lot of my childhood still, but I know a worried West when I hear one.

"Hey, West," I murmur, relaxing into the water as I prepare for his questions.

"Are you okay? What game have you just done? Please tell me you haven't lost anyone. Are you resting today?"

"My god, West, calm down. I'm fine, honestly, I'm okay. We had The Tunnel, I hadn't heard of it before we got here."

"The Tunnel? I haven't either, I'm sorry I couldn't prepare you for it beforehand. Is everyone, uhh, still alive?" he asks, and I can feel him cringe at the question, but under these circumstances, it is very valid.

"West it isn't your fault. You helped me as best as you could, and I appreciate it. We're all still breathing, but there are potentially three students dead. One might be because of me too," I whisper, wanting to be honest with him as I try to find the same sense of friendship we once had.

"It is not your fault Luna Moon, you do what you have to do to survive, do you hear me?" His voice is filled with steel and determination, and I'm grateful for his protective instinct.

"I hear you, now calm yourself. You'll be throwing off some alpha vibes, and Red is likely drooling over you like a character from one of her books or something," I say with a grin, and he chuckles in response.

"Can I have my best friend back now?" Red asks in the distance, and I really miss her sass.

"Sunshine wants you back, Luna Moon. Be safe, okay?"

"See you soon," I respond, before Red's voice fills the room again.

"I miss you, captain."

"I miss you too, Jess. Are you sure everything is okay? I can leave the bag for another time if it's inconvenient?" I murmur, trailing my hands through the water, worrying about her there without me.

"Everything is great, Luna, honestly. Now, let me get this arranged. Speak soon, okay? Now, stay safe," she calls out before the line goes dead.

Releasing a sigh, I mentally start to prepare myself for what lies ahead today. Finally seeing what's inside that bag may be able to answer some questions for me. Quickly washing my body, I step out of the tub, wrapping a towel around me so I can head to our bedroom to get dressed.

Stepping into the lounge, I jump at the sound of the main door opening at the same time. A girl bounces in, with Oscar chasing behind her.

"Stop being a little brat, Niamh," he grunts, but she doesn't respond. Instead, she stands on the other side of the sofa staring at me.

"Oh, hey, baby girl. You look edible, let me get rid of the brat, and I'll show you how much," he winks, making this girl gag.

"That's fucking disgusting, Ozzie. A girl that pretty does not let you near her flower, no way." Her head whips between us, and it takes me a minute to catch on that this must be his sister. They're the double of each other, she's just a younger female version of him.

Her long blonde hair is perfectly straight, and her bright blue eyes sparkle just like Oscar's do, full of mischief and trouble.

"Shut up, Niamh. She's my wife, of course she does," he growls, frustrated as he swings his arms out wide, looking for backup. As if on cue, Parker steps out of the kitchen.

Niamh looks me straight in the eye, serious as hell. "You should have married that one." Her head turns back to stare at Parker, who looks like a deer caught in the headlights. I can't stop myself from chuckling at her. I can guess where she gets her humor from.

Finally finding my voice, I smile, "I did. I married all of them." I feel too pleased with myself when I say those words out loud and she gapes back at me.

"You greedy bitch," she mutters in a state of shock, and I laugh hysterically.

"Niamh, I swear to god…" Oscar's rant is cut short when Kai and Roman step in, tops off, and sweat glistening on their perfectly chiseled bodies. I momentarily forget what's going on as I just stare at them.

"You had these three hot specimens, and my brother somehow convinces you to still include him. Are you crazy?" Niamh questions, not moving her eyes from Kai and Roman either.

"Niamh, get out right now." Oscar scowls, finally wrapping his arm around his sister and leading her back out. "And you two, cover yourselves up. She does not need any more encouragement," he grumbles, slamming the door shut behind them.

Even with the door shut, I can still hear her scream goodbye down the hall. Well, that was an experience. No one else has moved, still trying to catch up with what just happened.

"I need to speak to Rafe, and Ian is going to bring my

bag from the vault over so I can finally see what's inside," I say, bringing everyone to the present.

"Whatever you need, princess. We're in this together," Roman says, walking toward me. When he stands in front of me, he lifts my chin, planting a chaste kiss on my lips before checking my wound.

There is something playing on his mind, I can see it in the way he crinkles his eyes and the constant frown line marking his forehead. Maybe leaning on him to finally open the bag might encourage him to lean on me with his thoughts too. Otherwise, I'll get him to talk the only way I know how, in the ring.

OUR BLOODLINE

FIFTEEN

Luna

Red: Hey, captain. Ian has the bag and should be there in the next hour or so. If you need me just call. Be safe!

Luna: I will, thank you. Any issues with Maverick just let me know, I can always speak to West. I also forgot to mention on the phone earlier, there is some guy here, in The Games, named Conor Starker. He says Trudy sent him in, to be of assistance if needed. Something to do with making up for the fact she screwed me

over. Let me know if you hear anything on your end.

Red hasn't messaged me back since and that was over forty minutes ago. I'm sure if she needs me, she'll tell me. I'm just looking for a distraction until Ian arrives, trying to calm my jittery nerves.

Roman sits back in the corner, with me situated right in between his legs. Kai to my left, and Parker and Oscar relax to my right. I love seeing them in their casual clothes, no uniforms or combat outfits required. Although, they forgot how much I like the grey sweats club today, opting for Henley's and jeans, except Parker, who at least still has his grey shorts on.

I've tried to relax since Oscar got back, but I haven't been doing a very good job of it. No one, including Roman, would spar with me to help occupy my mind. Apparently, that's not an option with another round of The Games tomorrow. So, we spent the rest of the morning, and a lot of the afternoon in our new-found bubble, snuggled together on the sofa. There's something about getting lost in a movie, allowing it to pull you from surroundings, letting you enter their world.

I imagine this is what Red is like when she's reading her smutty books all the time.

"Do you want Rafe here when Ian drops the bag off, or would you prefer it to just be us?" Kai asks, no laptop in hand as he watches The Italian Job on the television.

I consider his words, and I know deep down that I need Rafe. I can't even remember if I told him about the bag to begin with. Moving to stand, Roman's arms grip me tighter to his chest, as Kai grabs my phone from the table.

I smile in thanks, as my nerves take over a little. Hitting Rafe's name, the line rings.

"Hey, darling, everything okay? How's your face?" he answers, frazzling my mind for a moment with all the directions his questions are taking me in.

"Uh, hey. My face is fine, I just have something I want to talk to you about." My heart beats rapidly in my chest as I feel myself starting to freak out, trying to figure out how to bring up the bag to begin with.

I look around at the guys, floundering for what to say.

"Is everything okay, Luna?" Rafe's concerned voice fills my ear, but I can only stutter.

Get a fucking grip, Luna, I scold internally, as I feel Roman tap me on the shoulder. Meeting his gaze, I instantly understand what he's offering, as he holds his hand out for the phone. Slowly, I pass over the phone, feeling the anxiety and nerves that were coursing through my veins begin to dim instantly.

"Meet me outside, Rafe," he murmurs, before passing the phone to Oscar. "Together, remember?" I lean into him even more, taking the strength he's offering.

"Thank you," I whisper, and the gentle smile on his face settles my internal wrestling.

"You're welcome. I'm assuming he doesn't know about the bag?" Roman asks, stroking my uninjured cheek and I shake my head. "Okay, well I'll explain it to him and pick up the bag at the same time." Kissing my lips, hard and demanding, I relish in his touch.

Too soon, he pulls away, but I'm too distracted with the taste of him on my lips to worry. Oscar's arm wraps around my shoulder, and pulls me sideways, resting my head in his lap. His fingers instantly stroke down my neck, goosebumps rising along my skin, making me shiver at the contact.

"I love this part," Parker murmurs, watching the television, as the red, white, and blue Mini Coopers race through the streets in the movie.

"Hmm, I love Jason Statham," I answer without thinking, suddenly feeling three sets of eyes on me.

"Baby girl, none of us look even remotely like Jason Statham," Oscar says, confusion laced in his words.

"What does that have to do with anything?" I ask, unsure where he's going with this.

"Well, I'm just saying, he doesn't represent any of us, and we are not adding any more to this harem you've got going on. We're married now, end of discussion." He raises his eyebrows at me expectantly, and I can't help but chuckle at his little outburst.

"No adding to my harem. Understood," I say, agreeing. "But just so we're clear, he's an adrenaline junkie just like you. With the whole brooding thing going for him like Roman. While Seth is the technology king, obviously second to my Kai, and Wahlberg has the whole 'all-American boy-next-door' vibe, with a hidden dark side, just like Parker Parker."

Completely pleased with my characteristic breakdown, I continue to watch the movie as no one answers me back.

Not much time passes before the door bursts open, Rafe steps into the room first, followed quickly by Roman.

"Darling, you should have told me. This isn't for you

to go through alone, okay?" Rafe asks, rounding the sofa as I push myself to sit up, wrapping his arms around me as soon as he nears. I squeeze him back tightly, appreciating the calmness that washes over me.

Kai pauses the movie. "This is at your pace, Sakura. If you need us to stop or move along, just say the word. We are all here for you." I smile softly at him, appreciating how he can always read the situation. I love seeing him calm and relaxed compared to yesterday. He looks like his usual self, in full control. Although, I love the dominant side of my quiet and observant man that only I get to see.

Looking at Roman, my eyes fall on the bag in his hand, and I lick my dry lips as I rub my hands down my yoga pants. Without question, Oscar drags the coffee table closer to where I'm sitting, and Roman places the bag down on top of it.

Rafe moves back and takes the seat beside me. He doesn't touch me, or encourage me along. He simply offers his silent support as always, allowing me to make the decision for myself.

Meu Tesouro fills my vision, drawing me in as my fingers slowly trace the white stitching on the large black duffel bag. It doesn't look heavy, or even half full, but in my mind, it contains the deepest corners of my soul. The material feels rough under my touch, but I'm not sure whether that's my imagination taking over the situation, making it seem worse than it is.

Wrapping my fingers around the zipper, I freeze for a moment, physically unable to move as I try to calm my breathing. My heart feels as though it's about to beat from my chest, as the sound of the zip pulling fills the room. The second it hits the end, my hands pull back as if they're about to catch fire.

"It's okay, angel. Take a minute," Parker murmurs from the other side of Oscar. Hearing his voice calms my nerves enough to reach out for the two white envelopes that are now poking out of the top.

Thick black ink is scrawled across the front, one saying Luna, the other, Rafe. My eyes instantly turn to Rafe, seeking his guidance as he too notices our names. His eyes are watery as he stares unblinking at his envelope, slowly taking it from my hand.

His other hand slowly strokes over the writing, and as I watch a tear slowly fall down his cheek, I know who wrote them. Seeing the love mixed with the pain in Rafe's eyes breaks my heart, and my eyes well on their own accord.

Finally bringing his gaze to mine, he offers a soft smile. "Open yours first, darling," Rafe whispers, his voice catching on my nickname, and I lightly nod in agreement.

Looking past him to Roman, he offers a nod of encouragement like I need, and I unseal the envelope. I don't know what to say or think, but that won't change until I see what's inside. Slowly unfolding the paper, I watch as the same style of writing covers the sheet.

Blinking back tears, I look to the ceiling as I try to control myself. A hand squeezes my knee, and I know it's Oscar, silently offering his strength to help get me through this.

Glancing at the first few lines, I scream. Dropping the offensive letter to the ground, my head falling straight into my hands as I feel my soul crush into a million pieces. I don't know whose arms wrap around me tight, all I know is they're keeping me connected right now, stopping me from completely disappearing into my mind.

I hear Rafe begin to cry beside me, but I can't begin to look at anyone. "I can't do this!" I cry out, "I can't." My words barely pass the uncontrollable blubbering coming from my mouth.

Pushing my hair out of my face, I rest my hands on my

head, finding Kai's face inches from mine.

"It's okay, Sakura. Take deep breaths." He cups my cheek, wiping my tears away as I continue to feel my heart break on a loop.

"Luna, darling. I need you to read, please," Rafe says, holding the paper out to me again. "I've read it, Luna." He sobs the words out, feeling all the emotions I am, maybe even more, but I can't process that.

Trusting him, as I always have, I take the paper from his hands and find the strength to read it in full. Kai remains in front of me, his hand across from Oscar's on my other knee, as Roman and Parker join them. Their touch is calming my erratic mind.

Glancing at the paper in my hands, I read.

Meu Tesouro,

I will never be able to explain how much pain it causes me, writing this letter, and what it must mean for you to read this.

My beautiful girl, I'm not dead.

Please don't tear this letter up just yet, let me explain.

There are only four people in the whole world that know I am alive, and I am very sorry you and Papa aren't included in that number.

I will always do whatever it takes to protect my family, and as much as it has pained me, keeping my distance and remaining 'dead' has kept a lot of people at bay.

I was able to convince an old friend to place this bag for you in the vaults when I found out you were being recruited, whether we wanted it to happen or not.

I don't know what you remember from the day our lives changed forever, but it was the best birthday I could have wished for with my girl. Maria, your grandmother, said your memories are repressed, and I hate that you are dealing with that without me there to comfort you and tell you that everything will be okay one day.

That day, Meu Tesouro, they came for you. I would never allow our beautiful darling girl to live the life Veronica and Totem wanted for you. A puppet on a string, helping to build the corrupted world they longed for, along with Totem's actual daughter.

I swear to you Luna, I fought that day with all I had as they stormed our home. My only saving grace was the fact they were being monitored by the FBI, who followed them in. I now know that Totem and Veronica managed to get away. Leaving behind the men I killed who tried to take you.

What I didn't know, in my beaten state, is that the FBI managed to save my life, but paused when coming back to get you because Papa came home. A part of me will forever be grateful that they didn't take you too. Papa wouldn't have survived without both of us.

I hope you gave him hell, Meu Tesouro, for all the times he forced us to watch those damn Teenage Mutant Ninja Turtles on the television, always saying it was your choice.

I promise you our time is coming, and I pray that you will one day see the whole picture and the sacrifices I made to protect my beautiful family.

I have written another letter for Papa, please make sure he gets it.

If you ever need anything please speak to Ian, he drives one of the Ace Rolls Royce's and I trust him to protect my daughter. As a complete last resort there is Special Agent Dominic Bridge, I have placed his telephone number in the bag.

I love you to the moon and back, Meu Tesouro

Daddy

SIXTEEN
Parker

My heart is breaking, and I'm not even the one reading the letter. Watching Luna cry as her eyes scan the paper in her hands, hurts me deeply. I feel helpless, we need to do something, anything, to make it all okay.

Looking at the others, they're all in a similar state of stress. Roman looks as though he wants to rip someone's head off as he watches our girl break down. Kai is monitoring her every movement, trying to read her enough to know what to do next. While Oscar is gripping her knee like his life depends on it, emotion thick in his eyes at her distress.

I catch Rafe's gaze, watching as he silently weeps. Whatever is going on, it's enough to bring this man to his knees. He nods at me, but I don't understand what he's indicating.

Worrying we're crowding her too much, I go to move my hand from her leg, so I can give her a little space, but lightning fast, her hand comes down over mine. The piece of paper is forgotten as it drifts to the floor. Luna searches my eyes, trying to find the words to explain what's going on, but all that comes out is more sobs. All I can see is how her beautiful green eyes are screaming for help.

Nudging everyone out of the way, I wrap my arms around her, lifting her to me as I blindly search for the coffee table behind me. I sit back with Luna wrapped tightly around me as she cries into my shoulder, chest to chest, our hearts beating as one. I hold on for dear life, pinning her body to mine, letting her know I'm here as she lets her emotions take over.

Nobody argues, instead they all sit on the sofa and wait patiently. Rafe nods again with a smile this time, and I think this is what he was encouraging me to do a moment ago.

Luna's legs wrap around my waist, while her arms

are around my shoulders. Stroking a hand down her back, I try to console her as her body shakes, but I worry I'm not doing it right. Her grip on me only grows tighter, as my shirt gets wetter from her tears. I've never watched someone I love hurt like this, with no physical pain, only emotional turmoil.

Rafe knows what the letter says, but none of the others even glance in its direction, wanting Luna to tell us when she's ready.

Her hold on me slowly starts to ease, until she's leaning back, looking straight into my eyes. 'Thank you,' she mouths, and I kiss the corner of her lips. I cup her face gently in both of my tattooed hands and brush away her tears with my thumbs, avoiding her bandaged cheek. Slowly unhooking her legs from behind my back, she turns to face the others while remaining in my lap. She laces her fingers through mine, squeezing tight, as words finally tumble from her mouth.

"He's alive," she whispers, her voice hoarse from crying, and it takes a minute to comprehend what she is saying. Alive?

"Bryce is alive?" Roman asks, shock etched into his features. His mouth drops open in surprise as his eyebrows raise, looking repeatedly from Luna to Rafe who nods, as a hiccup rattles through my angel's body. I squeeze Luna's hand tighter, knowing it won't settle her emotions, but hoping it will show my support.

Her father is alive? After all this time? What on earth could have kept him away from his daughter for so long? I don't want to throw all these questions at her. Not when she's dealing with her own thoughts to process, and she likely didn't gain all the answers she needs from the letter either.

Bringing our intertwined fingers to her stomach, I wrap my arm around her too, cocooning her in. Her head falls back onto my shoulder as she tilts it toward the ceiling with her eyes closed. Oscar looks helplessly at me, but none of us have the answers to fix this for her.

"One of you read the letter," Rafe murmurs. "She won't be able to re-read it to you right now." Standing to his full height, his movement catches Luna's attention. "Are you okay, darling?" he asks, but she doesn't know how to answer. Lifting from my lap, she stands to hug him tight. "I didn't know, Luna. I didn't know," he says on repeat, as they cry on each other.

Their moment feels almost too intimate for us to be

watching, but we promised to be here through everything, and that includes the emotionally tense scene between them.

"I know, Dad, I know. I just wish we'd known, but then I think we'd have gone searching, right?" she whispers, and Rafe agrees.

"You know it, darling," he murmurs, stroking her hair behind her ear. "Are you okay here? If so, I'd like to read my letter in private." He leans back, looking into her eyes as he speaks.

"Of course, yeah. I'll have a look at what else is in the bag, then I think I want to lie down," she responds, patting his arm, trying to let him know she will be okay with us.

"I can stay while you check everything else out," Rafe offers, but she instantly shuts him down.

"No, I can do that with the guys. You go, read your letter, but make sure you talk to someone. I know I might not be the right person, but make sure you talk to Juliana or Maria, okay?"

Planting a kiss on her forehead, he tries to offer a smile to the rest of us before leaving the room, the door clicking shut behind him.

Roman stands in front of Luna, tilting her chin up to

see her eyes, but she breaks the silence before he does.

"I'm glad I killed her, Rome, that bitch did this, her and Totem. I just wish I'd drawn out her death. She deserved to suffer, just like I have, like both of my dads have." Anger and vengeance laces every word.

"I know, Luna. Let's focus on the here and now, okay? Process all of this first. I don't want you going into the second Game with your mind consumed by this. Tomorrow, I need you to be 100% present," Roman says, wrapping his arm tightly around her small shoulders.

"You're right." Taking a deep breath, I watch as she tries to gain some form of control over her emotions, but it's a struggle. Tilting her head back, she inhales, holding her breath for what feels like forever, before slowly exhaling through her nose.

"Baby girl, come sit with me, and we can go through the bag together. Then we can go lay in bed, if you'd like?" Oscar offers, and I think even I could be onboard with that plan right now.

Roman is reluctant to let her go, as she picks the letter up from the floor, and turns to Kai. Folding it up, just as it was, she holds it out for him to take.

"I'll go through it when you're napping, Sakura. Right

now, we're all here for you," Kai mutters, and she smiles down at him, swiftly leaning over to place a kiss on his lips before turning back to the bag beside me.

"If it's too much, angel, I can pull the items from the bag, and then you can take them if you want to, or I can put them back," I offer, and she nods, tears pooling in her eyes again as she sits beside Oscar.

When she finally mutters, "Okay." I look into the bag, my heart pounding with nerves as her trust washes over me. I can't curb the worry of invading her privacy, so I quickly pull out the first item, a soft orange blanket.

"Oh my god!" she calls out in surprise, grabbing the blanket from my hands. Oscar, Kai, and I all watch in surprise as she brings the blanket to her nose. Inhaling its scent, she looks down at it with wonder. "This is my blanket from when I was a baby. God, I remember how much I loved this thing. A memory has never come so naturally to me before."

"Loved that thing? Princess, you brought it everywhere! It was the most annoying thing, Meu…" he cuts himself off instantly, frozen in place at the slip of his tongue. Clearing his throat, Luna stops him.

"It's okay, Roman. I'm not saying I can handle hearing

the words every five seconds, but don't stop yourself from saying it," she whispers, and he drops to his knees before her. He strokes the blanket in her lap, basking in his own memory for a moment.

"I'll do whatever it takes to make you happy, Luna." Looking up to search her eyes, he continues. "I said those same words to you when I was five years old and you got this damn blanket stuck on a branch when you tried to climb a tree. Nearly broke my leg trying to get it back for you," he murmurs, and she lightly chuckles.

"I remember."

Without pause, he kisses her. I can feel the happiness coming from him that she remembers a shared memory, one which doesn't cause her pain. Finally pulling back, Luna looks at me with glossy eyes, encouraging me to pull something else out of the bag.

Peeking inside the bag, I'm surprised only a stack of what look to be family photos remain.

"This is everything that was in the bag," I say, as I hold out the pictures for her to take. Her fingers stroke over the top picture, as tears begin to fall again.

"I know this is a lot for you, Sakura, but we're all really proud of you," Kai tells Luna, and I couldn't agree more.

As I remember back to Washington, and how she handled learning Roman's secret then, it's a massive difference to now. She's come a long way emotionally since then, we all have.

"Thank you, all of you. I can't tell you how much it means for you to be here with me." She smiles, going back to the pictures. She seems lost in her own world as she flips through them. No one says a word as we watch her smile grow with each passing photo. When she's finally looked through them all, she holds them to her chest, as a sense of calmness seems to wash over her.

Yawning, she glances at Oscar. "I want to lie down now."

He nods in agreement. "Of course, baby girl. Why don't you get comfortable, and I'll be there in a second, okay?"

I'm surprised he doesn't go instantly, it's not like him to leave her be. Luna doesn't seem to mind, smiling and heading straight for the bedroom. I stand to follow her, because I really don't want her to be alone. Oscar's hand clamps down on my shoulder, holding me in place until she's left the room.

"Kai, I need you to read that letter, then I need you to

research the safe house they want me to blow up for my assignment. I've held off on it, and now I'm glad because something doesn't feel right about it, and I don't think it's a coincidence," Oscar whispers, concern building around us.

How is it, every time we find an answer to something, ten more questions form?

OUR BLOODLINE

SEVENTEEN

Luna

Waking up this morning with my new-found knowledge has me feeling a little off-balance. My father, Bryce Steele, is alive. Alive. My heart still leaps out of my chest every time that word bounces around in my head. I can't help but feel frustrated with myself for not opening the bag the second I arrived at Featherstone. I just wasn't brave enough to open it, not until Special Agent Dominic Bridge told me to.

Taking a deep breath, I remind myself that everything happens for a reason, and I wasn't meant to learn of this until now. Fixing my hair in a secure bun at the top of my head, I glance over myself. Wearing a pair of skin-tight khaki green combat pants with a long-sleeved black t-shirt tucked in, I lace my boots up. I'm as ready as I'll ever be to take on the second round of The Games.

Stepping into the lounge, the guys are whispering, and I instantly know they're trying to keep something from me.

"Spit it out!" I shout over their discussion, and they all instantly freeze, not a single one of them willing to turn around to look at me. Hands on my hips, I sigh, annoyed we're here again. "I thought our connection was stronger than this now, am I wrong?"

"No, baby girl," Oscar instantly responds, as they all finally look in my direction. I don't say anything, just continuing to stare at them with my eyebrows raised does the trick.

"Just tell her," Parker murmurs, and Roman sighs, making it clear he's going to have to be the one to do the talking.

"Oscar asked Kai to have a look into something last night, after you went to lie down. Kai's found out a little more information, but not enough for a solid answer. We didn't want to tell you and distract you from today, in case it's not what we think," he says, looking into my eyes the whole time.

I rub my palms over my hips as they start to sweat with my nerves kicking in. That's not going to be enough information for me, and they know it. I call their bluff, not needing to utter another word for them to come clean.

"So, I don't know if you remember our assignments," Oscar starts, and I roll my eyes.

"Of course, I remember. Kai had to hack into DCM's tech systems. Parker had to make working grapplers, like he's Batman or something, and an undetectable tracking device. Which was one of your birthday gifts, Kai," I say, dropping where I got his birthday gift from, and I catch his glance in surprise at Parker. "Roman had to confirm a business contract with DCM Tech and provide surveillance on Special Agent Dominic Bridge. Leaving you to create a stimulant shot and destroy a safe house for the agency." I smile at myself, pleased I reeled that off so confidently.

Oscar shakes his head, likely surprised I remembered everything. "Right, well, you obviously know Kai hacked their system, and Rome provided surveillance on the agent because they helped with your assignments."

"Have you read the letter?" I ask, going off topic a little.

"I read it, Sakura, like you asked, and explained it all to everyone else," Kai answers, and I smile appreciatively, a weight lifting off my shoulders I hadn't even realized was there.

"Good, I'm worried Totem played a part in sending me to get Dominic Bridge on the books because he knows he is linked to my father, with him mentioning Dominic in his letter. It worries me that Dominic also mentioned I wasn't the first Featherstone student to approach him," I breathe out, as I reveal what's been playing on my mind.

"Well, before Kai read the letter I asked him to look into something for me because I had a bad feeling, and I think I'm right. Which is why we were discussing it just now, and not wanting to worry you with it," Oscar replies, running a hand through his already messy hair.

"Just tell her, Oscar, dragging it out is only going to make it worse," Roman grunts, nodding his head in my direction to encourage him along.

Oscar looks helplessly at me for a moment, before he sighs. "Can you take a seat then, let someone hold your hand or something? I have a feeling you might need comfort." I frown in confusion but take a seat on the sofa with Parker who sits beside me, lacing our fingers together.

I glance at them all, but no one wants to continue. I know if I keep my gaze on Roman he'll just blurt it out like he always does, but I feel like this needs to come from Oscar, so I sit and wait patiently for him to find his tongue.

"So, Parker completed both of his assignments as well, and Roman did confirm a business agreement with DCM Tech too. Which just leaves me." Clearing his throat, he sits on the coffee table facing me, and Kai squeezes his shoulder in support. "I've made the stim shots for temporary paralysis, but I haven't handed over the formula yet. I didn't want it to be used against us in The Games, but the details are all in my suitcase, on an encrypted microchip." His words catch me by surprise, and I can't help but glance in the direction of the bedroom as if I'll see what they look like from here.

Looking back at him, I watch as he nervously bounces his leg. His facial expression is grim, as beads of sweat begin to dot his brow lines.

"That just leaves the safe house," I murmur, looking down at my lap, realizing that's the only thing left to discuss. He nods in agreement, but I'm racking my brain trying to figure out why it has him so worked up.

We'd already discussed how all of our assignments

seemed to interlink somehow, so where does this fit in? My grip on Parker's hand tightens, as it slowly dawns on me.

"My dad. You think my dad is at the safe house," I whisper, as my heart beats so loud it pounds in my ears. Trying to gain control of my rapid breathing as panic kicks in, I look at Oscar. "Did… did you, do your…" I can't even finish my sentence, as I feel myself starting to hyperventilate.

"No! No, Luna!" Oscar shouts, dropping to his knees before me, his hands cupping my face tenderly. "Baby girl, breathe for me. I haven't done it. I haven't completed the second assignment yet." He frantically searches my eyes as I watch him take deep breaths to encourage me.

"Princess, follow his breathing," Roman says from somewhere to my right, but I can't pull my gaze from Oscar to look at him.

Copying his movements, I feel my heart start to calm and the lightheaded feeling subsiding.

"That's it, keep going. Now tell me, what can you feel?" Roman asks.

Clenching my hand tighter, I answer, "Parker. I can feel my Parker Parker," I whisper, and Oscar smiles at me.

"That's it, princess. Now, if you can tell me what you

can smell, and see, it'll help too," Roman murmurs, as I take another deep breath.

"I can see Oscar's dreamy blue eyes," I respond automatically, Oscar's grin widens, as I internally scold myself for sounding so fucking girly. I take a deep breath. "And all I can smell is vanilla since you Aceholes keep using my body wash."

"There she is," Kai murmurs, and I glance at him. The movement easing the tension building inside of me.

Every time my father has ever been mentioned before, it has sent me in a downward spiral as my brain refused to remember my history. Panic kicks in. I'm only just learning my father is still alive, and there's a chance Featherstone could be trying to turn him into ash. My mind went into a state of shock at the thought of something happening before I got to see him again.

"Baby girl, I'm sorry for scaring you like that. When we heard the rumors that The Games were being brought forward, I decided I would only go through with the explosives assignment if I made it through The Games." I turn my gaze to him, my eyes softening as I take him in. "Like I said, last night, I asked Kai to look into it because it just didn't feel right suddenly, and once Kai read the letter and did some digging, I think I'm right."

"Don't get used to it," Roman mumbles, and it makes me chuckle in surprise, lightening the mood that surrounds us.

"Shut up, *baby*," Oscar grumbles in response, using my nickname on him. "Kai found a general location of where the safe house might be located, which is two states over, and was able to pull footage of Dominic Bridge in the area after you met him at the diner."

I digest his words and what they mean. If he went there after I approached him at the diner, then called me on Saturday to agree to help me, he could have gone to see my father.

"Okay, what do we do? I don't want him out there unprotected if Featherstone knows where he is. We need to keep him safe," I say, as I release Parker's hand to stand, my head throbbing with the swift change in my mental state.

"Should we tell Rafe?" Parker asks, and I nod in agreement.

My phone is still in the bedroom, but as I head to grab it a knock sounds at the door. Shit, what time is it? I'm not ready for The Games yet, I need to get something in motion here first.

"I'll grab it," Kai murmurs, opening the door to see Rafe on the other side.

"I was just about to call you," I say, as he steps into the room. The dark shadows under his eyes tell me he's barely slept, at least he seems to have showered and is in fresh clothes. "Dad, what's wrong?"

"Sorry, Luna. I know I'm a half-hour early, but I have some more information," he says, wrapping me in his arms. I can't believe hugging wasn't the norm for us until recently. The calming effect it has on me is indescribable.

"It's okay, the guys found something too, which is why I was about to call."

Pulling away, he looks me over. "First, how are you, darling? I know yesterday was a lot, even for me, and I want to make sure you're alright." His deep voice washes over me as I try to explain my true feelings.

"Honestly? I'm so fucking pissed that he's been alive all these years and we've been left to believe this giant lie." I release a breath, refusing to let my emotions get the better of me again. "Yet, my heart glows, knowing that he's out there and I have a chance to see my dad again, instead of fighting with my memory to piece him together."

Rafe squeezes my shoulder in comfort. "Darling, I completely understand. When we see him again, I'll get him in a bear hug while you beat the shit out of him for all of our heartache, okay? Just after we've soaked in all his love because I know he will have been hurting too."

I nod at his words as I fight back my tears. My mind overwhelmed that this is even a possibility.

Turning to the guys, Rafe asks, "So, what details did you happen to find?"

The guys all look around at each other, deciding who should be the one to explain and Roman sighs.

"One of Oscar's assignments, which he did not complete yet," he turns to Oscar with a 'this is how you say it' look, before turning back to Rafe. "Was to destroy a safe house, which we believe is where Bryce could be staying." Simple, blunt, and straight to the point. My perfect Roman Steele-Rivera. The words make me smile, a complete contrast to the woman having a breakdown earlier.

"In Ohio?" Rafe asks, and his response catches me by surprise.

"Yeah…" Oscar murmurs, clearly surprised too.

"It was in my letter," Rafe says, answering my unasked question. "I sent a team in with Reggie last night. I couldn't go myself and leave you here." He smiles softly at me, and I can't bring myself to argue with him. I'm coming to learn he's going to put me first, every time, whether I like it or not. "But when the team got there, the place was bare. No sign of forced entry or anything, just simply empty."

I sigh as I scrub a hand down my face. The closest thing to a lead we have and now it's gone.

"Don't worry, darling. I've had the team out there take pictures of everything for me to go through. If he was there, he would have left something as a sign. If I don't see it in the pictures, when this is all over, I'll head out there myself, okay?"

"Together," I respond. I'm not being kept out of this, Featherstone be damned.

"Together," Parker says, and my heart swells with the love I have for my family. Through thick and thin they're here for me, for each other.

"Not to burst our bubble," Kai murmurs, "But we need to head down for the second game."

Fuck. I shake the negativity from my mind. We just promised together, and that means in everything, including this.

Love. Family. Freedom. That is what I want, and I'll do

whatever it takes to get it.

OUR BLOODLINE

EIGHTEEN

Kai

Dark grey clouds fill the sky as we make our way over to the next location for The Games. Zipping up my black hoodie, I nervously rub the sleeves.

The SUV comes to a stop in front of what looks like a giant warehouse. When we arrived at the main room, where Luna shot Veronica, there was a sign on the door advising everyone to make their way to Zone F in the SUVs provided.

Following Rafe's lead out of the SUV, I look around at our surroundings. Apart from the warehouse, there is nothing but the border of the property that's around us. The high brick wall is topped with wrought-iron and barbed wire to our left, while trees lead off into a forest to our right. Making the warehouse look completely out of place.

"Great, a creepy warehouse in the middle of nowhere. Just how I wanted to spend my Wednesday," Oscar murmurs, as we slowly approach the double steel doors where two guards stand waiting for us.

As we near, I notice the metal detectors and security scanners, which I'm assuming we're going to have to go through to get inside. Harris Franks steps out in front of the security guards, his arms outstretched wide.

"The Steeles, how are you?" he greets, tucking his hands in his pockets. "Sorry about the new security measure, but after Mr. Steele's trigger-happy finger, we've decided to limit everyone's access to weapons outside of the actual game."

I follow his gaze to Parker, who simply smiles and shrugs his shoulders in response. No remorse or apology evident on his face. His confidence boost makes me grin, but Luna and Oscar get all the blame for his new behavior.

"So, place all guns in the boxes please, then walk straight through the metal detectors." He points in the direction of the table just before the entry, where we silently lock our guns away in the metal boxes. Squeezing Luna's hand as I pass her, I step up to the armed security guards first, both of which are wearing the classic black hoodies with the bright red F.A. embroidered on the front.

The guard on the left nods for me to continue through the metal detector and the light stays green. Sadly, it doesn't stop the second guard from stepping up to pat me down. I stand still, my legs shoulder-width apart, as he makes quick work of patting up my arms, down my abdomen and legs. He yanks the bottom of my combat pants up as he pats my ankle, finding my blade neatly tucked in my ankle holster.

"Harris, you need to be more fucking specific. Guns *and* knives in the box," he grunts, pulling my blade out and putting it in another box. I keep my facial expression neutral, as I glance over my shoulders at the others.

Harris scurries around collecting the blades from Luna, Roman, Parker, Oscar, and even Rafe, before rushing them through the security.

"Let them through, I've got it all here. They'll be late," Harris mutters, and the security guys wave them through. "Go to your right, then take a left at the end." We don't hang around.

"Rafe Gibbs, you absolute mastermind," Oscar whispers, a wide grin on his face as he lightly taps under his right arm. Indicating where they each have hidden the undetectable guns West had given us before The Games. Rafe mentioned the new security measure before we left, so they all carried them except me, and Featherstone's security fell straight into our trap.

Roman brushes his arm against mine when we step around the corner, out of sight, handing mine over. I quickly hide the gun in my holster too, under my arm, discreetly hidden by my hoodie.

"Thanks," I murmur, as I slow my pace to walk with my Sakura before everything gets crazy in here. As if anticipating my move, her arm wraps around my waist from behind, her lips planting a light kiss to my cheek without missing a step.

My arm goes around her shoulders, and I return the touch, kissing the crown of her head. Approaching the doors at the end of the hallway, noise seeps through from the other side. The level of chatter and music instantly has me on high alert compared to the eerily quiet setting of The Tunnel.

We glance at each other, silently communicating our

love and appreciation, before Rafe pushes open the door. My eyes scan the room, trying to take everything in at once, but there is too much happening. Blinking, I take a deep breath, categorizing what is going on.

Even though we entered the warehouse on the ground floor, it's all open. From the ground to the ceiling is possibly four stories high, but the floor opens below, a further five stories deep, reminding me of a Roman Colosseum. The center looks like where The Game will actually take place, on the other side of a metal fence.

There are Featherstone associates everywhere, people pushing and shoving to get a good view. When I glance back up, there are people looking down from all levels, watching what will happen below. If they don't have a clear view, there are large television screens that display a countdown on them, with the words 'The Slums' flashing across the screen too.

"This way please!" some guy yells in front of me, and I follow his lead, dropping my hand from Luna's shoulder to take her hand, squeezing tight. I feel eyes observing us as we pass through the crowd and down the metal staircase to our right.

As soon as we hit the ground level, the members of The

Ring and the other students watch as we enter the space.

"How nice of you to join us," John Dietrichson complains, but no one pays him any attention, although I see Luna rolling her green eyes in annoyance.

"Welcome to The Slums!" Harris Franks calls out from behind us, breathing heavily as he tries to catch his breath, worn out from running down the stairs. I walk us over to stand with the other participants, as Rafe stays with the other family members.

Luna waits beside Taylor Doherty, who is giving Parker some flirty eyes. I don't want to point this out to Luna right now, she'll likely have Taylor's head before we even get inside. The girl is lucky Luna doesn't catch her.

"Who is ready for The Slums? Room upon room, all different in sizes, jam-packed with different dangers that await you. The aim is to survive for the next hour, as The Slums take your blood, sweat, and tears." He points his hand behind him to large steel doors that have six different types of locks, ensuring they stay shut when all of us have entered.

"When the horn sounds, the game is over. Weapons can be found inside, since we took your weapons upon arrival. Any questions?" He looks at each student, but no one offers a response. Some are bloodthirsty, while others look nervous. "Okay then, if you'd like to walk around the perimeter, each group has a separate entry. The televisions above the door will count down to notify you when you can enter." Clapping his hands, he's done.

Luna pulls me to follow her, and the guys step up beside us.

"We read about The Slums," I murmur, trying to remember what we learned.

"I remember," Parker says, and we all slow our pace as we try to prepare ourselves. "From what the experiences said, it's literally a maze leading from room to room. I think someone said there are a lot of Featherstone members in there ready to attack, and it's one of the bloodiest games there is in The Games."

No one says any more, as we see the television above the next set of doors with STEELE flashing across the screen.

This is it. Game two of three, all we have to do is survive this, by any means necessary. Kissing Luna's knuckles, I release my hold on her as I bounce on the balls of my feet, preparing to enter together.

That's what matters the most, being together. Strength

in numbers, in family.

Red numbers suddenly pop up on the screen, and I glance at my brothers and my Sakura. We're all focused and ready to go. Determination is clear on everyone's faces.

Three… Two… One…

OUR BLOODLINE

NINETEEN
Roman

The screen flickers green as it reads 'GO,' turning into a live feed of what's happening in The Slums. I can't see exactly what is showing on there, since we're being forced inside. Kai stays in front of Luna, while Oscar and Parker stand at her side, and I take up the back. We know she can handle herself, but it's still instinctive to protect what's ours, and she is everything we have.

The doors slam shut behind us, and I hear the locks activate. It's dark in here, not pitch black like The Tunnel was, but the lighting is sparse. The room we've stepped into is tiny, it's barely able to fit us all in, with five blades and five blunt objects lined up on the wall for us to choose from. The hard cement floor makes the room feel colder almost, as the smell of oil and smoke fills my lungs. It's eerily quiet in here, but the door straight ahead will lead to chaos, I can feel it.

Luna steps up to the wall first, eyeing the end of each silvery blade before choosing the slim Japanese dagger style option, just like she had in The Pyramid when she killed Tyler. She moves over to the opposite wall, leaving us to decide on our blades. I catch sight of a hunting knife, similar to what I had to hand over upon entry. Its brown leather handle feels good in my hand, as the steel blade almost shimmers in the darkness. Adding it to my knife sheath, I move out of the way.

In silence, we prepare ourselves for what may come, all stocked up with our weapons of choice. Each of us with a different type of blade, along with our blunt objects. Oscar has a baseball bat, Kai holds the wooden martial art tonfa, Luna has her kali sticks, while Parker is gripping the end of a baton, and I have my hammer.

Static sounds from behind us, gaining our attention. A television also hangs on this side of the door, and we watch as Harris Franks comes into focus.

"I hope you are all ready, because your time starts," he looks down at his watch, dragging out the whole thing before grinning at the camera. "Now." As the words pass his lips, the door at the other side of the room swings open, revealing flickering lights in a room painted with red walls.

Luna goes to step through the door first, but Parker is quick to move in front of her. I can't see her reaction, but I'm ninety-nine percent sure she's rolling her eyes at him.

As I follow them into the new room, the heat surprises me. The decor reminds me of a scene pulled straight out of a sixties horror movie. An old-fashioned bedroom with dark wooden dressers and an armoire pushed against the wall. I also notice black and white pictures taped to every surface. Literally everything, the walls, the dresser, only the floor is clear. A bed is set up in the corner of the room, old floral bed sheets covering it, and straightened to perfection. As I continue to assess the room, I spot the next door across from us. We appear to be alone, but it's something in the photos that catches my eye.

Stepping in front of the dark oak dresser, my stomach drops at what each picture shows. That sick motherfucker, I'll kill him when we get out of here. My pulse thunders in my ears as rage engulfs me. I feel Luna step beside me, a slight gasp passes her lips, and I hate that there is nothing I can do to stop it.

Every single photo shows Luna, Oscar, and Parker fucking. Pictures upon pictures of the moment they shared, knowing Rico might have been watching. We'll never know if he watched them live or not, but from the photo's before us, he captured every intimate moment. From the second they stepped into the room, to the still frame of me aiming my gun at the camera.

"Holy shit," Oscar whispers, and Luna giggles, fucking giggles.

"Hot, right?" she responds, and it takes me a moment to catch up.

"Wait… You're not upset?" I ask wearily, looking at the others for confirmation, as Luna moves both of her sticks to one hand so she can squeeze my shoulder.

"Baby, we stepped into that room knowing he would likely see us, and I don't regret it. Look at them," she says, stroking a hand over a picture of Oscar and Parker standing beside the bed, Luna between them, as they both thrust inside of her. Luna's head is thrown back in ecstasy, with pleasure evident on each of their faces.

She's right. It's hot as hell, intimate, perfect. I look

down at her to see she's already smiling up at me. Oscar and Parker look completely unfazed too. I take an extra moment to study Parker's face, making sure he's not internally breaking down, but he offers a grin, showing he's okay.

"They placed these here to catch us off-guard, send us into a fit of rage and make us sloppy," Kai mutters, and I nod in agreement.

"We're not going to let them get to us like that," Luna insists. "And if we had time right now, we'd fuck against these pictures just to show them we don't care, but we have weapons for a reason." A smile ghosts across her lips.

"And I'd rather Granny Steele and Rafe didn't castrate me when we get out of here," Parker adds, and I shake my head.

A boom sounds from the other side of the next door, breaking our conversation and sending us all on high alert, weapons raised and ready for action. Hardcore, heavy bass music suddenly surrounds us, thumping in our ears, stopping us from being able to hear anyone approach. Something hits the other side of the wall, which ricochets in front of us.

Kai walks up to the door, gripping the handle. Luna

is right behind him, as Parker and Oscar stand further in the room with me. He looks to us for confirmation before swinging the door open. Luna jumps back as a body flops to the floor at her feet.

"Is that…?"

"Yeah," I murmur in response to Luna, as we all look at Neil Portman, with his hands chopped off, and eyeballs gouged out. Blood pours from his body like a river, as we stand there and stare in shock. We've barely been in here for fifteen minutes. How the hell does he look like this already?

Suddenly, an axe comes flying through the open door, skimming past Kai's head as it lodges into the dresser behind us.

What. The. Actual. Fuck.

Without missing a beat, we all rush to help Kai, but with his usual calm demeanor he pulls the blade from the holster at his waist, and with a casual flick of his wrist, the knife leaves his hand. Racing to the door to support him, I watch as a guy dressed in a white lab coat covered in blood, drops to his knees on the opposite end of the room.

Kai's blade sticks out of the assailant's chest, right where his heart is, and he's looking down at the wound in shock. Watching the color drain from his face, red seeps into his lab coat, and I sigh in relief. Standing before Kai, I check him over, making sure he wasn't cut. With a shake of his head, I know he's fine. Patting him on the shoulder, I step further into the room, alone.

Blood splatter is on every surface, with what looks like intestines and other organs cluttering the countertops. A hospital bed lays in the center of the larger room, Neil's hands, eyeballs, and tongue thrown casually on top. There doesn't seem to be anyone else in here, as I scan every inch of the hospital like room. I notice bloodied tools haphazardly placed across a silver tray on the countertop, which were likely used on Neil.

Fuck, this scene is even making me queasy.

A television flickers on, hanging from a wall mount in the corner of the room, with Rico's face filling the screen. Darkness surrounds him, giving nothing else away.

"I'll put fifty thousand dollars on the table for whoever kills Parker fucking Manetti, and another fifty thousand dollars to whoever hands over that sweet piece of ass, Luna Steele," he sneers. "Totem may want you for the movement, little moon, but I want to hear you scream when I fuck you raw." His words make me cringe as the screen goes black again, leaving us to stand in shock.

Wide-eyed, I turn back to see Luna step through the door with Parker and Oscar right behind her. The music seems louder, making it harder to think, never mind trying to have a conversation, forcing us to shout to each other.

"I'll kill him with my bare hands," Oscar growls loudly, and I'm onboard with one of us forcing him to take his last breath, especially after he just put a hit out on Parker.

"Are you okay?" Luna asks, running a hand up his chest to cup his face.

Nodding in response, I'm surprised to see Parker so calm and collected, as he smiles down at her.

"Honestly, angel, I'm okay. Fuck him and his threat."

Searching around the room, we need a plan. It doesn't help that we don't know what is beyond the next door, or how many people are actually in The Slums, with the exception of the Featherstone Academy teams.

"Everyone have your weapons ready. If people weren't coming for us already, they are now," I shout over the music, and everyone focuses. Gripping my hammer in my right hand, I pull my blade into my left hand, ready for whatever happens next.

We were fucking made for this, trained for this, no one

gets to stop us now. Staying here isn't an option, because we're still too close to our entrance. If anyone is familiar with the layout of The Slums, they'll know where to find us.

Walking to the door, I look back at everyone, standing as though they're in a cage, ready to fight. I take that as my cue to move forward. Kicking the door, it flies open, bouncing off the wall. A revving sound groans out over the pumping music, and I try to place the noise.

"Is that a chainsaw?" Kai asks, and my jaw drops a little at the fact he's right. I shouldn't be surprised by the lengths Featherstone will go to, but a chainsaw, really?

Stepping cautiously through the door, I'm surprised to find a hallway instead of another room. Nothing but flickering lights to my left, I turn to check to the right. The space is too dark to see clearly, the walls painted black, absorbing all the light from the space.

Looking further to the right, I notice a guy with a damn chainsaw running, arms raised high in the air. He's coming from the dark abyss, the chain reflecting off the minimal lighting we have. The whole scene is straight out of a Halloween movie.

Noticing my movement, he starts to head in our

direction, picking up speed as he approaches.

"Watch out!" I shout, ducking as he reaches us. I feel a forceful breeze brush the side of my face, as the guide bar cuts through the air. Not wanting to trip him into the others, I manage to back myself against the wall, lowering even more as he swings the chainsaw down toward me. As it comes down, the nose lodges into the wall above me, stopping his movement.

Not missing my opportunity, I thrust my blade straight into his stomach, the rev of the chainsaw cuts off as he releases the throttle, screaming in pain. Pulling the blade back, I stab him again, readying my hammer.

I don't look to see where the others are, I just need to end this threat right now. With adrenaline kicking in even higher, I bring myself to my feet in one swift motion, swinging the hammer around with me. The crunch as it connects with his skull is swallowed up by the music pumping around us. I watch as his body slumps down the wall, blood splattering in his path.

My breathing is heavy as I try to focus on everything else around me. Parker is crouched on the other side of the dead guy, while Kai is at the opposite end of the hall, holding Freddie Richards back, as they swing their weapons at each other.

I catch sight of Luna sweeping her hair out of her face as the door to her left opens. Taylor races out, covered in blood and screaming. In slow motion, I watch Luna step to the side as a guy dressed all in black with a ski mask on, runs out of the room from behind her, a butcher knife in hand while he lunges for Taylor.

Luna doesn't question what to do next, she jumps, wrapping her arms around the murderous guy's neck, dropping her wooden kali sticks in the process to pull her blade from her hip. As he pins Taylor to the wall, ready to bring the knife down on her, Luna drags her blade straight across his throat.

Blood bursts from the wound, instantly covering Taylor in her attacker's gore, who stares in shock at the scene in front of her. Stumbling back, his hands grip his neck, while Luna falls to her knees beside him. This is turning into a serious bloodbath, and all I can hear is Taylor's screams echoing in my ears.

Oscar, where the fuck is Oscar?

A bang from behind catches my attention, and I spin around to find Oscar using his baseball bat to repeatedly beat down another one of Featherstone's men.

Behind him, a door opens, and I ready my body to attack and defend, only to see Wren step out, blood smeared all over her face. My eyes catch on the silver barrel as she slowly walks down the hall, past Oscar, raising a gun. How the fuck did she sneak one in too?

It could be trained on anyone, but I refuse to let her pull the trigger and hurt my family. Crouching low, I charge at her, lifting her off the ground at her waist, but it's not enough as I hear the sound of the bullet leave the barrel. Spinning with her in my arms, I carelessly drop her to the floor behind me as I frantically search in the direction she shot. She drops the gun when she falls, and I blindly kick it out of her reach.

Fear coats my skin as I track everyone. Kai's head spins in my direction, as well as Parker's, clearly both okay, forcing me to find Luna. Her back is pushed against the wall, her eyes wide in shock.

No.

Moving around the bodies on the floor, I rush to her side, but she isn't looking at me, she's looking at Taylor who is pressed up against her. Luna turns Taylor's body around, and I catch Taylor as Luna lowers her to the floor. Luna brushes the bloodied brown hair from Taylor's face while assessing her wound.

"Taylor, can you hear me? Stay with me, okay?" Luna shouts down at her.

"What a fucking hobo," she struggles to breathe out, her eyes flickering to Wren in disgust.

Confused, I try to process what's going on. Luna pulls her long-sleeved shirt over her head, leaving her in just a sports bra and presses the cloth on Taylor's stomach.

"Roman, help me. She took the bullet," she rushes out desperately, focusing on the dying girl before us. "She threw herself in front of me, Rome. She saved my life." Luna finally looks into my eyes, and I nod in understanding.

Looking over me, her frantic eyes suddenly freeze, fire burning in her pupils as she focuses on something.

"Take care of her, Rome," she murmurs, cupping my cheek, her fingertips smearing blood on my face, but I don't care. "She's going to pay for this." Luna stands up straight, determination clear in her eyes as she steps over Taylor, who looks up, pleading with me to save her life.

I continue to apply pressure as I track Luna's movements. She's heading straight for Wren, who is leaning against the wall, a dazed look in her eyes as she rubs her head gingerly. Blood touches her fingertips, likely from the way I dropped her carelessly before.

Parker looks to me for guidance, trying to figure out where he can help. Right now, standing amongst the blood, gore, and death, I don't even know myself.

OUR BLOODLINE

TWENTY

Luna

Leaving Roman to help Taylor, I stalk toward Wren. This bitch is done. Taylor was still in a state of shock from watching me slit the guy's throat in front of her, but the appreciation and respect had been evident in her eyes. I think that may be why she threw herself in front of me as she screamed to look out, clearly seeing Wren raise the gun before I did. She won't die for blindly protecting me in return, not at the hands of Wren Dietrichson or Featherstone.

Stepping over lifeless bodies that scatter the blood covered floor, I use my arm to swipe at my face, trying to remove some of the blood and sweat so I can see better. Wren looks disoriented as I near her, and I'm not usually one to kick a bitch when she's down, but there's no getting up for her. I'll make sure of it.

Grabbing the collar of her peach top, I drag her to her feet. Releasing some of my rage, I throw Wren through the open door to my left, opposite to where I came out with the guys. The sound of a table crashing fills my ears, the music not as loud in here. I step into the room behind her, leaving the door open. She's quicker than I expect, jumping to her feet in a crouched stance, sneering at me, but I just grin. Thinking about everything this girl has done in the past three months fuels my anger, and I'm happy to let my rage takeover finally. There is no tutor here to stop me.

Looking down at myself, my blade and gun are in clear view now that I don't have a top on, but I don't care. My sticks are somewhere on the ground, currently of no use to me at all.

"You should have fucking listened, whore," Wren growls, and I laugh, standing still, faking calm and carefree, but ready to react at any second. "You're fucking with everything! This is bigger than you, but you walk into Featherstone, thinking you're some queen. All because the other heirs of The Ring, Roman, Parker, Kai, and Oscar, worship the ground you walk on!" Her voice carries over the bass of the music, and I can hear the slight tremble in her words.

"I can smell your fear from here, Wren," I murmur, before running at her. The longer we stand, the more time she has to come up with a plan, and I refuse to let that happen. She lifts her arms to block the swing of my fist, but I still manage to connect with her cheek, her head snaps to the side with the impact.

Falling to her back, she surprises me, kicking her leg round, catching me right at the back of my knees and knocking me forward. What the fuck? My hands break my fall as I drop to my knees beside her. Bitch. Swinging my fist to the side, I hit the side of her head, making her grunt before she can overpower me.

Throwing my leg over her waist, her fists come up to hit me. I grapple with her to stop the attack, pinning her legs down with mine, as I fight to stay above her. Her fingers wrap in my hair, and I'm furious at the fact she's fighting dirty, trying to pull my hair like we're children.

Still hovering above her on the ground, I lift my fist and punch her in the stomach, causing the wind to rush out of her, as she tries to curl up in a ball. It reminds me of the time I was attacked by Wren and her friends, forcing me to curl into the same fetal position. All while they rained blows down on my body, over and over again. Payback's a real bitch, bitch.

Leaning over her, I continue to hit her face, blow after blow. Until she manages to land a fist in my side, weakening my grip, and allowing her to push me off. Rolling to my feet, I'm ready as she crouches low. Extending my leg, I watch as she pulls a knife from her hip, and just as my combat boot smashes into her face, she manages to slice my calf.

I feel the pinch, but the adrenaline coursing through my veins masks the extent of the injury.

Watching Wren's body fly back from the impact of my boot doesn't offer me enough satisfaction. Although, the blood covering her face as she holds her cheek in pain makes me smile. The fact that she manages to still stand though, fucking infuriates me. She quickly runs for the door behind her, running from me, but I'm not put off by a little chase.

Before I can follow after her, a television flickers on in the room, grabbing my attention as the music completely shuts off. I wipe my hair from my face, making the most of the calm before the storm, as I watch Juliana's frantic face fill the screen.

"Luna? Kai? Roman? Anyone!" She steps to the left, and I catch a glimpse of a wall filled with security cameras. It's as if she's searching for us on there. "Where the fuck are you, Luna? Totem is in there!" She yells in frustration, her eyes looking back to the camera.

Wait… what? Totem?

My heart rate picks up, and I feel my eyes glaze over, my defensive senses kicking in as I stand ready to fight. Of course, that motherfucker shows up here when we're at our weakest.

"Luna! Luna!" I hear Oscar yell from the hallway, but my eyes are fixed on the screen. Behind Juliana, I can see Rafe pinning Rico to the wall, his hands around his throat. The look on his red face is one I've never seen before, his eyes burn with anger, and his jaw is so tight he could cut glass. I watch as he pulls his gun from his back pocket, pressing the barrel into Rico's head, right in between his eyes.

Too much is happening all at once, but I can't take my eyes off the screen. Some of Rico's men go to charge Rafe, but it's too late. I watch in slow motion as Rafe pulls the trigger, the smirk on Rico's face instantly falling, along with his lifeless body as he drops to the floor. Swiping Rico's blood from his face, he glances down at his shirt, seeing even more of it, and he shrugs.

My heart pounds in my chest, watching my Dad kill someone with vengeance in his eyes. We'll never know what role Rico played in everything, but he deserved to die. I just wish I'd been able to do it, for everything he did to Parker. I hope he rots in hell.

"Luna! Fuck! I've been screaming your name," Oscar rushes out as he steps into the room, wrapping me in his arms.

"Did you hear Juliana?" I ask, and I feel him nod against me.

"I didn't see a monitor, but her voice was coming through the speakers. I heard a gunshot too." Leaning back, he cups my cheek, his eyes scanning over me. "We need to get you out of here, baby girl."

A boom rings in my ears, an explosion knocking us to the floor. What the fuck is happening?

My vision is blurred as I try to focus, but I can't gain my balance to even bring myself to sit up on the floor. My mind screams for Oscar, for Roman, Kai, and Parker, but I can't get the words to pass my lips, only a whimper, as my body deals with the impact of what is going on around us.

Helplessly, I manage to prop myself up on my hands and knees, the ground rattling around me. Why is it suddenly so bright? Forcing deep breaths, I push through the throbbing pain that's coursing through my body.

A hand squeezes mine, and I try to open my eyes again, just focusing on what is right in front of me. Oscar's hand holds mine, and I slowly trail my eyes up his arm, my vision staying clear enough to see his face. He looks as though he's reacting just as badly as me, concern in the crinkle of his eyes, but we need to find the others.

Oscar manages to gain enough balance to stand, letting me crawl up his body to stand beside him. Lacing his fingers with mine, we stumble toward the door where the others were. Using the walls to guide us, I see Parker and Roman to our right, coughing with the smoke that surrounds us, helping each other to their feet. It's the flickers of red and orange reflecting off the walls that draw my attention to the other end of the hall.

Glancing in the other direction, my heart drops as flames burn brightly, consuming everything in its path.

Looking back into the room, I see the door Wren left through, and it looks like the safest option right now.

Still unable to find my words, I pat Oscar's arm to gain his attention and point to where we need to go. Nodding in agreement, we make our way as quickly as we can to Roman and Parker, but where's Kai?

Roman scans me from head to toe, watching us approach, relief evident on his face as he takes me in. I glance between the two of them, Parker checks me over too, but he must see the question in my eyes. Parker points further down the corridor to another door where Kai must be, thankfully, in the opposite direction of the fire.

Dropping my hand from Oscar's, I steady myself against the wall, slowly making my way down the hallway, hopefully, to find Kai. My fingers wrap around the door frame, pulling me into view, and when my eyes fall on Kai, my heart sinks.

Sound finally fills my ears, but only to hear a man screaming. "Kill him! I said fucking kill him, Wren!" he seethes. "An eye for an eye, or it's your mother I'll take as repayment for the death of Veronica!" he spits out, but Wren remains frozen in place.

Kai lays injured on the floor, blood pouring from his

right shoulder, as I realize someone has already shot him. I can see his fingers slowly moving toward his gun, but with their gazes on him, he's going to have to be quick. That's going to be difficult when it's his shooting arm that's injured.

"I said, do it, Wren! No daughter of mine should fucking hesitate like this!"

My brain tries to process what they're saying, or who this motherfucker even is, and slowly it pieces together in my jumbled mind.

Totem.

Wren is the heir.

It should have been obvious, but my brain can't focus on that when Kai's life hangs in the balance. Clearly done with waiting, he goes to rip the gun from her hand, and I react on instinct.

Pulling my gun from my underarm holster, the safety already off before I have my target in sight. I aim and shoot without question, but in my rattled state I'm not as accurate as usual. The bullet sails through the air, followed quickly by another as my finger continues to pull the trigger.

As if in slow motion, Wren turns toward me at the sound of the gun going off, the bullet hitting her in the thigh, followed by the second in her back. As she tumbles to the floor, the third bullet lodges into the wall at the other end of the room. The fourth bullet making contact with Totem, not enough to cause serious damage, but it's a clean shot in his arm he's holding his gun in.

He sneers as his eyes widen with fury. "Soon, you'll be mine, little moon."

Glancing behind me for a moment, he suddenly scurries from the room, and I drop to the floor. Out of rounds, and lacking energy, I try to crawl toward Kai as he frantically tries to get to me as well. He feels too far, I need to lie down, just for a minute, my head is throbbing, the adrenaline starting to wear off.

The strength in my arms goes, but someone catches me before my face smashes into the floor, turning me to lay on my back.

Blinking up at the person who caught my fall, I know I must be dead, but at least I'll die with a smile on my face as I peer into the same green eyes as my own.

If my eyes weren't brimming with tears, I'd scream right now, but I'll take peace instead. The peace you get from seeing a loved one again, after your heart is broken, never truly healing.

My tongue is dry in my mouth, but I manage to speak a single word before darkness seeps in.

"Dad."

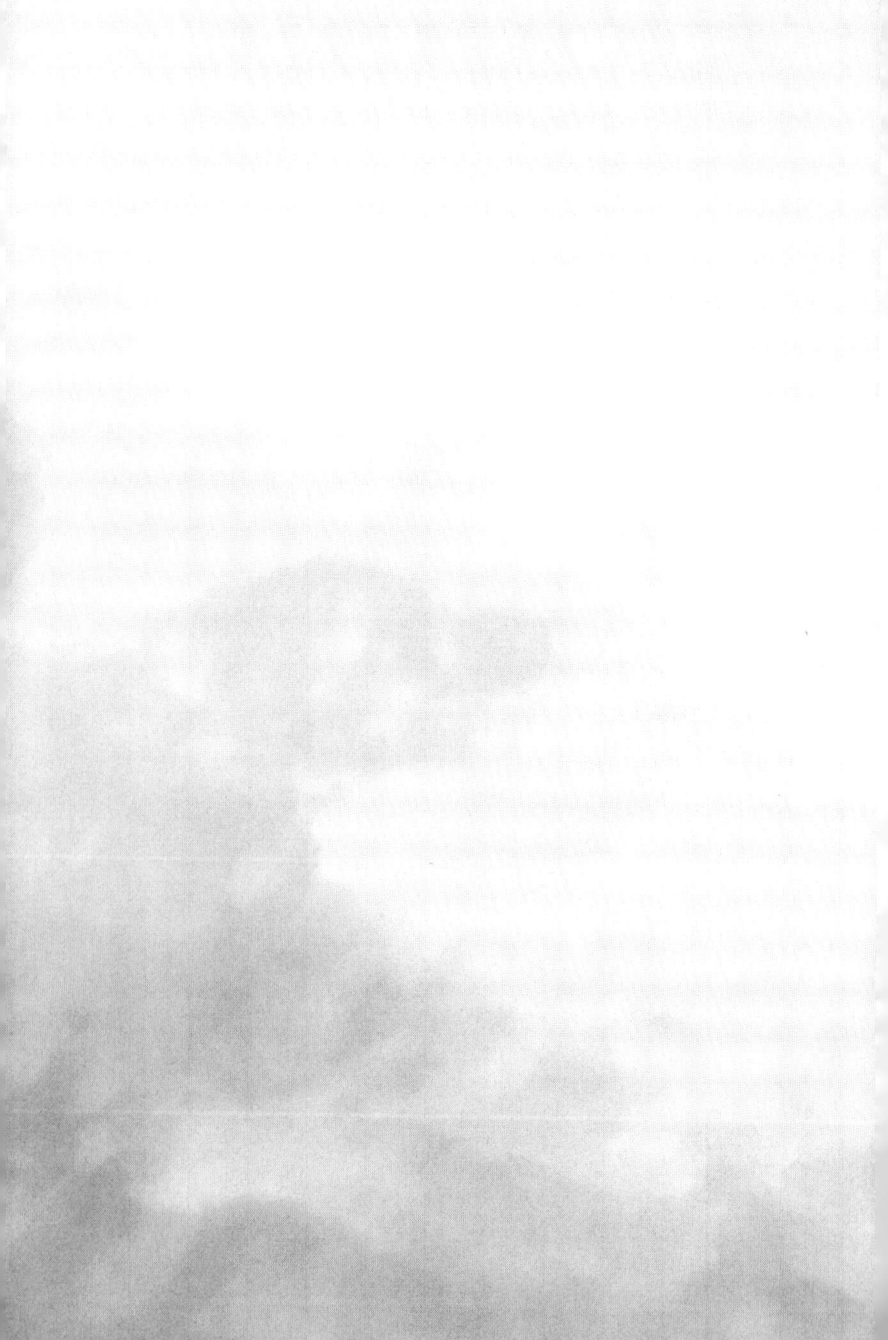

TWENTY ONE

Roman

My head jerks in the direction of the door Luna stepped out of, struggling to swallow past the rock stuck in my throat, fear consuming me. The hairs on my arms stand on end as I glance down at Taylor. She's still breathing, but I need to get to Luna. She's my priority right now.

I catch sight of Parker and Oscar following behind me, but I come to an abrupt stop as I enter the room, taking in the scene before me.

The door at the other end of the room slams shut, clearly someone running away, but with Kai rushing to

Luna's side, that's where my focus stays. Luna. Her body is held from dropping to the floor by a man, but before I can charge at him to get him off her, I hear the word she breathes before passing out.

"Dad."

Dashing to her side, I watch as her eyes close, slipping into an unconscious state. Cupping the back of her head, I look to the man hovering over her, and my eyes widen in surprise.

"Bryce," I murmur, instinctively touching his arm to feel he's really here. He smiles at me, tears in his eyes, as he looks back down at his daughter, my beautiful wife.

"We need to get out of here before the whole place explodes." He glances toward Kai, "Are you okay to move?" Kai nods in response, also at a loss for words.

I slip my hand under Luna's legs, but Bryce squeezes my shoulder. "Roman, you're still disorientated from the explosion. Let me carry her, okay?" Looking deep into his eyes, I know it's the right choice, but I'm scared to let her out of my sight.

"You don't go anywhere without me. Where she goes, I go," I grunt, accepting his help, but before he can lift her, shouts sound from the hallway. I instantly know who's coming, and I don't think I'm ready for this, and the gulp Bryce takes tells me his emotions are coming all at once too.

"Luna? Luna! The explosion destroyed the camera feed!" I hear someone call out, fear in his voice. "Where the fuck is my…" Rafe's voice trails off as he steps into the room, his eyes falling to Luna, limp between Bryce and me, before his eyes finally take in who is beside me.

If Luna hadn't melted my black heart, I would never have appreciated the love before me, instead turning a blind eye to what matters most in this world. We are literally in a burning building, the sound of wood splintering, and floors collapsing around us. Yet it's the sight of his love, Bryce, that brings Rafe to his knees. Literally, his legs give out from under him, knocking him to the floor.

Bryce stalls beside me, not wanting to release Luna, but needing to go to him. I nudge his shoulder, pushing him to go as I hold her. Oscar quickly fills his spot as Bryce drops to his knees in front of Rafe.

I know this is their moment, intimacy, and vulnerability wrapping around them, but I can't look away as they cry freely. Tears coating their cheeks as Bryce rests his forehead against Rafe's. If Luna were awake right now she'd cry at their display of love too. I just know it.

Parker stands awkwardly at the door, glancing over his shoulder, before taking a deep breath and interrupting. "I'm really, really sorry, but could we do the whole reunited thing when we have Luna safe? We're about to burn to death."

His words kick everyone into action. Bryce lifts Luna from my arms and heads out of the opposite door. We follow behind them, making sure to keep up as smoke fills the rooms, blocking our view, and filling our lungs.

Rafe steps in front, throwing a door open to let everyone out. The light that fills the room burns my eyes as we step outside. It takes me a minute to understand where we are. I expected us to still be in the warehouse, but the door led us straight to the forest.

"Straight down this path, there's an SUV waiting which will take us to the jet," Bryce calls out. Taking off down a makeshift path, barely noticeable amongst the trees and foliage. A boom sounds from behind us, as fire burns from the windows of the warehouse, black smoke darkening the sky.

"Rome, come on!" Oscar shouts, as he keeps up with the others, and I jog to catch up.

Walking beside Kai, I try to check his wound. He's losing quite a bit of blood, and he looks pale.

"Hopefully not too far now, man," I say, and he nods.

"I'm okay," is his response, but his voice sounds weak too.

Looking in front of us, the forest opens up to a break in the trees. A large black SUV is parked idly in the middle of it, with the driver's door still open.

"I'll drive," Rafe calls out, opening the rear passenger door for us. Bryce climbs in, laying Luna across the seats facing the back.

Kai sits facing her, resting his head on the back of the seat, pain evident in his expression. Parker climbs in beside him, as Oscar rounds the car to sit up front with Rafe. Before Bryce can sit with Luna, I climb in, lifting her legs onto my lap.

Jumping in behind me, he shuts the door and takes the seat beside Parker. Without wasting a moment, Rafe's in the driver's seat and flooring it. I release the breath I didn't even realize I was holding as I look down at Luna. We need to have a chat about the inconvenient times she's unconscious.

My leg feels cool, almost wet, and when I swipe a

hand over it, my fingers feel the sticky substance of blood. Quickly glancing to Bryce, his arm is covered in blood too. Lifting Luna's leg, I see the slice in her combat pants and the wound beneath it.

Before I can take my jacket off to wrap her leg, Bryce's t-shirt is being dropped into my lap. I try to smile in appreciation, but my focus is on stopping the bleeding. Tying the shirt as tight as I can, I keep the pressure on, catching sight of Parker helping Kai.

What a complete shit show this has been, but we're all here together, alive, and that's what matters.

Luna

A slight rumble beneath me tries to lure me back to sleep, but the pounding in my head is unbearable, forcing me to stay awake. Flickering my eyes open, the cream leather sofa in front of me makes me frown. Wetting my dry lips, I try to work out what the hell is going on.

Swiping a hand down my face, I notice the dirt and blood ingrained into the grooves of my fingers and nails, making me pause.

"She's awake," Roman whispers, and I glance down at the sofa I seem to be laying on. Where my legs are propped up on his lap. Well, at least I'm not alone. He smiles softly at me, his tired eyes checking me over as he gently strokes my leg. "Hey, princess. How are you feeling?"

I try to process how I feel, but everything is just one giant ache. The throbbing in my head and my leg slightly outweigh everything else, but overall, I *think* I'm fine. Trying to remember why I would be in this condition takes me a moment, but the second I see Totem's face in my mind, back in The Slums, my heart starts pounding in my chest. Kai. Kai was bleeding, I need to make sure he's alive.

"It's okay, princess. Kai's fine, the doctor took care of him. He's sleeping," Roman answers, clearly I was talking out loud again. The grin on his handsome face tells me I still am.

Totem's piercing brown eyes and slicked back dark hair flashes on repeat in my mind. I won't be able to forget what he looks like, the scar that runs down the side of his eye, all of the way down to his chin, is unmistakable. Add to the fact, a thick black cursive tattoo covers his neck, completely one of a kind, reading 'Totem.'

I scoff as a vivid memory comes to mind. "I had the craziest vision, baby. My Dad was there," I chuckle. "It must have been all that talk last night, and this morning, hmm?" I say, glancing back at him, but he doesn't meet my gaze.

Clearing his throat, he stumbles over his words, "Uh, about that." He rubs the back of his neck nervously, and it sets me on edge.

"What's going on?" I ask, but he looks across the room, panic in his eyes.

"I think he's trying to find the words to tell you I wasn't a vision, Meu Tesouro."

My heart pounds rapidly in my chest, and I feel like I can't breathe. I have the vaguest memory of that voice, and it definitely isn't one I expected to hear when I woke up. An invisible weight sits on my chest as I struggle to process what's happening.

Covering my face with my hands, I can't hide the sob that passes my lips. I'm too scared to move a muscle to find out this is a fucking dream.

"It's not a dream, Luna," the voice murmurs, and I curse myself out for still thinking out loud.

"Shut up a minute, will you? You're going to make her pass out again, dickhead," Oscar grumbles, and it makes me snort behind my hands. "See, she needs to hear *my* voice. I make it all better. Right, baby girl?" Oscar continues, his voice right beside my ear, as he strokes my hair from my face.

Like a scared little girl, I peer through my fingers as I tilt my face to look at Oscar, who smiles down at me. "Is that my dad?" I whisper, and he nods lightly in response. "You just called my dad a dickhead." The shock is clear in my voice, and he shrugs his shoulders.

"I'll do more than that if he makes you pass out again, baby girl. I've been worried." I grin like a madwoman at him, and he kisses my forehead. "No more of this hiding business," he mutters, pulling my hands fully from my face and helping me to sit up.

Sitting beside me, Oscar sandwiches me in between him and Roman, who laces his fingers through mine. Finding the courage, I look around, finding us on a freaking plane. My eyes first falling to Rafe, refusing to glance anywhere else. His puffy red eyes surprise me and do nothing to calm my nerves.

"Hey, darling. At least you woke up in transit this

time." He grins, trying to lighten the atmosphere, and I smile at the effort.

"It's the being awake when we enter the vehicle I seem to have an issue with, and a plane, again, really?" I murmur, catching movement beside him, begging me to look. My eyes well up with unshed tears, as I find the strength to look to his right.

My father, Bryce Steele, sits beside Rafe with his brown hair swept to the side just like I remember. Tattoos peek out from underneath his collar and trail down his arms. Meeting his stare, his green eyes glisten with unshed tears, just like mine. I crumble under his gaze, overwhelming emotions taking over, but he quickly moves to his knees in front of me.

Before his hand can touch me, Roman grips his wrist loosely.

"Remember what I said, only if she's comfortable," Roman mutters, no bite to his words, as he slowly releases his hold on him.

My father looks at me, trying to figure out what would be the best thing to do here, but I let my instincts take over, throwing myself at him. My leg throbs with the movement, as my knees hit the floor in front of him. Wrapping my arms tightly around his neck, I can't believe he's actually here right now.

He squeezes me back just as tight, the sense of home washing over me, just like it does with Rafe and my Aceholes. There is so much to talk about, but right now I allow myself the comfort I've craved all these years.

I don't know how long we stay like that, but when we pull away, it doesn't feel like it was long enough. Wiping my tears away, he smiles down at me.

"Hey, Meu Tesouro," he says softly. "I know there is so much to talk about, and we will, I promise. I've already been warned papa bear's going to pin me down so you can beat me up." He rolls his eyes, amused with the whole thing, and it makes me smile. "The plane is descending, and we should be landing in about fifteen minutes. When we get home, we can do whatever you need, at your speed, okay?"

I nod in response, as Parker and Kai step through a door to my left.

"I'm glad you're awake, angel," Parker says, as he places a kiss on my head and sits down across from Roman. I'm so confused by the fact this is a plane right now, but I won't complain at the luxury seating and not being packed in like sardines. At some point, I may even ask who it belongs to.

My father squeezes my hand and retakes his seat next to Rafe, and they instantly lace their fingers together. Kai slowly sits beside me, his injured shoulder on the other side, Oscar shuffles along to make space for him. Leaning my head against him, I look into his eyes.

"Hey Sakura," he says with a tired smile, and I relax into him, happy he's okay.

Now to get off this plane and figure out what the fuck happened back there.

OUR BLOODLINE

TWENTY TWO

Kai

The pain in my shoulder is irritating more than anything. The doctor said the bullet went straight through, so I'll have an exit wound to deal with too. It beats the bullet being lodged in my shoulder and needing surgery though.

Sitting in the back of another SUV, my body wants me to sleep, but I refuse to while we're in transit. Luna sits to my left, her fingers laced through mine, and the guys sit facing us. She's just as tired as I am, her eyes struggling to stay open. So, I hope when we get to our destination, we can get some rest.

Rafe is driving with Bryce beside him as we make our

way down a coastal road. The water's edge and the beach up above to our right, and small town buildings to our left. We have no idea where we are, putting all of our trust into Bryce.

"Where are we again?" Oscar asks, arms braced on his thighs as he looks out of the window.

"I'm surprised Roman or Luna haven't recognized it yet," Bryce murmurs in response, turning to smile at Luna. I can see her brain trying to work overtime to piece together where we are until Roman interrupts her thought process.

"Holy shit, princess," Roman whispers, looking to her with wide eyes. "We're going to the beach house."

"Beach house?" she asks, her nose wrinkling as she tries to catch up. Roman searches her face, trying to think of something that might jog her memory.

"The peacock, princess. This is where the peacock came from." Her hand squeezes mine in response, eyes brightening with his words. "We must be less than five minutes away now."

"Thank you," she whispers to him, and he smiles softly back at her. Glancing around at the rest of us, she must notice that we don't know what they're talking about. It's the first time they've really discussed something from their childhood. "Roman gave me a peacock brooch a few weeks ago, one that I used to steal for him. When he placed it in my palm, it jogged a memory of the place we're going to."

She smiles as she talks, but I can see the nerves in her eyes, and her grip on my hand hasn't loosened. Feeling the SUV begin to slow, I look out of the window to my right, watching as a gated community comes into view.

"Well, when the FBI Special Agent Dominic Bridge, mentioned you'd been sent to him for an assignment, it was agreed we had to move quickly." He sighs heavily, emotion in his voice. "And this was where we were always at our happiest," Bryce murmurs. I watch as Luna swallows heavily at his words, unable to respond.

Someone up front must press something because the black iron gates open before us. Driving down the gravel driveway, lined with trees, a house comes into view. It's dark outside, but the house is fully lit up. Roman doesn't hang around, sliding open the door and jumping out to stretch his legs. Parker and Oscar follow behind him, and I wait for Luna to step out before I do.

The smell of the ocean, and the sound of the waves crashing in the distance has me shutting my eyes for the briefest moments. A little more of the tension in my body floats away with the sea breeze, and I finally feel as though I can relax.

"Luna, I need you to stay with Kai. He's going to need you, Meu Tesouro," I hear Bryce say, and I open my eyes to glance at him. Why would he tell her that?

Luna steps toward me instinctively at his words, but I can see the question in her eyes too.

"There is a lot to discuss, remember?" Bryce responds, squeezing Luna's shoulder in support, before looking at me. "I didn't want to say anything on the way over, it wasn't the right thing to do, because we couldn't get here any faster, but…"

He doesn't finish his sentence as a door slams open from the house behind him.

"Kai? Oh my god! Where is he, Bryce? You promised!"

My heart thunders in my chest as her high-pitched voice washes over me. This can't be real, it just can't. The soft smile on Bryce's face doesn't help as I push him aside, my movements frantic, and the pain in my shoulder long forgotten.

Everybody is frozen in place as I finally see the entryway and the owner of that voice, without anyone blocking my view. My feet move on their own accord, my brain trying to play catch up with what I'm seeing. In a floaty blue beach dress and bare feet, she moves toward me. Her dark eyes search mine frantically, as she throws herself into my arms.

I wince at the pain to my shoulder, but it doesn't matter, none of it matters because she's here.

Mia.

Wrapping my arms around her, she sobs on my shoulder, holding me back just as tight. Fuck, I would take a hundred bullets if it meant being here right now. How is this even happening? My brain feels like it's short-circuiting as I try to grasp at the fact my sister is in my arms. My sister, the one I have spent years searching for, is here with me.

Keeping her in my arms, I turn back to the others. I don't know what I need from them, but I need something. I can't control my breathing. I'm in too much shock. I think I'm hyperventilating. Everyone except Bryce is staring at us with bright eyes and slack jaws, just as shocked as I am. Luna has tears in hers, and I want to console her, but I don't know how to move from this spot.

I can barely hear anything over the beating of my own heart until Mia pulls back a little, her smile wide.

"Hey, baby brother." My tongue refuses to work as I

continue to stare at her in disbelief. Patting my chest, she makes me relax my hold on her as she drops to her feet before me. "It's okay, Kai. We have so much to catch up on, but I'm perfectly okay."

Her eyes fall to the blood seeping through my fresh t-shirt from the plane, and panic sets in. "It's okay," I whisper quickly. "Nothing that won't heal."

She glares at me, a crappy job at that, but I see the worry in her face. "You should have told me before I jumped at you, shit-for-brains."

I hear Oscar laugh behind her, and I'm sure he's adding that to his own list of creative insults. "Don't you start with the swearing, I don't use those words because you never liked them," I grunt, and she laughs at me.

"Kai, that was when we were small children. I'm a grown-ass adult. If I want to swear, I motherfucking will, okay?" She smiles up at me, and it breaks my heart that we lost out on the transition from small children to adults together. Now she's an adult, but I still recognize the little girl who left.

Squeezing my arm, she looks around to the group who are all watching us.

"Oh my god," Luna murmurs, wiping tears from her

face. "Mia? Shit. Mia!"

They throw their arms around each other, holding on for dear life, and I'm confused with what is going on.

"Wait, what's this?" I call out, waving my finger between them, and the pair of them smile through their tears.

"She's as confused as you," Mia says with a grin, keeping hold of Luna. "When Daddy sent me away, I spent the first year living with a couple named Moira and Francis, who have a son, Jake. Jake had a friend at school named Luna, and she became my forever family too. Until people began searching for me, and it wasn't safe anymore. Then, Maria Steele brought me to Bryce, and I've been keeping his ass safe ever since."

I shake my head at everything she just threw at me. We're going to need to go a lot slower with all this information.

"How about we take this inside?" Bryce asks, and I stare at him with new eyes. My sister stands before me happy, care-free, and alive. It seems I have this man and Maria Steele to thank for that, although there are definitely more details needed.

"Thank you," I say honestly, with every ounce of

gratitude I have. Smiling at me, he approaches, minding my injured shoulder as he pats me on the back.

"There is nothing to thank me for. I'm only sorry we've all had to suffer apart," he murmurs, steering me toward the house, and I go willingly. The sound of stones crunching behind us, tells me the others are following, but I'm too lost in everything that's just happened.

Looking over at my sister, I still can't believe my eyes, but she's right. This is it, this is our forever family.

Luna

Mia.

Mia is here. When Rafe and I ran, and he finally set me up in school, I made friends with Jake. One day he showed up with a girl who befriended me too. What does Jake know about this world? How far did Rafe and I actually run, if she was placed so close to us anyway?

There are always more questions, no matter how hard we fight for answers.

Twenty-four hours ago, I was relaxed on the sofa with

my Aceholes, and now we're in the same room as my father and Kai's sister. Two people we never thought we'd see again. I have so many fucking questions, but I don't know where to begin.

"Princess, I can see your brain working overtime. Let's go inside and get cleaned up. I think we'll need to plan and organize our questions into categories before we go in demanding answers," Roman murmurs, throwing his arm around my shoulder as we step into the house behind Kai and my father.

Stepping through the large glass doors, I gape in surprise at the wide-open entry, opening straight into the lounge. An arched partition leads into the open lounge, with stairs leading upstairs at both ends. Glancing up, the glass panel balcony leads off in different directions. I can see the sea from here, through the floor-length patio doors on the other side of the lounge, while the kitchen is off to the left.

My feet instinctively step away from Roman, moving to the doors leading out back. The grassy garden comes into view, leading down to the beach below and a small dock reaching out to sea. A strong sense of home, and belonging, washes over me as I take it all in.

"Where are we again?" I ask, lost in my surroundings.

"New Haven, Meu Tesouro. New Haven, Connecticut." How the hell do I feel at home here? I shake my head in disbelief, as I look at my father's waiting gaze. "Would you like anything to eat or drink before I show you to your room?"

"I'll take a water, if you have one, please," I answer, struggling for words as I process the mundane conversation I'm having with Bryce. He smiles as he goes to step away, but my hand reaches out on its own accord, checking to make sure he's real.

My emotions are getting the better of me again, as my eyes well with more tears. How have they not dried out yet? I've never cried this much, ever.

"It's okay, Meu Tesouro. So much has happened and is *still* happening right now. I don't expect this to feel normal for some time, but please know that I am here for you, no matter what."

"You better be," Rafe grunts, stepping up beside me, his arms reaching around us both. My heart is in my throat as they both squeeze me tight. I can't return the hug, my arms trapped between us, the love pouring from them, warming my bones.

"Never again, Meu Amor," he whispers to Rafe, who squeezes us tighter. Stepping back, Bryce's love shines brightly in his eyes. "Raphael, grab our Meu Tesouro a water while I show them to their room." Rafe nods in response, a grin on his face as he looks over at my guys, a sparkle of mischief in his eyes.

I try to offer my thanks, but my brain has stuck on a thought. If I call Rafe Dad, how the hell do I address Bryce? So much has changed, there is so much to process, and all I can think about is how to address the man I assumed was dead for the past twelve years. Shaking my head, I follow his lead, focusing on the here and now.

"Watch that blonde one though, B, he's the troublemaker. Jess, Luna's best friend, warned me about him." He winks at me before hurrying off to the kitchen, leaving Oscar gaping at us. I can't help but chuckle at the banter Rafe has with my guys, and I hope Bryce will have that kind of relationship with them one day too.

"I've got my eye on him already, don't you worry!" Bryce shouts after him.

Walking back toward them, Kai and Mia are murmuring quietly to each other, shock still on their faces as they come to terms with being reunited.

"Defend my honor, baby girl," Oscar says as we approach, his arms out wide, making me roll my eyes.

"Big mouth, you already called my father a dickhead. Your big mouth dug that hole all on its own. There is no way I'm helping you get out of that." Turning his gaze to Roman and Parker, looking for their help, he comes up short as neither of them make eye contact with him. It's clear they reacted that way on purpose, just to rile him up.

"This way," Bryce says, walking through the doors at the opposite side of the lounge to the kitchen. The corridor has a few doors leading off, but he stops at the end one. "We got here five days ago, and I had Mia help with your room. Although the bed frame is the same one that's always been here, I just got a new mattress. Maybe I should have taken the hint when you begged for it at four years old," he says with a smile, my eyebrows wrinkling in confusion at his words.

Pushing open the door, he steps inside, nodding for us to follow. The room is massive, light grey, and pale dusty pink furnishings give off a relaxed vibe in here. With white furniture filling the room, it's the bed that holds my attention. It's just as big as the one back at Beechwood Hall, if not bigger.

Understanding dawns on me at his words, and I smile, pleased with myself.

"Clearly, I always knew what I wanted," I say, shrugging my shoulders, and everyone chuckles.

"Well, I'm sure I'll get a chance to know everyone soon enough, but for now, please try and relax, get clean and comfortable. I'm going to need to check in with your grandmother and Dominic, so we can see what else is going on."

Planting a kiss on my forehead, he leaves the room. Mia offers a shy wave before following him. I sigh in relief, enjoying a moment to just be myself with no expectation, or new knowledge being thrown at me.

"Come on, angel. Let's take care of you and Kai. After, we can have a chat amongst ourselves, then tackle the bigger shit out there," Parker whispers, gently kissing my temple, and I lean into his touch.

One day we'll get to relax without caring for somcone's injuries.

TWENTY THREE

Oscar

Stepping out of the shower, I grab a towel from the towel bar, quickly running it through my hair before I wrap it around my waist. I'm the last to get cleaned up, which means there are some heavy conversations ready to be had.

My mind still can't process what has happened today. Even though nothing life-changing has actually happened to me, Luna and Kai are my family, and whatever affects them, affects me too. Walking out of the en-suite and into the bedroom, it confuses my brain that the sun is still out, and it's only mid-afternoon. I feel as though I've lived a thousand lifetimes today already.

Luna is lying on her side in the center of the bed, with Kai lying on his back in front of her. Parker snuggles in behind her with his eyes closed, while Roman is out on the patio talking on the phone to his father.

Luna helped Kai shower, making sure to keep his wound dry, and a fresh round of bandages have been applied. I watch as her fingers delicately trace patterns along his chest, relaxing both of them. She's wearing a band tee with a pair of shorts, and I notice the guys are all in fresh sweatpants with no t-shirts on, but I'd like to know where the fresh clothing came from.

Parker opens his eyes as if sensing my confusion, and points to the open suitcase by the door. "Maria already sent it to Bryce when she organized our room back at Beechwood," Parker murmurs, answering my unasked question. That woman is very helpful, always thinking of the little things in our time of need, always one step ahead.

I feel like we need to start labeling our clothes, otherwise we're just going to be sharing everything between us at this rate. I smile at that thought, who would have known the Ace's would be reduced to sharing clothes and our woman? I don't know, but I fucking love it.

"What's got you grinning like a Cheshire cat?" Luna asks, pulling my attention to her, and I smile wider.

"I'm just thinking about how us Aceholes like to share," I answer, holding up my sweatpants and winking at her. She rolls her eyes at me, instantly knowing I'm talking about her as well. Stepping into them, I watch as her pupils dilate, watching me put them on with nothing else underneath.

Glancing back down at Kai, she places a kiss to the corner of his lips, "Do you want Mia to be here, or would you rather go and have a chat with her while the rest of us talk?"

His hand lifts, cupping hers on his chest as he looks up at her. "We can talk first. I need a minute to wrap my head around a few things, but thank you for considering her, Sakura," he whispers, a gentle smile playing on his lips.

With Roman still outside talking on the phone, I climb on the bed behind Parker, draping myself over him as I squeeze tight. My arm wraps around his chest as I throw my leg over his.

"Fuck, Oscar, I can't breathe," he grumbles, but his ass wiggles back, snuggling against me at the same time.

"You love it, so shush your mush," I murmur, and

he doesn't argue, but I loosen my hold on him slightly. "You're such a little snuggle slut," I whisper, burying my face in his neck and closing my eyes.

I feel Luna's hand squeeze my leg, as Parker chuckles at my words. "Just shut up and hold me, asshole." I fucking love this. Luna holds us together, enhancing the bond we already had, taking us all to the next level.

I'm caught by surprise when the bed bounces behind me, as Roman joins us. "Stop hogging all the love, Oscar," he moans, laying behind me with his arm reaching all the way across to hold Luna's hip. "And stop trying to start a dick chain, Parker," he mumbles, as Parker pushes into me more, forcing me to press up against Rome. Fuck, if that doesn't make my dick twitch, but now is not the time.

Parker glances over his shoulder, pouting at him, which only makes Roman lean over and kiss his lips. Fuck. "You guys are killing me. Stop," I whine, and Roman grins down at me. Without warning, his mouth comes down on mine too. I barely get to respond before he's pulling away, winking at me before he stands.

"Okay, let's get some distance, otherwise we'll never get this talk over with," Roman says, slightly adjusting himself through his sweatpants.

"Party pooper," I grumble, wetting my dry lips and adjusting myself too. I see Luna and Kai shake their heads at us as Parker sticks his tongue out at me.

Following bossy Roman's orders, I sit up on the bed, the others following suit as we get comfortable. "Where do we even begin?" Luna asks, and no one has an answer.

"How about we just discuss things that only involve us? Otherwise, we're going to have the same conversation twice, and they may have more information out there," Kai says, pointing to the door.

I nod in agreement. We don't need to put ourselves through this more times than we need to, but we all need to be on the same page with the information we have.

"I feel like I need to explain how I know Mia," Luna says quietly, her eyes tracking Kai's, who smiles appreciatively in response. "When Rafe and I ran and finally settled down, Rafe enrolled me in school, which is where I met Jake."

"Was he the guy with Rafe that time on the phone?" Roman asks, and she nods.

"Yeah, he's always had a soft spot for me, it just got more uncomfortable as we got older, when he developed feelings, and well, I didn't. I've kept my distance since I was dragged to Featherstone, wanting to keep him safe. Although, it seems there must be some kind of connection now if Mia stayed with him."

She runs her fingers through her hair, trying to piece it together in her mind, but Bryce may have more details on that for us. I reach out, squeezing her fingers in support, and she smiles.

"One day, when I must have been eight, maybe? Jake came to school with a little girl by his side. He's older by a few years, so we were never in the same classes, but he introduced Mia to me straight away." Her eyes close as if replaying the memory in her mind. "She was sad, like me, and I think that's what drew us together," she murmurs, looking up at Kai, who looks just as devastated as she does.

Lacing his fingers with hers, he encourages her to proceed.

"She cried all the time for her brother, while I locked my emotions away, yet we bonded. It must have been twelve months, I think. When one day, Jake didn't come to school with her anymore, and that was the end of that. No reason or explanation, just gone, but I always remembered her words, 'forever family,' and that's what my tattoo says."

She turns, showing us her back as she lifts her t-shirt up, revealing the five small symbols that trail down her spine. It reminds me of the day we were at the beach, and she pointed to each of her tattoos. I remember her saying it was a saying an old friend used to say, and it makes me smile.

Kai's fingers instantly stroke over the ink, emotion thick in his eyes as he processes the fact that his sister and Luna met in their darkest times. Offering each other comfort when it was needed most, I feel like my heart could burst.

Just then, a knock sounds at the door, "Hey, we're up to date with as much information as we can be right now. Do you want to come out so we can go through it all together?" Rafe calls out from the other side of the door.

"Yeah, we're coming," Luna shouts back.

"I fucking wish we were," I mumble, making Luna and the guys laugh as we head out together.

Let's see what Featherstone fucked up today, and how we move forward.

Luna

Following the smell of burning charcoal, I find Rafe, Bryce, and Mia outside relaxing on the outdoor furniture, with the grill burning away in the corner. Everyone wrapped up tight in big thick coats, courtesy of Maria Steele, as always. Bryce is hovering over it, trying to control the flame. Rafe takes a drink of water, with Mia sitting uncomfortably on the sofa. As much as we know each other, that was a long time ago, and we likely look a little overwhelming walking out all together.

Slipping my hand from Roman's, I take a seat beside Mia. Not only is she my old friend, she is Kai's sister, and I want to make sure she feels comfortable around us. Kai smiles appreciatively at me as he sits on her other side, and I feel the slight tension evaporate quickly.

"Luna Steele, is my brother one of your boyfriends?" Mia asks, with a wiggle of her eyebrows, and I chuckle.

"Husbands," Oscar says, sitting beside me, with Parker and Roman on the other side of him. We fill the large cushioned seating area, leaving the chairs empty for Rafe and Bryce to use.

"Husbands? As in plural?" she splutters, and we all

grin at her reaction.

"Husbands!" Bryce shouts, his eyes comically wide as he looks between Rafe and I. Rolling my eyes, I look back at Mia.

"You know how picky she is, B. I couldn't even argue, especially when these wannabe bad boys go all soft for her. It's hilarious, you'll see," Rafe says, patting my dad on the back, before taking a seat in the chair facing me. "We may as well get the big chat over with so we can try and enjoy a normal evening, okay?"

"That sounds like the best idea I've heard all day," Parker answers, relaxing back into the cushions.

"Okay, where would you like to begin?" Bryce asks, pulling a chair closer to Rafe before taking a seat.

I try to think over everything that's actually happened today, but I know deep down what needs to be addressed first. One glance at Kai, and I'm certain it's the right direction to take.

"With you and Mia." My voice is calm, but I can feel my nerves kick in as I watch, waiting for his response. I see Mia squeeze Kai's hand while I clasp mine in front of me.

"Don't shut yourself off, baby girl, it's not allowed,"

Oscar murmurs against my ear, moving my hair from my face. "Your body is rigid with tension, Luna. Relax."

Taking a deep breath, I turn to look in his ocean blue eyes. His fingers pry mine apart as he holds my hand, comforting me without words. Looking me over one more time, he nods, happy with my change in demeanor.

Leaning back, I turn my stare back to Bryce, who is staring at Oscar in surprise. When he finally looks back at me, he smiles softly.

"Well, Rafe said you read the letter, so I won't recap that bit, it's hard enough," he swallows, rubbing his hands down his jeans. "But, when I was healed, Dominic Bridge explained to me all the information he had on Totem and the movement. What their plans were, and how it impacted our family. Ultimately, the longer Totem, Veronica, and everyone else he got to follow him believed we were dead, the better our chances of survival and retribution would be."

He looks to Rafe with unshed tears in his eyes, who reaches between them, stroking his arm in comfort, offering him the strength to continue. I can't even imagine how either of them must feel right now. They have a lot to discuss without us here, but their priority, as always, is me.

"So, I stayed dead. My mother found me, all too easily really, but when she understood the bigger picture and the impact it could have on the both of you, she agreed to my plan."

The shock is clear on Rafe's face, knowing Maria knew all along must hurt him more than it does me, she's only just come back into my life.

"From there, I lived off the snippets of information Maria could give me. The smallest of insights into how you guys were." Swiping at his face, nobody even breathes, letting him continue at his own pace. "Then, one day, she reached out needing my help." He glances to Mia, before continuing. "She needed me to protect a girl, who was at risk of being used the way they planned to use you, Meu Tesouro. He always wanted another heir to The Ring to stand beside him for the movement. Specifically wanting you, and when he couldn't have you, he went after Mia, but never any of the male heirs."

His words catch me by surprise, my other hand instinctively reaching out for Mia, whose hand falls on mine. I look at her, and she simply nods. Clearly already knowing this.

"My father knew it was coming and pulled me from

our family home on Kai's birthday before they could hunt me down. That's when I came to live with Jake. I didn't really understand, but you were there, and everything wasn't as hard. You were two years younger than me, but your eyes were haunted all the same," she murmurs, and I feel all of our old pain floating to the surface. "Then the movement somehow got wind of where I might be, and what that meant for the both of us. So, my father trusted Maria to help, and I've been with Bryce ever since."

Kai's arm wraps around her shoulders as he slowly processes that his father really was protecting his daughter, refusing to explain anything to anyone in case someone got wind of it.

I'm sure there is a lot more detail we could go into, but right now, the main points will do.

"Princess, whatever is on your mind, talk about it, don't bottle anything up," Roman murmurs, holding my eyes captive.

Clearing my throat, I nervously glance to Rafe, who nods, encouraging me to speak my mind. It's crazy how I can feel like a badass bitch, but the second I have to talk about my hurt feelings, I want to run and hide.

"I, uh, this is in no way against you Mia, so please

remember that, but." I look to Bryce, letting my mask drop, and the pain in my eyes seep through. "You had enough strength to protect Mia, and I'll forever be grateful for that, even more so now Kai is in my life. But I can't figure out for the life of me why you couldn't have come for us. The only thing stopping us from all being together, was you."

I watch as he stutters and stumbles over his words, looking to Rafe for guidance, but none comes. "I thought I was doing what was best," he whispers, tears welling in his eyes as I continue to stare at him.

"I can understand that, but I don't agree with your actions. Am I happy you are sitting in front of me right now? More than you will ever know, but I'm not happy with the reasoning behind all of this. It's going to take me some time to process my emotions fully."

He nods solemnly, as Parker smiles proudly at me for sharing my feelings.

"Whenever you want to dig more into this, darling, I'll be by your side. We spoke a little," Rafe says, pointing between Bryce and himself, "But, your emotions are completely valid, and I support you." He's trying to soothe us all, and I smile admiringly at him, my rock, always.

I nod in thanks and turn my gaze back to Bryce. "So

where does the Special Agent fit into all of this? Why were they looking into Totem, but also willing to hide someone else from Featherstone?"

"There are informants that work for the FBI, allowing Featherstone to continue to operate under their radar. The FBI arrested someone who offered Totem to them on a platter in exchange for a lesser sentence. Even the informants knew he was flying off the rails and jumped at the chance to lock him down." He moves to brace his arms on his thighs as he unloads all of this information. "Dominic, is one of the few who refuses to waiver from his role, and for that, he was chosen to lead up the investigation, since he was against everything Featherstone stood for."

"So he wasn't in a position to be swayed by Totem?" I ask, and he smiles with a nod.

"Exactly, only the more he dug, the more he was led back to us, through Veronica, which is why a highly trained team literally set up watch the day everything went to hell. So, he was only ever allowed to take down Totem, and he actually became a friend, much to his dislike." His eyes glisten with emotion. "He was the one to help plant the bag in the vaults for you. I need you to know, Meu Tesouro."

"We're all here now, B," Rafe soothes, squeezing his

shoulder tightly.

Clearly sensing a shift in conversation is needed, Kai speaks up. "What's the update from The Slums?" he asks, moving the conversation along, and I can't get my words out quick enough as I remember.

"Wren is the heir!" I shout uncontrollably, looking to the guys to my left, surprise on their faces.

"That's why she shot me," Kai adds. "Totem was pushing her to prove herself, but she's a shit shot."

My heart aches as the memory of him lying on the floor, blood pouring from his wound as they towered over him, replays in my mind.

"It's okay, princess. He's alright," Roman says, pulling me from my thoughts, as he leans over Oscar to rub my knee. I shouldn't love how much their touch affects me, but I love the feeling of calm they give me.

"Do we know if she made it out? If anyone else actually made it out?" I ask, looking to Rafe and Bryce, who glance at each other before answering.

"The Slums is a complete wreck, but a thorough search was done of the premises, and her body hasn't been found." Mumbled cursing fills the air around us since we're all frustrated she got away.

"And Totem definitely got away," I murmur, internally yelling at myself for missing my shot. "What about the other students?"

"Well, we saw what happened to Neil Portman," Roman says, a shudder running through me at the memory. "My father also mentioned that Eliza Walker, his partner, was also found nailed to the wall."

Oh my god, I think I might be sick. "Anyone else?" I ask as Oscar wraps me in his arms.

"Freddie's dead, at my hands" Kai mutters, looking down at his hand in Mia's, and I remember them fighting in the hallway.

"Whatever it takes to survive, remember?" I say, smiling at my handsome, and his lips tip up in response.

"I spoke with my father, and he said they managed to get Conor and Taylor out. Taylor's in surgery, I asked for him to keep us updated." I love that he has updates on things he knows will be important to me. For some reason, that girl took a bullet for me. I know it's my responsibility to make sure she's okay.

"And the rest of the members of The Ring?"

"All safe. Everyone's focus right now will be Totem. Killing Rico was a crazy move, but I couldn't sit there and do nothing," Rafe explains, glancing at Parker before looking deep into my eyes, and I can't argue with his actions. "Dietrichson will be hiding for sure, especially now we know his granddaughter is Totem's heir."

"We'll do whatever it takes to be together," Bryce says, determination in every word. "They've taken enough from us. I refuse to let them take anymore. So we plan and take them all down. Once Totem falls, the rest will crumble."

I nod in agreement, already feeling my blood boil with anger.

"We need a minute to catch our breath, relax, and heal. Then we can go at them at full force," Parker says, and as much as I want to go after them now, I know he is right.

"Agreed. Now, feed me, B. I'm starving," Rafe says, ending the heaviness of the conversation.

Leaning further into Oscar, I let the stress of today drift away, enjoying the company of my loved ones, old and new, the calm before the storm.

TWENTY FOUR

Luna

I love waking up and being able to sit outside, wrapped in a thick blanket to keep the chill at bay. With a coffee in my hands and the sound of the waves crashing nearby, it's my new favorite thing to do. For the first time, I woke up before the guys, sneaking out of our giant bed while they slept.

With everything going on at the moment, I couldn't stop my mind from falling down the rabbit hole but being out here definitely helps calm me. Hugging the blanket tighter, I take a sip of my hot coffee, my eyes closing as I enjoy the moment.

It's a little after nine in the morning, and there are people on the beach walking their dogs and enjoying the autumn sunshine. I wish I could enjoy that level of normalcy right now. I miss just being Luna Steele, high school bitch and a tattoo apprentice. I know I'll never get that normal routine back, but I'd love to be able to spend time like that with my Aceholes, Red, Mia, and my fathers.

Laughter from behind me catches my attention, and I twist my head to see Rafe and Bryce in the living room together through the floor-length glass doors.

They haven't noticed me, too wrapped up in each other, and it warms my heart. It's going to take a long time to find a new normal for them, but it's clear to see that they will do whatever it takes, without question. I can't remember a time I saw Rafe with anyone, not a soul, and it seems that's because his heart always belonged to Bryce.

Rafe stands a little taller than Bryce, but it fits them perfectly, as my dad kisses my other dad on the forehead, both of their eyes closing at the contact. I know it's an intimate moment for them as they hold each other close, but it feels like déjà vu to be watching them like this. My mind surprises me with a heartwarming memory.

The teenage mutant ninja turtles show plays on the

television as I snuggle down on the sofa with my favorite orange blanket. The leather sofa beneath me tells me we're at our family home, before everything went to hell. My head is propped up on Papa's thigh, and his giant hand rubs my shoulder comfortingly, our sole focus on the television.

"Michaelangelo is the bestest ninja!" I shout, watching as they save the day once again.

"No way, darling, Raphael is the king of the turtles for sure," Papa says, and I giggle as he tickles my side.

The sound of the front door shutting in the distance makes us freeze, but only for a moment before we're fighting to get up as quickly as possible. Jumping to my feet, Papa lifts me in the air as soon as my feet touch the floor.

"Noooo, Papa, no fair!" I cry out, wiggling my arms and legs to fight against his hold, but he only laughs as he holds me high in the air.

"But I can't win if I let you down, Luna," he protests, looking up at me with wide eyes.

"Please, Papa," I whisper, giving him my best attempt at puppy dog eyes, and the love written all over his face warms my soul.

"Just this one time," Papa whispers back, placing me

on the floor. Turning straight for the front door, I stop in my tracks as Daddy comes into view.

"Mine!" I yell, my little legs racing toward him, arms out wide as he crouches down to catch me. As soon as I'm in his hold, my arms cling to him tightly.

"Hey, Meu Tesouro," Daddy whispers in my ear, and my eyes close, soaking in his love. "Hello, Meu Amor," he adds, speaking to Papa, who wraps his arms around the both of us.

"I'm glad you're home, B. We missed you, didn't we, darling?"

I nod frantically, releasing my tight hold on Daddy, to wrap an arm around Papa's neck too. Holding me between them, Papa leans in and kisses Daddy on the lips, and I can't stop the sicky noise that leaves my mouth.

"Ewwwww," I groan, my nose wrinkling as my face scrunches up. They pull apart and chuckle at me softly, Papa rolling his eyes at me.

"I think Luna wants kisses. What do you think, Papa?" Daddy asks, and Papa nods in agreement. Before I can protest, they lick their lips and plant sloppy kisses on my cheeks at the same time, and as much as it grosses me out, I love the attention and the moment all the same.

Frozen in place, I blink away the memory. As if sensing my presence, they look outside, smiling when they see me. Rafe pats Bryce on the back before heading into the kitchen, and Bryce makes his way outside, a thick hoodie on as he shivers with the cold air. I watch his every movement, unable to pull my eyes away. The six-year-old in me is scared I'll blink and he'll disappear again. I don't miss how he nervously pulls at the neck of his hoodie as he takes a seat beside me, and I place my coffee mug on the table. He looks tired and worn out today, like my words from yesterday hit hard. Rafe likely had a lot to say in private too, but he must have known it wouldn't all be sunshine and roses.

We sit in silence for a moment, both looking out to sea, happy to just be near one another.

"You know, when you were little, we always caught you peeking. With wonder in your eyes, you would always ask, 'is that true love, Daddy?' and I would always say, 'Meu Tesouro, true love is what I feel for you and for Papa, and one day, you'll feel it for someone else too.'" His eyes meet mine, a soft smile on his lips. "And every time you would ask how you would know, I promised you that you would feel it in your bones, in your heart and your soul."

His hand finds mine, squeezing in comfort as his words hold me captive, memories floating to the surface. "Is that what you feel for those men in there?"

I nod subconsciously, my mind already knowing the answer to that without having to even consider it. "I do. They complete me in ways I never knew were possible. They push me and challenge me, even fucking annoy me. But most of all, they accept me for who I am, never trying to change me." I smile at my own words, feeling the truth behind them.

"That's all I want for you, Meu Tesouro. I want you to feel all the love you deserve, and I'm going to spend forever annoying the hell out of you too, to make up for all the time we've missed out on." He takes a deep breath, sadness in his eyes and a frown on his face. "I'm sorry, Luna. For protecting you by staying away. I hope one day you can forgive me for all of the damage I've caused."

I squeeze his hand back, my eyes welling with emotion too. "I forgive you. I forgave you the moment you caught my fall in The Slums. I thought I was dying, but it was okay because I saw your face." My words are barely a whisper as he pulls me closer, wrapping his arms around me and holding me tight. "You just have to be patient with me. Papa is my Dad, my everything. He filled the hole that was left behind, and it's going to take some time for me to adjust. I don't even know how to address you. It's been tumbling around in my head, and calling you Dad too would just get confusing, and he damn well deserves that title."

I feel him nod against me as I squeeze him back when someone hugs us from the side. "I completely understand, Meu Tesouro. Everything will make sense between us one day. I don't care what you call me, as long as I get to hear your voice, that's all I care about. I love you guys so much," Bryce murmurs, and my heart feels full.

"I love you too, and my darling most," Rafe says, and I remember those words from being a child, sparking my own response.

"I love you three, for infinity and more."

"God, I've missed hearing that," Bryce says, leaning back to glance between us, and we all smile. We have a long way to go as a family, but we're definitely on our way.

Rafe takes a seat on the other side of Bryce, wrapping a blanket around them both. I'm glad they're giving me room to breathe and wrap my head around it all. Sitting in silence, we watch the waves and the birds flying in the distance. One of the dogs on the beach holds my attention as it plays fetch with its owner.

"Steele Security," Bryce murmurs, and I glance at him. "They're all part of the security team I used to run. Maria helped with that while I was gone." I glance back to the beach, surprised that there are at least twenty people down there, and he's saying they're all on payroll.

"Remember when I said he was the security man? I wasn't kidding, darling," Rafe says, and I shake my head.

"What else have you put in place?" I ask, intrigued by the extent he has gone to keep us safe.

Clearing his throat, he recalls every security measure put in place. "There are twenty-four people on the beach, twelve watching the front of the house, with six of those twelve in the trees, all personnel rotating. Then there are motion detectors set up around the property, all of which I've synced with everyone's facial recognition too. That just leaves the shutdown function on the home if anyone tries to get in, the whole place turns into a safe room."

My eyes widen as I glance between him and Rafe, who rolls his eyes. Is that where I get that from?

"Well, that's definitely plenty," I say, and Bryce shakes his head at us.

"I'll get more if I have to. Don't underestimate the lengths I will go to, it'll make me question if it's enough," he says with a tight smile, as Rafe pats him on the back.

"Calm down, B. You are all over it. You need to talk to Kai too, his tech skills are good."

As if hearing his name, Kai steps out onto the patio, a calmness in him that's never been there before. The likely factor being that his sister is alive and sleeping under the same roof as him.

"Good morning, Sakura," he murmurs, kissing my head as he takes the seat beside me. Wearing only a pair of grey sweatpants and a long-sleeved fitted white top, he shivers. Damn, he looks too fucking good this morning. Lifting up one end of the blanket, he's quick to snuggle in tight with me, warming up.

"How is your shoulder?" I ask, and he grimaces.

"I'll be fine, it's just going to need time to heal." I smile sadly at him, wishing I could take the pain away. "But I don't think *you* will be fine if you don't speak to Jess soon. Mia had a charger that fit your phone, and it's been going off all morning."

Oh shit.

I scramble out of my seat and rush inside, hearing

them laugh behind me. Running into the bedroom, I smack straight into a hard chest, arms instantly catching my fall before I hit the ground. Blinking open my eyes, Roman grins down at me.

"What's got you in a rush, princess?"

"Kai said Red had been calling non-stop," I say, trying to catch my breath, but he doesn't release me.

"You aren't speaking to Jess. Not until you've said good morning to me properly."

In one swift move, he pushes me up against the wall beside the door, pinning me against it as his lips come down on mine. Moaning into his mouth, my arms wrap around his neck, bringing him closer. His grip on my hips tightens as I tangle my fingers in his hair at the back of his neck.

"Fuck, if you two could just get naked, that would be the best porn ever to wake up to, thanks," Parker says, his voice gravelly with sleep, and it only makes me hotter.

Biting down on my bottom lip, Roman pulls away, leaving me gasping for more.

"Good morning, princess," he murmurs with a wink, and heads out of the door.

What the fuck just happened? I slump back into the

wall behind me, needing the assistance to keep myself upright.

Looking at Parker sprawled out on the bed, he grins at me as he adjusts his thick length in his boxer briefs, and I groan.

"Screw you, Aceholes, and your fucking hotness."

Flipping him off, I find my phone charging on the dresser near the doors leading outside. Disconnecting it from the cord, I step outside, already hitting the call button on the fifty-plus missed calls and text messages.

"What the hell, Luna!" Red screams down the phone, and I cringe. "Do you know how damn worried I've been? You promised to call after each game, that was yesterday, Luna. Yesterday!"

"I'm sorry. It was beyond crazy, Red. I don't even know where to begin."

"Well, we can start with the fact that you're still alive. Is everyone else accounted for?" she asks, her voice calming down a little.

"Yeah, we're all here, but Kai was shot in the shoulder."

"What!"

"Red, will you calm down, you're not helping," I grind out. "I know you're worried, but a lot of shit happened, and

I need you to relax if you want me to tell you everything."

Silence greets me for a moment, until she finally sighs. "Okay, I can be calm." I take a deep breath.

"Thank you," I whisper, before preparing to tell her everything. "The Games went to shit, Red. Totem showed up, there was a huge explosion, and Wren shot Kai. She's the heir. She's been the fucking heir this whole time." My free hand balls into a fist at my side, growing annoyed with myself for not seeing it all before, even using her mother's surname. Even though deep down, I would never have known.

"That bitch," Red fumes, and I couldn't agree more.

"Yeah, so we aren't at Beechwood. Everyone has gone into hiding from the sounds of it, including us. At least until Kai can heal a little, and we come up with a plan."

"I'm just glad you got out of there, Luna."

Bracing my hands on the stone wall's edge around the patio, I take a deep breath as I find my next words. "Jess, my father, he's alive, and he's here."

"Oh my god, Luna," she cries, emotion in her voice as she takes in my words.

"Yeah, I just, it's all crazy. Rafe killed Rico too."

"Are you okay though, Luna? This is all a lot to take

in, and it didn't even happen to me," she asks, and I smile at her concern.

"I'm good, Red, honestly," looking out at the ocean, I let it calm me along with her voice. "Hey, Red? Do you want me to arrange for you to come out here?"

She goes quiet on the other end of the phone, until she finally answers, "I'll stay here. You focus on getting Kai back to full health, and spend some time with your dad," she says quietly. "Just expect daily phone calls, and I'll be right here, okay?"

"Okay, but if you change your mind, just say so, alright?"

"Of course, I'll let you go. I love you, captain."

"I love you too, Jess."

TWENTY FIVE

Roman

Sighing, I glance at my phone. It's a little after six in the evening, and Luna still isn't back yet. Apparently, her and Mia thought it was a good idea to have some girl time and get out of the house. Nobody listened when I said that it was a stupid idea, but what do I know?

I feel better knowing Bryce sent them with so much security, even the president would be jealous. I don't want to seem clingy, but they left hours ago, and coming down to the water's edge hasn't helped like I'd hoped.

We've been here for five days. Five whole days in our own little bubble, and not a single word from Totem or the

Dietrichsons. I still can't believe Rico's dead, he fucking deserved it though. I just wish I'd been more involved in taking his life.

Shaking my head, I change my focus, not wanting to lose myself to Featherstone's drama again. We need a plan though, and we need one soon because we're all done with constantly glancing over our shoulders. Running isn't our way, we just need a little more time for Kai to heal.

The tide is slowly coming in, the water touching the tips of my boots as I sit in the sand. Raking a hand through my hair, I get ready to stand when a cold hand covers my eyes, catching me off guard. Before I can react, I hear a voice.

"Guess who?"

I instantly relax, hearing Luna's voice and recognizing her delicate fingers on my face.

"Princess Luna of Lunaland, Queen of the trees, and…"

"Warrior of the seas," she finishes, catching me by surprise. "Oh my god, I made you say that all the time," she adds. Dropping her hand, I tilt my head back to peer up at her.

"You were very demanding," I agree, and she sticks her tongue out.

"Well, I'll take this back then." Lifting up her other hand, she wiggles a clear plastic cup at me, with 'Baby Acehole' scrolled across it in black ink.

"Is that a dragon juice from a coffee shop in town?" I ask, and she nods in agreement. "I take it back, I swear. You are in no way demanding, princess."

She giggles at me as she hands it over, and I'm quick to get rid of the lid and straw, downing half of the juice in one gulp.

"Thank you."

"You're welcome," she says with a smile. Every day her smile gets wider, and her eyes get greener. That's why I want to find Totem and put an end to his shit, so I can watch her happiness grow more.

"You found him," Oscar calls out, as Luna takes a seat a little further back from the water's edge, patting the sand beside her for me to move up. I plant myself beside her, as Parker and Kai trail behind Oscar down the steps.

As they get closer, I notice she brought us each a drink and had our nicknames written on the cups. 'Handsome Acehole' for Kai, 'Big Mouth Acehole' for Oscar, and 'Parker Parker Acehole' for Parker. She catches my grin and kisses my cheek.

"I have something else to show you guys too," she whispers, her eyes twinkling with nervousness I haven't seen there before, but she has me intrigued. Parker, Oscar, and Kai sit with us, automatically forming a circle.

"So, I uh, did a thing," Luna murmurs, rubbing her hands on her knees nervously. "And I was completely confident with my decision until I sat down, now I'm…"

"Angel, just tell us. You're doing that thing again where you talk in circles and make our anxiety kick in too," Parker says, a smile on his face. She takes a deep breath and slowly exhales, closing her eyes for a moment.

"Okay," she mutters to herself before suddenly whipping her t-shirt off. Her breasts are bare, her nipples pebbled with the cold chill in the air. What the hell is she doing? We're in public, likely with security guards watching right now.

"What the fuck, Luna, don't…" Kai's hand stops mine from grabbing her top and forcing it back over her head, and I growl at him as my blood pounds in my ears.

Shaking his head lightly at me, he points at her bare chest. Confused, I look to see what he's showing me, and my heart stops. A quick look to Oscar and Parker too, and their jaws are wide open also.

Four small paint blobs, in different pastel colors, mark down between her breasts, and on top of each color is a symbol. At the top sits a purple paint mark with the outline of Pac-man tattooed in the center. A green one follows, with a skull etched on top.

My pulse rings in my ears as I continue taking in what she's done. Two more paint splashes mark her skin, pastel blue and pink, with a moon tattooed in one, and a feather in the other.

Holy fucking shit. Our girl, our *wife,* has marked herself with a small replica of tattoos we each have on her skin.

Parker leans forward, kissing Luna's lips and murmuring to her, but I can't hear what he's saying. Oscar follows suit, and I see her smile up at him. Kai releases my arm, going to her, while I sit back on my knees, willing my brain to catch up.

As soon as Kai moves, my body does too, on its own accord, crushing my mouth to hers. I can't find the words for how this makes me feel, but my body does. She opens for me willingly, all the self-doubt, everything I feared is all for nothing. She marked me on her skin, she wants me to be here. This isn't her just honoring some old family agreement, she needs me like I need her.

Pulling back to rest my forehead to hers, I frantically search her eyes. I can barely breathe, and my mind feels like it's about to explode if I don't speak.

Taking a deep breath, my lips graze hers as I look deep into her eyes. "I love you, Luna Steele," I whisper.

Her hand comes up to cup my chin as she smiles brightly at me. "I love you too, Roman Steele-Rivera." My heart swells with love and need. I didn't know how much I needed to say those words, let alone hear them in return.

I need her. I need her right now, but not in the sand. Putting the top over her head, I cover her back up.

"Kai, Oscar, I need you to take one for the team and distract the parents." I hear Oscar moan and grumble in response, but they both stand as I move back from Luna.

Kissing her lips, Oscar helps her to her feet. "Well, I'm fucking walking her up if you're keeping her to yourself. But you better remember this when the time comes," he says, and I pat his back, giving him the luxury of walking with her.

Heading straight up the wooden steps, I cut across the grass and climb over onto the patio outside of our room. As I push open the door I left cracked, Parker calls out to me before I step inside.

"Why didn't you tell me to distract them too?"

I can't help the grin that takes over my face at his question. "I told you why, when I watched you fuck our girl with Oscar, remember?" He frowns for a moment before realization dawns on his face, his pupils dilating as he searches my eyes.

"Now, get the fuck in here and bring our hot wife with you."

Parker

Holy fuck, holy fuck. Holy. Fuck.

My palms are sweating, I'm itching to get in there, but Oscar is taking his sweet-ass time getting over here with Kai and Luna. I glance back to the patio door Roman left open, and my dick strains against my jeans. Squeezing myself through the denim, I try to ease the ache, but there's no use.

Oscar catches the movement, his eyes heating as he somehow manages to walk slower.

Fuck this.

Marching over, Luna looks at me in confusion as I pull her arm from Oscar's.

"Not fair, asshole, you leave me with the guy who doesn't care for experimenting," he grumbles, and I grin at the want in his voice.

"Oscar, we'll play again soon, I promise." I wink over my shoulder, before lifting Luna over the stone wall surrounding the patio and follow behind.

Pulling the door shut behind me, I lean against it for a moment, watching as Roman pulls his top over his head. Revealing his chiseled abs and full back skull tattoo, I can't decide which side of him I'd rather be staring at.

"Close the curtains, Parker."

Luna glances between us at his order, desire in her eyes as she takes us in. I blindly close the curtains behind me, not wanting to miss a second of the action. Roman places himself behind Luna, turning her to face me, as he runs his hands up her side. Slowly trailing his lips up her neck, he bites down on her earlobe when he reaches the top.

"I have a vision, princess, and I want to make it happen," he says against her ear, and she nods eagerly in agreement, without even knowing what it is. "I want Parker between us, princess. Me fucking him, while he's deep inside of you."

I watch as she shudders at his words, her eyes looking me over from head to toe. Leaning back against the curtain, I undo the button on my jeans, squeezing the head of my cock to stop myself from coming too early. Ever since he whispered those words in my ear, I've wanted to feel them both at the same time.

Luna looks at me, trying to gauge my reaction to what is being suggested. "I really want that, if Parker wants it too," she moans out. I can't stop my cock from rocking up into my hand at her voice.

"I really, really want that, angel."

"Good," Roman murmurs, pulling her top back over her head, revealing her pierced nipples and her brand-new ink. She looks stunning, as always, but her little symbols to represent each of us sets me on fire. "Let's tease him first, shall we?" He looks at me with a grin on his face as his hand cups her breast, careful not to touch her newly marked skin.

Luna moans in response, watching as my hand disappears beneath my boxer briefs. "But, I want to touch him, baby." Licking her lips, she looks at me through half-mast eyes, sexy as sin.

"This is the one time you get to call the shots, so if you want to touch him, tell him." His hands run down her sides, slipping into the top of her yoga pants, and trailing them down her thighs.

Without moving her gaze from mine, she kicks off her sandals and steps out of her pants. Standing before us, oozing confidence in only her lace panties. Urging me forward with a waggle of her finger, I'm happy to oblige. Not wasting a second, I cover the distance and bring my mouth down on hers. Bringing us chest to chest as Roman stays at her back, sandwiching her in, giving her a taste of what they're going to do to me.

Her fingers wrap around my neck as she pulls me closer, and I feel one of Roman's hands grab my waist too. Moans fill the room, but they could be coming from any of us. Trailing my lips to her neck, Roman pulls her face to the side, crushing his lips to hers. My fingers find her nipples as she arches into me, and my cock pushes into her hip.

Just as I'm about to take her taut nipple into my mouth, I feel a hand tug at my hair, pulling me back up to full height. It's Roman's hand in my hair, as Luna's fingers trail up my chest, lifting my Henley top as she goes. Seeing the unspoken demand in her eyes, I lift my arms above my head, letting the top fall away when she lifts it off.

Her gaze trails from the feather tattoo on my arm to the Steele family emblem on my hip, and I watch as her eyes darken. The head of my dick is peeking out of my boxer briefs and unbuttoned jeans, making her lick her lips. Before I can say anything, my face is being pulled forward as Luna sinks to her knees, taking my clothes with her.

Roman's lips touch mine, my eyes closing instinctively, and the contrast between him and Luna only adds to my desire. Where Luna's lips are soft and delicate, Roman's are fuller and more demanding. My mouth already feels close to bruising, before he bites down hard on my bottom lip, drawing a moan from me. At the exact same moment, Luna licks a trail from the root of my cock, all the way up to the tip, my legs almost buckling under me.

Knowing the impact they're having on me, Roman pulls back, and it takes me a moment to open my eyes. When I do, I find him looking down at Luna, her hand trailing up my thigh to squeeze my balls as she deepthroats my length in one swift move.

"Fuck!" I pant. "Luna, I'm going to cum too quick if you don't stop," I hiss out, and she pulls back with a proud grin on her face.

Letting me catch my breath a second, she turns to Roman while still on her knees, but he shakes his head. "Not yet, princess. Watching you both has me as close as Parker."

"But I want you naked too, baby," she purrs, and even he can't refuse her as she licks his abs.

"Princess, you're playing dirty," he murmurs, and I love seeing her bring him to his knees, killing his usual dominance because he needs her so much. "Lay down on the bed," he whispers down to her, and she's quick to comply.

Watching as she lays down, dead center with her head on the pillow, my eyes go back to the tattoos. So close to her heart, so specific for each of us, I love them. Luna's eyes widen, and it has my eyes tracking where she is looking.

Turning to my left, Roman stands with his shorts at his feet, his hard length holding my attention. How the fuck am I supposed to take him? I look back at Luna, who must be able to read the worry on my face, as she giggles. Kicking my jeans off, I discard them, as I try to gain control of my beating heart.

Deciding I need to focus on Luna, I step toward her,

but she shakes her head. "I want to see you together first." Heat burns bright in her eyes, her fingers stroking down her stomach, heading straight for her clit. My face flushes, watching her arousal increases my own.

Turning to face Roman fully, he wastes no time lining our bodies up. My lips move the short distance to his as his hands grip my waist, pulling me closer. The movement has my dick brushing against his, and I can't help but hiss in pleasure at the contact.

Holy fuck. I hear Luna moan, but Roman doesn't give me a chance to look her way. With one hand on my hip and the other against my chest, I get lost in his touch.

"More," Luna begs from the bed, and Roman moves to wrap his hand around both of our lengths, squeezing us together. Goosebumps rise all over my body as I throw my head back in ecstasy.

"Fuck, Roman," I groan, pulling my lips from his, but our faces stay millimeters apart, watching each other fall apart at the touch.

Luna's moan pulls my gaze away, and the show she's offering in return has me biting my lip. Laying bare before us, with one hand pulling at her nipple piercing, the other glides over her clit and down to her entrance, slowly over and over again.

Perfect. She is utter perfection.

"Taste him," she breathes out, and before I can drop to my knees, Roman does instead. My mouth falls open as I stare down at him, on his knees before me. Looking up at me with hooded eyes, I could orgasm from the sight alone, especially combined with Luna on display before me.

Keeping his eyes on mine, he wraps his lips around the head of my cock and sucks hard.

"Shit," I breathe, my cock pulsing for more. Usually, Roman will draw everything out, wanting control and a little delayed gratification, but even he can't hold back from the arousal in the room. Without warning, he takes the rest of my length, my cock hitting the back of his throat, and I forget how to breathe.

My hand instantly reaches out, gripping my fingers in his hair for balance. The sharp pull against his scalp has him humming around my cock. Fuck. The desire in his eyes screams for more. Tightening my grip, I hold him in place. Thrusting past his lips to the back of his throat, taking everything from him, like he always demands from me.

Trapped in his gaze, he works his lips up and down my

length, his grip on my thighs only adding to the intensity. I don't know how I'm supposed to last, hearing Luna moan at the show she's getting has me close to bursting. On the verge of making him stop before I cum, he releases me with a pop, a sinful grin taking over his face.

"She doesn't get herself off when we're in the room," he whispers, turning his gaze to Luna, whose chest and neck is pink as her arousal prickles her skin. I nod in agreement, somehow managing to lift my knee up onto the bed.

At my approach, Luna widens her legs, letting me in, as I wet my lips. Knowing the connection I just felt with Roman, as he looked into my eyes, I do the same to my wife. Maintaining eye contact, I lick slowly from her entrance to her clit, and she shudders beneath me. Her body is coiled, ready to explode, and she will, beneath me.

Grabbing the globe of her ass with one hand, I trail the other to her core, teasing her entrance as I lap at her clit.

"More, Parker, I need more," she pleads, and I can't bring myself to deny her.

Thrusting two fingers into her tight pussy, I graze my teeth against her swollen clit. She moans loudly, but we're too far gone to care. Not relenting on my assault, her core grips my fingers, wanting just that little bit more.

The next time I thrust into her, I twirl my fingers, finding her g-spot, and her hand wraps in my hair, holding me tighter to her. Roman's hand grips my ass, which is up in the air as I taste my queen. His other hand is cold with some form of lube on his fingers, as he traces my hole. Pressing his finger against me, it catches me off guard, and my teeth clamp down harder on Luna's clit. She cries out as her orgasm tears her apart.

I stifle my own groan against her, as I make sure she rides out every last wave of pleasure. All while Roman toys with me, stretching me to take him.

"Breathe, Parker," Luna whispers as she cups my face. "Relax, I know it's uncomfortable, but it'll be worth it." Releasing her from my grip, she looks past me, watching what Roman is doing, and the desire in her eyes only increases.

"Crouch up on your knees, Parker," Roman murmurs from behind me, as he removes his finger. I follow his guidance, as I hear the click of a lid and watch as he pours coconut oil that he retrieved from the bathroom over his fingers. "Don't worry, I googled the best oils to use, and this is high up on the list," he reassures me, but I'm still shocked and appreciative that he cared enough about my comfort to google it.

His fingers trace me again, and this time he slowly pushes two fingers inside me. I can't stop my body from tensing up, but Luna kisses my lips, distracting me from the discomfort.

"Push back," Roman says, and I do, all while Luna consumes my lips and wraps her fingers around my cock. I feel him scissor his fingers inside me and mixed with Luna's touches, I can't take much more.

"I'm going to cum too soon," I mumble against her lips, and she smiles.

Dropping to her back in front of me, Luna shuffles forward, her intent clear. Roman pulls out of me again, and I feel the loss this time, I need more. My cock glistens with pre-cum as I line myself up at Luna's entrance, just as Roman does the same to me.

Pulling me down on top of her, Luna lifts her hips off the bed, forcing my cock deeper. Her hands grip my shoulders as she moans out in pleasure.

Roman slowly begins to push inside of me, and I freeze inside of Luna, too tense to move at all. Remembering what he said about pushing back, I do it again. This time his cock stretches me out, my groan dying on my lips as I slip almost all of the way out of Luna.

Nobody moves as Roman sits deep inside me. I take deep breaths, adjusting to the fullness that washes over me, as Luna stares up at me in awe and Roman curses behind me.

"Holy fuck, Parker. You're so tight, so hot," he mumbles incoherent sentences, and I manage to smile at Luna. Finally, ready for more, I push forward, filling Luna up, making her moan as she cups my face.

Roman doesn't move as I pull back from Luna, impaling myself on his thick length. The drag against my walls as he stretches me wider is like electricity. He holds still while I repeat the motion a few more times, the three of us moaning in sync.

I feel the shift in him as his hands tighten on my hips. Holding me in place, he drags himself almost all the way out before slamming into me, hard and deep. The chain reaction has me thrusting home in Luna, who cries out with the impact.

"Fuck," someone says, but I couldn't be sure who. Roman does it again, and again, sinking all the way home. My skin prickles with pleasure as he increases in tempo, his skin slapping against mine, which in turn slaps against Luna's.

She stares wide-eyed between us, falling apart at the seams with pleasure as she watches Roman fuck me. His weight pushes down on my back, bringing me closer to Luna, who manages to tilt her hips up, taking me deeper, our lips grazing as we moan together.

From the tips of my toes, my movements become erratic, the force of my orgasm building. The feel of Roman's fingertips digging into my skin, mixed with the softness of Luna beneath me, sends me over the edge.

The most earth-shattering orgasm rips through my body, seemingly taking everyone with me. All I see is white, as Luna crushes her lips to mine, swallowing my cries. Her pussy clamps down on my cock, as Roman's length stutters inside of me, filling me with his cum.

I ride the waves of pleasure for what seems like hours. When I finally start to get my vision back, I hear Luna murmur.

"That was the single hottest thing I have ever experienced. But the weight of you both on top of me is going to kill me."

Blinking my eyes, I register Roman fully at my back,

and the pair of us piled up on top of her. She smiles up at me, and I shudder at the loss of Roman as he slips out of me. My cock twitches inside of her, and she gapes up at me.

"Roman, what have you done to him? His dick is stirring again," she says with a chuckle, as I pull out of her, and try to stand at the bottom of the bed.

"Oh, give me a little time. I'm all for round two, then I get to take you, princess," Roman says, pulling my gaze to him. The heat and appreciation in his eyes catches me by surprise.

"I'm going to be too sore for that, but next time we'll trade places."

He grins and winks at us both, before stalking off to the en-suite. The sound of taps running is like music to my ears. Looking at Luna, she comes to stand beside me.

"I fucking love you, Parker Parker." She plants a kiss on my lips, and I grip her hips.

"I fucking love you, wife."

OUR BLOODLINE

TWENTY SIX

Luna

Sitting in our little all seasons room, sipping coffee with a blanket wrapped around my shoulders, is my new favorite way to start the day. The sea calls to me, and I could listen to waves crashing against the shore in the distance for hours. Wherever we go after Featherstone, I'd love for it to be like this. Calming and safe. A real home, with the water on our doorstep.

Nobody else is awake yet, but it's almost ten in the morning, so someone will stir soon. Sitting alone has my mind wandering, and I can't help but replay last night with Parker and Roman. I could have orgasmed without being touched as I watched them together.

Remembering the look of pure bliss on Roman's face as he sank into Parker, I know I want to see it again, and again. Especially as I watched Parker's body coil up tight as he orgasmed. Feeling the force of Roman fucking Parker, as he sank into me, has me hot all over again.

Hearing the door creak behind me, I look over my shoulder to see Oscar and Parker both stepping outside. They both smile softly at me, but Oscar goes back to frowning at Parker. Sitting on either side of me, on the rattan sofa we have in our own private space, Parker sighs, and I glance between them.

"What's going on?" I ask, and Oscar's frown only deepens.

"Parker won't tell me what you guys were up to last night? I mean, I kept the 'rents away and no one wants to tell me the details. I know it was good, I saw all of your faces at dinner." He pouts at me, and I can't stop the grin from spreading on my lips. Damn right, it was good, it was perfection.

"What exactly do you want to know?" I ask, turning to face him.

Parker catches me by surprise, turning with me and

propping a leg up on the sofa, so he can pull me back between his legs. I only have a long t-shirt on, and the blanket around my shoulders, so the movement offers Oscar a glimpse between my legs. A shudder runs through me as the slight chill in the room kisses my bare skin.

"You give in too easily with him, angel," Parker murmurs in my ear, and Oscar scoffs in response, not moving his eyes from my pussy.

"I want to know everything, baby girl." Licking his lips, Oscar finally looks back up at Parker's face. The grin on his lips tells me he knows exactly what he's doing to me. While Parker kisses my neck, making goosebumps pop up across my body.

"From start to finish?" I ask, and the devilish smile on his face is all the answer I need. "Roman and Parker sandwiched me between them, taking turns kissing my lips." His eyes burn with fire as he stares at my mouth. "Then, as Roman took Parker's lips, I dropped down to my knees between them, taking Parker to the back of my throat."

He hums in appreciation as he adjusts himself in his pants. I feel Parker stiffening behind me at the memory too, his hands gripping my waist.

"Then what?"

"Then, I asked for a show." His gaze goes to Parker as he registers my words.

"Tell me what kind of a show, baby girl," he whispers, releasing his swollen cock from his boxer briefs with his right hand, as his left slowly strokes up my leg. Parker peppers kisses along my neck and shoulder, making my back arch at their touch.

"I watched them get lost in each other's lips before Roman dropped to his knees too."

"Fuck." His chest moves rapidly, as his breathing becomes choppier. "You got Roman to his knees?" He asks as Parker trails his hand up my chest. Cupping my breast in his hand, he reveals more of my body to Oscar.

"He went down all on his own. Stopping just before he brought me to the edge, all while Luna was lying in the bed, touching herself," Parker adds, and Oscar groans in response. I watch as Oscar tightens his grip on his length, pulling hard as our words create a visual in his mind.

My hand comes up over my head to cup the back of Parker's head, as he traces his fingers against my skin. "Then Parker spread me wide and licked me to orgasm as he rubbed my g-spot," I moan, as Oscar's fingers ghost against my clit. "Do you want to know what made him bite down on my clit, and bring me to orgasm?"

He nods enthusiastically as he slowly teases a finger inside of me and Parker touches my clit.

"Roman started stretching him out."

His movement falters as he grips his cock tight, pre-cum leaking from the tip. "Holy shit, why was he stretching you out, Parker?" he asks, and I feel Parker smile against my skin, his fingers circling around my clit, forcing me to push down more on Oscar's fingers.

"Because, while I fucked Luna." He grinds into my back, and my skin burns at the tension he's building. "Roman fucked me."

"Fuck." His eyes frantically search between us as his hand drops from my body, and he stands. Parker instantly pushes me forward and flips me over, so I'm on my knees before him.

My body screams in protest, begging for more, as Oscar comes to stand beside Parker's head, his cock aimed in his direction. I can't stop myself from nodding in agreement.

Hands suddenly grip my hips, catching me by surprise, as a cock presses at my entrance, sinking all the way home in one thrust. Crying out, I look over my shoulder to see

Kai. With one leg propped up on the cushions, he gazes down at me with hooded eyes, as he pulls out and slams straight back in again.

My mouth falls open as I try to mute my moans, bringing my hands to Parker's shoulders to prop myself up. Movement catches my eye as I see Roman step up behind Oscar, pulling Oscar's boxer briefs the rest of the way down.

Fuck, we're completely out in the open. Luckily we're secluded from the main space of the house, but I'm sure a security guard somewhere is catching a good glimpse at us. I can't bring myself to care. Not as Kai drags his length all the way out before slamming straight back in.

I watch as Parker takes Oscar in his mouth, his cheeks hollowing out as he sucks hard, and Oscar's head falls back on Roman's shoulder. Blindly searching, I feel Parker's cock beneath me, and I wrap my fingers tight around him as I spread his pre-cum down his length.

"Remember what I whispered to you the last time your dick was in his mouth, Oscar?" Roman murmurs against his ear, and he nods frantically. "His ass was like heaven, just like I said it would be." Parker moans around Oscar's length, making Oscar groan with pleasure.

Even Kai's grip tightens on my waist as he fucks me harder. I'm close, so fucking close. Squeezing Parker's cock, I want to bring him with me.

I see Roman's hand glisten as he trails his fingers between the globes of Oscar ass. Understanding dawns on me, as he slowly pushes an oiled-up digit into Oscar. His eyes fall to mine as his neck flushes red, and he moans, deep from his toes.

It's too much. Roman teasing Oscar as Parker sucks his cock. While Kai brutally fucks me from behind, as I pull at Parker's dick. Unable to keep myself up any more, I drop chest to chest with Parker. Kai follows me down, his thrusts growing erratic, as he adjusts me a little so my clit is rubbing against Parker's cock.

I can barely tilt my head to see as Oscar loses his control, his orgasm ripping him from the inside out. Roman and Parker don't relent, draining him, taking every last ounce of pleasure. The friction between my clit and Parker's cock, and demand of Kai's length inside me, pushes me to my own climax.

I groan low and deep as I ride through the waves of ecstasy. Parker moans below me, as he grinds his cock up against my pussy, coming all over us. Kai settles deep inside of me, filling me with his cum too.

Oscar sags beside me as he pulls himself from Parker's mouth, and Roman steps back, coming to stand right beside me. Pulling his cock from his boxer briefs, it takes only a few jerks before he's coming all over my back and the side of my face. Painting me with his pleasure.

"If we're going to tell dirty stories, princess, you get to feel all the ecstasy you caused," Roman murmurs, and fuck if that doesn't make it even hotter.

Collapsing against Parker, Kai kisses down my spine as he slowly eases himself from my body.

"Good morning, Sakura," he whispers against my ear, and I smile.

Damn straight it's a good fucking morning.

"Fuck. Is that what we're calling a quickie now?" Oscar asks, making everyone hum in response.

Kai

Damn. I could wake up like that every morning. Hearing Luna tease Oscar with what they did last night had me hard, simply from hearing the lust in her voice alone. When I saw Roman walk out of the bathroom putting oil on his hands, I knew I wanted in as well.

I love how we're slowly finding ourselves. With Luna by our sides, anything is possible, even finding my sister, which still blows my mind.

Freshly showered, I throw on some jeans and a loose navy hoodie and head to the kitchen where everyone else will be, fighting for breakfast.

"Morning, Kai," Mia says, as I step into the lounge where she's relaxing on the sofa, and I smile wide at her. Waking up to hot sex with my wife, and knowing my sister is alive definitely puts a spring in my step.

"Good morning," I murmur in response, taking a seat beside her. "Have you thought any more about speaking with Mom?" I ask. We've broached a few subjects over the past week, but ultimately we've just been learning more about each other, putting off the heavy stuff.

"Not really." She shrugs. "Bryce always got updates on Luna and you, so he could tell me all about the Kai you were growing to be, and that was always enough for me."

It warms my heart to know that she may not have been with me, but she was safe. Bryce took care of her better than I could have prayed for, and I'll be forever thankful for that. He talked about me all the time with her, but she never wanted to know about our parents, and I can understand the impact their actions would have on her. Now she knows it was to protect her, she may change her opinion, but I won't push her to make any decisions. We've had enough people's thoughts dictate our lives already.

"Hey guys, Bryce and Rafe have some information they want to go over with us," Roman calls from the kitchen door, and we stand to follow him inside. My arm instinctively wraps around Mia's shoulders protectively.

"You know I'm two years older than you, right? I should be protecting you," she mutters, and I smile down at her.

"I still have the height advantage, and it will always be our job to protect each other. Forever family, remember?" She stops in her tracks, wrapping her arms around my waist, and I squeeze her back. Leaning her head against my shoulder, she takes a minute, and I'm happy to give her all the time she needs.

One final squeeze, and she leans back. "I'm good now." Brushing her hands down her floaty pink dress, she smiles up at me before heading into the kitchen. God, sisters should come with a warning label.

Everyone is sitting at the kitchen table, pancakes stacked sky high at every seat. The table seats twelve, so there is plenty of space for the eight of us. Oscar, Parker, Luna, and Roman sit on one side of the table, nearest to the windows, while Bryce and Rafe sit with their backs to us. I let Mia sit beside Bryce as I take up the end seat, facing Oscar and his shit-eating grin.

Bryce has clearly made breakfast again, loving to feed us. There are pancakes in front of me, then the center of the table is filled with syrups, fruit, whipped cream, and chocolate sauce for us to customize our toppings. Nobody speaks as we all dig in, enjoying each other's company.

"So, what details have you got?" Luna asks, not wasting any time once everyone has finished eating, and we all look to Bryce and Rafe expectantly.

"Maria called this morning, and The Ring has made a few decisions. Well, everyone except the Manettis and the Dietrichsons," Rafe says, glancing at Parker as he says his bloodline, but Parker doesn't react. "Sorry, Parker, I feel like I should apologize or something. We haven't talked, and with what happened at The Slums, and I know you had a difficult relationship with…"

"If you're apologizing because you killed him before I could, then I'll accept it, but nothing else requires forgiveness. Especially when I already agreed you could," Parker says with a smile, and the tension in Rafe's shoulders relaxes.

"Well then," Rafe mutters in response, as Roman pats Parker supportively on the back. "So, The Ring, and Featherstone as a whole, want to draw Totem out so we can put an end to this once and for all."

I process his words, and a sinking feeling in the pit of my stomach tells me it links back to us. "What are they wanting us to do?" I ask, and Bryce looks at me in surprise.

"What makes you…"

"Dad, he's the observant one. If he knows, he knows. So, please explain," Luna says, waving her hand at him, her trust in me making me smile.

"They want to take the fight to the academy, so they can try and control it the best they can," Bryce says, keeping his eyes on me as he speaks.

"So, they want to use us as bait," I state, and I get the plan and reasoning behind it, but I want to hear it confirmed.

"Yes," Rafe finally says, when Bryce can't bring himself to answer. I hear the guys scoff in annoyance from across the table, but I remain focused.

"And what does that exactly entail?"

Bryce continues to eye me warily, "Are you not going to argue with me first?"

I look to Luna across the table, who grins at me, while Mia murmurs, "You haven't changed one bit, Kai." Patting my thigh, she looks to Bryce. "Kai here is the level-headed one. He's isn't going to waste time with unnecessary emotions when he can just get straight to the point."

The others chuckle as her description is spot on, but I won't get distracted right now. I raise my eyebrow at Bryce, and he shakes his head with a smile.

"We takeover the Ace block, letting everyone think it's just you guys, like normal. When in actuality, there'll be a lot of trained people in every room, ready for their attack. Because there will be one, so why not have it on our terms?"

Luna and the guys nod in agreement, as I consider the situation from every angle, my fingers tapping absently on the table as I do. "Once this is over with, what will our lives look like? Without Totem in the picture? We're not going back in The Games or completing any outstanding assignments if they expect us to put our lives at risk to protect Featherstone."

Rafe's hand slams down on the table as he shouts, "Yes! New favorite. Kai's my new favorite, I called it." He smiles at me, and even I can't stop myself from smiling back. "That's exactly what I said, and they agreed." He finishes.

"Alright, old man," Luna says, making him glare at her. "When are we expected to leave?"

"Today," Bryce answers. "We all go today."

OUR BLOODLINE

TWENTY SEVEN

Luna

"Look at me!" I call out, gaining everyone's attention, but more specifically, Rafe's. He looks at me confused, as I jump up and down at the top of the steps leading to the private plane waiting on the tarmac for us. "Fully alert and completely aware I'm about to get in a vehicle with you, Dad!" I yell. He shakes his head as he smiles up at me.

"Get on the damn plane, brat," he grumbles back, and I smile as I step inside. This time around, I can appreciate the interior and luxury of the plane. Cream leather seats sit facing the front in pairs. The sofa-like seats behind them face each other from each side, seating eight in total. The memory of waking up on that same sofa, and seeing my father again, runs through my mind.

Just beyond that is a small kitchen area and two doors. One is leading to the bathroom, the other to the fully furnished bedroom Kai laid in after he'd been shot.

The flight should take around four hours, so we should arrive at the Academy around dinnertime. Sitting on the sofa, I get comfortable and buckled in, ready for us to go over a few details when we arrive back at Featherstone.

Roman takes the seat to my left, as Oscar cuts in front of Parker to take the seat to my right.

"Sharing is caring, Parker Parker," he sings, but Parker just gives him the finger and takes the seat on the other side of him.

"It would work in your favor if you were nice to me. You know, so when you want to play and experiment, I'll be more inclined to say yes," Parker whispers, as Kai steps onboard, with Mia and my dads behind him.

Roman can't contain his laughter as Oscar gapes openly at Parker, making me chuckle along with him.

"Having sex has given you some big balls there, Parker, and I think I like it," Oscar says back, quickly planting a kiss on his cheek in response. "But we both know you want in my ass, sweet cheeks, so stop with the high and mighty bullshit, it doesn't suit you."

Clipping himself in, he smiles brightly as if nothing was just said, and makes conversation with Rafe, who sits across from us.

"What have you done to us?" Roman whispers against my ear, and I whip around to look at him.

"Don't blame me," I say, my eyes widening, but I see the humor in his face.

"I definitely blame you. None of us are the same since meeting you, princess. You've changed all our lives, even before falling in love and marrying you. We barely joked or smiled, always focusing on the next task at hand. Now, we have hope, a sense of freedom, and you. Always you." Brushing his lips against mine, my heart swells at his words. I definitely love me some romantic Roman.

"Have you spoken to Jess?" Rafe asks, and I nod.

"Yes, her stuff is packed, and she'll be there when we arrive too." I can't wait to see her, I've missed her so much, but it was always the safest option. I'm not totally set on her being in Ace if there is a chance of Totem attacking, but there will be a lot of us there to protect her.

"Great, I spoke with Maverick too. Him and a few of the guys he's had watching over her are also going to come to Ace as well." Good, the more people on our side, the better. "So, you guys will all stay in Luna's dorm. Maria said, 'you're welcome,' she sorted your bed situation out." He rolls his eyes, but I silently thank the greatest grandmother of all times. The waggle of Oscar's eyebrows tells me he thinks the same.

"Reggie, Travis, and Patrick are going to set up in Roman's dorm," Bryce says, glancing up from his phone as the plane starts to move. "While Juliana is going to share the Morgan's with Betty and Maria. Rafe and I will be in Parker's, and the Dietrichson's dorm will be filled with security guards." Glancing at us all for confirmation, he continues, "Maverick and his guys are going to go in with Jess, so we can assign security guards to Oscar's and Kai's space as well. That way, we can have a good rotation of fresh guards at all times."

Mia looks around nervously, but Rafe catches her gaze. "We want you to be able to choose where you stay, doll. You can stay with us, or the women."

"You aren't handing me off to my father as soon as we get there?" she asks quietly, and Bryce's eyes nearly fall out of his head.

"Never, Mia. If you want to see him, that's your choice, but I will *never* force you." She nods, sighing in relief, as Kai squeezes her hand.

A part of me questions whether I should be jealous of the relationship she has with my biological dad, but ultimately, they saved each other. I'll be forever grateful that neither of them were alone, or dead.

"Okay, whatever works out, I'm not fussy."

"Great, are you getting anything on the security feeds yet?" Roman asks Kai. Bryce gave him a laptop after breakfast, and he's been working his magic ever since.

"A few of the verified guards are already showing up at Ace, but nothing else out of the ordinary. You were right, Barbette is nowhere to be seen either," Kai answers, glancing to Rafe when he mentions Bitch Dietrichson. My blood boils at the sound of her name alone.

"Okay, well, let's make the most of relaxing, because once we land we need to be on high alert."

Kai goes back to the laptop, tapping away as he tracks every security camera on campus, and the surrounding areas. Roman slouches back in his seat, stretching his legs out as he closes his eyes. Parker pops the headphones

Bryce gave him in, The Violence by Asking Alexandria, blaring through them.

Lost in their own conversation, Bryce and Rafe zone us out, as Mia leans her head on Kai's shoulder, watching as he works. Which just leaves me and Oscar.

"Do you want to Netflix and chill, baby girl?" he asks, shaking the laptop from his backpack in front of me. "I know, we can't do the chill part, but I'm game for some binge-watching if you are."

"I'm in," I answer, as he wraps his arm behind me, pulling me close and setting the screen up for us.

The calmness that settles over me, in this steel can floating in the sky, has me thankful I was dragged to Featherstone. Otherwise, I wouldn't be here with my Aceholes.

The SUV drives through the gates of Featherstone, and my body is ready for an attack. Although, an ambush as soon as we drive onto campus is highly unlikely. Parker squeezes my hand, as my eyes scan the grounds. Dad is driving, and Bryce is wearing a baseball cap to hide his face from any footage, in case Kai can't delete it quick enough.

We're driving in like ghosts, Kai erasing our trail, but no one knows my father or Mia are alive, and we want to keep it that way for a while longer. Roman sits across from me, searching for any signs of threat, just like I am. Kai and Mia sit beside him, as Oscar takes the seat on the other side of Parker.

Silence fills the car as we slowly crawl through the grounds. Watching as the blocks come into view, it feels like we've been away for years. It's a little after six in the evening, so classes are out, and there are a few students relaxing outside.

No one really pays any attention to the SUV as we drive past, but the blacked-out windows help keep us covered in the rear. The garage door opens, security guards waiting on the other side, as Rafe parks the SUV. We all stay inside the vehicle until the garage door shuts behind us, then we all begin to climb out.

Rafe and Bryce greet the security guards as we make our way into the lobby. The glass windows in the lobby have been tinted, so no one can see in, making it feel too dark. Especially without having Thomas here to smile at us, but Rafe said they'd encouraged him to take a vacation, so he didn't end up caught in the crossfire.

Standing in the lobby, near the main doors with his hands crossed behind his back, is Ian. Without question, I run straight at him. He doesn't step out of the way, only relaxing his arms to his side. I don't know what he expects, but when I jump, throwing my arms around his neck, it takes him a moment to hug me back.

"Thank you, Ian. Thank you for everything. But if you keep secrets again, I'll karate chop you so hard in the throat, you won't be able to speak for a week. Understood?"

"Yes, Miss Steele," he mutters, and I drop down to my feet.

"And quit that shit, you call me Luna, or I'll think of something else to weakly threaten you with, okay?" I plant my hands on my hips, trying to muster a glare as I stare at him, but he just shakes his head at me.

"To call you Luna would be unprofessional, but I'll consider it."

I nod and turn back around, my Aceholes waiting for me. Bryce and Rafe step around the corner, seeing Ian straight away. Leaving them to greet each other, Mia heads back with them, as we step into the elevator. The elevator quickly takes us up to the fourth floor, where there are two security guards walking around.

Unlocking my door, the guys follow in behind me. As the door clicks shut behind us, I sigh in relief. Kai's arm comes around my shoulder, and he kisses the crown of my head.

"Sakura, I'm going to set the tech up on the kitchen table. If you need me, just call." With that, he stalks off, determination in every stride. We want to get these fuckers, and sooner rather than later.

"You guys better not be fucking! I've missed my girl," Red says, stepping out of my bedroom and charging toward me. "Hey, captain," she murmurs, wrapping her arms around me and holding me tight.

"Hey, Red," I respond, squeezing her back just as tight. "I've missed you," I mutter back, and I hear someone huff behind me.

"I haven't," Oscar adds. I can tell she's giving him the finger behind my back, and I roll my eyes at the pair of them already. Pulling back, she glances at my face, noticing the cut from Becky, and her eyes darken.

"I'm all good, Red," I say, trying to reassure her, but she still stares me down a little longer. "The guys are going to grab a few things from their rooms before the others get situated, and Kai is going to set up all the tech stuff in the kitchen. Do you want to order food with us? You can catch me up on everything that's been going on while I've been gone."

"Oh my god, yes. I want pizza. Lots and lots of pizza." She claps enthusiastically, and I glance back at the guys who are already heading for the door, not ready to deal with an excited Red right now. Even Kai runs toward them, winking as he shuts the door behind them. Aceholes.

Turning back to her, she grins wide at me. "I'm not actually *that* excited, but I wanted you to myself for a while," she chuckles, and I can't stop the bubble of laughter that passes my lips.

"You crafty, bitch!" I cry out, and she just laughs harder.

This is exactly why I've missed my girl.

OUR BLOODLINE

TWENTY EIGHT

Luna

I'm not ready to pretend everything is back to normal today, but here we are, getting ready for classes like Totem isn't out there wanting to get his hands on me. My hands shake with fury as I think about it again, but I need to pull myself together.

I loved spending time with Red last night, her presence has a good effect on all of us, including Oscar. Kai still insisted on walking her to her room, which she now has to share with Maverick and a few others apparently. She seemed to be putting on a brave face, but I can tell this is all getting to her.

Sighing, I finish brushing my hair up into a ponytail and move away from the vanity, minimal make-up on my face. Looking down at the uniform I'm forced to wear again, I frown in annoyance. The blouse shows too much cleavage, the split of the skirt rising high up my leg, and the blazer pulling my waist in tight. It's all a load of bullshit. I love my body, but I'm not just here to put it on display like this uniform encourages.

Glancing to the rows of heels in the closet, I've reached my limit. Fuck them. I'm not wearing those damn heels anymore, especially if I'm expected to react to a sudden threat at any time. I bypass all the black court heels with red soles and roll on a pair of ankle socks. Slipping my feet into a fresh pair of combat boots, I instantly feel more comfortable. I dare someone to fucking question me today. What is on my feet is the least of anyone's worries.

"Angel, come eat before we have to leave," Parker calls out from the kitchen, and I move toward the sound of his voice.

Stopping at the door leading into the kitchen, Kai, Oscar, and Roman are already sitting at the table, while Parker carries over plates of eggs and bacon for everyone. I want to capture this moment, everyone relaxed and smiling at each other. Kai taps away on his laptop, grinning at Oscar winding Roman up, flicking the end of his nose like a child, and Parker smiles as he takes care of everyone.

"Fuck, baby girl, you're turning me on in those combat boots," Oscar says, his eyes scanning over me from head to toe. I roll my eyes at him, as the rest of my Aceholes follow his gaze.

"Damn, princess, he's not wrong," Roman murmurs, and their attention has me blushing a little.

"Sakura, you're getting all flustered, and it isn't helping the situation," Kai adds, and I watch as his hand drops below the table to adjust himself. Fuck.

Taking the seat beside him, his other arm instantly comes around my shoulders. "How is your other shoulder?" I ask, my hand instinctively resting on his thigh.

I watch as he grimaces at the question, but answers honestly. "Not too great, Sakura. Movement in general isn't that bad, but too much strain, and it burns." He sighs. "But, I'm here with you, and that's what matters." I melt at his words, lifting up to place a kiss to the corner of his mouth.

"No more distracting our wife, she needs all the energy she can get. We want to be at our best when they come,"

Parker says, putting a plate of food in front of me, and I smile up at him. Kai moves his laptop so Parker can place the other plate in his hand in front of him. Rushing to the counter and back, Parker takes the seat beside me, offering me a hot mug of coffee as he does. Mumbling my thanks, I bring the caffeine goodness to my lips.

"What's the schedule for today?" Oscar asks, and subconsciously we all look to Kai.

Shaking his head at us all, he reels off classes for today. "Weaponry for us all this morning. Followed by Science for Oscar, a free period for Roman, and Tech for the rest of us. Then we've all got Combat this afternoon."

"Perfect, a good bit of training is what we need," Roman adds, and I couldn't agree more. "You'll be able to try your range of weaponry with your left hand, Kai," he murmurs, and Kai nods in agreement.

"I will. I've also blocked the security feeds, so we are the only ones with access to the cameras, and Rafe put a few more up last night. We haven't found any blind spots, but we just need to stay vigilant," Kai responds, and the determination in his voice fills me with confidence.

A knock from the front door stops our conversation. "Come on, bitches!" Red yells from the other side of the door, and I can't help but grin.

"You heard the woman, come on, bitches," I sing, rising to my feet to go and let her in.

She bombards me as I swing open the door, rushing inside and slamming the door shut behind her.

"What the fuck? Where's the threat?" I panic, checking her over, but she just waves a hand at me.

"No threat. I was just excited to see you." I stare her down, watching as she runs her fingers through her hair. There is definitely something different about her, I just don't know what. I'll give her some time to figure it out, then she better spill it.

"If you say so. Have you eaten?" I ask, and she nods in response.

"Oh my god, I love the boots. *So* you, captain," she says with a grin, holding her hand up for a high five, which I reluctantly meet. "Are you ready to show everyone their queen is back?" Rolling my eyes, I glare at her. "What? You are! And you have to introduce me to your bio Dad too."

"God, Jess, one thing at a time. Throwing everything at her at once will put her in a foul mood," Roman says, placing his hands on Red's shoulders from behind and guiding her to the door. While Oscar wraps his fingers with mine, pulling me along too. Kai and Parker follow behind us, as Roman opens the door.

"She would not be in a foul mood with me, Roman," she argues back, glaring over her shoulder at him.

"I mean in general. My father warned me to avoid upsetting my wife at all costs, and if that means shutting you up, then so be it." She stops dead in her tracks, her smile reaching from ear to ear.

"You just said wife," she whispers, and he frowns down at her. Turning to face him fully, she pats him on the arm before hugging him tightly. "The little twinkle of love in your eyes is adorable," she adds before spinning around and heading for the elevator.

"What the fuck?" Roman mutters to himself, looking at me with wide eyes, but I just grin because it really is adorable.

"I'm starving," Parker moans, like we're not heading for lunch.

This morning has been busy, but Weaponry with West was good. He literally just set us up in the far corner, having us practice with all the guns he'd had stored in Ace. So we were familiar with everything we would have on hand.

Kai was surprisingly okay with his left hand, not as fast or accurate as he would be with his right hand, but still on target. I can see the stress in his eyes. I heard him mumble something about being useless earlier, but I quickly shut him down. Kai still does so much for us, especially the tech side, and even if he didn't, he deserves a moment to rest his injury. Tech was free rein, meaning we spent the whole time making sure we were on top of the security feeds and tweaking anything slightly out of place.

The three of us walk out of the building and wait for Oscar and Red to finish up in Science. People stop and stare, seeing us outside of a classroom properly for the first time today. It's too cloudy to put my sunglasses on to hide the annoyance in my eyes, so they'll just have to deal with my resting bitch face.

I'm glad we have Combat after lunch, hopefully I'll be able to beat some of this tension out of my system. My phone vibrates in my pocket, pulling my attention from everyone around us. Kai and Parker seem to be trying to block me from everyone, but it's not doing much.

Roman: Hey, princess. I've got our table ready in the lunch hall. Hurry your ass over here, I miss you.

I smile down at my phone. Since he said those three words, it's like his head and heart are in the same place. Now he's open to sharing his emotions with me, and I love it.

Luna: Bossy much? We won't be long. I've missed you too.

Roman: Damn right I am. Less texting, more moving.

Roman: I LOVE YOU <3

Oh my, did he just love heart emoji me? Who the hell is this guy? This might be my favorite side of Roman.

Luna: I love you too, baby.

"What are you smiling at?" Parker asks as I put my

phone away.

"Nothing. Roman just sent me a love heart emoji." I waggle my eyebrows for added effect, and I see the surprise on his face too.

"I didn't even think he knew they were a thing," he murmurs, placing a hand to his chest dramatically, and I roll my eyes, but a growl from the entryway of the academic building stops our playfulness.

"I said, back the fuck away." I know that voice is Oscar's, but what the hell is going on?

Looking around the other students, I spot Oscar jogging down the steps, Red running along with him as he holds her arm. The anger on his face is prominent in the frown lines marking his face and the grinding of his jaw.

Instinctively, I move toward Oscar, but he signals for me not to as he walks our way. "Get in the Rolls, now."

"What? Oscar, slow down, talk to me." I put myself in his path, my hands landing on his chest as he stops right in front of me. Looking over me, he speaks with one of the guys.

"Get Jess in the car." Dropping her arm, she looks frantically between us.

"Somebody, please tell me what the fuck is going on,"

I grind out, my body zinging with adrenaline, ready to attack whatever has upset Oscar.

"It's me," a voice says quietly behind Oscar. He tries to block my view, but I step to the side, finding Trudy. My blood instantly boils as she stands before me, guilt written all over her face.

"You've got some fucking nerve," I spit out, and she remains completely still, as fear flashes in her eyes.

"The nerve, baby girl," Oscar grunts beside me. "Is that she was trying to get Jess to sweet talk you, soften the blow of her betrayal and all that."

I glance back at Red as Ian opens the door to the Rolls, shame on her face too. Is this all a joke? Taking in the scene around me, I notice every pair of eyes on us right now, wanting to see me air my dirty laundry in their faces, all for the love of gossip.

Stalking toward Trudy, she flinches back, ready for me to hit her. So, I'm sure it surprises her when I growl in her ear instead. "You better show up to Ace. Tonight, seven p.m. You've got some fucking explaining to do. When I kick your ass, it'll be for my pleasure, not for the enjoyment of bystanders."

She nods frantically as I lean back, walking toward the

same Rolls as Red. I feel Oscar go to protest, but I just glare at him. Climbing in, I slam the door shut behind me before Ian can help.

"Luna, I—"

"Shut up, Red!" I shout, unable to control my anger right now. "This is the kind of thing I expect you to tell me about, Jess. I don't expect to see shame on your face because you fucking know you should have said something sooner."

I need to get myself under control. Leaning my head back, I glance up to the roof of the car. Inhaling slowly through my nose, I hold my breath, before slowly exhaling through my mouth. I repeat the process a few more times, finally feeling my heart calm and logic return.

Taking one more calming breath, I look to Red. "Do I want to hear what she has to say?" I ask, looking her in the eye. She clamps her lips shut, simply nodding in response.

Great, another shit show to add to my snowball effect. Just push me down the mountain now.

"You've got the car ride over to the food court to catch me up to speed, and tell me what the fuck has been going on," I murmur, searching her eyes for any more secrets.

"Trudy didn't say what happened, but there is a haunted

look in her eyes that wasn't there before, darker than I've ever seen. Aiden mentioned she hasn't been sleeping at all, lost to the fear that now rests inside of her." Her words are deep, barely above a whisper, as they carve themselves into my soul. If Red believes it, I trust in her to at least offer Trudy the chance to explain. Especially after what Conor mentioned in The Tunnel.

"I'll listen to what she has to say, but I'm not promising more than that," I say, and Red nods lightly. I'm surprised to see a weight lift off her shoulders at my words, not understanding why it matters so much to her. "So, what else have I been missing out on?"

"Uhh, not much really. Maverick had me like a damsel in distress, training at every available minute, and not willing to let me out of his sight or those he trusts. Which meant I've done a whole lot of nothing, except reading."

"And who does he trust?" I ask. There's something missing, that she's not telling me, I can feel it, but I can't put my finger on it.

"Not many people apparently. Although, since staying there his circle seems to have expanded." She rubs her hands down her skirt nervously, and I can tell by the crinkle between her eyes something is playing on her mind.

"Talk to me, Jess. Whatever is going on you can talk to me you know?" I say, softening my voice, compared to the rage I had moments earlier.

Searching my gaze, she clears her throat. "I, uh, well…"

Before she can respond, the car door on my side flies open, and Roman peeks his head in. I didn't even realize the Rolls had come to a stop, and before I can continue to process anything else, Roman unclips my seatbelt and pulls me from the car.

My legs instinctively wrap around his waist as he presses me against the side of the car.

"What took you so long, princess?"

"We—"

His mouth takes mine, not waiting for a response. My fingers curl in his hair at the back of his neck, as I get lost in his touch, letting him consume me, instead of all the stress I just felt.

"Don't keep me waiting like that, princess. I missed you," he growls against my lips, and I can't help but smile at his possessive streak. I shouldn't love his bossy tendencies but I just can't get enough of him.

TWENTY NINE

Oscar

Sitting down on the bench, sweat trails down my face as I pull my top over my head. Training in Combat didn't seem to be enough for any of us, so we came back to Ace, and we've been in the gym ever since.

Swiping my face with my t-shirt, I watch as Roman and Luna spar together in the cage. The fury and tension building inside of her is not subsiding, no matter how hard she pushes herself. We're all mad at Trudy for what she did, and the fact she was trying to get Jess to back her up, fucks with my head. There should have been no reason for Jess to even consider entertaining the idea, let alone keep quiet about it. I know Red hasn't actually tried to talk to Luna about it yet, but she didn't say anything at all.

Shaking my head, I glance to Parker, who is still running on the treadmill. Kai is the only one not here, wanting to spend some time with his sister.

Grabbing a bottle of water, I down half of it in one go, glancing at the clock. "Ten minutes, baby girl," I call out, distracting her, which leaves her open for Roman to get her around the waist, dropping her to the floor.

"Fuck, Oscar," she grumbles from the mat, but Roman smiles at me.

"Thanks, man." Dropping on top of her, he touches his lips to Luna's, who doesn't resist at all. She can thank me later.

"Hey, Parker, wanna make out too? My lips are lonely," I shout to him across the room, but he just gives me the finger. "I'll just play with myself then." I groan, and his head whips around lightning fast, making me grin. I just give him the finger back, take that, asshole. I wonder if I look that good in loose grey shorts hanging off my hips? Who am I kidding, of course I do.

The door creaks open, and Red pops her head around the door. I try to glare at her, but it's pointless, we're all too damn soft on her. She looks straight to Luna until she sees her beneath Roman, then her eyes glance anywhere else.

"Are you here for the show?" I ask, and she runs her hands down her thighs.

"I'm here to support Luna," her voice is surprisingly full of confidence. She takes the seat beside me, looking me straight in my eyes. "I know I didn't tell Luna what Trudy was asking me to do, but don't underestimate my loyalty to her." Her eyes stray to Luna, who is still grinding against Roman. "She is one of the most important people in my life, Oscar. She was taken by her own mother, who she had to kill, and has since been attacked in The Tunnel and The Slums." Her fiery eyes turn back to mine. "So, I'm sorry if it wasn't at the top of my fucking list, but I was worried she wasn't coming back," she snaps, leaving me to gape at her in surprise.

Well then.

"Okay," I finally manage to say, making her look at me, confused.

"Okay?"

"Yeah, okay. I believe you," I respond, watching as Roman helps Luna up off the mat.

"As simple as that?"

"I'm not a parrot, Jessikins." I give her a bored look, and she shakes her head at me, a soft smile playing on her lips.

"Thanks, Ozzie," she murmurs, nudging my arm with hers.

Roman throws a towel at Luna as she comes to stand in front of us, dripping with sweat and giving Roman her sexy eyes. Hot as fuck. I can see her Pac-man tattoo peeking out just above her sports bra, and goosebumps spread all over my skin, just like every other time I catch sight of it.

Not wanting to be outdone, I grab a bottle of water from beside me, unscrew the cap, and hold it out to her. Smiling down at me, she takes it from my hands.

"Are you two good now?" she asks, tilting the bottle between Jess and me, making me frown. Seeing the question in my eyes, she takes a seat on my lap, my arm instantly wrapping around her waist, as she sips her water before continuing. "Red and I talked it out in the car, making sure we fully understood each other. She then bet me twenty bucks that she would have to explain herself to you too."

My jaw drops, is she for real? I look to Jess, who shrugs unapologetically at me.

"I can see your brain thinking over whether you should be insulted or not," Jess says, and I raise an eyebrow. "You shouldn't, but you just don't want to admit it." She winks at me as Luna kisses my head.

Roman grins down at her words, squeezing her shoulder, showing her the support she always shows us. I can't even fucking argue, so I don't intend to.

Just as Parker steps off the treadmill, the door to the gym swings open. Conor Starker steps in, followed by Trudy and Aiden behind her. Conor's facial expression doesn't change at all as he takes in his surroundings, while Trudy looks nervously at Luna, and Aiden glares at Roman.

Luna stands to her feet, slowly moving toward Trudy, and no one moves. Just as Luna nears her, Aiden steps in front of his sister protectively, making me rise to my feet too.

"You don't get to fucking kill her," he grunts out, and Luna laughs, raising her eyebrow at him.

Trudy steps around her brother, coming to his side and making Luna shift her position. As she goes to open her mouth, Luna swings her arms back and punches her straight in the face, watching her drop to the floor. She hits her right on her cheekbone, so there's no blood, but there is going to be a black eye in the morning.

"Who said anything about killing anyone?" Luna huffs out, crouching down to Trudy's level.

I try to adjust myself privately, but the shake of Parker's head beside me tells me he caught it. It's not my fault our wife is so fucking hot when she's angry.

Luna

I shake my hand out, enjoying the throb that pulses through my hand. Crouching down before Trudy, I rest my arms on my thighs. I'm surprised when she doesn't stay down, instead rising to her knees before me, dropping her hand from her cheek, as if preparing for the next hit.

Why is she doing that? Openly taking what she expects me to throw at her. I glance at Red, who nods ever so slightly, and I sigh.

"Get up."

She does a double-take at me, making sure she heard me right, as I stand to my feet. Conor stares at me with a raised eyebrow, but I don't miss his clenched hands by his sides. While Aiden openly glares over my shoulder.

"I said, get up," I repeat, when she's still gaping up at me. Quickly scrambling to her feet, she looks at me nervously. "Conor, go and get her an ice pack before her face swells too much," I murmur, catching the surprise on his face before he turns and leaves without question. "Aiden, I don't know what you're glaring at, but your frown is giving me a fucking headache."

He sighs as he glances at me from the corner of his eye. Shaking his head, he walks over to Red and the guys sitting on the benches. "Hi Jessica, long time no see. Why don't you extract yourself from Roman and sit with me?" There's a slight growl in his undertone, but I don't have time to deal with the usual bullshit with him and Roman.

Glancing over my shoulder, Red looks like a deer caught in the headlights as she glances between the two of them. Roman is still standing beside her, his hand resting on her shoulder from when he was comforting her earlier, while Aiden glares at him.

The confusion on Oscar's and Parker's faces likely match mine, but we haven't got time for petty shit like this. "Aiden, either sit down and shut up, or leave, you aren't helping," Trudy mutters, and he sighs dramatically as he takes a seat beside Red on the bench.

"I was fucking sitting there," Oscar grouches, waving his hands around in protest, but Aiden just shrugs his shoulders.

"On your feet, lose your seat." Aiden grins back at him, leaving Oscar to glare at him.

I shake my head at them, we're getting completely off topic, so I turn back to Trudy, as she stands before me. Red said she is worth listening to, so this is her one and only chance.

Conor steps in with what looks like a frozen bag of peas wrapped in a towel, handing it off to Trudy, who smiles in thanks.

"I want the fucking truth, and if I ask you a question, you answer. Understood?" She nods frantically, wincing as the cloth touches her already bruising cheek. "Tell me what the hell happened?"

She looks around at us all for a moment before taking a deep breath, trying to relax her nerves. "So, after you and Kai came to the tents to set up the cameras, Barbette Dietrichson showed up. Apparently, she had video footage of Aiden and I coming over to your room the day we discussed setting up a spot at the party for you to get Brett.

She also watched Kai set the camera up in the tree, and wanted to know why."

She looks behind me, and I follow her gaze to Aiden, who nods encouragingly to her, his hands clasped together as he leans forward on his knees. "Tell them, Tru. You promised," he murmurs, and l look back at her.

"I told her I didn't know what she was talking about. That you and I were friends, but she wouldn't believe it." Her hands start to shake as she tries to find the right words. "Then Rico, the member of The Ring, showed up." I watch as she gulps, her hand coming to her chest. "I'm still waiting for him to come back and finish what he started. Now he knows I didn't do everything they asked me to do," she whimpers, tears forming in her eyes.

What the fuck did he do to her? The pained, haunted look in her eyes has me trying to console her a little. "He's dead, Trudy. He won't be returning."

Her eyes shoot to mine, and when she only sees the truth in my words, she breaks down, the ice pack in her hands dropping to the ground. Face in her hands, she sobs as Conor slowly puts his arm around her. I want answers, but I can see she needs a minute.

"When did this happen?" Conor asks.

"In The Slums, I watched my father do it over the camera feed," I answer, and he simply nods in response.

"The only camera feed I saw was when Rico put a bounty on Parker's head. The rest of the time, I was knee-deep in dead bodies," Conor responds.

I glance at Parker, checking he's okay with the mention of his father, and he offers a small smile in reassurance. Although, I can still see the concern in his eyes for whatever he did to Trudy. Finally having the strength to carry on, Trudy clears her throat.

"He, erm, he was quite forceful in his mission, to get me to help, and I was too weak," she whispers, swiping her hands at her cheeks. "But, uh, he wanted me to help catch you off guard, and he knew my bloodline is in Science. So, he wanted some paralysis stim shots, because the one's they'd been banking on, hadn't come through."

Oscar growls behind me, knowing it was his assignment they were waiting on. I look at him, but Parker is whispering in his ear, trying to calm him already.

"We weren't paralyzed, Trudy," I murmur, confused. "We weren't far from the Academy before we were awake again."

"I know," she sniffs, her face blotchy and red. "I gave

them vitamin shots instead. I knew I wasn't strong enough to go against them, but you are."

Holy shit.

I nod, letting her words wash over me. "Okay, you guys can leave," I say, believing her words. "I don't trust you, but I believe you."

She nods, wrapping her arms around herself as Conor steps back. Not needing to be told twice, she heads for the door, Aiden slowly passing me to follow.

"Trudy, can I ask what Rico did?" Parker asks from behind me, making her stop. Turning to look at him, her usually blue eyes are almost black.

"You seem like a sweet guy, Parker Steele. Rico has tainted enough of us already, I won't add to your pain, this is my burden to carry." With that, she turns and leaves.

Fuck. It must have caused irreversible damage to her soul.

KC KEAN

THIRTY

Luna

We've been back at Featherstone Academy for two weeks. Two fucking weeks, and Totem still hasn't shown his face. My irritation is growing as the situation continues to drag out. I can feel the tension building, and that's likely what he wants. Let us fall into a false sense of security, so that he can catch us by surprise.

We've moved one of Roman's sofas into my room so we can fit Red and Mia in comfortably and watch a movie. I can't seem to focus on the screen though, I need to do something, anything to keep my hands busy.

I can't imagine how Mia must feel, she hasn't left Ace

block since we've arrived. Only coming to our room to hang out or staying with Bryce and Rafe in Parker's old room. She's working hard to avoid her father at all costs, even though Kai says he is desperate to see her, their father is at least respecting Mia's wishes for now.

Mia and Red are whispering on the sofa beside me, likely coming up with girly shit they can force me to do. Since meeting each other, that's all they have done. If they force me into one more mani/pedi sleepover with chick flicks, I'll scream.

Roman and Kai are relaxing on the other sofa, while Parker and Oscar are down at the gym. Deciding I need to get out of here, to try and shake the agitation from my bones, I jump to my feet. "I'm going to go out and clean Dot," I announce, the girls ignore me and the guys look at me with a frown.

"You did that last weekend," Roman states, but I roll my eyes.

"And? She gets dusty down in the garage. Besides, I can't just sit here, it's driving me fucking crazy. I've already been to the gym this morning, and you've put a ban on going down twice," I moan, and he raises his eyebrows at me.

"Princess, I'll go down if you want me to *go down*." His eyes rake over me, and I get the innuendo. Acehole.

Rolling my eyes, I pretend I didn't hear him. "Yeah, yeah, I know. Overworking my body won't help," I say in a monotone voice, already knowing what he's about to say.

"Do you want me to come down with you, Sakura?" Kai asks, and I shake my head.

"No, you're okay, but thank you for asking, handsome." Stepping in front of him, I lean over to kiss his head, but he tilts his head back to kiss me too. Our soft, sweet kiss turns heated the moment his hand touches my waist, but gagging noises from Mia and Red ruin the moment.

Kai glares at them as I step back, only to be pulled into Roman's lap instead. "Kiss me too, princess," he whispers against my lips, and I can't say no to him. His hands on my ass pull me closer to him, my legs on either side of his hips, grinding me against the growing length in his pants. Since I'm only wearing a long band tee as a dress, I feel every inch of him.

"Eww, get a room," Mia cries out, giggling along with Red.

"We have got a room, you just happen to be sitting in it," Roman groans, but I smile down at him as I try to stand. "Since we can't train, fight or fuck," his glare aimed at Mia and Red. "How about you tattoo me, princess?" he asks, and I freeze.

Smiling up at me, he brushes a loose strand of hair from my face as I look him in the eyes. "For real?" His simple nod in response is all I need. Standing, he lets me go, taking my hand. I don't hang around, pulling him into our bedroom and slamming the door shut behind us.

As I lean my back against the door, excitement builds inside of me. I watch as he walks into the closest. He steps back into the room moments later with my black case, filled with my equipment. Roman places the case at the side of the bed and stares expectantly at me.

"Do you have any idea of what you want?" I ask, my fingers itching to paint his skin again. I loved marking him with my bloodline emblem, but this feels even more personal since he's the one asking.

"I do." He moves over to my bedside table, and the second he picks the object up, my heart starts to pound in my chest. Turning to face me, he holds it in the air, a soft smile playing on his lips. "I want you to tattoo a peacock on the inside of my right forearm."

I nod slowly, unable to form words at his request, I feel

too raw. Sitting down beside the suitcase, I methodically start preparing everything I need. I send Roman to grab a few bottles of water and a chair from the kitchen. Bringing the nightstand closer, I take a moment to calm myself. The peacock brooch lays beside me on the bed, and my fingers run along the little green and blue gemstones.

Roman silently enters the room again, getting comfortable on the bed as I shift into the chair, drawing out a quick sketch. I show him my template, and his face lights up. Holding his forearm just right, I transfer the sketch onto his skin. I shake my hands out, calming the excitement that still runs through my veins.

"Ready?"

"Always, for you, princess."

I roll my eyes at him. "That's some cheesy shit I'd expect from Oscar, but from Roman the brooding Acehole? Never," I say with a smile, and he grins back at me.

"What can I say? You bring out my cheesy side."

Shaking my head, I line the small ink cups up on the nightstand and pick up the gun. Looking him in the eyes one more time, I get to work. Getting lost in the flow of the art and the buzz of the machine, I mark his perfect skin.

While the gun glides across his skin, I can't stop

the question that comes to mind. "Why a full back skull tattoo?"

I feel his eyes cast over my face, but I don't lift my gaze from his arm. "It's my bloodline. The Riveras are known as the grim reapers of Featherstone. I just always wanted a back tattoo and decided to combine the two," he murmurs, and his words surprise me.

Lifting the gun from his skin, I meet his gaze, noting the hint of concern in his eyes as he tries to read my reaction. I let the small smile naturally take over my lips as I get back to his tattoo.

"So I've had a kiss with death and lived to tell the tale, huh?"

There is a slight pause, but I feel his body relax. "This is one of the reasons I love you so much, princess. Always accepting me, no matter what."

"I love you too, baby." My eyes flicker to his again as the words fall from my lips before we fall back into a comfortable silence.

I don't know how much time passes, but he holds perfectly still the entire time, as I go through detail after detail to replicate the brooch as best as I can. Finally, leaning back, I look at my work. The head of the peacock sits just under his elbow, with its elegant green and blue feathers stretching out across his forearm, down to his wrist.

"Princess, it's fucking beautiful," he whispers in awe, and I smile up at him. "Thank you."

"No, thank you." I sigh, looking into his eyes. "For not giving up on me when I wanted to push you away. For putting me first every single time. You were supposed to be a quick fuck in the ring, then like an amateur, I went and fell in love." The smile on his face is full of admiration. "Then came all the secrets, and fucked up shit, and you're still here. Where I want… no, where I *need* you to be."

Using his free hand, he cups my chin, tilting my head back to bring my lips to his. It's the sweetest, softest kiss he's ever given me. My skin flushes at his touch.

"I love you, Luna," he mutters against my lips, making my heart soar. "Now clean me up, so I can show off this masterpiece to the others."

"I love you, too," I answer automatically, before cleaning him up. The air around us is filled with giddiness. No angst, or fear, or anxiety, just love and happiness. I want more of this feeling, with all of my Aceholes.

As I start to get rid of the used materials, he plants a

kiss on my lips and heads for the door. Perfect timing has Oscar swinging it open before he gets there.

"Hey, shit for brains. Where's my baby… Holy shit, did Luna do that?" he shouts, his eyes fixed on Roman's new tattoo, who's grinning like a Cheshire cat.

"Hell yeah, she did," he says with a wink at me, before walking around Oscar to show the others.

Oscar's gaze finally meets mine as he remains standing in the same spot, shock on his face. "I want one too, baby girl," he pouts, walking toward me.

"You want what? A tattoo?"

"Yeah. All of the others have received personalized tattoos from you. Except me." Dramatically dropping to his knees in front of me in only his grey shorts. I heat at his touch, as he trails his fingers up the back of my thighs. He slowly lifts his face, his big blue eyes looking up at me, my fingers running through his hair.

"What did you have in mind?"

"Whatever you're offering to draw, I don't care," he responds instantly.

Pretending to think, I grin down at him. "How about 'Property of Luna', right here on your forehead?" I ask, stroking my finger across the spot.

"If that's what you want, baby girl, I'm in."

I frown down at my crazy Acehole. "I'm joking, but I think I have the perfect idea. If you're up for a surprise?"

Oscar

The excitement in her eyes is hard to say no to. I wouldn't ever say no to her, even if she was mad. She can do whatever she pleases, as long as her mark is on me, that's all I want. The bloodline doesn't really count, it's an expectation, a formality of a Featherstone marriage, to wear the emblem. I want something on my skin that she chose to put there, from her heart.

"Tell me where to sit, and I'm all yours, baby girl."

She taps a spot on the bed, taking a seat in the chair facing it, and I sit across from her like an obedient little dog. Smiling at me, she gathers a few of her things scattered around. "Give me a few minutes to get everything fresh for you, and we'll be good to go."

I watch her ass sway as she leaves the room, leaving me to wonder what surprise she has in mind. She's quick to come back in, heading straight to her kit, and going through the process of setting everything up again.

"Last chance to back out before you give me free rein to brand you," she murmurs, making me smile.

"I'm all set, surprise me, Luna." I love trusting her. Knowing she would never do anything to hurt me fills me with so much happiness, it's indescribable.

"Close your eyes," she whispers, and I'm happy to oblige. "Don't open them until I say so, and no peeking, okay?" I nod silently, trying not to move with the anticipation building inside of me.

I hear the hum of the needles moving, but she doesn't touch me for what feels like ages. What is she even doing? When I'm just about to see what's going on, she shouts, "Oscar Steele-O'Shay, don't you even think about it!"

I instantly clamp my eyes shut, but I can't hold in the grin at the sound of our combined surnames. The sound of the gun stops for a few minutes, but I refuse to open my eyes, not wanting to get in trouble again. When it starts up again, she takes my hand.

"Get ready for the little prick," she murmurs, and I chuckle.

"You'll never have to worry about a little prick again,

baby girl."

I can see her eyes roll in my mind, as the needle pierces the skin on top of my finger. I don't know where I expected her to tattoo me, but my hand definitely catches me by surprise. Within minutes she's done, and I'm left a little confused with how quick she's finished.

"You can open your eyes now," she whispers, emotion recognizable in the lilt of her voice.

Slowly opening my eyes, I look to her first, seeing uncertainty in her eyes.

"Baby girl, what's wrong?"

"Nothing. I just, it seemed like a good idea at the time, and now I'm worried you won't like it." I frown at her, and she nods down to my hand, still in hers.

There across my fingers are small roman numerals 'XXII'. What do they mean? That's when she flips our hands over, showing me hers. Just above her wedding ring, the family heirloom from her grandmother, she has 'VIII' freshly inked into her skin.

"It's the date we first met," she breathes out, barely a whisper. "August twenty-second," she continues pointing to her finger first, then mine. "After I pushed Wren in the water fountain, you picked up my I.D. box. I remember thinking you were hot as hell, and then you opened that damn mouth of yours." She smiles up at me, the memory playing between us, as I continue to gape at her.

Glancing down at her hand again, I look at the black ink, as it slowly dawns on me where the location of the tattoo is. Flipping our hands over, so mine rests on top, the numeric symbols boldly holding my attention. Moving our wrists again, I look up at her, and she's already looking right at me.

"You tattooed it on your ring finger," is all I can finally say, and she nods. "And on my ring finger."

"Do you…"

I crush my lips to hers, trying to convey how she makes me feel. It takes her a moment, but her lips respond just as forcefully to mine. Pulling her toward me, flipping her on to her back, my hands find their way under her long t-shirt dress. My brain malfunctions when I feel her bare pussy beneath me. She hisses as my fingers stroke over her clit.

Leaning back slightly, I pull my lips from hers so I can pull her dress over her head.

"I'm taking this as a sign that you like it," she murmurs, and I grin down at her.

"Luna, I fucking love it," I say, quickly standing to drop

my shorts to the floor, my cock hard, and aimed straight at her already. As I crawl back onto the bed, she beckons me closer, her legs wrapping around my waist. Her mouth calls for mine, and as I drop down to brush my lips against hers, my cock teases at her entrance, she flips us over.

My surprise is overpowered by the way her pussy slips down my length, slowly taking every inch of me. "Holy fuck, Luna," I pant. "Foreplay, we need foreplay," I chant, as she stretches my arms above my head.

"Have you felt how wet I am from simply inking my guys? I don't need foreplay," she whispers in my ear as she grinds against me.

"Fuck, baby girl. I do, otherwise I'm going to explode." The fire in her eyes burns brighter as she leans up, my cock sinking even deeper inside of her.

"Good," she moans, rocking against me. "Show me how I affect you too."

Her hands go to my chest, using me as leverage as she slowly lifts up, slamming straight back down. The cords in my neck tighten as I groan deeply, fighting against the pleasure taking over me, gripping her hips like my life depends on it.

"Luna, I swear to god. You need to stop for a damn

minute, before I cum in less than sixty fucking seconds," I grind out, but she just moans louder. Rocking back and grinding against my cock again and again.

"But Oscar, I've got all this pent-up need inside of me." Her moves become erratic as my cock swells inside of her. Fuck. She's driving me crazy. I refuse to come before she does. Bringing my hand to our joined bodies, I stroke my thumb against her pussy, her body jolting at the touch.

Catching sight of her small Pac-man tattoo, my body moves on its own accord. Sitting up, our position shifts slightly, as my lips find her ink.

Pinching her throbbing clit, I look up as she shatters around me, wave after wave of her orgasm rolling through her. The way her core tightens around me leaves me no choice but to join her, my cock slamming up into her as we fall off the cliff together.

Luna's body goes limp above me, her breasts pushing up against my chest, and I love the feel of my girl against me. Slowly holding her up, I slide up to lean my back against the headboard, turning her to lie against me, her back to my front.

Coated in sweat, her hair sticking to her face, she looks back at me with the most beautiful smile on her face that

I've ever seen.

"I swear to god, if you tell anyone you milked me that quickly, you'll be in deep trouble," I fake growl, and she grins up at me as she laces our fingers together.

I look down at our joined hands, our tattoos side by side, and my heart feels like it could explode.

"I love you, Oscar."

"I love you too, Luna."

We lay quietly together for a moment, enjoying the serene bubble we're in, when she grumbles. "I need to move, I'm starting to make a mess."

"Nah, don't worry about it, baby girl, we're laying in Roman's spot anyway."

THIRTY ONE

Luna

My back hits the mat as Roman pins me down. His chest glistens with sweat, and his shoulders rise and fall with heavy movement while he tries to catch his breath. He grins down at me, mischief in his eyes as he pins my hands and gets comfortable sitting on my thighs. I'm too exhausted to try and get out of his hold. We've easily been down here training in the Ace block gym for over an hour, matching each other blow for blow.

"I love watching your chest heave as you lay beneath me," he murmurs, heat in his eyes as he looks me over.

"I love that you're always willing to go toe-to-toe with

me, and not treat me like a delicate flower when it comes to the mat," I respond honestly. No matter what, he always pushes me, treating me like the equal opponent I am.

"You're the owner of my delicate flower," he says with a grin and a wink. "But you, my wife, are a warrior, and I love you because of it." Leaning down, Roman places a gentle kiss to my lips, my back arching off the mat needing to be closer to him, as he suddenly bites down on my bottom lip. I can't stop the moan that leaves my lips, but my joy is short lived when he jumps off me and stalks across the training ring to grab his water.

"You fucking tease." I scowl, which only makes him grin wider as he rolls a bottle of water toward me.

"For you to cool down, princess."

"I'll remember this, Acehole."

"Don't be dramatic, princess, it's almost time for us to have dinner with everyone. As much as I want you naked and stretched out beneath me, we'll be late, and I'd like to keep my balls, thank you very much. Maria likes me, I'm not ruining that," he says, holding a hand out to help me to my feet. I'm in agreement with his response, but I still roll my eyes at the fact our fun was cut short.

The sound of the gym door opening catches our

attention, and West steps in wearing sweatpants and a hoodie with a winter hat and headphones on his head. I take a big gulp of water as he lifts the headphones from his head and smiles at us.

"Hey, moon, Roman," West says with a smile, and I'm surprised by the fact I'm happy to see him, realizing I've missed his presence.

Dropping the water bottle at my feet, I jump down from the ring and make my way toward him.

"Hey, West." I smile, wrapping my arms around his neck, and it takes him a minute to respond to my hug, gently placing his hands in the middle of my back.

"Is this normal?" he asks, surprise in his voice, as Roman chuckles.

"She's full of surprises, aren't you, princess?"

I hum in response as I step back and look over my shoulder at my man.

"I guess you guys should have a minute. Walk her up for me, okay?" Roman says, as he approaches, kissing me on the head as he passes.

"Uhh, you're okay with that?" West frowns, confused by Roman's relaxed demeanor, and he shrugs in response.

"She's my wife, West, that changes everything." It

warms my heart hearing his words and seeing the love shine in his eyes at me. "But you guard her with your life, or I'll kill you." Without a backward glance, he's gone, leaving West to gape at the closed door.

"Who the fuck was that, and where is Roman Rivera?" I chuckle at him as I take a seat on the benches by the wall, patting the spot beside me.

"So, wife, huh?"

"Yeah," I sigh happily.

"It suits you. Even Roman apparently," he murmurs, and when I look in his eyes I'm glad to see only happiness there.

"It feels right too," I whisper, slipping my ring back on, loving the weight of it on my finger.

"Well, I'm glad my moon is alive and happy. We just need to get our hands on Totem, so you can actually enjoy it all." I nod in agreement as we sit side-by-side in comfortable silence. Any negativity I felt toward West because of the secrets that surrounded me are gone. He has shown nothing but support and care toward me, even when I didn't always understand it.

"Thank you," I breathe out, resting my head on his shoulder, and he wraps his arm around me comfortingly.

"For what?" he asks, a hint of confusion in his voice.

"For everything. For always being there for me as a child. For never giving up and finding me again. It always blew my mind how we became instant friends when you showed up at Rafe's gym, and it was because even though I didn't remember you, my mind knew I could trust you." I lean back to meet his gaze, and he's already smiling at me. "And thank you for being here right now, for finding me when I was attacked and helping me the best you could through all this shit."

"Anytime, Luna. That's what friends are for, right?"

"Right," I agree, rising to my feet. "Now, we need to find you a girlfriend because I want you to feel this level of happiness too," I say with a wink, and it's his turn to roll his eyes at me.

"I do not need your help, I can find a girl all on my own. I might have even done so already." He calls out over his shoulder as he heads for the door.

"Who? What? When? Tell me all about her," I call out, but he shakes his head.

"One day, moon, but for now, let's not keep your men waiting, shall we?"

"Remind me why we're having dinner here again?" Roman groans from our bedroom as I step into a pair of black skinny jeans and a band tee I stole off Kai. Bypassing my boots, I roll on my fluffy slipper socks, feeling comfortable and relaxed.

"Because you went all alpha ape-shit on everyone about Luna's safety," Oscar shouts back, which only makes Roman curse under his breath.

Stepping into the bedroom, I watch as he flops back on the bed with an exaggerated sigh. "What's wrong, baby?" I ask, moving closer to him.

"I just want you all to ourselves, I can cope with sharing you with the guys, but I can't do naughty things to you when others are here," he pouts, making me giggle.

"Did I hear naughty things? I'm down for that," Parker says as he leans against the door frame with a grin on his face, his hungry eyes looking between us.

"Don't encourage him," I mutter, moving toward him as a knock sounds at the front door. They both groan, knowing they're definitely out of luck. So, I lift my t-shirt up to my neck, flashing my breasts in the black see-through bra I'm wearing and wink. Before they can respond, I stick my tongue out, drop my top, and brush past Parker quickly, so he can't stop me.

Kai holds the door open for Dad, Bryce, Maria, and Juliana, who are thankfully all dressed casually too. Dad smiles wide when his eyes catch mine, and we instinctively gravitate toward each other.

"Hey, darling." He wraps his arm around my shoulder, rubbing his knuckles against my head and messing my hair up. I try to whack him away, but we both end up laughing as he tries to get me in a headlock. Who the hell is this fun-loving guy? I've missed this side of him.

"You two were always play fighting, can we not act like civilized adults now?" Maria calls out, but I hear the humor in her voice. Finally separating, Bryce stands before us, his arms instantly wrapping around us. I love the feel of their embrace, their love, and the sense of family they offer.

"Let me see my niece," Juliana whines, pulling me from their hold. She links her arm through mine and pulls me toward the kitchen, Maria right behind us.

Kai and Parker moved another dining table into the kitchen, so there was enough space for us all to sit together.

Nothing matches, since the added furniture has come from Roman's old room, but it serves its purpose, and the covered plates already set have my mouth watering from the workout earlier.

Glancing over my shoulder, Bryce and Dad follow in behind us, then in step my Aceholes and somehow my heart manages to feel fuller. I take a seat in the middle, my back to the wall, Roman and Kai sitting to my left and Parker and Oscar to my right. From left to right, Juliana, Maria, Bryce, and Rafe sit across from us, and it surprises me how natural it all feels.

Maria opens a bottle of wine, pouring a glass for herself before handing it to Juliana. All the while, staring at my guys.

"So, you four men are now Steeles," she breathes, her face void of any emotion as she looks them over with a stern gaze. The silence stretches out amongst us, and I start to worry when she smiles wide.

"Oh shit, she's going to say it," Rafe chuckles, and I look to him in confusion.

"Mother, do not…" Bryce starts, but she lifts her hand to stop him from continuing.

"Only men with big dicks can be Steele's, you know."

Rafe, Juliana, and Maria burst out laughing, as Bryce cringes, and the rest of us stare at her in shock.

"We do not want to know. This is my Meu Tesouro we are talking about," Bryce exclaims, and I chuckle along with Rafe.

"Aww, well, I was born to be a Steele, Mrs. Steele," Oscar chimes in with a wink, and the table roars in laughter, all except Bryce and Rafe, who realize too late they don't need to know about my sex life.

"Nope. Stop the conversation right there. You're always the trouble maker," Rafe says, pointing a finger at Oscar.

Parker squeezes my thigh, and in this moment, with all the crazy going on around us, I feel like I'm home.

THIRTY TWO

Roman

If Kai doesn't shut his fucking alarm off, I'm going to break the damn thing. It's too dark outside for me to be awake right now. When I hear the tapping of a keyboard, but the alarm still continues to ring, I pry my eyes open and glare at him.

Lying at the other end of the bed, with Luna, Parker, and Oscar between us, I see the frown on his face from the glow of the laptop. My body tenses instantly, my gut telling me something is wrong. I don't want to alert the others if it's actually nothing, so I slip out of my side of the bed and silently throw on some sweatpants and a t-shirt, before coming to sit beside him.

He doesn't acknowledge me, he's lost in whatever is happening on the screen, so I try and wait patiently for him to respond. When his frown deepens, and his tapping gets faster, I can't take it anymore.

"Kai, what's going on?"

He lifts his gaze from the screen, as if he's just noticing me, and shakes his head. "The camera feed from the main gates has cut off," he murmurs, just as his phone starts to vibrate from the bedside table. He rushes to grab it, the screen flashing with Rafe's name.

"Hey. Yes, I'm seeing that. Are you sure?" He jumps from the bed, raking a hand through his hair. "We'll be ready in five." Throwing the phone down, he presses the internal system to blackout the windows and turns on the lights. Frantically searching for some clothes, he still tells me nothing.

"Kai, what's…"

"Rafe thinks it's time, he believes Totem is here," he rushes out. "Help me wake them." Pointing in the direction of the bed, I look at Luna and the guys.

"Shit." I have to shake my head to wake myself up a little more. Of course, they're coming in the night, when we're fucking tired and completely caught off-guard.

"Can you guys shut up? I can't sleep," Oscar grunts. "And someone turn that fucking alarm off." Curling himself more around Luna, his lips brush her shoulder as he tries to settle back down, and he goes back to ignoring us.

"Oscar, we need to get up, there's been a security breach," Kai says, but Oscar doesn't respond.

Parker and Luna both stir at all the noise, and I lean over, giving their shoulders a nudge, encouraging them awake. When that doesn't work, I clap my hands, giving up with the soft approach.

"Security breach, bitches! We think Totem could be on campus. Now get your asses out of bed."

Luna instantly sits up, wiping sleep from her eyes as she processes my words. Without saying anything at all, she gets out of bed and walks straight into the closet, while Parker and Oscar slowly start to come round. Kai finally shuts the damn alarm off, allowing my brain to function a little more.

Strolling back into the bedroom, wearing a pair of black pants, a long-sleeved black top, and her combat boots, Luna is ready to go. Parker and Oscar finally start to catch up, pulling themselves out of bed. They're going to need to move quicker than this if we plan on fucking defending ourselves.

"Good morn—" Oscar goes to wrap his arms around Luna, but she places her finger on his lips, stopping his approach.

"I need coffee," she grumbles, turning on her heels and leaving the room.

"Hurry the fuck up and get dressed," I grunt, following after her.

Stepping into the kitchen, I find Kai already there. When did he even leave the bedroom? Shit, I need some coffee too. The kitchen table, and the wall behind it, are covered in all of Kai's tech set-up. Six monitors come to life as he powers everything on, tapping away at lightning speed.

What is going on? I need more information. I feel helpless standing around waiting for something to happen. Swiping a hand down my face, I watch as Luna pours herself a cup of coffee. Grabbing a mug from the cupboard, I do the same, hopeful it will make me more alert.

Just as I bring the steaming hot coffee to my lips, a boom sounds from outside.

I watch as every single one of Kai's screens flickers to black, and all the electricity cuts out around us. "They've blown the main electrical panels," Kai murmurs, as I rush to the living room to glance through the window.

Darkness fills the surrounding area from where I can see, but a flicker of orange lights the night sky, and that feeling in my gut feels stronger than ever.

"Another explosion and fire? I'm not over the last one," Oscar frowns, stepping up beside me as he runs his fingers through his hair.

Kai's phone starts to ring again, and I look to him as he answers it, not even glancing at the screen to see who it is.

"Hello. What? No, she's with you." I watch as the color slowly drains from his face. His eyes fill with despair as his frown lines deepen. "No. No, no, no, no."

"Kai, what's going on? Look at me." Luna stands before him, hands cupping his face as she helplessly tries to understand what on earth is going on.

Looking around at all of us, his phone slips from his hands, bouncing across the floor.

"Totem's already here, and he has Mia."

Luna

"What? How?"

Kai looks down at the phone on the floor hopelessly. The tightness in his jaw is a complete contrast to the pain in his eyes. His head and heart are at war with each other, one wanting to go in gun blazing, while the other wants to assess the situation to make precise decisions.

Grabbing the phone, I hear Rafe calling for Kai on the other end. "Hey, Dad, what's going on?"

"Luna! Please tell me Kai is still there? We don't understand the full situation right now, and I don't want him charging into dangerous territory."

My hand instantly reaches out to squeeze Kai's hand as he stands before me, lost in his own mind. "He's here, but we need to act fast. How do we know he has her?" I ask, trying to stay calm.

"We couldn't sleep, so Bryce and I were down at the gym, and when we got back to our room, the door was ajar. Mia was gone, and there's a small totem figurine on the coffee table," he murmurs, and my heart breaks. Everything we have all done and sacrificed to keep this man at bay, and he still finds a way to tear us apart.

"What about the security cameras and the guards? We need to cover every inch of Ace, figure out where the fuck he got in, and how, without us knowing until it was too late."

I squeeze Kai's hand tighter, forcing him to meet my gaze. "I want everyone up and alert. We're wasting time. We'll start from the roof and make our way down while you wake the others." Not wanting to listen to him argue with me about this, I put the phone down, throwing it to the sofa beside us. "Kai, I need you to focus. I need your brains, we'll be the brute force when the time comes, but let's get a better understanding first, okay?"

He surprises me when he nods instantly. "Okay. I'll get all the tech rebooted with my emergency generator. Luna and Roman, start at the roof. Oscar, alert Red's room, we need to keep her safe, then join them. Parker, I could use an extra set of eyes."

My body hums with adrenaline, feeling the determination come through stronger in his voice the more he gives out orders. Not wanting to waste any more time, I lean up on my tiptoes, kissing him hard but quick on the lips.

Stepping back, I'm already heading straight for the

door when I hear him call out. "Phone, gun, and blade." Like they're general items to carry with you. Grabbing my hunting blade, already in its sheath, I quickly wrap it around my ankle. Before preparing my handgun, making sure I have enough ammo and flicking the safety off.

Standing by the door ready, I look over my shoulder to find Roman geared up too. Taking a deep breath, I let all my emotions wash away, focusing on the task at hand. A I pull open the door, Roman's hand stops it from swinging any further.

"Princess, let me lead." It's not a question, but the concern in his eyes makes me pause. We need to be focused on what we need to do, he doesn't need the extra worry. So, if that means I let him lead, then that's what we do. I nod, stepping to the side for him to go through the door first.

Raising his gun, he checks both ways before giving me the sign to follow. There isn't a security guard out here like there usually is, and the reason why makes sense as Roman steps into the stairwell. The dead security guard lays across the bottom steps leading up, a thin rope is wrapped around his purple bruised neck, his face still red. Roman leans over him, checking his pulse, and the look in his eyes is all the answer I need.

Moving around him, we jog quickly up the stairs leading to the roof, the emergency fire exit door wide open. Securing the roof, no one's here, but it seems this is where Totem entered and then escaped. I just don't understand how we didn't hear anything.

Turning to head downstairs, Oscar appears in the doorway.

"Nothing?" he asks, and I shake my head. "Rafe's with Kai and Parker. Bryce, Travis, and my father started clearing the building from the ground up."

Fuck. How the hell did he sneak in, take Mia and manage to get out again unseen or un-fucking-heard? Even helicopters make a hell of a lot of noise.

Stepping back inside, I feel my phone vibrate in my pocket. I pull it out, my heart pounding in my chest as Mia's name flashes across the screen. I turn the screen to show the guys, before quickly answering, putting it straight on speakerphone. I don't speak, that's what he wants, to hear the fear in my voice.

"Little moon," he sings, dark and gravelly. "Where are you, my little moon?"

"Where is she, Tony?" I ask, refusing to give him the satisfaction of using his nickname. It's almost funny how his actual name doesn't hold nearly as much terror in comparison.

"She will be given back when I get who I actually came for."

I don't ask who that is, already knowing he means me. Roman growls before me, anger building around us, and I'm only going to add to it.

"Tell me where to go, and I'll be there." His eyes burn mine, the feel of Oscar's just as strong.

"I want you at the Main Hall, alone. I'll know if you're not. Your loved ones might want to head to the library before it burns to the ground with Mia inside. There's probably only five, maybe ten minutes left before it blows completely."

The phone cuts off as I stand frozen in place, staring down at it.

"How can we even trust she'll be there? Luna, I swear, you are not…"

"I know, I know. I think I have a plan, but we're going to need everyone."

Everyone and a fucking miracle.

OUR BLOODLINE

THIRTY THREE

Kai

"Anything?" Rafe murmurs, as he taps away beside me. I don't answer, because I can feel it in my fingertips that we're close. Totem has some tech talent on his side, that's for sure. I'm sitting here trying to hack back into my own damn systems.

"Close," I hear Parker reply as he watches me work. The tension in the room continues to grow as I make the mistake of allowing my emotions to build. What I need to do is keep calm and let my logical brain assess the situation. "In. I'm in!"

Glancing up from the keyboard, I watch the monitors

come to life around us. Dozens of camera feeds reappear, filling the screens. My eyes don't know where to search first, there is so much we need to be on the lookout for.

"Kai, you focus on the two screens in the middle, Parker and I will focus on the ends. Our main focus is looking for Mia, Totem, any of the fucking Dietrichsons, and we are all protective assholes, so when you see Luna, shout."

I nod repeatedly in response as my eyes scan the screens in front of me. Each monitor is linked to four camera feeds, so clicking into each one will give us a better view of what's going on.

A knock sounds at the door, but I can't pull my gaze away. I'm thankful when I hear Rafe move to answer it. Murmurs from the other room let me know he's let them in, but nobody interrupts my search.

"Luna and the guys are up on the roof," Parker mumbles, pulling my gaze to where he's pointing. My eyes instantly see her wavy brown ponytail floating in the breeze, as they all stare down at her phone. The anxiety building in my chest eases slightly at the sight of my Sakura.

Focusing back on the monitors in front of me, I zoom in on the library, smoke billowing from the roof as fire licks the exterior walls. Is that what the explosion was?

Rafe steps up beside me. "It was Maverick. Jess is safe in her room, but he's here to help, West too." I nod, unable to explain how much I appreciate their instant willingness to help. "What's this?" he then asks, zooming in on one of his screens.

I watch as the Main Hall comes into view, fully lit up on the ground floor. John Dietrichson stands on the steps leading up to the entry, a cigarette in hand as he grins down at the phone in his hand. Quickly tapping away on my laptop, I pull up the cameras we have in Barbette Dietrichson's office.

The room fills the screen, Barbette leaning over the desk as she seethes at Wren. I don't have time to flick the audio link-up before Wren storms out of the office, slamming the door behind her. I see the fear, anger, and rage in her eyes, just like it was there when she stood over me, her gun trained in my direction.

Commotion comes from the lounge as I hear Luna with Oscar and Roman. Dragging myself away from the laptop, I follow Parker and Rafe to see what on earth is going on.

Stepping into the lounge, Luna and the guys aren't the only ones here. Maverick, West, Bryce, Reggie, Patrick, and my father all stand before me too. Luna's face is lined with worry, concern etched in her eyes. My feet instantly move me toward her, needing to know what's playing in her mind.

"Sakura," I breathe out, my hands bracing her shoulders as I look down at her.

"Totem wants me to trade myself for Mia."

"No! Fuck, no!" I growl instantly, refusing to entertain such bullshit.

"We have to, Kai," the pain in her eyes sears my soul. "She's in the library."

The library? It's on fire. She's in the burning building. My heart rate kicks up as I look helplessly at Luna. It feels as though the floor is sinking beneath me.

"Kai, I need you to go to the library now." She looks around at the silent room as everyone takes in her words. "Travis, Patrick, Maverick, Bryce, all of you. Go with him, please, we don't have long. Ian already has cars ready to move." They begin to move around us, but I'm frozen in place. "Kai, go."

"But what will you…" She cuts me off with a kiss, her lips feel like heaven against mine.

"I love you, Kai. Don't worry about the rest; get your sister. Go."

Releasing my hold on her, I look to Roman, who nods for me to do as she says. Grabbing a gun off the table, I look at my Sakura once more before rushing from the room.

I race out of Ace in a blur, diving straight into the SUV Ian has running outside, my father and the others right behind me. The tires screech as Ian floors it before the rear door has even been shut. Adrenaline courses through my veins as I try to keep my fear at bay. I watch as the library comes into view, the flames brightening the night sky, and my pulse quickens. We have to find her.

"We will get her out, son. I promise you." I look to my father, his dark eyes filled with despair, matching my own. I can't even manage a nod in response, my mind wandering back to Luna and the guys. I shouldn't have left her without knowing what the full plan was, but I also need to save my sister.

As the SUV slows in front of the library, Maverick quickly opens the door, leading everyone out. "I can't tell where the fire started. I'll enter the front with Kai and Patrick. While Travis and Bryce search the perimeter and enter from the second door to the rear," he says, continuing his approach to the building.

Without question, my father and Bryce take off to the left-hand side of the building, as Maverick tests the door. Watching as it slowly opens, my heart drops. Smoke fills the whole space around us. The high walls filled with books are engulfed in flames as I frantically search for Mia.

"Mia! Mia!" Patrick calls from beside me as he steps further into the space. I still can't process why these people are so willing to help, but I'm thankful they're here.

Moving further into the room, I feel water sprinkle on my face. I try to see where it's coming from, but the thick smoke blocks my view. It's as if the sprinklers have come on, having been activated by the smoke, but the fire continues to roar around it.

"Mia!" I shout, along with the others, but I hear no response as I stand even further in the room. The smoke is starting to burn my throat, my chest heavy from inhaling it. I barely see the desk in front of me, catching my leg on the corner of it as I pass.

I hear my father's voice call out Mia too, but it seems pointless when we're not getting a response. The sound of splintering wood followed by a ground-shaking rumble has me glancing behind us. Watching as one of the supporting beams hits the ground, blocking where we entered, flames torching the doorway.

The red and orange flames are the only light offered to us in the now burnt, black library. I feel lost, slowly sinking into the pits of hell as I choke and splutter on the smoke around us.

"I've found her! Mia! I'm here. Mia!" I hear my dad yell over the roar of the fire. Looking to Maverick and Patrick beside me, a wave of relief washes over us. But now we need to continue in the same direction because we can't leave the same way we came in.

Maverick pulls his arm around, covering his mouth with the inside of his elbow, encouraging us to do the same. Slowly navigating through the room, I hear Patrick cough uncontrollably from behind. Glancing over my shoulder, he drops to his knees, allowing the smoke to consume him. Refusing to let anyone die in here, I force my arm under his, dragging him to his feet.

"I can see the exit," Maverick calls from ahead, as I slowly pull Patrick along with me.

My shoulder screams in pain as I take more and more of Patrick's weight, his body growing limp beside me. My body feels heavy as the smoke surrounds me, forcing me to inhale more with each breath I take. My steps slow, the exit in view, but it feels like an endless tunnel to reach it.

A boom sounds beside me, more wood and debris falling to the floor around us. I can't take anymore, the strain on my shoulder from carrying a now unconscious Patrick, the smoke filling my lungs. I just need to sit down for a minute. It's too fucking warm in here.

My eyes grow weak as I lay Patrick on the floor beside me, black ash smeared all over his face and clothes. Falling to my knees, I barely catch myself on my hands, breaking my fall before my face smashes into the floor.

"Oh no, you don't, son." I hear, but my eyes refuse to open. I feel weightless, my breathing shallow as my feet drag along the floor, the sound of falling wood the only noise in my ears until the heat subsides a little, the chill of the night air teasing my skin.

"Stay with me, Kai. I've got you." My father's voice rings out around me, but I can't find the strength to open my eyes. I need to check on Mia, and my Sakura needs me, but the darkness' pull is too strong. My last thought before it all goes black is of Luna whispering she loves me, and I never said it back.

OUR BLOODLINE

KC KEAN

THIRTY FOUR

Luna

I watch as Kai races out of the door, taking a piece of my heart with him, but he's out of the room before I realize he didn't say I love you back. There is too much shit going on around us right now, but I refuse to die without hearing those words from him. The whole place is going up in smoke, literally, and even when we are on our own turf, Totem still manages to pull the rug out from under our feet.

Feeling a hand rest against my shoulder, I glance back. Rafe stands before me, offering the same comfort he always does, calming me in my moment of need. There is a mixture of trepidation and pride in his eyes, but I know he can see the slight hint of uncertainty on my face.

"Where's Red?" I ask, glancing at Oscar.

"She's in her room. Maverick said there were two guys there he trusted her with. So, he came to help knowing she is safe."

I nod absently, glad there was less for me to worry about. Feeling time slip through my fingers, I can't seem to shake myself out of the frozen state I find myself in. I need to get my shit together and end this now.

"What do we do, Luna?" Parker asks, pulling me from my mind, even though he already knows what the answer will be, from the way I charged down here a moment ago.

"We give him what he wants," I answer simply, and Roman growls.

"He can't always get what he fucking wants, princess! That's not how this shit works. How about I get what I want? Which is for you to be safe!" Oscar nods frantically in agreement, as Rafe and Parker already stand with resigned looks on their faces, knowing what's inevitably going to happen.

Stepping out of Rafe's hold, I plant myself right in front of Roman, chest to chest. I lean my forehead against him, for just a second, feeling the weight of the world on my shoulders. Inhaling his woodsy scent, my hands grip his waist, taking every ounce of strength from him I can. I slowly lift my gaze to his, to see he's already staring down at me.

Feeling his hands pull me tighter against him, I find my voice. "Roman, you know I'll never be able to stand by when someone's life is in danger. That's not me, and you wouldn't love me as fiercely as you do if it were." He sighs, his eyes closing to slits, knowing the truth in my words. "I can feel our future, Rome. It's within arm's reach, our fingertips brushing against the seam. But we're not going to get it with him still breathing, he's going to do whatever it takes to rip us apart. I refuse to let him control us like that."

It feels like he's peering into my eyes, pulling my soul apart piece by piece and trying to decide if he wants to put it back together again. "If anything goes wrong, I'll kill you myself, princess," he whispers, before taking my lips with the most brutal force. All too soon, he steps back, "Let's go," he grinds out, determination in his voice, wanting this to be over with just as much as I do.

Oscar's hands cup my face, touching his lips to mine, drinking me down as if feeding his fire with my own.

Releasing his hold, he winks and storms out after Roman. Rafe shakes his head, following them out of the door, leaving me with my Parker Parker. He smiles softly down at me, tilting my head back gently with his finger under my chin.

"I love every inch of you, angel, but you need to explain on the way over how this is going to go down because that fucker dies, tonight."

Rafe parks the SUV behind the trees facing the Main Hall, headlights off as we're blocked from view, the eerie silence surrounding us. Without a word, I step out of the SUV, walking as quickly as I can toward the stone steps. I can already see John Dietrichson and two bodyguards at the top, but fuck them if they think they're going to scare me.

Taking the steps one at a time, they can see I'm here, so they don't need to accelerate anything over at the library, and I'm alone, just like Totem asked. Dietrichson catches sight of me first, his glare washing right over me as I carry every ounce of confidence I have with each step I take.

"The rebellious bitch finally shows," he taunts, but I don't miss the tightness in his jaw, or the mess of his usually combed grey hair. The two bodyguards stare me down with matching grins on their faces, their leering eyes grazing my skin. Neither of them holds the butt of their gun with caution, completely unfazed by my appearance, underestimating me as always. How fucking refreshing. Clearly, they think they have me backed into a corner, more fool them.

It takes everything within me to smile wide, not rising to his bait, as I breeze right past them. Pushing the double wooden doors open and letting them slam shut behind me, I feel the breeze at my back as they do, gaining Totem's instant attention. He stands on the bottom step of the grand staircase, twirling a knife in the banister.

The grin that takes over his face as he takes me in unsettles me. He's wearing black pants, with a loose-fitted white shirt, unbuttoned to his belly button. His hair gelled back, a gold chain hanging around his neck, and his scar shining with the light. Totem is dressed like an old-school mafia gangster, and it takes a lot of restraint to not roll my eyes at him.

"Mrs. Luna Moon Steele," he calls out, his arms swinging out wide as he jumps off the step, "Has finally arrived." He claps his hands, applauding me with fake glee as he slowly steps closer. "And, I have been waiting for quite some time."

I don't move an inch, refusing to show him the fear his eyes beg for. But I decide silence is on my side right now, he seems the type to want to fill in the quietness surrounding us, and the longer he talks, the more time I have.

"What's the noise for? Oh, the little whore has arrived," Barbette sneers from the open hallway leading to her office. Her usual stylish appearance is on full display in a yellow skirt suit. Yellow, like a fucking canary. She glares at me when she gets no response, her whiny voice ringing through the air as she hits a sickly sweet tone, batting her eyes. "Tony, grab her, and let's go."

"No, no, no, Barbie. I want to share a moment with my little moon first, there is so much to show and tell." He grins between us as she remains standing in the hallway. Rushing to one of the dark wooden coffee tables, with dark leather seats surrounding it, he grabs a remote. I'm too busy staring around me, waiting for the chaos to happen, as sound comes from the monitor.

The television screen flickers to life on the far wall, close to Barbette. It takes me a moment to understand what I'm seeing. My heart instantly feels as though it's breaking in two as I watch the library burn. The surveillance they've set up shows a view of the front of the library. Catching the full view of the building crumbling to the ground.

Kai, I scream internally, but I refuse to let them see me react, maintaining my neutral expression, even though my soul screams to know whether Kai is okay, and if he found Mia in time. I don't see a single person on the screen.

"Come now, little moon, tell me how you feel. Watching as you lose one of your husbands before your very eyes? Hmm?" His smile stretches wide across his face, reaching his eyes as glee takes over his features at my pain.

I use every ounce of strength I have to shrug my shoulders in a care-free manner. Totem's face instantly falls, anger building in his eyes, as his nose flares in rage. Lightning fast, a knife whirls past my face, slamming into the door I walked through. I don't flinch, I don't even fucking breathe for a moment, denying him again of the fiery reaction he wants from me.

"How dare you! You walk in here, as though you haven't spent the past twelve years fucking up my whole life one breath at a time!" His whole body rattles with fury as he picks up the closest chair to him, smashing it into the side of the banister.

Barbette slowly steps toward him, "Tony, honey, don't…"

"Shut the fuck up, Barbie!" he growls, and I watch as she visibly gulps, edging back away from him. "This little bitch keeps taking from me! No more!" His eyes find mine, his hands fisting his hair, as I rub my thumb against my palm, encouraging myself to remain calm. "Your mother promised me another heir! The second heir to my empire, after one of the twins died before Barb gave birth, Veronica promised me you. Power in numbers and I wanted two heirs."

"I'm sorry, Tony, but that's not really my issue. Veronica's dead, whatever she promised, doesn't fall on my shoulders," I finally speak, but my words only make his face turn red with anger.

"That's where you're wrong, little moon. Would you like to guess why?" he cries out, flipping the coffee table in rage. I don't answer, he's just like Veronica, so he's going to tell me whether I want him to or not.

"Do you really think I wasn't fucking Veronica? When they convinced her to go through with the artificial insemination, I'd already cum in her cunt more times than you could believe, little moon!" he screams, my blood running cold at his words.

No. Never. A shudder runs down my spine, uncontrollably, and he catches the movement.

"That's right, I'm your daddy, and you'll do whatever I fucking tell you to do," he spits out, as I hear the slightest gasp from Barbette, who's practically cowering on the spot.

"Rafe is my father before all else, rotten sperm doesn't determine who my father is," I reply, holding my ground, not wanting his words to affect me. I can feel the shake in my voice slightly, the distress he's causing in the revelation is evident.

Ignoring my words, he pushes on with a different tactic. "Little moon, we could rule the entire criminal underworld, not just in the U.S. but across the ocean, infiltrating every continent," he preaches, arms out wide. "You could be number one, I see a fire in you I've never seen in Wren. She could learn a thing or two from you."

I scoff at his attempt to persuade me, but he does have me slightly intrigued. "Is this the movement I've heard so much about?" I ask, remembering what Veronica said.

He claps with excitement, a manic gleam to his wide eyes. "Yes. Exactly! I spent all my time at this damn

Academy as a fucking underdog. A Club through and through. I refuse to let anyone else look down at me," he growls. "Imagine the power we would wield, the destruction we could cause. I've worked hard to get us to this point, little moon. I've balanced Barbie and Vee, ensuring Wren was raised exactly as I wanted, but now I need your obedience. We have people on our side all over the globe, ready to move when I say go."

He stares me down, bouncing on the balls of his feet as he waits expectantly for my response.

"Thanks for the offer, but it'll have to be a no from me."

"Don't defy me, Luna!" he yells at the top of his voice, raking his fingers through his hair. "You'll fucking listen to me, or I'll force you to do as I see fit. It's your choice."

"Let me say it slower for you since you don't seem to be hearing me. I. Said. No," I drag it out, but I think he's reached his limit with me.

Storming toward me, I hear the magical words spoken in my ear, "Three, two, one."

Doors slam open from behind me, and the opposite entryway on the other side of the room as Rafe, Roman, Oscar, and Parker step into the room from all angles. Each covered in mud and splatters of blood, they aim their guns at Totem, who simply raises an eyebrow at me. Rafe and Oscar are in front of me, and Parker stands with Roman at my side.

"I'm going to kill every last one of these fuckers, and after I'm done, you're going to come with me. I'm not afraid to beat a little obedience into you." Before I can respond to his words, he pulls a gun from the back of his pants, pointing it straight at Rafe, all while maintaining eye contact with me.

No. The hairs on my arms stand on point as fear rushes through my body, my legs stumbling over themselves as my brain tries to speed up my response.

Bang. A simple fucking sound, so easily changing the course of our lives, holds me captive. As if in slow motion, I watch Totem stumble as a bullet blasts through his knee cap. In shock, he glances down at his leg, a pained cry ripping from his lungs as he drops his gun to the floor.

"Tony!" Barbette cries, dashing across the floor, but she doesn't make it to his side as a bullet shoots through her shoulder, the impact throwing her backwards. The second gunshot finally kicks me into action, pushing me to grab my own gun from its holster. I pull the trigger on instinct, raining a succession of bullets at Totem, feeling every inch of my pain release with each click. My eyes unwavering as each one hits its target, his stomach, leg, and face exploding with blood. A sick sense of satisfaction washes over me as his eyes glass over and he drops to the floor.

Tearing my gaze from him, Barbette's wild eyes frantically search around her as rich red blood pours from her wound, seeping into her god awful yellow suit. I aim my gun at her, smiling wide, I go to pull the trigger, but another shot rings out. The bullet hits right between her eyes, and her lifeless body drops to the floor right along with Totem. I glance at the guys, and Rafe for a moment, knowing that some of the gunshots weren't from any of us, but when I look up to the balcony on the second floor there's no one visible.

The silence that surrounds me feels odd, as my mind adjusts to the scene. It's rare to see the dead bodies around us, without a single drop of blood on me. My heart pounds in my chest as my mind processes what my eyes are seeing. Totem is dead. Holy shit. The usual pressure, wrapped tight around my neck, is gone.

Parker is quick to spin me around, scanning me from

head to toe, making sure I'm okay before bringing his lips to mine. I feel more arms wrap around me, not a word spoken as we bask in each other's presence.

The door behind me bouncing off the wall breaks the moment, sending us back on high alert as Maverick splutters before us, covered in ash. Hands braced on his knees, he barely glances at the mess of bodies around us, his eyes finding mine.

"It's Kai."

THIRTY FIVE

Luna

Charging into the Combat building, with the guys close behind me, I head for the door Maverick told me to go through. I barely hear them ricochet off the walls, as my eyes frantically search the people before me. I never knew there was a full medical center on campus. Although, I do remember when I knocked Wren out in our first Combat class, there were medics readily available.

A handful of nurses and doctors stop in their tracks around the reception area, staring me down. I must look like a madwoman, but I am, and I don't care. All I care about right now is getting to Kai because Maverick said he wasn't good.

"Luna!" Bryce calls out from the far corner of the room, and I bypass everyone to get to him. His hands instantly wrap around my body, holding me tight. I can feel him sag in relief against me, and it fills me with a strong sense of comfort, just like when Rafe holds me. It still doesn't quench my need to find Kai, though. Stepping back, he glances over my shoulder at the guys behind me.

"Where is he?" I ask, needing to see him with my own eyes.

"Kai is through there," he murmurs, pointing at the door to my left. "He's sleeping right…" I don't hear the rest, my feet automatically moving toward my handsome.

Pushing the door open, there are two nurses and a doctor checking Kai over. Hearing me enter, the doctor frowns. He doesn't look much older than me, messy blonde hair swept across his forehead with hazel eyes assessing me. Straightening the collar of his doctor's coat, he sighs.

"No one should be in here right now, but I have a feeling you're not going to accept that instruction." I raise my eyebrow at him, he knows me well already. "Okay, Luna. Take the seat by his bed, but the others are going to have to wait outside." I start to argue, but he cuts me off. "Don't push me, Ace boys or not, that's the rule. Kai needs to sleep right now anyway, maybe the others can get cleaned up, and have someone bring some fresh clothes or something."

I look over my shoulder, Parker's eyes trail over Kai's sleeping form, but he nods reluctantly. Smiling softly at me, he steps out of the room, and I watch as Bryce wraps an arm around his shoulders. Oscar looks helpless, but nods and steps outside, leaving Roman to glare at the doctor.

"The second he wakes up and is truly conscious, you fucking notify me and don't think one of us won't be standing at this door at all times. This is our wife, and that is my brother," he grunts, pointing a finger first at me, then at Kai. "You do what you have to do to help him, and I won't kill you for trying to order us around." The doctor looks nervous at the thunder in Roman's voice, as he nods gently in agreement.

Always pushing boundaries and rules, Roman steps up to the side of me, lifting my gaze to his and crushing his lips to mine. "I love you," I whisper, and the fire in his eyes calms a little.

"I love you too, princess," he murmurs before stepping out.

I don't miss the nurses checking out my Aceholes as I take the seat beside Kai, but my brain can't focus on anything beyond his health right now. He's covered from head to toe in soot, black ash marking him everywhere. I can't see any physical injuries, but Maverick mentioned it was smoke inhalation.

"How do you know my name?" I ask, unable to pull my gaze from Kai, wondering how he called me Luna a moment ago.

"Because when Kai is briefly alert, he's calling out for you, then falls unconscious again." His words hit me with a mixture of emotions. It warms my heart knowing he's calling for me, but it splits my soul in two, knowing how alone he is right now, lost to the darkness.

I intertwine my fingers with Kai's, stroking my thumb against his soft skin. An oxygen mask sits on his face, trying to pump pure oxygen into his lungs. His long eyelashes brush against his cheeks as he sleeps, and my heart aches. I want to do something, anything to make him wake-up.

"What has been done so far?" I ask, glancing at one of the nurses, who offers a soft smile in comfort.

"He's already had a chest x-ray, we're just waiting on the results back from that. We've drawn blood so we can run a few different tests, including an ABG, uhh sorry, an arterial blood gas test." She comes to stand on the other side of him, pointing down at his left hand, where a small device sits on his finger. "We also have a pulse oximetry on him, so we can see how well oxygen is getting to his tissues. The oxygen mask is the most important part, if we feel it's not working as well, we may move it to a tube down his throat, but that'll be the last resort."

I nod along to her words, but a lot of it goes straight over my head. The details she offers though, show me they're working hard on him, and that's what matters.

"We haven't had to do a bronchoscopy so far, and his vitals are slowly starting to return to normal. All the signs are looking positive for him," the doctor adds, scribbling on the clipboard in his hands. "We'll leave you to sit with him. If he wakes, just press the button on the wall to your left, and someone will be here."

The room dips into silence as they leave the room, only the sound of the machines working surround me. I squeeze Kal's hand tighter, my mind needing to make sure he's still there. A lot has fucking happened in the past few months, but tonight was life-changing.

Totem is dead. Barbette Dietrichson and her father

too. Maverick mentioned Travis Fuse was the one to find Mia and pulled her from the burning building. Then, he ran straight back in to save his son. I'm seeing him in a completely different light. There is a lot to discuss now, like what all this means for us, but my sole focus right now is Kai.

I just need my quiet and observant Acehole to wake the fuck up.

Parker

Glancing through the glass in the window, I watch as Kai sleeps in the bed, his chest rising slowly with each intake of breath. My beautiful angel sits beside him, her hand wrapped around his as she sleeps, sitting up. It doesn't look the most comfortable, but no one dares to move her.

We've been here for hours, they're even offering to set cots up for us, but we won't sleep while they are. Taking turns, we have all showered in the Combat side of the building, changing into the fresh sweatpants and hoodies that Jess arranged for us, and had Maverick bring over.

Kai's father, Travis, is resting in the room next to him, Mia, by his side. Risking his life for his son means a lot to everyone, so I'm glad he isn't alone right now.

Rafe walks through the main doors, freshly showered and with a serene look on his face. He took charge of the major clean-up needed up at the Main Hall, but he was more than happy to do it. Bryce jumps to his feet, throwing his arms around Rafe's waist, and they hold each other tight. Whispering in their own little bubble, I have no clue what they are saying, but happy tears streak their faces.

"Hey, old man, talk to us," Oscar says loudly from the seat beside me. He's slouched down in his chair, legs spread wide as he bounces his knee like he owns the place.

Rafe glares at him for the nickname, but at least he knew Oscar was talking to him. Walking over, he claps hands with me, patting me on the back, doing the same with Oscar and Roman as they stand too. While Luna was inside with Totem, as a team, we stormed the perimeter of the Main Hall, taking down every person in our way. John Dietrichson and all the damn muscle they had circling the place are now dead, and I don't feel bad, not even a little bit. That's what they fucking deserve for playing their part in the shit show Totem started.

"Has everything been taken care of with the bodies?" Roman asks, and Rafe nods.

"Yes, just like I said it would be. So, don't stress," Rafe says, clapping him on the shoulder. "How is your father?" he asks, looking to Oscar for a response.

"He's good. They've set him up across the hall," he responds, pointing at the door at the opposite end of the room. "My mother and sister are in there with him at the moment."

Oscar's relationship with his father is beyond complicated, but I can see the relief in his eyes knowing his father will be okay.

"Has anyone figured out how Totem got in Ace block yet?" Roman grunts, asking the question on all of our lips, but Rafe shakes his head.

"Honestly, I don't think we'll ever know. Unless, we get any answers from interrogating the staff. I feel like he had help on the inside, and even though the roof door was open, it just doesn't add up." He sighs, rubbing the back of his neck. "Hopefully, we can try and recover some of the blocked footage, and get some answers."

Movement from the corner of my eye catches my attention as Rafe continues to speak, but I cut him off.

"He's awake," I whisper, my feet moving on their own accord, seeing Kai's eyes frantically search around him.

Pushing the door open, I don't look behind me. "Hey, it's alright, Kai. It's okay," I murmur, stopping his hand from clawing at his face in an effort to get rid of the face mask. His breathing increases as he frowns at me, trying to speak, but the sounds of the monitors going crazy distracts us all.

"Kai," Luna says from across the bed, sleep and emotion thick in her voice. "Hey, handsome." She leans over him, stroking his hair from his face as tears well in her eyes.

Kai's gaze settles on Luna, a calmness washing over him. Raising his hand to her lips, she kisses his knuckles, soot marking her lips as she does.

"Luna," he muffles from behind the face mask, pulling his hand from my grasp to lift it away from his face. "I love you…" he rasps before he starts to cough uncontrollably. Luna surprises me, instantly slamming the button at the side of his bed, as she forces the mask back over his mouth. The rest of us stand frozen in place, watching him try to catch his breath.

She murmurs sweet encouraging words as she brings

her face close to his. She always has the magic to take care of us, aiding, and guiding us when we need her. I feel a hand squeeze my shoulder, looking behind me to see Roman smile comfortingly at me.

The doctor enters the room, a nurse behind him, staring at us with a raised eyebrow. We all step back from the bed, all except Luna, and the doctor shakes his head, but doesn't utter a single word. We can be compliant when we want to be.

"Mr. Steele-Fuse, nice of you to join us," the doctor says, and Kai glares at him. "Much more responsive too." He taps away on the tablet in his hands, and Kai starts to growl. I think he's the worst patient out of all of us. "Okay, how about I check you over, and we can see how quickly we can get you out of here?" the doctor asks, and Kai nods furiously.

Luna chuckles from beside him, making him look up at her. The love and admiration in his eyes, even touches me, the power of our feelings for our wife affects us all. Slowly, he lifts the masks from his face, and nobody dares to stop him again.

"I didn't say it in the room before we left," he breathes, trying to not agitate his throat again like earlier. "I love you, Sakura. With all that I am, I love you."

"Oh, you say that now, but wait until I get you home. You are in some serious shit for scaring me like this," she warns, but the smile on her face overrules the stress in her voice. "I love you, too." She looks around at all of us, touching us with her fierce love.

This is where I want to be forever. Everybody has an addiction, mine just happens to be love.

Wren

I rush from the medical center waiting room, not wanting anyone to see me. My heart beats rapidly in my chest as the fresh morning breeze wraps around me, making me shiver. I'm in no state to be seen right now, covered in filth with my hair a mess, my mother would kill me for looking like this.

Leaning against the side of the Combat building, I take a deep breath and close my eyes. I did it. I can't believe I actually fucking did it. My hands shake before me, as my mind replays the bullets hitting my father, then my mother, my trigger finger repeating the motion. She can't break me down, and he can't ruin me anymore.

I need to leave, and I need to do it now. I should have left straight away, but I wanted to make sure no one else died at the hands of that monster. I refuse to be a product of his making, a puppet on his damn string.

"I'm surprised you haven't run already," a deep voice rumbles beside me, and my fight or flight instincts kick in. But when I open my eyes, Rafe Gibbs stands before me with his hands raised slightly in surrender.

I don't dare move, staring him down as he slowly slips his hand into the front of his jeans, quickly retrieving an object. My confusion must show on my face, but he says nothing.

"I saw you," he murmurs, and my breath catches in my throat. "What you did, back in that Main Hall… This is me saying thank you." He stretches out his hand, offering me the key and a slip of paper I hadn't noticed earlier.

"What's this for?"

"It's a safe place to stay."

He must be joking. After all the shit I did to Luna, this has to be a fucking lie, but the gentleness to his eyes tells me differently. It's hard to remember that not everything comes with a price like it does with my father. My *dead* father.

I slowly take them, and he steps back. "I will tell her," he says, and my heart sinks. "It'll be up to her what she does with that information, but for now, we both know you need to leave. Just remember this is Featherstone, so there isn't really much point in running. Trust me, I would know."

With that, he turns and leaves. I'm left standing alone, and for once in my life, it feels like heaven. No expectations or harsh consequences. Just me, Wren Dietrichson. I just have no clue who the hell that actually is.

KC KEAN

THIRTY SIX

Luna

The sun glares in my eyes, pulling me from the best damn dream of my life. Heat and pleasure still ripple through me from the hot sex playing in my mind as I slowly wake up. Stretching my arms above my head, I sink further into the mattress, gasping as fingers trail softly against my clit.

What the fuck? Lifting the quilt, Roman peers up at me, hunger in his eyes with a wicked grin on his face. Damn, it wasn't a dream after all. Even better. Not speaking a word, his tongue follows the same path as his fingers. A shudder runs through my body, my mouth falling open as a moan slips from my lips.

Hot damn, that mouth. Wrapping my legs around his head, I grind against his face, taking everything he has to offer. Happy to oblige, he sinks two fingers deep into my pussy as he sucks against my clit. Holy shit. I think this is my new favorite way to wake up. One hand wraps in Roman's hair as the other squeezes my pierced nipple, and within moments I reach my climax.

Roman plays my body perfectly, drawing every ounce of pleasure from me, leaving me in a sex induced haze. Slowly kissing my thighs, my body quivers beneath him, while he trails his lips all the way up to mine.

"Good morning, princess," he murmurs against my lips, and I smile.

"Good morning, baby."

"We have a surprise for you today." He grins against my neck, his lips brushing against my pulse.

"What surprise?" I whimper, feeling my body react to the length of him against me.

"It wouldn't be a surprise if I told you now, would it? So, get your cute ass up. I've drawn you a bath. Jess will be here soon." Kissing my lips with brute force, my hands hold him close until he shuffles back down the bed.

Kissing my clit one last time, he gets up and walks out of the room, but I don't miss the strain of his cock against his boxer briefs. Good morning to me.

Finding the strength to rise to my feet, I finally notice no one else is in bed. The sound of the front door shutting makes me frown, and as I step into the lounge, it's empty. Straining my ears, the sound of Christina Perri, A Thousand Years, plays gently through the sound system. Stepping further into the room, my eyes fall on vases and vases full of red roses.

What on earth is all this?

Petals line the way to the bathroom. Following the trail, I can barely contain my beating heart. Standing at the open door to the bathroom, I see candles flickering on every surface, bubbles up to the top of the tub, and the smell of vanilla fills the room. Stepping into the tub, I smile wide at the hot mug of coffee perched on the side, waiting for me. Damn, they know me too well. Sinking into the water, the bubbles up to my chin, I feel giddy.

I can't bring myself to soak in the water forever, like I usually would, wanting to get out and find out more of what this surprise is. Never would I have believed my Aceholes would do this for me, but I shouldn't really be shocked. Now, I'm intrigued.

Wrapping a towel around my body, I make a fresh cup of coffee and head back into the bedroom to put some clothes on. Placing my mug on the bedside table, my phone vibrates.

Red: On my way up, wear your pjs!

Shaking my head at her sassiness, I throw on one of Roman's longline t-shirts and a pair of shorts when the knock sounds at the door. I rush to the door, swinging it open to see her holding large white boxes in her hands.

"What the hell, Red. What's all this?"

"This is Project Queen. No, I didn't get to name it, but it'll be worth it. Even if it does have a stupid name," she says, rolling her eyes dramatically, and I chuckle. I'm rubbing off on her way too much. "Well, don't just stand there. You guys all overslept, and Roman refused to wake you. So now we have about forty minutes." She shoos me into my walk-in closet, as I glance at the time. How the hell is it two in the afternoon already?

Making sure to grab my coffee on the way, I take a seat at the vanity, and watch as Red places the boxes on the floor and starts pulling all the make-up out of the drawers that I never use.

"I have to wear make-up?" I ask, but not really bothered, becoming more curious with what's going on.

"Nope, they actually told me to give you the choice, but screw them. I deserve some fun too." I raise an eyebrow at her, taking a quick sip of my coffee before she gets to work. She knows I'll let her do this even if I couldn't really be bothered with it.

Relaxing into my chair, I think about everything that's happened in the two weeks since Totem died. It was agreed that finally eliminating Totem was a good enough substitute for the third round of The Games. Now we get to enjoy the rest of the school year, and at the end of the final term, discussions will be held to determine when we will step up and take on more responsibility as members of The Ring.

Not that it was really needed, but Bryce and I did a DNA test to squash the slither of doubt Totem placed in my mind. Needless to say, it came back a definite match. I'm glad that man no longer holds anything over my head anymore.

"How's Kai doing? You know when I ask him, he just shrugs me off," Red asks, as she applies eye shadow to my lids.

"He's actually doing really good. He completely refused to take any medication, but it helped having him use the oxygen machine daily in the beginning. He doesn't have any scarring on his lungs or throat, so we just have to make sure his shoulder heals properly, and we're all good." I answer, feeling lighter than ever. Twice I've come close to losing him, and against all odds, I still get to stand by his side.

"Done," Red murmurs, and I blink, catching tears in her eyes.

"Red, what's wrong?"

"Nothing, nothing," she says, waving her hand at me. "Just emotional, that's all." A knock sounds from the door as she sniffles. "Would you look at that, saved by the door. You grab it, I'll get the boxes ready."

I stare her down for a moment, but I know she's not going to talk, so I head for the door. I did not expect to see Rafe standing on the other side in a suit. A perfectly fitted grey suit against his olive skin, and his hair is even brushed back neatly into a man bun at the back of his head.

"Right, drop the shit. What the fuck is going on?" I demand, my pulse picking up as I try to process what's happening. Rafe smiles wide at me, love and pride radiating from him.

"Your Aceholes, as you like to call them, wanted a proper celebration of your marriage, so here we are."

Holy. Shit.

"What does that mean?" I whisper, my heart pounding in my ears.

"It means you need to get dressed, darling," he says softly, and I nod, walking back to the closest in a daze. When I step into the bedroom, Red stares nervously down at the bed, a white lace gown lying on top of the quilt, with a pair of rose gold heels on the floor next to it.

My breath catches as I take it all in. I bite my lip, hard, to stop myself from crying, but it's really fucking difficult.

"So, uhh, all this was their idea?" I murmur, and Red smiles brightly.

"Everything, except for the dress. They actually listened when I said they shouldn't see." I nod along with her like it all makes perfect sense, but my mind is blown.

Trailing my fingers against the lace of the dress, I feel like I could burst.

"I'll give you a moment while I change in the bathroom." I hear the door click shut behind her, but my gaze doesn't pull from the dress.

Slipping out of my clothes and into the layers of fabric, I pull the body-hugging dress over my hips, and the spaghetti straps over my shoulders. The back is all open, with the zipper stopping at my hips, and the sweetheart cut at the front dips low between my breasts. I'm thankful it hits the ground at my feet, but there's no train behind me.

Stepping into the low heels, I take a glance at myself in the floor-length mirror. How is this me? So happy, and smiling, my heart full of love. I head for the lounge, close to tears if I stay in here much longer. The second I open the door, Rafe stands to his feet, twirling to see me.

"Darling," he whispers, swiping at his face. He's close to setting me off too. I force myself to look at the ceiling, steadying my breathing as I fan my face.

"Oh my gosh, will you guys stop!" Red cries out, a tremble to her voice too.

"We are the biggest set of fucking pansies," I grouch, and they laugh, forcing a smile from my lips too.

"Let's go. I should never have given them all my number. I can't deal with one more message from them," he mumbles, his eyes wide in disbelief, and it makes me relax. I want to get out of here and see my Aceholes.

Taking the elevator down, Ian waits by the door, a tear in his eye too. I'm going to kill them when I get my hands on my guys. I am in no way ready for this level of emotion. I can't hold it in much more.

The sky is clear, with a few clouds scattered around, but the chill in the air is ice cold. Ian chauffeurs us over in a Rolls, with Rafe sitting upfront with him. I can't speak the whole ride, squeezing Red's hand tight, but my heart stops as we pull up beside my little secret garden. On autopilot, I step from the car and head for the opening, but Rafe catches my hand, slowing my pace. Red waves before stepping past the hedges and my heart is in my throat.

As I walk down the aisle, which is covered in scattered petals, Oscar, Kai, Roman, and Parker all stand under the gazebo, in matching navy suits. Heaters blast from all corners, warming the space, and I can't feel the usual chill in the air. I catch the lyrics of All of Me by John Legend, playing softly in the background, and goosebumps prickle my neck.

I don't know how I make it to the gazebo, bypassing a handful of people, but I don't see them, only seeing my four men. My Aceholes. When I stand in front of them, all lined up next to each other, Parker strokes his thumb against my cheek and I'm shocked to realize I'm crying.

"Don't cry, angel. This is good, right?" he asks, worry in his hazel eyes, and I manage to nod in response.

Clearing his throat, Bryce stands before us. "So, it was all their idea for me to officiate your ceremony. Is that okay with you, Meu Tesouro?"

"Of course, Pops," I murmur, unable to say more than a few words.

I get lost in the words we murmur to each other. I hope someone records this because their eyes hold me captive, and I can't digest everything properly.

"I guess you may now kiss the bride, who I might remind you is my daughter," Bryce says, emotion in his eyes too, as the small crowd giggles. Roman leans in and kisses me first, his full lips devouring mine. When he steps back, Kai fills the space before me, stroking his finger down the side of my face, goosebumps rising at his touch. He kisses me softly, and I feel light-headed. I hear someone clear their throat, and Kai reluctantly moves. As Oscar moves toward me, Parker spins me to him, his lips crushing mine in an instance. My hands clutch the fabric of his suit jacket, but he's pushed to the side.

"These fuckers are winding me up on purpose. Kiss

me, baby girl," Oscar groans, and I smile wide at that damn big mouth of his. Stepping into his arms, I lift on to my tiptoes, joining our mouths. Hearing the claps and cheers around us, our moment is cut short, but the heat in each of their eyes holds a promise for later.

"Let's get the party started!" Aiden calls out, and suddenly I'm being whisked over to the Weaponry building, where the whole space has been transformed like the Main Hall was for the Fall Ball. Rose gold and white flowers fill the room, with matching decorations covering the walls. A huge billboard size picture of the guys and me all smiling wide at the camera while we were at the beach house, is propped up against the long wall.

Intimate tables cover the outer area, with a dance floor in the middle. This, this right here, is perfection. I never asked for a day like this, yet they delivered me one anyway, and it makes my heart glow brighter. A DJ booth is set up in the corner, blasting out the latest hits.

I spot Bryce standing side by side with Rafe as Mia sits with her parents, lost in a deep conversation. West waves from the other side of the room, and even Maverick nods in greeting as we pass.

When the time comes for us to dance, Silence by

Marshmello floats out through the speakers, and I feel the words in my veins as we all huddle together.

"To new beginnings," Kai says, smiling at me without the weight of the world on his shoulders, and I grin back.

"To hot sex on every surface," Oscar adds, and I laugh as he wiggles his eyebrows at me.

"To freedom." Parker squeezes my hip a little tighter, as his words ring out around us.

"To family," Roman murmurs with a cheeky wink, his playful side showing.

"To never kneeling for others. And, more importantly, to love." The guys holler at my words, and I grin wide. Some motherfuckers wanted to take everything from us, piece by piece, but I'm in this *Featherstone* business to stop people like Totem from deciding how I live… if I live. I can't control that this is my destiny, but I much prefer my life in my own hands.

I've found more than I ever dared to dream about. My forever. My solace. My Aceholes.

OUR BLOODLINE

EPILOGUE

Red

My heels click against the stone flooring in the quiet hallway as I step away from the loud bustling hall where the party continues. I can't stop the smile from gracing my face, remembering the pure love and happiness in Luna's eyes today, a complete contrast to the girl I first met.

I want that so much, the love you only read about in books, but my love life is in complete shambles.

As I push against the cool wood of the bathroom door, my hand is pulled to the side, and I'm whirled around. My back hits the wall softly, my eyes closing, as the knowing scent of leather and sandalwood invades my senses.

"You look beautiful tonight," he murmurs huskily, my legs shaking at the feel of his knuckles grazing my cheek. I swallow hard, feeling his body heat surrounding me, his thumb stroking my bottom lip before his mouth meets mine.

Slowly, his lips consume me, my palms stroking up his chest, feeling his heart beating just as frantically as mine. The grip on my waist tightens, as the door to the hall opens and the music fills the space around us.

"Somebody better start fucking explaining what's going on here," Oscar growls, ruining the moment.

As I finally open my eyes, I know the secret is out… but I can explain.

OUR BLOODLINE

AFTERWORDS

HOLY MOTHERFUCKING SHIT!!!!!!!!!

I'm so fucking emotional right now, that the time to lay these Aceholes to rest has come!

The journey Luna and her men have taken me on is one I will never get over.

Back in May, riding the COVID wave, I decided I was going to put pen to paper and give this a try, and it has been the best decision I have ever made <3

Boy have these guys had me on a rollercoaster! The love, the heartache, the pain and rage. I've felt every ounce of their emotions and I've loved every second if it.

I know this doesn't really offer a HEA and more of a HFN vibe, but that's because Featherstone Academy has so much more still to offer. Will there be another Luna & The Aceholes book? Never say never, but for right now, no. Val is probably sick of hearing me say, I never want to over do something and everyone gets bored, because I somehow got repetitive. Besides, I think they need a minute to breathe LOL

With that being said, did you see the epilogue????? Does it mean what you think it means??

HELLLLLL YEAHHHHHHH

Oh my days, from the second I wrote her into My Bloodline, Red has screamed at me for her own book LOL so here we finally are. Our red-headed, quick witted BFF is getting her time to shine. But with who you might ask? Well, we all know I like to tease, so you'll only know this if you read it here - She's got three men vying for her attention, and YES you have already met them all <3 I refuse to say anymore for now though LOL

If you've read this far I'm impressed LOL I'll shut up now and get back to typing!

THANK YOU

I want to start this time with saying the biggest thank you to YOU! For picking My Bloodline up and making it this far! I wouldn't have carried on writing if it wasn't for you!

To my partner, and two beautiful children, who are used to mummy going off into the world of Featherstone, and not returning for a few hours <3 Your patience, understanding, and love helps push me to continue finding my dream <3

I always call her my Alpha Queen, and damn she is, but Valerie is my partner in crime. The friend I never knew I needed, and my biggest supporter. Your random thoughts, and uncanny ability to live inside my brain blows me away! Thank you for putting up with me, and the crazy things I say and do. Thank you for always participating in my GIF wars, but mostly, thank you for loving these Aceholes just as much as I do <3

Where are my BETA bitches at??

Kristen, Hope, Emma, Monica and Katy <3 My favorite ladies!

Thank you so much for your eyes and your minds. Somehow taking lesson from Valerie and clawing a further 3k words from me LOL

Your effort and love for the Aceholes means so much to me, I can't even begin to explain. Thank you for being here, this has been a crazy ride, and I show my appreciation with the next installment of Featherstone Academy! Haha!

My Aceholes for life;

Noreah, Rachel, Michelle, Samantha, Nicole, Kyndal, Kathryn and Lauren.

Thank you for putting up with my crazy and loving Luna and her guys so much <3

ABOUT THE AUTHOR

KC Kean is the sassy half of a match made in heaven. Mummy to two beautiful children, Pokemon Master and Apex Legend world saving gamer.

Starting her adventure in the RH romance world after falling in love with it as a reader, who knows where this crazy train is heading. As long as there is plenty of steam she'll be there.

ALSO BY KC KEAN

Featherstone Academy

(Contemporary Reverse Harem Academy Romance)

My Bloodline

Your Bloodline

Our Bloodline

Red

Freedom

The Allstars Series

(Contemporary Reverse Harem, Sports Romance)

Toxic Creek

Tainted Creek

Twisted Creek - September 14th

Printed in Great Britain
by Amazon